A Mother's Wish

Dilly Court

A Mother's Wish

arrow books

Published by Arrow Books 2009

2 4 6 8 10 9 7 5 3 1

First published in Great Britain in 2009 by
Arrow Books
Random House, 20 Vauxhall Bridge Road,
London SW1V 2SA

www.rbooks.co.uk

Addresses for companies within The Random House Group Limited can be found at:
www.randomhouse.co.uk/offices.htm

The Random House Group Limited Reg. No. 954009

A CIP catalogue record for this book
is available from the British Library

ISBN 9780099538769

The Random House Group Limited supports The Forest Stewardship
Council (FSC), the leading international forest certification organisation. All our
titles that are printed on Greenpeace approved FSC certified paper carry the FSC logo.
Our paper procurement policy can be found at www.rbooks.co.uk/environment

Mixed Sources

Product group from well-managed
forests and other controlled sources
www.fsc.org Cert no. TT-COC-2139
© 1996 Forest Stewardship Council

FSC

Typeset in Palatino by Palimpsest Book Production Ltd, Grangemouth, Stirlingshire
Printed and bound in Great Britain by CPI Mackays, Chatham, ME5 8TD

For Anne, Jean and Beryl,
the best of friends and inspiration.

Chapter One

Three Mills, East London, 1870

The last sack of grain swung perilously over Effie's head as it was hoisted into the House Mill on the banks of the River Lea. The narrow-boat rose a little higher in the water as if relieved to be divested of its heavy cargo, and a thick layer of dust settled on the decking like a generous coating of sugar on a sticky bun. Effie held her hand to her aching back, peering into the gathering gloom to catch sight of Tom, her younger brother, who had gone to collect their horse, Champion, from the patch of waste ground nearby.

'Tom,' Effie shouted, cupping her hands around her mouth in an attempt to make her voice carry above the splashing of the water-wheel and the grinding of the millstone, which was silenced only at low tide. 'Tom, we're ready to move.'

A faint answering cry confirmed that he had heard her, and from the cabin the high-pitched wailing of her infant son made Effie forget everything other than the need to tend to her child. Despite the fact that she had been on her feet since dawn, navigating the vessel through seemingly endless locks on its journey from the Essex countryside to Three Mills, it only needed a plaintive cry from Georgie to galvanise her tired limbs into action. She made her way along the empty deck to the cabin, and a wave of heat from the cast-iron stove hit her forcibly as she opened the door. She stepped down into the confined space where the family lived cheek by jowl. Privacy was not a familiar word in the lives of canal people.

Her father-in-law looked up, scowling. 'You took your time with the unloading,' he grumbled. 'You need to see to the child. You can't expect me to run round after young Georgie now he's toddling. It's woman's work.'

'I'm sorry, Father-in-law,' Effie murmured, biting back a sharp retort. 'But I can't be in two places at the same time.'

'That's enough backchat from you, girl. I may be a cripple but I'm still the boss round here.' Jacob Grey fumbled in his pocket, producing a battered tin snuffbox from which he took a pinch of the brown powder and inhaled deeply. He wiped the excess off his upper lip with a handkerchief that might once have been white but was so stained with snuff that its colour matched that of the polished wooden bulkhead. 'That young limb has had his fingers in everything,' he added, glaring at his grandson.

'Georgie is just a baby,' Effie protested, bending down to scoop her eighteen-month-old son up in her arms.

'What took you so long?' Jacob's eyes watered and he sniffed, wiping his nose again and eyeing Effie with a scornful curl of his lips. 'I wouldn't put it past you to be sizing up the next man now that my boy has gone to his Maker. I always said you were a conniving trollop.'

'Mama.' Tears welled up in Georgie's blue eyes and he wrapped his chubby arms around his mother's neck.

'There's no need to raise your voice, Father-in-law. You're scaring Georgie.' Effie held her child close, stroking his soft brown curls away from his forehead. 'There, there, darling, it's all right.'

'Don't change the subject.' Jacob glared at her with a belligerent outthrust of his whiskery chin. 'What have you been doing all this time?'

Effie held her breath, mentally counting to ten as she faced her father-in-law's overt antagonism with an attempt at a smile. 'There was a full load. I couldn't leave Tom to see to it on his own. He's only a boy.'

'He's thirteen,' Jacob snapped. 'My Owen was working the boat from the age of ten.

He was a wonderful son and he could have done better for himself than marrying a girl from the workhouse.'

The accusation hit a nerve, drawing a swift response from Effie. 'If I was in the workhouse, it was through no fault of my own.'

'You were a barmaid and that's even worse. You set your cap at Owen because you thought you'd have an easy life with him, and you would have if he hadn't been carried off by the same illness that took his ma. It was a bad day when he fell for your big brown eyes and all that yellow hair. I've always suspected that it's dyed.'

'I was born with hair this colour,' Effie protested. 'Living as we do it would be impossible to keep it secret if I put anything on it other than lye soap.'

'Don't you dare grumble about the way we live, my girl. You were quick enough to accept Owen when he proposed marriage. You didn't complain about the cramped conditions then so don't you dare start now. This is my boat and I can send you and your brother packing any time I feel so inclined.'

This harsh remark brought Effie's chin up. 'And how would you work the canals on your own, crippled as you are?'

Jacob's eyes flashed angrily. 'That's right: throw my misfortune back in my face. I was a strong fellow before the accident that broke both my legs and I wouldn't have sat here listening to a scrawny wench criticising my vessel. As it is I only keep you on out of respect for my dead son.'

'And you never miss an opportunity to remind me of that fact,' Effie cried, close to tears at the constant reminders of her husband's premature death. 'You never let me forget that I am beholden to you.'

'And you would leave me to fend for myself at the first opportunity, don't pretend that you wouldn't.'

'All I want is a decent life for Owen's son, and you're right, Father-in-law, if I had a choice in the matter I would leave you and this wretched narrowboat and take my son with me. All I wish for is the chance to raise my child properly and give him the opportunities in life that were denied to me. Surely that's not too much to ask?'

'Poppycock! You want everything given to you on a plate. One day you'll flutter those long eyelashes at some poor bloke and he'll fall for your pretty face just like my boy did. You'll be off so fast it will make my head spin, no matter that Owen would have wanted you to care for his old father.'

Effie turned away, sighing as she put Georgie down on the padded seat which at night doubled for their bed. She knew that she would lose this argument as she had lost so many in the past. She moved to the stove and lifted the lid from a bubbling pan, selecting a wooden spoon from an earthenware pot and stirring the beef bones and vegetables that had been stewing gently all day. 'We'll have supper as soon as we've moved the boat to our berth in the canal basin,' she said, in an attempt to steer the conversation onto safer ground. She had learned long ago that attempting to gainsay her father-in-law would only lead to further conflict. Jacob had ruled his family with a rod of iron and Effie was convinced that Owen had secretly been afraid of his father, even after the old man had lost his physical strength.

'You should have seen to that the moment the last sack of grain was taken off,' Jacob said impatiently. 'Where is that good-for-nothing brother of yours?'

'He went to fetch Champion.'

'Then for God's sake go out and hurry him along. The boy dawdles at the best of times.'

Effie did not dignify this unfair remark with an answer, and Georgie slid from the bunk to clutch at her skirts. He smiled up at her as if in his baby way he understood that she was under verbal attack. She bent down to kiss his chubby cheek. 'Let's go outside, Georgie. We'll find Uncle Tom and maybe he'll let you ride on Champion's back.'

'And the child will fall off and break his neck,' Jacob muttered. 'You'll be quite free from the Grey family then.'

Refusing to be goaded, Effie swung Georgie into her arms and climbed the steps leading out of the suffocating heat into the cool night air. It was twilight and the scent of hawthorn mingled with the aroma of freshly milled grain and the pungent odours emanating from the distillery. The bonded warehouse was sited on land below the mill and from there the narrowboat would be loaded with barrels of alcohol to be transported back to London. It was a circular trip that the Grey family had undertaken for the past twenty years or more, long before Effie met and married Owen. She smiled as Georgie twined his fat little fingers around a lock of her hair and she held him close, breathing in the scent of him as she gazed up into the sky. Noisy starlings swooped and soared, forming dense black clouds against the pale evening sky. Livid streaks of purple and fiery red were all that remained of the sunset, and a silver sliver of moon was accompanied by the evening star. Effie sighed. There was so much beauty in the world and yet so much sadness. She still mourned the loss of her husband. At just twenty-three, Owen had been too young to die, but the insidious disease that had rotted his lungs had taken him from her when she was still a bride and not yet a mother. Georgie had been born six months after Owen's death and the birth had not been easy, but Effie would have willingly suffered the pain again and again to hold her baby in her arms. He was so like his father, with blue eyes that smiled with delight every time he saw her and hair the colour of a sparrow's wing. Very early on he had smiled and this had developed into a throaty chuckle when something amused him. When Jacob was in a good mood he often claimed that Georgie was a true Grey, but to Effie he was all hers; the only thing in her twenty-two years that had truly belonged to her.

She came back to earth with a jolt as Tom hailed her from the towpath. 'Shall we cast off now, Effie?'

'Yes, Tom.' She set Georgie down on the deck and ran lightly to the bows to catch the mooring rope. Within minutes they were on the move, the narrowboat seeming to skim the dark water of the canal basin as Tom led Champion towards their berth for the night. First thing in the morning on the turn of the tide, they would be on their way back to

Limehouse Basin and the circuit would begin again.

Next morning when the first crack of light appeared in the eastern sky, Effie was at the tiller with Tom trudging along the towpath leading Champion. The heavily laden narrow-boat was low in the water but gradually gathered momentum and picked up speed as Champion plodded on towards London. The distinctive twin towers of the Clock House Mill and the now derelict windmill gradually faded into the distance and street lights shone like strings of glow-worms along the banks of the River Lea. As they left the river and entered Limehouse Cut, passing through brickfields and market gardens, the cool morning air was heavy with the stench from the manufactories. The mixed odours of varnish, chemicals, India rubber, manure, tar, alum and glue made from animal bones hung in a miasma above the murky waters of the canal.

It was still early morning when Bow Common Bridge came into sight and the gaudily painted Prince of Wales tavern where Effie had once been employed as a barmaid. Champion it seemed had already decided to make a stop here and he had his head down champing away on a patch of sooty grass.

Tom tethered him to a fence post, hitched a nosebag over Champion's head and came strolling back to the boat whistling a tune, his hands in his pockets. Effie had to hide a smile at her brother's insouciant air. Dear Tom, she thought fondly, nothing ever seemed to get him down. He often suffered the sharp edge of Jacob's tongue but he took it all with good grace and never seemed to let the unfairness of their situation bother him. Perhaps it was the hardship they had suffered in the workhouse that had inured him to such treatment, or maybe it was simply that Tom possessed a happy nature and a good heart. Whatever star it was that ruled him, Effie was very grateful for its benign influence as without Tom her life and that of little Georgie would be all the harder to bear.

'What d'you say to breakfast in the pub?' Tom suggested, grinning. 'I can smell bacon frying, hot toast and coffee.'

'I don't know, Tom. I don't think Mr Grey would approve. Since he gave up the drink he thinks that pubs are dens of iniquity.'

'Aw go on, Effie. We've made good time and if we arrive too early we'll only have to wait for a berth. Mr Ellerman is always late anyway.'

Effie acknowledged this truth with a reluctant nod of her head. Mr Ellerman was the agent for the distillers' company and he organised the carts to transport the barrels of alcohol to Clerkenwell where they would be rectified into gin. Effie's stomach rumbled and her mouth watered as she too caught a tantalising whiff of bacon which momentarily overpowered the noxious city smells. 'All right, Tom. I think we've earned a treat. Go inside and order three breakfasts. I'll share mine with Georgie.'

Tom held his hand out. 'It'll cost you, Effie.'

She put her hand in her pocket and took out a silver sixpence, the last of the money that Jacob had allocated to buy food for the week. He might not be able to work the barge but he still insisted on handling the business transactions, making it plain that he did not trust Effie with such matters.

Tom shot off in the direction of the pub and Effie made her way into the cabin, preparing for yet another battle of wills. She was not disappointed.

Jacob had raised himself on a cushion and his nightcap sat awry on his thinning white hair. 'You can't keep away from your old haunts, can you?'

'That's not fair, Father-in-law.' Effie glanced anxiously at her sleeping child and lowered her voice. 'All we want is some hot food and there is nowhere else between here and Limehouse Basin.'

'You are wantonly extravagant, my girl, wasting our hard-earned money on food that you could cook yourself for half the cost.'

'There is nothing left in the cupboard, not even a crust of bread, and we've been on the go since daybreak.'

'You were raised on gruel in the workhouse, but that's not good enough for you now, is it? You've got ideas above your station, and you'll ruin us before you're done.'

'So you don't want anything from the pub then?' Effie knew that she ought not to goad the old man, but he had pushed her too far this morning.

'You can wipe that smug look off your face, madam. I'll take breakfast although it will probably choke me, but at least I know I'll get a decent meal from the pub kitchen and not the slop that you serve up.'

Jacob's harsh voice must have penetrated Georgie's dreams, for he stirred and opened his eyes with a whimper that went straight to Effie's heart. She snatched him up from his nest of pillows and carried him out onto the deck, threading her way around the tightly packed barrels. She wanted to put as much distance as possible between herself and her tormentor. Sometimes she felt that she could not stand another minute of her father-in-law's cruel jibes, and for two pins she would have left the narrowboat to take her chances on land, but there was always Georgie to consider, and Tom. The threat of returning to the workhouse was enough to make her think twice before making any rash decisions.

Hampered by her long skirts and the weight of Georgie in her arms, Effie was having difficulty in getting onto the towpath when a hand reached out to help her.

'Why, if it isn't young Effie Sadler.'

Effie would have known that voice anywhere. She looked up into a pair of speedwell-blue eyes that twinkled with laughter and a weather-beaten face that denoted a life spent mainly outdoors. 'Toby Tapper!' she exclaimed. 'Where did you spring from?'

'From the tavern, my pet. I recognised Tom supping a pint of small beer and I couldn't believe my eyes to see how he'd grown.' Toby slipped his free arm around her waist and swung her off the deck, setting her gently down on the towpath. His smile broadened as Georgie reached up to touch his face. 'And who might this fine fellow be?'

'This is my son, Georgie.'

'I heard that you'd married a boatman.' Toby ruffled Georgie's curls. 'Your boy does you credit, Effie, but it's hard to believe you are a wife and mother. Your presence behind the bar is sorely missed, my dear.'

'You always were a smooth talker, Toby. I'm sure you say that to all the barmaids in every town you visit. Are you still trading horses?'

Toby took off his cap, brushing back a lock of dark, curly hair that gleamed like coal in the bright light. 'I'm Romany. No one understands horseflesh better than we do.'

'And do you still travel with the fair?'

He shook his head. 'No, we parted company some time ago.'

She had always had a soft spot for Toby and seeing him again lifted her spirits, reminding her of happier days. Questions bubbled on Effie's tongue like sweet sherbet, but Tom appeared in the pub doorway. 'Grub up, Effie. Come and get it while it's hot.'

Toby linked her hand through his arm. 'Allow me, ma'am. I think I might join you at the breakfast table, if that's all right with you and if your husband won't object.'

The years had rolled away and she had been Effie Sadler, but she returned to earth with a bump and her smile faded. 'I'm a widow, Toby. Owen died of consumption two years ago.'

'I am sorry, truly I am. I had no idea, or I wouldn't have made light of things.'

'You weren't to know.'

'Effie Grey, where's me food?' Jacob's voice boomed from within the cabin, reminding her painfully that life had changed, and not for the better.

'It's coming, Father-in-law.' She shot an apologetic glance at Toby. 'He's not the easiest person to live with.'

Toby raised an eyebrow. 'I can see that, ducks. Best get the old codger fed then.' He led her into the pub, settling her on a seat by the fire where Tom had already begun shovelling his food down at an alarming rate. 'Hold fast there, young fellow.' Toby picked up a rapidly cooling plate of bacon, eggs and buttered toast, thrusting it into Tom's hands. 'Take this to the old man.' He turned to the barman. 'A pint of porter, if you please, Ben.'

'The old fellah don't approve of drink,' Tom said nervously. 'He says it's the devil's brew and he'll only throw it at me.'

Toby strode to the bar and came back with a foaming tankard. He took a red-hot poker from the fire and plunged it into the pot. The beer hissed and fizzed, and he thrust the tankard into Tom's hand. 'Tell the old devil that this is purely medicinal; doctor's orders.'

'You shouldn't have done that,' Effie said anxiously as Tom left the taproom. 'Mr Grey has a fierce temper. He might not be able to walk but he has a long reach with his cane and a strong arm.'

'I'll wager that Tom is quick on his feet, and

maybe the mulled ale will sweeten the old man's temper.' Toby held his arms out to Georgie. 'Come with me, young man. I know the cook here and if we ask her nicely, I'm sure she'll give you a bowl of porridge with lots of sugar and cream. Shall we go and see?'

Effie half rose to her feet, but Toby pressed her gently down on the wooden settle. 'Don't worry, little mother, your boy is safe with me. I'm used to handling young colts, and, as you see, he is not afraid of his Uncle Toby.'

As if to confirm this statement, Georgie peered at the gold earring dangling from Toby's earlobe and he poked at it with a chubby finger, seemingly content to be held in a stranger's arms and quite happy to leave his mother and be carried off to the unknown. Effie did not know whether to be pleased by her son's newfound independence or upset by it, and she had to resist the urge to follow them. Even as she ate the tasty food, she found herself straining her ears in case Georgie should suddenly miss her and begin to cry, but it was Tom who returned first, bursting through the pub door like a whirlwind. He flung himself down on the settle and began to eat again, grumbling through each mouthful. 'Miserable old bugger. I'll kill him if he keeps hitting me with that stick.'

'Hush, Tom,' Effie said, glancing round anxiously to see if anyone had heard him. 'You don't mean that.'

Tom swallowed hard. 'Don't I just? He's an ungrateful old sod and I hate him.'

Effie pushed her plate away, unable to eat another mouthful. 'I know he's difficult, Tom, but we have to put up with him for now at least.'

'I could get a job, Effie. There's the chemical works across the cut, and the match factory back along the river. There's the gasworks and the alum factory, the glue works . . .'

'Stop it, Tom. I know you mean well but it's not as simple as that,' Effie said in a low voice, reaching out to cover his hand with hers. 'We would have to find a place to live and rents are high, wages are low. We would end up back in the workhouse or worse.'

'But he's a pig and a bully. I can't bear the way he treats you.' Tom wiped his sleeve across his face.

Effie's throat constricted at the sight of her brother's eyes magnified by unshed tears and she squeezed his fingers. 'I'll think of something, Tom, but for the time being we've just got to put up with things as they are.'

'Effie Sadler – or should I say Mrs Grey.'

A familiar voice from behind her made Effie turn her head and she rose to her feet, holding out her hand to the landlord. 'Ben. It's good to see you again. It's been a long time.'

'Too long, my girl. I've seen the *Margaret* pass us by on many an occasion and yet you never called in to see us.' Ben Hawkins wiped his hands on his apron and took Effie's outstretched hand in a large paw, pumping it up and down enthusiastically. 'I've just seen Toby in the kitchen and he told me you were out here.'

'We just stopped for a bite to eat,' Effie explained hastily. 'We don't normally have the time and my father-in-law doesn't drink, so that's why . . .'

Ben threw back his shaggy head and roared with laughter. 'You don't have to explain, ducks. Old man Grey is well known in these parts for being a bit of a miser. The other boatmen don't have much time for him by all accounts.' His craggy features smoothed to a look of deep concern. 'I heard about your husband, Effie. It were a bad business, girl, and we was all sorry to hear of your loss.'

Effie swallowed a lump in her throat and blinked as the ready tears stung her eyes. 'Thank you, Ben. I appreciate that.'

He turned to Tom, slapping him on the shoulder. 'And you've grown, young fellow. I hardly recognise you now.' He squeezed Tom's arm playfully. 'Look at them muscles! It's easy to see who does all the work.'

Tom flushed a rosy red beneath his freckles. 'That's right. I'm the one who leads the horse and works the locks where there's no keeper to help. I dunno what Effie would do without me.'

'You're a good chap, Tom,' Ben said, taking a silver threepenny bit from his pocket and pressing it into Tom's hand.

'What's that for?' Tom shot a sideways glance at his sister. 'I suppose you're going to say I shouldn't take it when I done nothing to earn it.'

'Then earn it you shall, my lad.' Ben ruffled Tom's curly hair. 'There's a delivery due any moment. You know the drill, Tom. Go and open the cellar door and make certain they drop off all the barrels as ordered.'

'It's like old times,' Tom said, leaping to his feet. 'They won't pull a fast one on me, guv.' He raced out of the door, shouting a greeting to the draymen.

'He's a good boy,' Ben said, grinning. 'And you know that you've always got a job back here, girl. I can find work for the pair of you, if you've a mind to take me up on my offer.'

Effie met his grey eyes with a steady gaze. 'Thank you, Ben. I'll remember that.'

'Ben, come here. I want a word with you.' The shrill voice that Effie remembered only too well as belonging to Ben's wife, Maggie, made Ben turn with a guilty start. 'Coming, my love.' He patted Effie on the shoulder. 'Enjoy your food, ducks, and don't leave it so long before you call in again.'

Effie's attempt at a smile was met with cold disdain from Maggie, who appeared in the doorway, beckoning furiously to her husband. Ben followed her into the depths of the pub like an obedient hound.

Poor Ben, Effie thought sadly. He was such a good-natured man and he didn't deserve a vinegar-tongued wife who watched his every move and no doubt nagged him half to death. From the first moment she had met him, when as bedraggled runaways from the workhouse she and Tom had arrived at the pub looking for work, Effie had always liked Ben. He had taken them in when no one else was willing to help two half-starved youngsters and he had been a kind and generous employer, but Maggie was possessed of a jealous nature. She had been convinced that Effie was a threat and nothing would persuade her to think otherwise. She had spied on Effie and had accused her husband of flirting with their young barmaid. Ben had fended off her hysterical outbursts with casual good humour, refusing to admit that the situation was making life difficult for Effie. Then one day Owen had walked into the taproom. Effie found it hard

20

to believe that the handsome young boatman had fallen in love with her at first sight. Things like that only happened in fairy stories and not to a poor girl from the workhouse. But Owen was not to be denied, and he had wooed and won her with his kindness and gentle adoration.

Effie had not been sorry to leave the Prince of Wales tavern when she married Owen. Even though he must have suffered strong opposition from Maggie, Ben had given them a good send-off. The bar had been garlanded with wild flowers and there had been food aplenty. Ale had flowed like the River Lea in full spate and Morris men had danced on the green. It had been midsummer and Effie had spent her wedding night lying with her husband on the deck of the *Margaret Grey* with a canopy of stars above their heads. She would never forget how gentle and tender Owen had been on that magical first night, or the joy she had experienced in their rapturous union. It had been a long, hot summer and they chose to sleep on deck rather than in the close confines of the cabin, making love in the moonlight with the musical sounds of the water and the nightingales singing their sweet songs above their heads. But as the days grew shorter so Owen's life had begun to ebb away.

It had been a cold and frosty night, but

Owen had insisted that he wanted to sleep beneath the stars once more. Effie had wrapped him in a patchwork quilt and lain beside him, holding him close. He had died in her arms, slipping away so peacefully and silently that he might have been asleep. It was then that she had felt the first flutter of their child in her womb, and even in the depths of her grief she had taken comfort from the knowledge that the love they had shared would produce a son or daughter who would carry something of Owen into the future.

'Well now, what's that sad face all about?' Toby demanded, setting Georgie down on Effie's lap. 'You've not finished your breakfast, Effie. Are you all right?'

Jolted out of her reverie, Effie wrapped her arms around Georgie and received a sticky kiss on her cheek.

'Honey,' Toby said, chuckling. 'The woman who does the cooking took a fancy to young Georgie and gave him some honeycomb to suck.'

Effie smiled. 'That sounds like Betty. She was always good to me.'

'She said she remembers you well, and you were a lovely bride. I only wish I'd been here to drink your health, or maybe I don't. I always thought you were too good for this place and should have thrown you over my saddle when I had the chance. I should have spirited you away to live the travelling life with me.'

She shot him a sideways glance. She had always found it hard to tell whether Toby Tapper was serious or merely teasing her, and today was no exception. His flashing smile and good-looking face had no doubt charmed many a young maiden into his bed, but she had always thought of him as a friend and nothing more. She was about to make a suitable rejoinder, putting him gently but firmly in his place, when a commotion outside made everyone in the taproom stop talking.

A youth stuck his head round the door. 'There's a man drowning,' he cried excitedly. 'Fell off the barge he did. Come quick or you'll miss the show.'

Effie was on her feet instantly. Clutching Georgie to her, she ran out of the pub.

Chapter Two

A small crowd had gathered on the canal bank and someone was thrashing about in the water. Effie could just make out Tom on the deck of the *Margaret* and to her horror he was leaning dangerously over the side with a boat hook in his hand. She broke into a run, pushing between the onlookers.

'There's a man overboard,' one of the draymen said calmly, as if watching someone drowning was an everyday occurrence.

Georgie began to wail and Effie held him even closer, murmuring words of comfort even as she felt panic rising at the sight of Tom so perilously close to falling into the filthy water. Her heart seemed to miss a beat as she saw the top of a head break the surface, and it was even more of a shock to realise that it was Jacob who was in the water. The question as to how such an accident could happen froze on her lips as someone jumped into the cut and swam towards the drowning man. It was only when she turned her head to speak to Toby that she realised he was not there. A cheer went up from the onlookers, and it was Toby who towed Jacob towards the steps, holding his head above the water until two hefty draymen climbed down to lift the half-drowned man to safety.

Effie saw Tom collapse onto the deck, burying his face in his hands. She was torn between the desire to comfort her brother and her duty to her father-in-law.

'Here, let me take the little 'un.'

Effie turned to see Betty, the cook from the pub, and as Georgie obviously recognised the kind person who had given him something nice to eat Effie had no compunction in handing him to her. 'Be a good boy, Georgie. Mama won't be long.' Flashing a smile at Betty, Effie edged her way through the crowd to where Jacob lay on the towpath, gasping for air like a landed pike.

'He'll live,' Toby said, wiping his dripping forehead on an equally wet sleeve. 'He might spew up a bellyful of dirty water, but I don't think he's badly hurt.'

'How did it happen, cully?' A drayman kneeling beside Jacob helped him into a sitting position. 'How did you come to fall overboard?'

Jacob coughed and brought up a copious amount of fluid. 'He tried to kill me,' he said, raising his hand and pointing to Tom. 'That boy tried to murder me. Fetch a constable.'

Effie threw herself down on her knees beside him. 'It must have been an accident, Father-in-law. Tom would never do such a thing.'

'He pushed me, I tell you. You both want me dead, so don't deny it.' Jacob hunched his shoulders, glancing around at the curious faces with a calculating look in his eyes. 'You all saw it. The boy tried to kill me. I'm a poor defenceless cripple.'

'Hold on there, mate,' Toby said sternly. 'If you're a cripple how did you move about on a deck packed with barrels? I don't think the boy could carry a man of your size.'

A murmur ran through the crowd with much nodding of heads.

Effie took off her apron and began to dry Jacob's face, but he snatched the cloth from her. 'Leave me be, you wanton harlot. I'll warrant you put the boy up to this. You want to get rid of me so that you can claim my boat and take up with your fancy man.' He jerked his head in Toby's direction. 'A didicoi. That's who she's after.'

Toby seized him by the shoulders. 'Why, you evil old man, I should toss you back in the cut for speaking to her like that.'

Effie rose to her feet. 'How can you say terrible things, Father-in-law? Haven't I looked after you well? I've cooked and cleaned and slaved away on your wretched boat, and never received a kind word or a penny piece for my labours.'

Jacob pointed a shaking finger at her. 'You're a Jezebel. I'm afraid to eat in case you put rat poison in me food.'

'You take that back,' Tom shouted, raising himself from the deck and leaping ashore. 'I never tried to kill you, but I wish you'd drowned.'

'Condemned out of his own mouth.' Jacob's face twisted with malice. 'You'll hang for this, Tom Sadler. They'll string you up outside Newgate for all to see.'

The crowd was growing and Effie reached out to clutch Toby's hand. 'Do something for God's sake, or he'll have Tom arrested.'

Toby gave her fingers a comforting squeeze. He raised his other hand, commanding silence. 'This man is out of his head with shock. I say we all need a drink, and I think it should be on Mr Grey in thanks for being saved from a watery grave. What do you say to that, my friends?'

Jacob's demand that the police should be summoned had been disregarded in favour of free ale, and a cheer rang out as the crowd surged back into the pub.

Effie took Georgie from Betty with a grateful smile. 'Thank you for looking after my boy.

You were always very kind to me, even when I was in trouble with Maggie.'

'Think nothing of it, ducks, but I'd best get back to work.' Betty kissed Georgie on the cheek and backed away, waving to him and chuckling when he copied her.

Toby hooked his arms around both draymen's shoulders. 'Thanks for your help, mates. If you'd be good enough to carry the old man back on board his boat, I'll stand you a round of drinks.'

'You're on, cully.'

Despite Jacob's protests, the draymen picked him up and carried him on board the *Margaret*.

'I wish the old bugger had drowned,' Tom said bitterly. 'He's a fraud, Effie. The cook lady asked me to fetch his dirty plate but he was out on deck when I got there. He'd managed to get himself right up to the bows and he was leaning over the side, trying to cast off. Don't ask me why, unless it was the pint of ale that he'd drunk making him crazy in the head. But when I tried to stop him he took a swing at me and lost his balance. I never pushed him. You got to believe me.'

'Of course I believe you, Tom,' Effie said, placing her arm around his shoulders and giving him a hug. 'But if he can get about on his own the old man must have been having us on all this time.'

'If he's a cripple then I'm the Prince of Wales,' Tom said with a rueful grin. 'What are we going to do, Effie?'

'We've no choice but to go on to Limehouse Basin. Mr Ellerman will be waiting for us and we've already stayed too long. Fetch Champion and we'll cast off right away.' Effie climbed on board, setting Georgie down on deck while she went to the bows to stow the mooring rope. She could hear the babble of voices and shouts of laughter emanating from the open pub door, but there was no sign of Toby. She knew she ought to thank him for saving Jacob but she was anxious to be away in case anyone had sent for a constable. Life, she thought, would have been much easier if Jacob had drowned in Limehouse Cut. She was immediately ashamed of having such wicked thoughts and a shout from Tom was a welcome distraction.

'Ready to go, Effie.'

'All right, Tom.' She hurried along the deck to where Georgie was absorbed in trying to pick up a large cockroach that had found its way on board. She scooped him up in her arms and made her way to the stern, sitting him down with a warning not to move as she took the tiller.

Soundlessly, gliding over the water like a swan, the *Margaret* moved on towards

Limehouse Basin, leaving the Prince of Wales tavern far behind. So many memories were contained within its walls, but it was only now that Effie realised how carefree she had been in those days. She had worked hard from dawn to dusk but she had not minded that, and when Owen came onto the scene her life had changed forever. If only he had lived . . .

Jacob's head and shoulders appeared suddenly above the cabin roof like a malevolent jack-in-the-box. 'You think you're very clever, don't you? But your plan didn't work.' He shook his fist at her. 'Try something like that again and I'll see both of you clapped in jail.'

'You're mad,' Effie said, keeping her voice down so that she did not alarm Georgie. 'You fell overboard. It was an accident.'

'It's my word against his, and who do you think would believe scum from the work-house?'

'Why are you being like this, Father-in-law? Haven't I looked after you these past two years or more? I've waited on you hand and foot and worked the barge even when I was carrying Georgie.'

'You've been fed and had a roof over your head, haven't you? Well now it's all going to change. I've hired a man to take your place and I don't need you any more.'

Effie stared at him in horror as the truth began to dawn on her. 'You planned all this, didn't you? You wanted Tom to be arrested for attempted murder and you were going to say that I put him up to it. Why, Father-in-law? Why would you do something so wrong and so cruel?'

'Use your head, girl. I never wanted my boy to marry you. He should have chosen a boatman's daughter, a girl born to the job instead of a puny little thing like you. I could've snapped you in two like a twig when I was in me prime, but now I'm lame I have to depend on a slip of a girl and a lazy lout of a boy.'

'You never were crippled, were you? It was all an act.'

'Shut your face. I don't have to explain myself to you. When we get to Limehouse Basin you and the boy are leaving my boat. Ellerman has found me replacements for the pair of you, but the child stays.'

'What?' Effie's throat constricted with fear. 'No, you can't mean that. I won't leave Georgie with you.'

'You've no choice, girl. Young Georgie is Owen's son and the *Margaret* will be his when he's a man. He'll carry on the tradition and you can go to hell.' Jacob disappeared as quickly as he had come.

Effie clutched the tiller, unable to let it go for fear of running the boat into the canal bank, but with her free arm she reached down to pick up Georgie who had begun to cry, frightened by the sound of his grandfather's raised voice. 'There, there, darling. Mama's here and she's never going to leave you.'

There was no stopping until they reached Limehouse Basin and Effie's thoughts were in a whirl. She was still getting over the shock of discovering that her father-in-law had been exaggerating his infirmity and must have planned his apparent accident down to the last detail. She needed to talk to Tom and warn him about Jacob's plan, but he was trudging on ahead, leading Champion along the towpath. She sat Georgie on the deck beside her, keeping an eye on him while she steered the boat. His face was still sticky with honey and he was smiling up at her with such love and trust that Effie felt her heart contract. If Jacob thought he could take her son from her then he was very much mistaken. There was nothing in the world that would persuade her to abandon her precious boy to his care. Nothing.

Ellerman was waiting for them, pacing the wharf with a cheroot clenched between his teeth. As they approached, he took a silver watch from his waistcoat pocket, tapping his fingers on the case as if to underline the fact that they were late.

Before Effie had a chance to explain or to warn Tom what was afoot, Jacob limped out of the cabin and leaning heavily on his cane he managed to climb ashore without too much difficulty. Effie could see the astonished expression on Tom's face as he unhitched the horse but she was powerless to do anything until the narrowboat was secured and the unloading began. She had to keep Georgie well away from the activity on deck and she held him in her arms, watching Jacob and Ellerman who appeared to be deep in conversation.

Moments later Ellerman and Jacob were joined by a brutish-looking man and a gaudily dressed woman with a mass of suspiciously red hair and equally unnatural scarlet lips. Effie strained her ears to hear what they were saying, but their words were lost in the general hubbub of the crowded dock basin. As soon as her path was clear, she climbed onto the wharf, holding Georgie in her arms. She saw Tom ambling towards them and she beckoned to him frantically. They must find out what devious plans Jacob had been hatching. She had not entirely believed his threats, but now she was not so certain.

Ellerman tipped his greasy top hat as she approached. 'Mrs Grey,' he murmured, baring his lips in an oily smile. 'And young Georgie too. What a fine boy he is, to be sure.'

'Mr Ellerman. Good day to you, sir.' Effie bobbed a curtsey, shooting a sideways glance at Jacob.

'You won't get anywhere by making up to Ellerman,' Jacob snarled. 'He knows all about you and your wicked ways.'

'How can you say such a thing?' Effie gasped.

'She plays the innocent so well, don't she?' Jacob appealed to the man and woman who stood silently at his side. 'You'd think that butter wouldn't melt in her mouth, but she's a vicious harridan and her devil of a brother tried to murder me. It's a wonder I'm here to tell the tale.'

'Who are these people?' Effie demanded. 'What is going on, Father-in-law? Why are you telling all these lies?'

'What's going on, Effie?' Breathless and panting from running the last hundred yards, Tom pushed past Jacob to stand at his sister's side. 'What has the old bugger said?'

Ellerman took the cheroot from his mouth and ground it beneath the heel of his boot. 'I see what you mean, Jacob. You will be well rid of the pair of them.'

'Shall us go aboard now, guv?' The unpleasant stranger, who had been silent until now, touched his forelock with an ingratiating smile. 'The missis would no doubt like to get settled and put the pot on for our supper.'

'Yes, by all means, Salter,' Jacob said, slanting a sly look at Effie. 'I'll look forward to eating proper food again after two years of pigswill.'

'You take that back,' Tom cried, fisting his hand. 'You shan't say things like that about my sister. Effie's a blooming good cook and I never heard you complain when you was stuffing vittles down your ugly old throat.'

Effie laid her hand on Tom's shoulder. 'Don't, Tom. It won't do any good.'

'That's what I've had to put up with,' Jacob said, casting his eyes up to heaven. 'Please make yourselves at home, Mr and Mrs Salter. The bunk by the stove is mine, but you can choose where you will sleep. It's cramped, but cosy.'

'We're born and bred to the canal life, guv. It was sheer misfortune what led us to lose our snug little craft. We was cheated out of it, but that's a long story and will keep for another time.' Salter doffed his cap to Ellerman before boarding the narrowboat.

Mrs Salter held her arms out to Georgie. 'Let me take you, young master. Old Sal will look after you just like a mother.'

Effie clutched Georgie even tighter as she backed away from Sal's outstretched hands. 'Leave my son alone. He has a mother and you shan't touch him.'

'Come come now, Mrs Grey,' Ellerman said, clearing his throat. 'Don't make a scene. You know it's for the best. Young Georgie will be cared for by Mrs Salter as if he were her own child. She comes highly recommended and you will not be in a position to look after the young fellow.'

'You won't take my baby, Father-in-law,' Effie cried. 'I would die rather than give Georgie to your care.'

'Shall I hit him, Effie?' Tom demanded, dancing about on his toes like a bare-knuckle fighter.

'Call a constable, Ellerman,' Jacob said, curling his lip. 'I want the young hooligan arrested for attempted murder and grievous bodily harm.'

'Give us the child, missis,' Sal urged. 'Don't let the boy witness such a spectacle.'

'Get away from me,' Effie screamed, rocking Georgie in her arms as he began to wail. 'Leave us alone. You shan't take my son from me.'

Jacob took a step towards her, his eyes narrowed to slits. 'The law is on my side, I think you'll find. I'm the head of the family and George is my grandson. Any court of law would agree that I am his legal guardian. You are just a woman and one of doubtful character to boot. There isn't a magistrate in the land who would grant custody to you.'

Effie howled with rage as Sal attempted to snatch Georgie from her arms and she backed away, looking desperately for a means of escape.

Ellerman laid his hand on Jacob's shoulder. 'We don't want a scene, Jacob. It's bad for business, particularly with a young child involved.' He glanced anxiously over his shoulder at the dockers and carters who had stopped work and were advancing on them with grim-faced determination.

'Very well,' Jacob snapped. 'Effie can come back on board and look after the baby, but the boy will never set foot on my boat again.'

Effie stared at her father-in-law aghast as his words sank into her confused brain. 'What do you mean? You can't turn Tom away. He's just a boy.'

'He was old enough to try to kill me. I'm being more than generous in giving him a second chance.' With a swift movement, Jacob caught Tom a hefty clout round the ear that sent him tumbling to the ground. 'Get out of my sight this instant or I'll send for a constable and have you arrested. Show your face on my boat and the same is true.'

Tom scrambled to his feet, holding his hand to his ear. His brown eyes swam with tears and his bottom lip trembled. 'Effie? What shall I do?'

Effie threw her free arm around him and they clung together. Her tears mingled with his and Georgie sobbed inconsolably against her shoulder. 'Best do as he says,' she whispered in Tom's good ear. 'Go to the tavern and see if you can find Toby. He'll look after you until I can think of a way out of this mess.'

'But, Effie, you can't live on board with those people,' Tom said, hiccuping on a sob. 'Come with me, please.'

She shook her head. 'I can't leave Georgie, you must understand that. We've no money and no one is going to take all of us in. I'll find a way, Tom. I swear on our mother's grave that it won't be too long before we're together again.'

'I'm counting to twenty,' Jacob said as if he were enjoying every moment of their agony. 'One, two . . .'

Tom pulled away from Effie's embrace, drawing himself up to his full height. 'I ain't afraid of you, old man. You couldn't count to twenty if your breeches was on fire.' He kissed Effie on the cheek and gave Georgie a tender hug. 'Look after your ma, young 'un. I'll see you again soon.'

Effie watched her brother walk away with a rebellious shrug of his shoulders and a defiant swagger. She could only guess at what effort this show of bravado must be costing him and her heart swelled with pride. 'Don't worry, Tom,' she called after him. 'We'll be together again before you know it.'

'You'll never see him again,' Jacob said, smirking. 'You will stay with me and look after my grandson until I think he is able to do without you. If you make any attempt to take the boy from me I'll set the police on your brother and I'll see that he hangs. Do you understand me, Effie Grey?'

Effie blinked away her tears, meeting Jacob's derisive grin with a toss of her head. 'Think of your son, Father-in-law. What would Owen say if he could see the way you are treating me?'

Jacob raised his hand as if to slap Effie's face, but this time Ellerman intervened, catching Jacob by the wrist. 'Hold hard there, Jacob. I wouldn't advise you to strike a woman holding a child.' He jerked his head in the direction of their audience of tough-looking men. 'They might be brutes but we don't want to antagonise them any further. I think you had better take your family problems else-where. The gin distillers wouldn't take kindly to a public scandal, if you get my meaning.

If you wish to continue doing business with us, then you'd better take heed, my good fellow.'

Jacob allowed his arm to fall to his side. 'You're right, Ellerman, and she isn't worth the trouble. Get on board, woman, and make yourself useful, but take this as a warning – one word out of you and Salter will toss you in the river.'

Unable to control the tears that coursed down her cheeks, Effie climbed on board the *Margaret*. Georgie was sobbing quietly against her shoulder and his small fingers clutched strands of her hair as she stood on deck, staring after Tom until he disappeared into the distance. She felt a sharp pain in her chest as though her heart had cracked and broken. Tom might be thirteen, but the harsh upbringing in the workhouse had stunted his growth and he was small for his age. She felt that she had failed him and now he was all alone in a world where everyday survival was a struggle for the poor. She could only hope that he would find Toby. Effie knew little of the Romany way of life other than the tales that Toby had told her when he used to frequent the Prince of Wales tavern, but she had learned that they looked after their own and were good to their young. She prayed silently that Toby would treat Tom like a brother.

'Go below, missis,' Salter said gruffly. 'Behave yourself and no harm will come to you or the boy. Cross me and you'll be sorry.'

Reluctantly, Effie did as he said. She entered the cabin to find Sal Salter sitting with her feet up. She had a clay pipe clenched in her teeth and puffs of smoke issued from her lips, curling up to the planked ceiling to merge with the steam from the kettle. 'Put the kid down and make us a pot of tea,' Sal said without removing the pipe from her mouth. 'And while you're at it you can make us something to eat. I'm bloody starving and me old man turns nasty if he don't get fed. There's a fresh loaf, cheese and a pound of butter in me basket. Jacob told me that you spent his money on yourself and half starved the poor old sod.'

'That's a wicked lie,' Effie said angrily. 'And I'm not your servant. I thought you were supposed to be the cook.'

'Well you thought wrong, ducks. I ain't going to lift a finger. You'll do the work and I'll watch.'

'You won't get away with this. Mr Grey won't pay you to sit around doing nothing.'

'I'm here to look after the boy, and I know how to handle men like Jacob.'

'You'll leave my son alone,' Effie hissed, snatching up a meat cleaver. 'I'll cook and I'll clean if I must, but you lay a finger on Georgie and you'll have me to deal with.'

Sal threw back her head and laughed, exposing a single tooth and an expanse of bare gums. 'We'll soon knock the spirit out of you, missis. Now get on with making that tea, and I have a fancy for bread and cheese with a couple of pickled onions.'

With Georgie clinging to her skirts, Effie made the tea, cut and buttered bread and sliced cheese, all of which Sal demolished in the blink of an eye and demanded more. Effie waited grimly for Jacob to return to the cabin, expecting him to erupt with rage when he saw Sal Salter sitting in his place, stuffing his food into her greedy mouth. But when he did put in an appearance he seemed to find Sal's antics more amusing than annoying and he slumped down on the seat beside her, placing his hand on her thigh with a throaty chuckle.

'I think we're going to get along passably well, Sal, me old duck.'

Sal fluttered her sandy eyelashes. 'No doubt about it, me old cock.' She took the pipe from her mouth and offered it to him. 'Want a puff, love?'

Effie could hardly believe her eyes when Jacob took the pipe and sucked hard on the clay stem. 'Good baccy, Sal. My old woman wouldn't let me smoke in the cabin.'

Sal nudged him in the ribs, chuckling. 'Well she ain't here to spoil our fun, guvner, so we can do what we likes.'

Jacob glared at Effie as he relinquished the pipe. 'What are you staring at, girl? Get out on deck and take the tiller. Salter has gone to fetch the old nag and we need to be on our way.'

Effie had to resist the temptation to fling the teapot at him, but somehow she held on to her temper. 'Is that how it's going to be then, Father-in-law? Are you going to let her do as she pleases while I do the work?'

'She ain't so stupid as she looks,' Sal wheezed, squinting at Effie through a pall of tobacco smoke.

'You chose to stay,' Jacob said with a humourless smile. 'But you'll abide by my rules. You'll eat and sleep on deck and you'll do everything that the Salters ask of you. And don't think you can slip away in the dead of night because if you do I'll have the law on you and that worthless brother of yours. The boy sleeps in here with us. Do you understand?'

Effie understood only too well, but that night it transpired that Georgie had other ideas and a will of his own. His howls brought Effie running to the cabin where she found Sal shaking him like a terrier with a rat while Jacob and Salter looked on.

'The boy's possessed!' Sal screeched. 'He's the devil incarnate.' She raised her hand as if to strike Georgie but Effie lunged at her, giving her a shove that sent Sal sprawling onto the floor.

'Why you little bitch,' Sal roared, scrambling to her feet and rolling up her sleeves. 'If you want to play it rough then you've picked the wrong woman.'

Salter took the pipe from his mouth and used it to poke his wife in the ribs. 'Stow it, Sal. Let her take the little bugger if she thinks she can stop him making that row. It's giving me earache.'

Jacob nodded his head, grinning stupidly, and it was only then that Effie realised that her father-in-law was drunk. He picked up a tankard and took a swig, wiping his mouth on his sleeve. 'He's got good lungs, I'll give him that.'

Sal hesitated, glaring at Georgie who had gone into a full tantrum and was lying on his back flailing his arms and legs and screaming. 'He needs a good slap,' she muttered. 'Spoilt little brat.'

Effie snatched her child up in her arms. 'Leave him alone,' she screamed as a bubble of hysteria rose in her throat. 'Touch him again and I'll kill you.'

'You're no better than me, you stuck up cow,' Sal snapped, pushing her face close to Effie's. 'I can't stand his noise. Take him outside and let's see what a night in the pouring rain does for you and your high and mighty ways.' She turned her back on Effie and lurched over to sit between her husband and Jacob.

Effie needed no second bidding and she stumbled from the cabin, clutching Georgie to her breast, only to discover that Sal had been right about one thing – the misty drizzle had turned into a downpour. She was soaked before she reached the bows where she had rigged up a tarpaulin to give her a little shelter during the night. She could only be thankful that it was May and not December as she settled down on the blanket that Jacob had grudgingly given her, wrapping Georgie in her shawl and cradling him in her arms until he fell asleep, sucking his thumb. The rain drummed a tattoo on the tarpaulin above their heads and it was a long time before Effie's clothes dried out and the warmth returned to her body, but at least she had her son safely cuddled up to her and eventually she drifted off into a fitful sleep.

Next morning she awakened to find the sun shining from a clear sky and steam rising from the wet decking. Georgie's small body was curled up in her lap, and as she moved he stirred and opened his eyes. A smile of recognition lit his face and Effie felt her heart constrict with love for him. He was so small and precious and she would do anything in her power to protect him.

A shadow loomed over them and a large hand reached down to pull back the tarpaulin. 'Get up, you lazy slut.' Salter leaned over them, his face dark with stubble and his breath stinking of onions and stale beer. 'I ain't starting the day on an empty belly so you'd best get into the cabin and make us some food.'

Effie did not dignify this order with an answer. There was much she could have said but there seemed little point in attempting to converse with an animal like Salter. He strode off along the deck and was about to climb onto the towpath when he turned his head to glare at her. 'Get a move on, girl. We've got these empty barrels to return to the distillery afore noon. You'll find things a bit different now that I'm running the show.' He leapt ashore, leaving Effie staring after him as he made his way to where Champion had been tethered for the night.

She knew now exactly what her life was going to be like on board the *Margaret*, and it was not an exciting prospect. She reached down to hold Georgie's hand as he tugged at her skirts to attract her attention. She had no idea how she would achieve it, but she was determined to make her escape at the first possible opportunity. But she would need money and getting her hands on some of her father-in-law's hoard of cash was not going to be easy. She knew exactly where Jacob hid his money, and that was in a leather pouch concealed beneath the planking that formed his seat during the day and his bunk at night. The main problem was that he so seldom left the cabin, and now she had the added complication of Sal Salter having taken up residence.

Effie made her way to the cabin and opened the door. The stench of sweaty bodies, stale ale and tobacco smoke hit her forcibly, making her feel physically sick. Jacob lay on his bunk, his jaw slack and loud snores shaking his whole body. Sal had awakened and was sitting with her skirts pulled up over her knees as she scratched her bare bottom. She squinted at Effie with bloodshot eyes. 'You took your time. Stoke the fire and put the kettle on. When you've seen to our food you can go ashore and fetch kindling. There's no milk left so you'll have to get some, but then you must know where the farms are around here.'

Effie nodded her head in response as she bent down to riddle the ashes in the stove.

At least there were still glowing embers and it would not take long to get the fire going.

Sal pulled a purse from the top of her stays and took out a coin, tossing it to Effie. 'Salter likes a rasher or two of bacon for breakfast and a couple of fried eggs, so best get some while you're about it. I dunno what you've been living on but there's not enough vittles in the cupboard to feed a mouse. My man likes his food, so bear that in mind.' She rose to her feet and stretched; a move that seemed to terrify Georgie who buried his head in his mother's skirts. 'What's the matter with him?' Sal demanded crossly. 'I think that kid's a bit simple.'

Effie drew the poker from the fire and turned to point it at Sal. 'You leave my son alone, Sal Salter. I've never hurt a soul in my life, but I swear if you lay hands on my boy once again, you'll be very, very sorry.'

Chapter Three

The days that followed were a living nightmare for Effie. If she had thought her life was
hard before the advent of the Salters, she
found it doubly so now. Salter himself seemed
to have a hold over Jacob and he took over
the day to day decisions as to the running of
the narrowboat. He dealt with farmers and
agents alike, accepting extra cargoes and
handling the money. Effie could not understand why Jacob allowed a complete stranger
to run the business that he had inherited from
his own father and had built up over the past
twenty-five years, but she had no doubts that
Sal was making herself available to Jacob in
the most basic way. The cries and grunts
emanating from the cabin in the afternoons
when Salter was leading Champion along the
towpath would have been evidence enough,
even if Effie had not come upon them once in
the middle of the day. She had left Georgie
taking a nap in the well of the stern while she
went to put the stew pan on the stove, and
she had entered the cabin without knocking.

She had found Jacob straddling Sal with his hands clutching her plump breasts and kneading them like bread dough as he took her with amazing vigour for a man who was supposed to be a cripple. Effie had backed out of the door before either of them had seen her, and her stomach had rebelled, causing her to collapse on deck and vomit over the side of the boat.

If she had thought it would alter her circumstances she might have told Salter what was going on under his nose, but on reflection she decided that he condoned his wife's promiscuous behaviour. Effie knew that at night the trio sat up till all hours drinking the raw spirit that Salter tapped from the sealed barrels. How he managed to get away with it she had no idea, but Salter was as slippery as the eels that thrived in the river, and she did not trust him an inch.

During the next few weeks, the only thing in Effie's favour was the weather. A warm and sunny May evolved into a hot, dry June, which made sleeping out on deck almost a pleasure. While she steered the boat, Effie kept a strict eye on Georgie as he played with the wooden bricks that Tom had made for him during long winter evenings. She was constantly on the alert in case Georgie became more adventurous, but he seemed content to keep close to her and actually thrived on the outdoor life. His hair was sun-kissed with blond streaks and his once pale complexion glowed with a healthy tan, although Effie kept a close watch on him in case his fair skin should burn. She herself worked from dawn until long after dusk, lighting the stove and making sure that the fire was kept going all day. She prepared and cooked all their meals, made tea and cleaned the narrowboat from stem to stern under Sal's cold-eyed supervision. All this was accomplished when the boat was moored and loading or unloading the various cargoes of grain, spirits, hay and farm produce. At all other times, Effie was at the tiller. Salter saw to it that she did not converse with any of the lock keepers along the way, warning her that if she tried to make trouble she would be set ashore without her child. Effie had no doubt that Salter and his hateful wife would carry out this threat with pleasure, but even so she risked everything once or twice by speaking to the lock keepers she knew well and asking if they had heard any news of Tom. She thought perhaps he might have left a message for her, knowing that the *Margaret* would have to pass that way. Once, she managed to speak to the keeper at Old Ford lock, but Salter had spotted her before she could elicit any information from the man, and she had been hustled back on board, sustaining a hefty clout from Salter on the way. All that was left to her was to bide her time and await an opportunity to get at Jacob's hidden cache of money.

Effie's chance came unexpectedly on midsummer's day. It had been particularly hot and Sal had complained bitterly about the stuffiness in the cabin. Effie had to hide a smile when she heard Jacob and Sal shouting at each other in the afternoon. It sounded as though Sal had resisted Jacob's advances for once and he was not at all happy. After a brief spat, Sal stomped out of the cabin adjusting her clothing with an angry twitch of her shoulders, and she had sprawled on a pile of sacks filled with grain, legs akimbo and skirts raised above her knees as she basked in the sun. Jacob had limped out of the cabin and continued to harangue her until she opened one eye and uttered a stream of such foul language that even Jacob was silenced, and he retreated into the cabin, slamming the door.

'What are you looking at?' Sal demanded, raising herself on one elbow and glaring at Effie. 'Keep steering this contraption or it'll be the worse for you, missis.'

Ill-temper had rolled around the boat for the rest of the day, growling like a distant thunderstorm, but late in the evening when they were tied up for the night it appeared that both Sal and her husband had had enough of quarrelling and somehow they persuaded Jacob to accompany them to the riverside inn. Effie spotted her chance. Having waited until they were safely out of the way, she checked that Georgie was sleeping soundly before making her way to the cabin. Her mouth was dry as she prised up the loose piece of planking. What would she do if Jacob had changed the hiding place or spent the money? Her hands were trembling as she felt about in the dark space, and she had to stifle a cry of relief when her fingers curled around a leather pouch, heavy with coins. She emptied the money into her apron, and from her pocket she took out a handful of small pebbles that she had collected on one of her forays ashore when she had gone to fetch kindling. Replacing the coins with the pebbles, she returned the pouch to its hiding place and slid the board back into position.

She hurried back to where Georgie lay sleeping, and settled down to count the coins. She was thrilled to discover that Jacob had amassed the princely sum of fifteen pounds. She knew she ought to feel guilty for stealing, but she comforted herself with the fact that having worked unpaid for two years, she had earned this money. If Owen had lived things would have turned out differently. But sadly he was dead, and however much she grieved for him, there was no altering that fact. She had their son to raise and she knew that Owen would have wanted the best for Georgie.

Effie tucked the money bag into the flour sack in which she had packed a few necessities and made herself as comfortable as was possible on the hard decking. The summer dusk was swallowing up the landscape and bats flew overhead making crazy circles against the darkening sky. Owls hooted and in the distance she could hear the mournful bark of a dog fox. The soft lapping of the water against the bottom of the narrowboat was rhythmic and soothing. She took Georgie in her arms and she settled down to sleep, planning to awaken before dawn and leave before the others were up and about. She had toyed with the idea of leaving as soon as they staggered back from the pub, but she had decided that it would be too dangerous to wander about in the dark, and Georgie was getting too big to be carried for any length of time. She must be patient for another few hours, and then she would head for freedom and she would go in search of Tom.

She was awakened by raucous singing and the crunch of booted feet on the towpath as Sal and Salter returned to the boat one on either side of Jacob, who was singing the loudest of all. They boarded the boat, narrowly missing a dunking in the river as they staggered and stumbled, laughing as they missed their footing and fell against each other.

'Wake the little bitch up, Salter,' Sal said, slurring her words. 'I wants a cup of tea.'

'I got better than that, my duck.' Jacob grabbed her round the waist. 'Let's have a proper drink.'

Sal gave him a shove that sent him stumbling into the cabin. 'You're drunk, old man.'

'And so are you, Sal,' Jacob said, clinging to the doorpost. 'Come here, my girl, and show me how much you love me.'

Salter moved towards Jacob and for a moment Effie thought he was going to do something violent, but to her surprise he swung Jacob up in his arms as if he weighed no more than Georgie. 'You need a lie down, old man, and that's what you're going to get.'

'Toss him overboard,' Sal said, chuckling. 'Get rid of the old devil.'

'Shut your face,' Salter snapped. 'D'you want the girl to hear?'

The rest of their conversation was lost as the cabin door slammed behind them. Effie sat bolt upright on the pile of sacks that had to suffice as a bed. Were they really planning to murder Jacob? Or was it just drunken chatter that would be forgotten in the morning?

There was no doubt that Salter and his wife were bad people, but Effie did not think they would risk the hangman's noose. She glanced down at Georgie in case the noise had awakened him, but he was sleeping peacefully. Effie's throat constricted as she gazed at her infant son; he looked so vulnerable, like a little angel, although that was far from the truth. Georgie might be little more than a baby but he had spirit and he was a normal, mischievous little boy. She experienced a surge of love so great that it almost choked her, and she knew then that she would give her own life to protect him.

She closed her eyes but sleep evaded her and at the first sign of approaching dawn she rose from their makeshift bed and made ready to go ashore. Georgie whimpered as she lifted him from his warm nest of blankets, but his sleepy head lolled against her shoulder and he did not wake. Moving stealthily as a cat, Effie tiptoed along the deck and stepped ashore. She could tell by the movement of the water that the tide had turned and on a sudden impulse she untied the mooring rope and tossed it back on board. Almost immediately the *Margaret* began to move, floating silently but swiftly downriver towards its confluence with the River Thames. She knew that it would get no further than the next lock, but by the time Salter realised what had happened she and Georgie would be far away. Salter would have to walk back to their night moorings to find Champion and that would take even more time. She smiled to herself as she pictured their faces when they woke up to find themselves in such a pickle.

Champion uttered a soft whinny of recognition as she walked towards him and Effie stopped to stroke his muzzle, whispering words of comfort to the old horse, and assuring him that he would soon be found. She realised that he did not understand a word of what she said, but she knew that Owen had loved the animal and she could only hope that Salter would treat him well. She had toyed with the idea of stealing the faithful old horse. It would have been so much easier to ride away from here, but she had no doubt that Jacob would inform the police and horse stealing was a serious offence, although no longer punishable by hanging as it had been in Jacob's younger days. Reluctantly, she said goodbye to Champion, and turned south, beginning her long walk back towards London.

It had not been an easy decision, but in the small hours of the morning when sleep evaded her Effie had made plans for their future. She was not a country girl and she knew nothing of farm work other than the fact that it was hard and paid very little. She had been born in Hoxton, so her mother had said, although the family had left there when Tom Sadler senior had lost his job as a journeyman carpenter. He had taken his family to Bow, where he had found work in the glue factory, and they had lived in one basement room sharing it with rodents, fleas and cockroaches despite all her mother's efforts to make the place clean and safe. As Effie trudged onwards with Georgie hitched over her shoulder, still half asleep, she remembered the flight from Hoxton with her family, which had then included her younger brother Stanley and her sister, Emily, who had both died in a measles epidemic which Effie had miraculously survived. It was then, when she was nine years old, that Tom had been born, almost costing their mother's life. Their father had succumbed to cholera shortly afterwards along with thousands of other city dwellers. With no means of support, there had been no alternative for the small family other than the dreaded workhouse. Effie shuddered as she remembered the day when their mother had given up all hope as they passed through the grim iron gates. She had not lasted the year out, and Effie had held three-year-old Tom's hand while they watched their mother slip away into the other world. Effie had prayed that Ma would be reunited with their pa, and despite her frantic pleas Tom had been taken from her and carried, sobbing his heart out, to the boys' section of the workhouse. She had been just twelve years old and had spent the next three years picking oakum until her fingers bled. Then, one winter's morning, she had snatched Tom from his bed and they had hidden beneath sacks in the night soil collector's wagon and made their escape from the workhouse.

As the first pale green light split the dark sky in the east, Effie would have known where she was if only by the stench of rendering fat as she trudged past the soap works with Georgie riding piggyback. She crossed the river at Five Bells Bridge and made her way towards Bow High Street. She was now on familiar ground and she stopped first at a dairy and bought milk, filling the tin can she had brought with her, and then called in at a bakery where she purchased a loaf of bread fresh from the oven. Georgie was crying from hunger but Effie did not stop again until they reached the market gardens in Campbell Road, where she set him on a patch of ground behind a wooden tool shed. The sun was high in the sky now, promising another hot, dry day, and Effie was close to exhaustion, but after making sure that Georgie had drunk some milk and was happily chewing a chunk of bread and cheese, she allowed herself to relax a little and eat. Her plan was simple. She would go to the Prince of Wales tavern and see Ben Hawkins. If anyone knew where she might find Toby, he would, and if she found Toby she hoped that Tom would be with him. She had thought no further than that, but she had to start somewhere.

Footsore and weary, with Georgie's arms tight around her neck as she carried him on her back, it was late afternoon when Effie finally arrived at the pub. She set Georgie down on the ground but as she caught sight of her reflection in one of the windows she saw a woman whom she barely recognised. Her corn-coloured hair was a tangled mess and her face was streaked with dirt and sweat. Her dress was frayed at the hem and spattered with mud, and the soles of her boots had parted with the uppers, exposing her bare toes. In fact, she looked like a beggar, and she knew she could not go in through the front entrance even though she had money in her purse. She went round to the back, and finding the scullery door had been left open to let in the air she went inside.

A startled girl, who could not have been more than ten or twelve, was standing on a box at the stone sink, up to her armpits in greasy water as she washed a pile of dirty dishes.

'What d'you want?' the girl asked, frowning. 'It says no hawkers or pedlars on the doorpost. You won't get nothing here.'

'I want to see Mr Hawkins,' Effie said, ignoring the girl's truculent attitude.

'The missis is in the kitchen, but don't say I didn't warn you.' The girl went back to scouring a plate with a bunch of twigs.

Holding Georgie's hand, Effie went into the kitchen. It had not changed in the years since she had left the pub. The ceiling was tar-coloured, an accumulation over many years of smoke and grease. The range was belching out heat and steam from the water boilers on either side, and the aroma of roasting meat mingled with the fragrance of hot bread and frying onions. Her stomach rumbled and she felt weak at the knees. Maggie Hawkins was standing in the doorway as if about to leave, but she stopped when she saw Effie and her thin features pinched into a scowl.

'Can't you read the sign on the door? We don't want your sort in here.'

'Mrs Hawkins, it's me, Effie Grey. I'm not staying: I've just come for some information.'

Maggie squinted short-sightedly at Effie. 'Oh, it's you. Turning up again like a bad

61

penny. Well, my girl, you can just turn round again and leave. My Ben doesn't want to see you and neither do I.'

Effie stood her ground. 'I'm looking for my brother. I think he might have passed this way. I was hoping that Ben, I mean Mr Hawkins, might have spoken to him, or that he would know where I might find Toby Tapper.'

'Nice company you keep, Effie. I always said you was a bad lot. Now go away and leave us alone. Mr Hawkins don't know anything about your brother or Tapper, so you'd best leave before I set the dogs on you.' She stalked out of the room with a swish of starched petticoats.

Effie turned to Betty, who had been standing silently stirring a pan of soup on the range. 'Is Ben about?' Effie asked urgently. 'I only need to have a few words with him.'

'He's gone to the brewery, I think. I daresay he'll be back in an hour or so if you can wait outside.'

'Oh!' Effie was suddenly overcome by a wave of exhaustion. She had expected Ben to be here, although she realised now that it had been a forlorn hope. She had received the sort of welcome she might expect from Maggie, who had made not the slightest effort to disguise her contempt.

'You look done in,' Betty said sympathetically. 'And the little mite is probably hungry.

My boys was always on the lookout for food.' She bent down, holding her arms out to Georgie. 'Come to Betty, love. She'll see if she can find you something tasty to eat.' Georgie smiled happily as she scooped him up in her plump arms. He tugged playfully at her mobcap so that it tilted over one eye, which seemed to amuse him hugely and made him chuckle.

Effie swayed on her feet as her legs threatened to give way beneath her.

'Sit down afore you fall down,' Betty advised, setting Georgie down on the kitchen table amongst the various pots, pans and vegetables. 'I'm sure that her majesty can afford to give you a bite to eat, just so long as she don't find out. She's a mean cow when all is said and done. She's got eyes like a hawk, counting everything down to the last potato peeling, but then you'd know that, wouldn't you, ducks? I mean having worked here yourself. I remember you well, although I only started just as you was about to marry that handsome young boatman.'

'It seems like a long time ago now,' Effie said dazedly as the room continued to swim around her in mystifying circles. 'Could I have some water, please?'

With a stern warning to Georgie not to wriggle about or he would fall off the table and hurt himself, Betty went into the scullery, returning moments later with a cup brimming with water. 'Sip this and I'll make us a pot of tea.' She hurried back to the table and proceeded to cut a generous slice from a loaf, buttering it liberally and handing it to Georgie who immediately sank his teeth into the bread and began stuffing large chunks into his mouth.

'Easy does it, young 'un,' Betty said, smiling. 'You'll choke if you ain't careful.' She set him down on a chair, ruffling his curls. 'You sit there, love. There's plenty more where that come from, and if you eat all your bread and butter Betty will give you some cake.'

Effie sipped the water and gradually the kitchen stopped spinning around her in a crazy kaleidoscope of colour. 'Thank you, Betty, but we mustn't stay or you'll get into trouble with Mrs Hawkins.'

Betty paused as she was about to pour boiling water into the teapot, and she grinned. 'She'll have gone for a lie down. Her ladyship always has a nap in the afternoons, so we won't see hide nor hair of her until she rings for her tea. It's like working for a blooming duchess.' She poured water onto the tea leaves and set the pot to brew. 'Now then, ducks. If you feels up to it, tell me how you come to be in this state. You was living on board the *Margaret* the last time I saw you.'

'It's a long story,' Effie murmured, as another wave of dizziness threatened to overcome her. 'Do you think I might have a slice of that bread?'

'I can do better than that.' Betty took the lid off a saucepan and ladled stew into a bowl which she put on the table in front of Effie, followed by a slice of bread generously buttered. 'There you are, get your chops round that and you can tell me everything when you've eaten. My rabbit stew is the talk of Bow and you'll not get a finer meal even up West.'

When she had eaten her fill, Effie faced a barrage of questions from Betty which she answered without holding anything back. Betty listened with her eyes widening and her mouth open. 'Well, I never did,' she exclaimed when Effie had finished. 'What a tale, to be sure. And I can tell you now that your brother did come here looking for that rascal, Toby Tapper. Now there's a charmer if ever I saw one.'

Feeling much stronger now, Effie reached out to clasp Betty's hand. 'Did Tom find Toby, and if he did, where did they go from here?'

Betty angled her head, frowning. 'Young Tom went off looking for Toby, as I recall. Whether he found him or not I couldn't say.'

Effie rose to her feet. 'Well at least I know

that Tom came this way, and it's a start. We have to go now, but I can't thank you enough for the food, Betty.'

'You're welcome, ducks. Her ladyship can afford to be generous although she wouldn't give you a sniff of a dishrag without charging for it. I don't say nothing against Ben, he's a good man to work for, but she's a pain in the arse, if you'll excuse the expression.'

'I know what you mean,' Effie said with feeling. 'I worked here for four years before I met Owen, and I could never please her, but Ben was kind to me and I'll always be grateful to him for taking me and Tom in.' She moved round the table to pick up Georgie, holding him at arm's length and chuckling. 'Look at the state of you, young man. There's more chocolate cake on your face than in your tummy.'

Betty looked round as the young scullery maid sidled into the kitchen, wiping her red and wrinkled hands on her none-too-clean apron. 'There you are, Minnie. I thought you'd gone down the plughole to the sea you've taken so long to wash them dishes.'

Betty's tone was jocular but the girl's eyes filled with tears. 'I done me best, cook.'

Effie felt instantly sorry for her and she gave the girl an encouraging smile. 'I used to do your job, Minnie. It's hard work and I'm sure you've done your best.'

'Me hands is red raw,' Minnie complained. 'Can I have me dinner now, cook?'

Betty filled another bowl with stew, placing it on the table. 'I reckon you got worms, my girl. I never knowed a child to eat so hearty and yet always be wanting more food.'

Minnie let out a howl. 'I ain't got worms.'

'She's a growing girl,' Effie said hastily. 'My brother, Tom, is just the same; always hungry.'

'I seen him,' Minnie said through a mouthful of stew. 'I seen your brother. He come here looking for that gypsy with the gold earrings and the bright blue eyes.'

'Heavens above,' Betty exclaimed, laughing. 'Don't say you've fallen for Toby Tapper at your age, girl.'

Minnie swallowed and sniffed. 'I dunno what you mean, cook. All I knows is that Tom was asking about the horse dealer and one of the blokes in the bar told him that there's a fair come to Bow Common. That's where Tom went. I'd swear to it.'

Effie set Georgie down on the ground and gave Minnie a hug. 'That's the best news I've had. Thanks, Minnie. You're a brick.'

Minnie's pinched little face was suffused with a pink glow at this unexpected praise. 'You're welcome, I'm sure.'

'Don't let a few kind words go to your head,'

Betty said severely. 'When you've finished your dinner you've got to mop the floor.'

Effie took Georgie by the hand. 'We must go now, Betty.'

'I hope you find your brother, ducks.' Betty picked up a cloth and bent down to wipe the smears of chocolate off Georgie's face. 'You be a good boy for your ma, young Georgie, and you can come and see me any time. There'll always be a slice of cake for you in Betty's kitchen.'

'Tell Tom I said hello,' Minnie murmured shyly. 'He was nice to me and I like him.'

'I'll be sure to pass the message on,' Effie assured her as she led Georgie out through the scullery, stopping to allow him to wave to his new friend before stepping out into the blazing afternoon heat.

It was not difficult to find the fairground. The sound of hurdy-gurdy music floated in the hot air, summoning the townsfolk to the fair like a Lorelei. Long before they reached the spot, Effie could hear the shouts of the stall-holders attempting to entice the wary public to sample their wares or to test their skills, and the excited cries of both children and adults. She could smell horseflesh and hay, hog roast and woodsmoke. Even if she had not guessed where the fairground lay, Effie could have found it by following the steady stream of people who were advancing on this island of pleasure in the centre of a grim and unforgiving city.

Effie had quite forgotten that it was Saturday and by now most people would have finished work and be ready for a night out, a fact that became clearer as she reached the packed fairground. On the outskirts, the gypsy caravans were grouped in a circle with the horses tethered safely inside. Camp fires sent plumes of smoke spiralling up into the sky and barefoot children with sun-tanned skins played with mongrel dogs. Goats were tethered a little way from the encampment together with the odd cow accompanied by its calf. Georgie had been moaning quietly but now his tiredness was apparently forgotten as he plugged his thumb in his mouth and stared in fascination at the lively gypsy children. Effie led him quickly onwards as they entered a wide expanse of common land filled with tents and stalls, noise and colour. Men on stilts wandered between the crowds towering above everyone on their ridiculously long legs, while musicians played fiddles and drums, competing with the steam organ on the merry-go-round and the lively tunes of the hurdy-gurdy man.

Effie wandered from stall to stall, asking the

traders if they had seen Tom or if they knew Toby Tapper. Although most of them seemed to know Toby, no one had news of Tom. After an hour of fruitless questioning, Effie was feeling exhausted and dispirited. With Georgie riding piggyback once again, her shoulders were aching and her feet were undoubtedly blistered and extremely sore. She was hot, thirsty and very close to tears. It was early evening and although it was still light, naphtha flares were blazing on the stalls adding to the intense heat which seemed to rise from the baked earth and crushed grass. Tiredness combined with anxiety and pent-up emotions threatened to swamp her and she stumbled, almost losing her footing.

'Oy, look out there. Knock me stall over and you'll have to pay for breakages.' The harsh voice of a raw-boned woman standing behind a stall piled high with fairings acted like a slap in the face, bringing Effie sharply back to her senses. She steadied herself by clutching at the wooden table, and the crudely made ornaments jiggled together.

'I said be careful.' The woman strode round to the front of the stall, but she came to a halt as Georgie began to wail. 'Goodness gracious, what d'you think you're doing dragging that baby round a place like this? Ain't you got a home to go to?'

Effie shook her head. 'No.'

The woman took a step backwards, staring at them with a frown wrinkling her weather-beaten brow. She folded her arms across her chest, angling her head. 'A runaway, are you?'

'No, I'm not,' Effie said angrily. It was too close to the truth to ignore and she resented being judged and criticised by a complete stranger. 'I'm looking for my brother and a man called Toby Tanner.'

The woman threw back her head and laughed as she chucked Georgie under the chin. 'That's his brat, I suppose. Come to beg him to marry you, I suppose.'

'Certainly not.' Effie slid Georgie off her back and cradled him in her arms. 'It's not like that. Toby is a friend and my brother went looking for him. Tom is just a boy and I haven't seen him for weeks.' To Effie's chagrin her voice broke on a sob. 'I'll not bother you any longer.' She began to walk away but the woman called her back.

'Here, you. Come back.'

Effie paused. 'What do you want? Have you remembered something?'

The woman held out her hand and Effie noticed that it was unusually large for a woman, sinewy and strong, as if she had spent a lifetime doing manual labour. 'They call me Leah.'

It seemed churlish to ignore this friendly overture and Effie found her hand clasped in a firm hold. 'Effie,' she murmured. 'I'm Effie Grey and this is my son, Georgie. My husband died . . .' She could not continue without breaking down completely.

Leah released Effie's hand and held her arms out to take Georgie, who had stopped crying and was eyeing her curiously. 'He's a fine fellow. I had one just like him, but my Eddie was taken from me afore he reached his second birthday.' She lifted Georgie from his mother's arms, holding him high above her head and laughing at his delighted chuckles. 'My Eddie used to love being swung about. Nothing frightened my Eddie.'

Effie watched anxiously. 'We'd best be on our way.'

'You look exhausted,' Leah observed, settling Georgie on her hip. 'How long have you been on the road looking for this brother of yours?'

'Not long,' Effie said truthfully. 'But I must go now. I need to find somewhere to sleep tonight.' She saw suspicion in Leah's dark eyes and this brought her chin up. 'I have money and I can pay for a night's lodging.'

Leah shrugged her broad shoulders. 'Keep your cash, Effie Grey. I've got a wagon of me own and a pot on the fire. You're welcome to share my supper and kip down for the night, if you don't mind the small space. Or you can sleep outside under the stars, which I often do on a night like this.'

'Oh, really. I couldn't put you to so much trouble.'

But Leah did not seem to be listening. 'Oy, Myrtle.' She beckoned to a woman selling toffee apples from a tray slung about her neck on a leather strap. 'Watch me stall for a moment.'

Myrtle took the clay pipe from her mouth and nodded, catching the purse which Leah tossed to her.

Effie was about to protest but Leah was already on the move with Georgie tucked beneath her arm like a bundle of washing. She disappeared between a tent advertising the charms of the bearded lady and another boasting of the largest rat in captivity. Effie felt panic rise in her throat to choke her as wild thoughts flashed through her mind. She had heard about gypsies and fairground folk kidnapping young children. She broke into a run . . .

Chapter Four

Pushing her way through the crowd, Effie stumbled over grassy tussocks and narrowly missed getting her foot caught in the guy ropes of a large tent where, judging by the thunderous applause and appreciative shouts and whistles, some kind of entertainment seemed to be in progress. Panic gripped her as she lost sight of Georgie, and she wanted to scream and shout at the smiling faces of families out for a pleasant Saturday evening at the fair. What right had they to be so cheerful when her child might have been abducted by a strange woman? Effie skidded to a halt as she came to the end of the attractions, reaching the place where the fairground people had set up their encampment. She was just in time to see Leah set Georgie down on the bottom step of a brightly painted caravan. He was smiling happily as he licked a toffee apple.

Leah turned to her with a nod of approval. 'He's a fine boy. Took to me right away he did.'

Effie controlled her erratic breathing with

difficulty. She did not want to make a scene, and she realised that she was receiving curious looks from some of the women who were nursing babies or simply sitting on the steps of their wagons. With her panic subsiding and commonsense reasserting itself, Effie moved closer to Georgie. She did not know whether to snatch him up and make a run for it, or to brazen it out with this bold and slightly mannish female.

Leah, however, seemed totally oblivious to the storm of unrest she had wrought in Effie's bosom and she was casually stirring something in a black cast-iron pot suspended over the fire on a tripod constructed from forked branches. She looked up and grinned. 'Fetch a couple of bowls from the van and we'll eat now. Zilla will eat later.'

'Zilla?' Effie stared at Leah in surprise. She had assumed that this rather odd person lived alone, but it appeared that she had been wrong.

'My pal Zilla, the bearded lady. You'll meet her in a while. Now, are you going to join me for supper or not?'

The thought of meeting a woman with a beard who went by the name of Zilla was so intriguing that Effie momentarily forgot her reservations and climbed the steps into the caravan, taking care not to tread on Georgie.

Used as she was to living in the cramped conditions on a barge, the interior of the caravan seemed little different. It was, she thought, as she searched for the bowls, much better organised than the cabin on the *Margaret* and it was spotlessly clean. The paintwork was as colourful inside as it was on the exterior, and there did not seem to be a nook or a cranny that was not brightened either with plump cushions, polished brasses or china ornaments, some of which Effie recognised from the fairings stall. It was, to her surprise, a most welcoming home: comfortable, cosy and unashamedly feminine. She hurried out with the bowls that she had found on the shelf of a wooden dresser.

The soup might not have been quite up to the standard of Betty's rabbit stew, but it was flavoured with wild herbs and tasted very good: Effie consumed two bowlfuls with no difficulty, sharing the first with Georgie, after which he fell asleep on her lap replete and smiling, with remnants of toffee stuck to his face. Leah sat cross-legged on the ground smoking a pipe, but she tossed it aside and scrambled to her feet when a large woman squeezed her wide crinoline between two caravans, swaying towards them like a giant bell. As she came closer, Effie realised that this could be none other than Zilla, the bearded lady. Much to Effie's astonishment, Leah greeted her friend with a smacking kiss on the lips, and, hooking an arm around Zilla's ample shoulders, she proudly introduced her. 'This here is my pal, Zilla. We've been together for more than twenty years, ain't that so, my dear?'

Zilla smiled and nodded, although the gesture was rather lost in the mass of grey beard that began at her hairline and tumbled in waves onto her large bosom. 'Pleased to make your acquaintance, young woman.'

Hampered by Georgie's weight, Effie was unable to rise but she nodded her head. 'Likewise, I'm sure.'

'This is Effie,' Leah said with an expansive wave of her hand. 'And the fine young fellow asleep on his ma's lap is Georgie. Don't he remind you a bit of my Eddie?'

Zilla's green eyes filled with tears and she wiped her face on her beard. 'Poor little mite. I knew him for such a short while, but he were an angel straight from heaven.'

'And that's where he is now,' Leah said, raising her eyes to the darkening sky. 'I like to think of my boy as a star, gazing down at me as I gazes up at him.'

Zilla patted Leah's gaunt cheek. 'You are so poetical, my dear.'

'And you must be starving, old girl.' Leah

cleared her throat with a loud harrumph and went to the fire to fill a bowl with soup. 'Sit down and eat up. I've got to go back to me stall before young Myrtle gets the hump.' She turned a stern face to Effie. 'Now don't you start talking nonsense about moving on at this time in the evening; your boy needs his sleep and you shall have the van. Zilla and me can share a bed beneath the stars as is our wont on a night like this. I shall look up at Eddie and Zilla will keep me company.'

Leah disappeared into the dusky shadows and Zilla lowered herself down onto the ground with her skirts falling about her like a deflated hot-air balloon. She tucked her beard into the front of her dress while she supped soup straight from the bowl. When she had drained the last drop she licked her lips and wiped her mouth on the back of her hand. She held the bowl out to Effie. 'I could do with some more, ducks. Would you? It takes me a while to get to me pins again once I've sat down and me corsets are killing me.'

Balancing Georgie over her shoulder, Effie rose to her feet and did as Zilla asked. As she took her seat again she couldn't resist voicing the question that had been on her lips ever since she first saw the bearded lady. 'Is it real, ma'am? I mean, did it grow on your face?'

Zilla's emerald eyes twinkled as she peered

at Effie over the rim of the bowl. 'Let's just say that it's like everything in the fairground, duck – an illusion.'

'So it's not real then?' Effie couldn't hide her disappointment.

'Oh, it's real hair all right. This beard was cut off a Barbary pirate just afore he was hanged at Execution Dock, or so I've been led to believe.'

'A pirate!' Effie could hardly believe her ears. 'A real live pirate?'

Zilla pulled a face. 'Well, he's dead now of course, but I was reliably informed by the man what sold it to me that it was the beard of Kemal the Cruel. Between you and me, ducks, I've a feeling the whiskers was cut off his old grandpa afore he croaked, but it's a good story and I'm sticking to it.'

Effie sat in silence; her head was spinning with the strangeness of it all and she felt as though she had wandered into a weird dream world where nothing was as it seemed. The camp fires burned even more brightly as the shadows lengthened and deepened into dark canyons between the wagons. The shouts and laughter of the children gradually died away as they were sent off to bed and the murmured conversations of their mothers were drowned by the noise of the fairground. The musicians played their instruments even louder as they competed with the barkers shouting out the attractions of the various stalls and sideshows. The scent of woodsmoke and damp earth struggled to overcome the heavy chemical-laden atmosphere that hung in a cloud over Bow Common, and overlying it all was the faint sweet smell of hot toffee and herb-scented stew. A strange feeling of lassitude made Effie's limbs heavy and she was finding it increasingly difficult to keep her eyes open.

'Best get yourself off to bed, girl,' Zilla said gently. 'You look done in and the poor little mite is already in the land of Nod.'

'Are you sure you don't mind giving up your bed for us?' Effie asked anxiously. 'Georgie and me have grown used to sleeping out on deck.'

'On deck, you say?'

Effie bit her lip. She had not intended to give so much away. Leah had asked no questions and Effie would have preferred to keep their history to herself in case Jacob had reported their absence to the police. She had a nasty feeling that he would stop at nothing in order to gain control of Owen's son. Shifting Georgie to a more comfortable position on her shoulder, she rose to her feet. 'It's a long story, Zilla. Would you mind if we left the details until morning? I'm very tired.'

'Of course you are. Anyone can see that.

I didn't mean to stick my nose into your business, my dear. Get some sleep and everything will look better in the morning.'

When she had settled Georgie for the night, Effie lay down on the bunk, curling her body protectively around her baby son. She had made up her mind to leave as early as possible next day in order to continue her search for Tom. She tried not to think of the dangers that might beset a thirteen-year-old boy travelling the rough streets of the East End alone and penniless. She could only hope and pray that he had found Toby who, despite his raffish lifestyle and reputation as a lady killer, would see that no harm came to her young brother. As her limbs relaxed and she began to drift off to sleep she remembered a conversation she had once had with Toby in the bar of the Prince of Wales tavern when she had graduated from scullery maid to helping Ben serve customers. As she recalled it was one of the rare moments when Toby had talked seriously about anything and in particular his past. He had spoken tenderly of his mother who had been a maidservant in a large house on the edge of Hackney Marshes. He had been born there, he said, but he had only been seven years of age when his mother died and he had been sent to live with her Romany family. Effie would have liked to know more about him, but Toby had not been very forthcoming. 'Where are you now, Toby?' she murmured sleepily. 'I pray to God that Tom is with you.'

Effie awakened to the delicious aroma of frying bacon, but her pleasure quickly turned to panic as she realised that Georgie was missing. She fell off the bunk and ran to the door but she stopped, holding on to the doorpost as she saw Georgie playing happily with a group of children. His laughter was a sound that she had not heard for some time and her eyes unaccountably filled with tears.

Leah was turning bacon in a soot-blackened frying pan and she looked up, waving the fork at Effie. 'Come and get your breakfast, ducks. There's tea in the pot if you'd like to help yourself. Zilla's had hers and she's gone to wash her beard in the stream. She says there's nothing like fresh water to keep the hair soft.'

Brushing her long hair back from her face, Effie was suddenly conscious that she must look a fright and she needed a wash, but she was hungry and she did not want to offend Leah by retreating into the van to make herself presentable. A quick glance around the encampment was reassuring in the fact that no one appeared to be in the least bit interested in her. In the distance she could see a man juggling brightly coloured wooden clubs, although he did not seem very good at it as he kept dropping them and starting again. Effie was about to turn away when a tiny woman, little taller than Georgie, clambered down the steps of a nearby caravan. Effie couldn't help but stare at the little person, who had the body of a child but a rather disproportionate head and a face that was lined and anything but youthful.

Leah slapped some bacon on a plate and thrust it into Effie's hands with a knowing grin. 'That's Margery, the midget. She may be small but she don't like to be reminded of it and she don't like people staring at her, which is odd because that's what they do all day when she's on show as the World's Smallest Woman.'

Effie felt the colour rise to her cheeks and she averted her gaze as Margery turned to look at her through narrowed eyes. 'I'm sorry; I didn't mean to upset her.'

'Don't worry about it, ducks. You'll find it a bit strange here at first but you'll soon get used to us and our funny ways.' Leah took a chunk of bread and tossed it in the bacon fat. 'Eat up, Effie. You could do with a bit more meat on your bones.' She stuck a fork in the fried bread and passed it to Effie. 'Get that down you and then you can help me unpack a box of fairings and set them out on me stall.'

With her mouth filled with bacon, Effie was not in a position to argue and she felt obliged to repay Leah's generosity. By the time she could speak Leah had wandered off to speak to a tall man with a bare chest that rippled with muscles as he performed a series of exercises with much jumping and swinging of his arms. Effie doubted whether he had much breath left to answer the questions that Leah appeared to be putting to him, but eventually he stopped leaping about and stood with his head bowed as he paid attention to her, all the while mopping the sweat from his torso with a none-too-clean towel. Effie turned her head to look for Georgie, not liking to take her eyes off him for more than a few moments, but he was still larking around with the other children and a couple of mongrel puppies. Their shouts and laughter echoed round the encampment together with the happy yapping of the small dogs. There had been little to laugh at on the *Margaret* and this was the first time that Georgie had been able to play with children of his own age. She did not want to spoil his fun.

She finished her food, washing it down with a cup of strong, sweet tea. She was immensely grateful to Leah but she knew that she could not stay here for long. She must renew her search for Tom. She would tell Leah the moment she had finished speaking to the muscular gentleman, who wore only a pair of ankle-length trouser drawers which left little of his manly shape to the imagination. Effie averted her gaze quickly, hoping that no one had noticed that she was staring at the extraordinary fellow, whose body seemed to bulge in most unexpected places. She concentrated her attention on the children, smiling at their obvious enjoyment of the game, which looked rather rough and tumble, but Georgie did not seem to mind. She was so engrossed in their play that she jumped at the sound of Leah's voice calling her name. Effie looked round and saw her new friend striding across the springy turf towards her. The muscular man had picked up a set of dumb-bells and was striking poses to an imaginary audience while the rest of the camp seemed to ignore him.

'Who is he?' Effie asked, when Leah drew close enough for her to question without raising her voice.

'Him?' Leah shrugged her shoulders with a dismissive snort. 'Thinks he's somebody, but he's not. Calls himself the Great Arnoldo but his real name is Arnold Hicks and he comes from Hoxton. He's the strong man act and the punters are impressed, but it's all show. He's afraid of his own shadow.'

'Oh!' Effie digested this piece of information

in silence, staring at Arnoldo and frowning. He looked every inch a man, but Leah was clearly unimpressed. 'Don't you like him then? You were talking to him for ages.'

'He owns two vans, his and the one that was used by the two-headed lady before she run off with the lizard man. Anyway, it gave me an idea which I'll put to our head man, Frank senior, when I've got a moment, but I'll not say any more for the time being.'

Effie was too concerned about the fate of the odd couple to take much notice of Leah's mysterious pronouncement. 'Did she really have two heads and was he really a lizard?'

Leah gave her a pitying look. 'Of course she didn't have two heads, one was stuck on, and he was only half lizard, all scaly and horrible. I dunno what the attraction was there.'

'At least they have each other,' Effie said, sighing.

'Forget them; we've got work to do. The punters will be arriving as soon as they've done their duty and been to church.'

Effie had quite forgotten that it was Sunday, but now as if to confirm Leah's statement church bells began to chime, their differing tones and timings making them sound as though they were calling to each other as in the old nursery rhyme, 'Oranges and Lemons', which Effie had learned at her mother's knee.

She closed her eyes, picturing her mother's sweet face and the soft sound of her voice as she sang.

'Stop daydreaming, Effie. Leave the boy here, no harm will come to him.' Leah marched off, hitching her skirts above her knees to accommodate her long strides.

Effie glanced anxiously at Georgie. She couldn't leave him here. What if he missed her and panicked, thinking his mother had deserted him?

'It's all right, dearie.'

Effie looked around and couldn't see the woman who had spoken, until someone tugged at her skirt. She looked down into Margery's grey eyes. 'Oh, I'm sorry. I didn't—' Effie clapped her hand to her lips. She had almost admitted that she had not seen the tiny woman, but just in time she remembered Leah's warning.

'You could leave the boy here, ducks,' Margery said with a smile that transformed her stern features. 'I'll keep me eye on him for you. He's having a lovely time with the other nippers. Why spoil it for him?'

'I've never left him before,' Effie murmured.

'There's always a first time. I got a nipper of me own. She's asleep in the van with her pa looking after her, but your little 'un will be safe here. We're like one big family and we all looks out for each other. You go off and help Leah. Your boy won't even know you're gone.'

Reluctantly, Effie left Georgie under the watchful eye of Margery, but she kept glancing over her shoulder in case he should suddenly realise that his mother was not there and start to cry. She was almost disappointed when Georgie showed no signs of missing her, but Leah was already out of sight and Effie had to quicken her pace as she tried to remember where the fairings booth was sited. She wended her way through narrow gaps between stalls selling everything from sweets to quack medicines. The stallholders were getting ready for a busy day's trading and the sun was already high in a clear sky, giving the promise of continued hot weather. The gilding and gaudy paintwork on the merry-go-round sparkled in the bright light and the wooden horses seemed to smile at Effie as she paused to admire their sleek beauty. Their names were painted on their necks and she found herself thinking of Champion, and hoping that Salter would treat him kindly.

She moved on and the warm grass crushed underfoot gave off the scent of new-mown hay. The sugary scent of toffee, boiled sweets, liquorice and peppermint made a heady concoction when mixed with the faint whiff of leather and horseflesh, cheap cologne and woodsmoke, but the sudden powerful odour of wood alcohol and a loud whoosh brought Effie to a halt as a plume of flame erupted from the mouth of a man holding a flaming torch. She uttered a faint scream, thinking that he must have exploded.

He gave her a toothless grin. 'Ain't you never seen a fire-eater afore, lady?'

Effie swallowed hard, holding her hand to her heart as it pounded against her tightly laced stays. 'Good heavens! Is that what you are? How do you do that?'

He pulled a flask from his belt, filled his mouth and expelled a fine mist into the torch which exploded into a fireball. He wiped his lips on the back of his hand. 'That ain't nothing. You watch me when I swallow flaming swords. I've entertained all the crowned heads of Europe in me time.'

Impressed and still feeling a little weak, Effie could hardly speak. 'Well, I never.'

'No, you never saw a fellow to equal me, I'll warrant.' He held out his free hand. 'Elmo the fire-eater.'

Effie shook his hand. 'I'm Effie.'

'Yes, I know. News travels fast around here.' With a dramatic wave of his torch, Elmo bowed and sauntered off leaving Effie staring after him, but a shout from Leah brought her back to the present and she hurried over to the fairings stall.

No sooner had they unpacked the crate of china ornaments and arranged them on the white cloth than the first punters began to wander through the fairground. Soon the place was alive with the sound of excited chatter, laughter and music. Effie watched in awe as Leah shouted out her wares, exchanged banter with the customers and persuaded parsimonious husbands to part with their hard-earned money in order to buy a pretty china ornament for their wives. Effie worked diligently, wrapping the delicate objects in brown paper and taking money while Leah concentrated on selling, but Georgie was constantly on Effie's mind and at the first opportunity she hurried back to the encampment. She found him sitting side by side with Margery on the steps of her caravan. From a distance they looked like two children, but Margery was holding a baby in her arms and she smiled proudly when she saw Effie.

'This here is my little 'un, Victoria, named after her majesty. Ain't she just the most beautiful baby you've ever seen?'

Effie nodded in agreement. 'Yes, she's just perfect. Thank you so much for minding Georgie.' She bent down to scoop him up in her arms and give him a cuddle, which he resisted, squirming and demanding to be put down.

'He's a fine boy,' Margery said, chuckling. 'He's got a mind of his own, I'll warrant.'

Effie set him back on the ground, watching him toddle off to disturb one of the puppies which were enjoying a nap in the warm sunshine. 'He takes after his pa,' she murmured, blinking away the tears that sprang to her eyes when she thought of Owen.

'Run off, did he?' Margery patted the baby's back as it began to whimper. 'Happens all the time.'

'He died before Georgie was born. He never saw his son.'

Margery made a sympathetic sound in her throat. 'That's hard, that is. Never mind, ducks, you got a lovely little chap there, and I don't doubt there'll be someone else waiting round the corner to sweep you off your feet. Unless, of course, it's Toby that you fancy and I wouldn't bet on him.'

'I don't want anyone else,' Effie said hotly. 'And it's not like that at all. I'm looking for my brother and I think he might be with Toby, who is just a friend.'

'All right, don't get in a miff. I was just surmising and meant no offence.' Margery scrambled to her feet, hoisting the baby over

91

her shoulder like a sack of potatoes. 'Now I got to get dressed for me first show.'

'Who will look after your baby?' Effie asked, suddenly anxious. 'I can't go back to the stall if there's no one to keep an eye on Georgie.'

Margery paused as she was about to enter her caravan, pointing her finger in the direction of a much older woman dressed all in black, who was stirring something in a cast iron pot over the camp fire. She looked so much like the illustration of a witch that Effie had once seen in a picture book that she caught her breath, but Margery seemed quite unperturbed. 'That's Gert. She used to be the fortune teller but she's getting on a bit now and her daughter, Laila, reads the cards. Gert watches over the nippers while the rest of us goes about our work.'

Effie bit her lip, staring anxiously at the old woman. 'Can she cope with small children? I mean, she might not be able to move quickly enough if they were in danger.'

Margery cackled with laughter. 'She's a fortune teller, ducks. If she don't foresee danger then no one can. You leave young Georgie with me and I'll make sure that Gert keeps an eye on him.'

Despite Margery's confidence in Gert's prowess as a child minder Effie spent an anxious afternoon, and when Leah put Myrtle in charge of the stall so that they could return to the caravan for their supper, Effie raced on ahead. She found a group of young children seated on the ground close to Gert, who was in the process of telling them a story. For a dreadful moment Effie was convinced that Georgie was not amongst them, but then she saw him sitting beside a girl of about six or seven. He was covered in dirt from head to foot, which made his eyes look even bluer when a smile of recognition lit his small face and he scrambled to his feet, running towards Effie with his arms outstretched. She caught him up and held him close. He lifted his face to give her a sticky kiss and she rubbed her cheek against his dusty curls. 'My goodness, Georgie Grey, what a state you're in.'

'It ain't nothing but what a tub of water won't wash away,' Gert said, apparently overhearing Effie's softly spoken remark. The fortune teller might be old, Effie thought, but there was nothing wrong with her hearing, and if it were true that Gert could see things in her crystal ball, she might just know where to find Toby.

Effie moved closer to the old woman, trying not to wrinkle her nose at the smell of her unwashed body and musty clothes. 'Madam Gert,' she began nervously.

Gert cocked her head on one side. 'You're

going to ask me the whereabouts of Toby Tapper, the horse trader.'

Effie felt her mouth drop open and she closed it quickly. 'H-how did you know that? Have you looked in your crystal ball?'

'You're an innocent all right,' Gert said, cackling with laughter. 'No, dearie, it's all round the camp that you're looking for Toby, and it ain't the first time that a young woman has come searching for the young devil.' Gert's smile faded into a look that bordered on the sympathetic. 'But I can see that it ain't so in your case.'

'I'm looking for my brother. He's only thirteen and not yet a man. I'm afraid that something might have happened to him.'

Getting to her feet, Gert thrust her hand into her pocket and took out a handful of dried herbs which she tossed onto the fire. She leaned over the smoke, inhaling deeply, and then subsided back on her haunches. She closed her eyes. 'I can smell marsh gas and mist. The fog is curling up around a boy and he's fading away . . .' With a convulsive shudder Gert opened her eyes, staring wildly around her. 'What did I say? Did I tell you where to find Tom?'

Effie was shivering violently. She felt ice-cold although it was a balmy evening and the heat from the camp fire was intense. 'How did you know his name? I never told you.'

'I dunno, ducks. It comes and goes, the gift; although it goes more often than it comes these days. You should get Laila to read the tarot cards and look into her crystal ball. She's got the sight now but mine is fading. What I can tell you is that there is a tall man waiting to have words with you.'

'Do you know his name?' Effie demanded, her curiosity aroused and a tingle of apprehension running down her spine. 'How do you know he wants to speak to me?'

Gert grinned, exposing a row of blackened tooth stumps. 'Because he's standing right behind you, ducks.'

Chapter Five

Effie turned her head and found herself looking up into the whiskery face of the Great Arnoldo. 'Did you want me, mister?'

'Arnoldo,' he boomed in a stentorian voice that reverberated off the wooden sides of the caravans. 'Everyone addresses me Arnoldo.'

'Except your ma who calls your Arnie,' Gert muttered.

'What did you say, old woman?'

'That's no way to address a lady, Mr Arnoldo,' Effie said angrily. 'I daresay as how you wouldn't wish anyone to speak to your ma in that way.'

He bent down to stare into Effie's face. 'You dare to speak to the Great Arnoldo like that?'

'I do, sir. Especially when I know I am in the right. Now, what is it you have to say to me? If you want me to leave, then I have to tell you that I have no intention of staying any longer than one more night.'

'Oh, well then you won't want the two-headed woman's caravan after all.' Arnoldo twitched his massive shoulders and pursed his lips, causing his moustache to quiver like a small furry animal clinging to his upper lip.

'She wants the van,' Gert said sternly. 'Don't torment the girl, Arnie. She's worked hard for her bed and board and she'll not find her young man for a while yet. I can tell you that for nothing.'

'If you say so.' Arnoldo seemed to shrink in stature and he bowed his head in deference to Gert's commanding presence. 'I suppose she can have the van until we find someone more permanent, but I shall expect something in return.'

'I can work hard,' Effie said firmly. 'I don't mind what I do.'

'You don't?' Arnoldo peered down at her, frowning thoughtfully. 'Then I have the perfect job for a small person like you. See me in the morning, but now I have a show to do.' He strolled off with his cloak flying out around him like the wings of a giant bird.

'Soft as butter,' Gert said, winking. 'He's afraid of his own shadow, but don't let on I said so.'

Effie's mind was bemused by the strange events of the day and she shook her head. 'Did he say I could have the two-headed woman's caravan?'

Gert rose stiffly to her feet, hitching up her long skirts to expose skinny legs bristling with black hairs and large feet encased in a pair of men's boots. 'Come with me and I'll show you. Best bring young Georgie too and then you can put him to bed. Leah will want you to help out on the stall this evening, so it's best to settle the boy first.'

Effie had to chase Georgie in order to catch him and he chuckled with glee, seeming to think this was all part of the exciting game of living in a fairground. With him firmly tucked beneath one arm, Effie followed Gert to a caravan just a few yards distant from the one owned by Leah and Zilla. It was by contrast very run down and verging on the dilapidated. The paintwork was blistered and peeling and when Gert opened the door Effie was appalled by the smell emanating from the interior.

Gert stood aside to allow her to pass. 'It's nothing that a bit of elbow grease won't cure, and a few buckets of hot water and washing soda.'

Effie stared at the chaotic jumble inside. It was evident that the two-headed lady and the lizard man had left in a hurry. 'Yes,' she murmured. 'I'll see to it in the morning.'

'Leave the door open when you've put the nipper to bed and I'll keep an ear open for him should he wake, but seeing as how he's been racing round like a lunatic all day, I think he'll sleep well tonight.' Gert wandered back to the fire, leaving Effie to explore her temporary home.

Holding her breath, she entered the caravan and set Georgie down on one of the bunks. It might, she thought, have been better had she seen it late at night when darkness would have disguised the torn curtains and moth-eaten covers on the squabs, which were stained and looked suspiciously greasy. The air was thick with the smell of decomposing food, human sweat and stale tallow from the candle stubs that littered the table and shelves. Effie opened the window to allow air into the van, and finding an old sack lying on the floor she swept the detritus off the table and floor into it, tossing it outside onto the grass when it was full.

Georgie was unnaturally quiet and she smiled at the sight of his rosy, dirt-smeared face as he lay sleeping where she had placed him. His dark eyelashes formed crescents on his cheeks and his soft brown curls, streaked golden by the sun, flopped over his forehead. He was so small and helpless and so dear to her that it almost hurt to look at him. She bent down to drop a kiss on his cheek and he stirred, smiling in his sleep. She would not normally have allowed him to go to bed in such a filthy state, but it would be a shame

99

to wake him now. She covered him with her shawl, tucking it around him so that he would not roll off the bunk. She was reluctant to leave him, but she trusted Gert to keep her word and listen out for any sounds of distress from the van. With a last, loving look at her baby, Effie climbed down the rickety steps to the ground and receiving an encouraging nod from Gert, she made her way to the fairings stall.

Next morning, Effie awakened to find Georgie tugging at her hair and she snapped into a sitting position. The interior of the caravan looked even worse as the sunlight poured in through the open window, and she clutched Georgie to her as a large cockroach scuttled across the table, falling to the floor where it joined the rest of its large family. Effie stifled a cry of disgust and she swung her legs over the side of the bunk, reaching down for her boots. She turned them upside down and gave them a shake; a small brown field mouse toppled out of one boot, stopped for a moment to stare at her with button-bright eyes and then scurried towards the door where it disappeared through a hole in the boards. To her relief the other boot was free from livestock and Effie crammed her feet into her well-worn footwear before standing up. Each time she took a step the roaches crunched beneath her feet like dry leaves on a forest floor. Georgie was fascinated by the moving carpet on the floor and not at all frightened by the shifting insect mass. He would, Effie thought with a shudder, have been quite happy to play with them as if they were clockwork toys, but she was not prepared to put her theory to the test. She lifted him in her arms and tried not to pull a face as she trod carefully across the floor. She opened the door, hesitating on the top step as she stared open-mouthed at the sight that met her eyes.

Below on the grass, Elmo the fire-eater was tending a fire over which hung a huge pot of bubbling water. He looked up and saluted her. 'Fire is my business, Effie,' he said, smiling and revealing a row of surprisingly white teeth. 'We thought you might need a bit of a hand this morning.' His expansive gesture encompassed a group of people that Effie had seen but not yet met.

A young woman wearing a rather theatrical version of a gypsy's costume, complete with a headdress decorated with shiny metal coins and a red scarf knotted around her slender throat, stepped forward. In her hand she held a poke filled with tea leaves and another containing sugar. 'I'm Laila,' she said in a deep, musical voice. 'Gert's daughter. We thought you'd want to start the day with a cup of split pea.'

Effie descended the steps and took the packets with a grateful smile. 'That's very kind.'

Laila beckoned to an older woman who carried a pail and a mop. 'This here is Annie. She's Dr Destiny's missis. He's the crocuser who makes and sells Dr Destiny's Elixir of Life, a cure for everything from warts to dropsy.'

Annie smiled shyly. 'The two-headed woman wasn't much inclined to cleanliness. I thought you might need a bit of help clearing up her mess.'

'Oh, yes,' Effie said earnestly. 'I would be very grateful. It smells like something died in there and it's full of cockroaches and mice.'

'We'll soon have those out,' Annie said, rolling up her sleeves as she climbed the steps and stood in the doorway, staring at the interior. 'I'll have them curtains down too, unless you've got any objections. I think I might have a spare pair in my van, and . . .' she broke off, but Effie could hear her tut-tutting as she disappeared inside.

'You can leave it to Annie,' Laila said cheerfully. 'And this is Frank Tinsley, he's the head man round here and he runs the merry-go-round together with his son, Frank junior. They do all the carpentry round here.'

Frank tipped his cap. 'Those steps are a death trap. Frank junior will fix them up for you afore you can wink an eye. We don't want you tumbling down them and breaking a leg or hurting the nipper.' Without waiting for a reply he took a tape measure from his pocket and the stub of a pencil from behind his ear. He picked up a scrap of paper from the ground and began jotting down numbers.

'You're all very kind,' Effie said, swallowing a large lump in her throat. She had become so used to being bullied and browbeaten by Jacob that to come face to face with such overt kindness was quite overpowering.

Elmo patted her on the shoulder. 'Water's boiling, missis. How about a nice cup of tea?'

Gert wandered over at this point, holding a jug of milk in her hand. 'Just milked the cow, so there's plenty here for the young 'un and for tea as well.'

Annie poked her head out of the window, flapping a piece of dusty rag. 'Jessie,' she shrieked at the top of her voice. 'Fetch a couple of slices of bread for the lady, and don't skimp on the butter.'

The small girl to whom this command was directed jumped to attention like a well-trained soldier, and ran over to a caravan with *Dr Destiny* painted in scarlet letters on its side. She went inside, reappearing moments later with two hunks of bread and butter which she presented shyly to Effie.

'Thank you,' Effie said, smiling as she recognised the child who had befriended Georgie the previous evening. 'That's very kind of you, Jessie.'

'I'll clean him up for you if you like,' Jessie murmured, jerking her copper-coloured head in Georgie's direction. 'Us played together yesterday. He's a poppet.'

Georgie obviously reciprocated this sentiment as he wriggled in his mother's arms, making it plain that he wanted to go to his new friend. Effie put him down on the ground. 'Georgie needs a good wash; can you do that, Jessie?'

Jessie puffed out her chest. 'I got two brothers younger than me and three sisters, older than me. I'm good with nippers, ain't I, Ma?'

The duster appeared out of the window followed by Annie's flushed face. 'A proper little mother is Jessie. She may only be seven but she's a great help. You can trust my Jessie to look after the little chap. She won't let you down.'

'I don't know how to thank you all,' Effie said, her lips trembling. 'You've been so kind.'

'You're one of us now, and you have the mark on you.' Laila spoke in solemn tones that brought a ripple of assent from the small crowd gathered around Effie.

Effie was not certain that this boded well. 'What does that mean?'

Laila tapped the side of her nose. 'All will be revealed in good time. Now I must get back to my tent and polish my crystal ball. Them bleeding punters put their sticky fingers all over it when they think I'm not looking.' She turned on her heel and waltzed off with her skirts swirling around her in a rainbow of colours accompanied by the merry tinkling of the coins.

Having eaten her own food quickly and given Georgie his breakfast washed down with a cup of milk, Effie made a pot of tea and took a cup into the caravan for Annie, who had taken down the curtains and was busy stripping the covers off the squabs.

'I always said that two-headed woman was a slut,' she said, holding up the stained material for Effie to see. 'She might have had two brains but I'll swear she never used either of 'em.'

'I've brought you a cup of tea, Annie.'

'Ta, ducks. Put it down on the table and I'll get to it as soon as I've tossed these disgusting rags out of the window.' With an energetic swing of her arm, Annie disposed of the offending material. She stood, arms akimbo, admiring her work. 'This is going to take me all day, and you'd best get off to Arnoldo's van. He don't like to be kept waiting.'

'What do you think he wants with me?' Effie asked, unsurprised by Annie's remark. She was getting used to the idea that the fairground folk knew everything that went on in their midst.

'He'll tell you soon enough,' Annie said mysteriously. 'Leave young Georgie here with us. Jessie will keep an eye on him and Gert is always there if they take a tumble.'

In the face of such a persuasive argument and with her curiosity running high, Effie brushed her hair and tied it back with a ribbon. It would have been nice to have a change of clothes, but she had left the barge with little more than a spare blouse and a clean pair of drawers. She had packed most of Georgie's clothes but her best gown, the one in which she had married Owen, was wrapped in tissue paper and stowed away in the cabin on the *Margaret*. Owen had insisted on having it made for her by the best dressmaker in Bow, and the woman had excelled herself. Fashioned from many yards of lavender silk, the full skirts had billowed out over a nine-hoop crinoline. It had been the most beautiful gown that Effie had ever seen, let alone possessed, and it had cost her much heartache to leave it behind.

'You look fine, ducks,' Annie said, as if reading her mind. 'Now get along with you. I'll throw a few vegetables in the cooking pot for you later, and maybe one of the lads will come back with a rabbit or a couple of pigeons. We share and share alike round here, as you'll soon find out.'

Effie smiled and nodded, completely overwhelmed by Annie's motherly concern. It was a long time since she had had any female company, and she did not quite know how to respond, but Annie had already turned her attention to cleaning beneath the squabs. She pulled out a single, dirty and much-darned stocking and tossed it out of the window with a disgusted snort. Effie left her to it, and having made certain that Jessie was taking proper care of Georgie she made her way to the Great Arnoldo's caravan.

She found him outside on the grass going through his elaborate routine with accompanying loud grunts and a great deal of posturing. He made her wait until he had completed a series of bends and stretches, and when he finally came to the end he untied a red and white spotted scarf from round his neck and mopped his brow. 'You're late,' he said in a matter-of-fact voice.

'I'm sorry,' Effie murmured, dropping a curtsey. He towered above her and she felt very small and insignificant in his presence, but his scowl was wiped away by a shy smile and he looked almost apologetic.

'I didn't mean to shout at you, little girl.'

'My name is Effie, and I'm not a little girl.'

He eyed her speculatively. 'Well, Effie, you are very small and that is what I have been looking for.'

'What is it you want, mister?'

Without saying another word, Arnoldo stepped forward and seizing her round the waist he spun her round and round like a Catherine wheel, ending by sitting her on his shoulders. 'Perfect,' he said happily. 'And I don't doubt that Nora's costumes will fit you like the proverbial glove.' He set Effie down on the ground but the world was still spinning and she struggled to regain her balance.

'What was all that about?'

He picked up a pair of dumb-bells. 'That was part of my act, until Nora decided to marry the local butcher. I tried to dissuade the poor girl, but she would have none of it and now she lives in Upminster over the butcher's shop with a squalling baby and another on the way. She gave up all this for that.' As if to underline his point, Arnoldo spat on the ground.

Effie blinked as the world righted itself and

her head seemed to re-join the rest of her body. 'Are you suggesting that I take her place?'

'That is the general idea,' Arnoldo said gravely. 'In return for lodging in the caravan and for a small remuneration, you would become my partner in the act.'

'And you toss me around like a spinning top? Is that it?'

'That is part of it. You would attract the crowd, who are always drawn to a pretty girl wearing a short skirt and a low-cut bodice.'

Effie stared at him in dismay. 'A short skirt, sir? Do you mean I would expose myself below the knee?'

'There would be nothing indecent, young lady. Nora used to wear long drawers fashioned from the most costly silk stockinette. They looked completely natural, but covered her modesty.'

'And you would expect me to do the same?' Effie closed her eyes, thinking of Owen and his horror if such a suggestion had been vaunted within his hearing; but then common-sense began to reassert itself. Owen had gone to a place where he was unable to help her now, nor could he be upset or offended if his wife was obliged to sacrifice her modesty in order to support their son.

'Of course,' Arnoldo said sternly. 'That is an

important part of the act. What is your answer, young Effie?'

She was tempted, but she knew she must move on as soon as she was rested enough to travel on foot in her search for Tom. 'I must be on my way as soon as possible, Mr Arnoldo. I thank you for your offer, but . . .'

He held up his hand. 'I have heard that you are looking for the horse dealer. There is no surer way to find him than to stay with the fair. Tapper turns up where and when he feels like it, but turn up he will.'

Effie bit her lip as she tried to make up her mind. She was reluctant to postpone her search for Tom, but she also had to think of Georgie's welfare. She had spent a little of the money she took from Jacob, but she would need every penny of it to set them up in a rented home of their own once she had found Tom. If she stayed with the fair for a week or two she could earn her keep and be on hand should Toby turn up as Arnoldo suggested.

'Well, don't keep me waiting all day,' Arnoldo said, flexing his muscles so that his naked torso appeared to move of its own volition. 'There are young ladies queuing up to be my assistant.'

Effie looked around and could see nothing other than the fairground people setting up their stalls and going about their daily routine.

Myrtle waved to her from the sweet stall where she was stacking toffee apples onto a tray, and Elmo winked at her as he sauntered past carrying a ladder. They were kind people and they had taken her in; Effie nodded her head. 'Yes, I'll help you in your act, mister. And thank you for giving me the opportunity.'

Arnoldo's shoulders drooped and he exhaled a great sigh, which could have been interpreted as impatience at being kept waiting or relief that Effie had accepted his challenge. He confirmed the latter by giving her a hug that almost knocked the air from her lungs.

'I'm so glad, Effie. I was afraid you'd turn me down.' He set her back on the ground, wiping tears from his eyes.

'Why, you're just a big soft thing after all,' Effie said, patting him on the arm. 'I was scared of you at first, but I'm not now.'

He gave her a watery smile. 'I wouldn't harm a fly, and that's the truth. I was given this big body, but inside I quake every time I face an audience and sometimes I just want to run away. It will be so much easier with you at my side, little Effie. You may be a half-pint, but you have a brave heart, anyone can see that.'

'Perhaps you'd show me the costumes I have to wear?' Effie suggested. 'I mean, they might not fit me and I would have to alter them.'

'Of course,' Arnoldo said, brightening. 'Come into my caravan and you shall choose which one you will wear tonight.'

'Tonight?' Effie ran after him as he strode towards his van. 'But I don't know what to do.'

'We'll rehearse all afternoon, my little chick. By this evening you will be Miss Effie, assistant to the Great Arnoldo.'

Zilla altered Nora's costume to fit Effie's small frame and she was ready for the second performance which began at seven o'clock. Dressed in a bodice embroidered with glittering spangles and with her legs encased in pink stockinette drawers under an alarmingly short, semi-opaque white tarlatan skirt, Effie waited nervously in the entrance of the large tent. She could see Jessie sitting on one of the benches in the front row with Georgie on her knee, and he was staring at her outlandish costume with obvious delight. Effie waved to him, forcing a smile and hoping that her nerves did not show. She was grateful for the fact that it was Monday and therefore the audience was small. If she made a complete mess of things there would be few people to see her make a fool of herself. She stood aside as Ethel the bareback rider cantered past on her horse, a sturdy piebald pony named Brag, who normally pulled her caravan but was quite happy to trot round the small ring with Ethel doing not very much other than displaying a lot of leg and a daring amount of décolletage. Eventually she managed to rise onto her knees and then briefly rose to her feet to tumultuous applause, especially from the men who Effie realised saw a great deal more of Ethel's plump body than was seemly.

Frank junior announced the acts and Effie thought him very handsome in his slightly green-tinged tailcoat and top hat. He had a commanding presence and a way with the audience that made them clap and cheer at the right moment. Although Effie had never visited a circus she found herself comparing this performance to those she had read about in magazines that Owen had bought to amuse her. There were no wild animals, unless you counted the World's Largest Rat, Charlie the capybara, whom Frank junior had just introduced to a stupefied and slightly scared audience. Effie had come across Charlie by accident that afternoon when she almost fell over him as he grazed placidly in a shady spot between two caravans. Her screams had attracted his keeper, Fernando, a South American seafarer who explained in charming broken English that he had brought the animal to England when it was small enough to sit in his pocket. He had hoped to sell Charlie for a fat profit to the Zoological Society in London, but they had refused to buy the creature and anyway he had become fond of his rapidly growing pet. Fernando had jumped ship and had ended up travelling with the fair showing Charlie and tending to the horses. He had calmed Effie down, introducing her to the huge rodent who he said was as gentle as a lamb and loved being stroked, which made him purr like a cat.

Fernando led Charlie past Effie, and the capybara stopped to sniff her hand, looking up at her with gentle brown eyes before being led outside to be fed on cabbage leaves and carrots. In ringing tones, Frank junior introduced Arnoldo, the World's Strongest Man, and Miss Effie, his beautiful assistant. As if in a trance Effie found herself following Arnoldo into the centre of the trampled grass ring.

'Mama, Mama,' Georgie trilled in his baby voice, causing a ripple of laughter to run around the tent.

Effie blew Georgie a kiss as she relieved Arnoldo of his red velvet cloak. A gasp of admiration was drawn from both males and females as they observed his bulging muscles and tanned flesh anointed with oil so that it glistened in the light of the lanterns that dangled overhead. Effie curtseyed and stationed herself in front of Arnoldo who picked her up and twirled her several times above his head. She came down to enthusiastic applause and she began to relax. Her job was relatively simple: she just had to remember in which order to hand his props to Arnoldo, and when to allow him to pick her up and spin her round or to toss her into the air and catch her as she plummeted back to earth. They were at the end of their act when something went drastically wrong. Arnoldo threw her up above his head, but somehow the timing went awry and as she came down she slid off his oiled chest and although he made a grab for her she fell to the hard-packed earth with a thud that winded her. She lay gasping and the audience rose as one to their feet. She could hear Georgie calling for her and his sobs echoed round in her dazed brain as she struggled to catch her breath.

Then, strong hands lifted her gently to her feet and she found herself supported by Frank junior. 'The lady is not hurt, ladies and gentlemen,' he announced calmly. 'Miss Effie has survived and lives to perform another day.'

Effie leaned against him, struggling for every painful breath.

'Are you all right?' Frank whispered in her ear. 'Try to smile for God's sake and I'll lead you out.' He turned to Arnoldo who was openly weeping. 'Get off, you jackass. Don't let them see you sobbing like a girl.' Frank hoisted Effie up in his arms and she managed a wave to the crowd as they left the tent to a round of sympathetic clapping.

Frank set her down on the ground. 'Are you all right now, Effie? Can you stand?'

'Yes,' Effie gasped. 'I'm fine. Thank you, Mr Junior.'

He threw back his head and laughed. 'My name is Frank. Unfortunately my pa decided to share his Christian name with me and I am burdened with the title junior, but only to those who do not know me well.' He took off the slightly battered top hat to reveal a fine head of hair the colour of ripe horse chestnuts and equally as shiny. His brown eyes gleamed with humour and he had a strong jaw. Effie was immediately attracted to him and instantly ashamed of herself for thinking of any man other than her beloved Owen. She felt the blood rush to her cheeks and she put a respectable distance between them. She was bruised and sore but that did not explain the rate at which her pulses were racing or why she was inexplicably lost for words.

'I have to go back inside,' Frank said, seemingly oblivious to the mixed emotions that raged in her breast. 'The punters will be getting restive and I have to introduce Elmo. You will be all right, won't you, Effie?'

The genuine concern in his eyes and the sincerity in his voice only added to her confusion, but she managed to nod her head. 'I'm quite all right, thank you, Frank. I'd better go and find Arnoldo; he seemed very upset.'

'You do that, but don't worry about old Arnie, he's always boohooing about one thing or another. His mother was Italian, you see. They're a very emotional race.'

Effie found that she could not take her eyes off Frank as he strode back into the tent. He was tall and broad-shouldered and despite the shabbiness of his clothes, he had an air about him as if he were meant for better things. She jumped aside as Elmo raced past her holding his flaming torches aloft and only narrowly missing setting fire to the flaps of the tent. Putting thoughts of Frank and the way in which he had swept her off her feet aside, Effie made her way to Arnoldo's caravan. She found him slumped over the table amongst the remnants of his evening meal, and judging by the odour of sour milk and rancid bacon fat he had not cleared anything away since breakfast or possibly his supper last night. Arnoldo's living space was a clutter of discarded clothes, books and old newspapers. His bedding lay crumpled on the bunk and the floor was littered with dumb-bells, barbells, boots and shoes.

Effie stood in the doorway, not knowing whether to enter or to go away and allow him time to recover, but his shoulders were shaking and she could see tears seeping through his fingers as he clasped his hands over his eyes.

'Are you all right, Arnie?'

He mumbled something unintelligible.

She picked her way carefully around the scattered items on the floor and, overcome with pity, she put her arm around his shoulders. 'I'm not hurt and the audience thought it was part of the act. Didn't you hear them applauding you?'

He stopped sobbing for a moment, gulped and sniffed. 'You're just saying that.'

'No, cross my heart and hope to die if I tell a lie. They loved you, Arnie.'

He dropped his hands to his sides and lifted his head, smiling at Effie as though she had given him the best news in the world. 'They loved me?'

She nodded vigorously. 'I just need a bit more practice. I expect it was my fault that I fell, and maybe you had just a little too much oil on your skin. You were a bit slippery.'

He jumped to his feet and gave her a hug that made her wince. 'You are a good girl, Effie.

We will begin in the morning and perfect our act. I will make a star of you, my girl, although you will never eclipse the Great Arnoldo.' Grinning like a happy child, Arnoldo swept the mess from his table, and scrabbling about in the tumble of bedclothes and cushions he produced half a loaf. 'Will you stay for supper, little one? I have some cheese, I think, and a pork pie somewhere amongst all this clutter. As you can see, I am not the best of house-keepers. Perhaps . . . ?'

The unspoken question hung in the air but Effie was beginning to understand her new boss and she smiled. 'I'll help you tidy up in the morning, Arnie, but now I must get back to my van and put Georgie to bed. But thank you anyway.' She left him searching for the rest of his supper and with a feeling of relief that she had been able to help him out of his black mood, even if it had entailed a few white lies, Effie made her way back to her caravan.

The sun had set and the fair was in full swing. Naphtha flares illuminated the stalls and the merry-go-round was crowded with punters, their faces shining with delight as the horses waltzed in dizzying circles to the sound of the Dutch organ. Despite the odd shriek of agony from the booth where Jed the black-smith was pulling teeth at a penny a go, the atmosphere was a happy one. Dusk was slowly swallowing up the world outside the brightly lit fairground, and the summer night was heavy with the mixed odours that were now becoming so familiar to Effie that she barely noticed them. She was still stiff and sore but the pain was lessening and she quickened her pace, eager to get home so that she could be there when Jessie returned with Georgie. It was comforting to know that they were safe here amongst the fairground folk. If only Tom were here, Effie thought as she threaded her way between the vans; how happy and excited he would be to share this life with her. She gazed up into the darkening sky where a silver fingernail of moon shone like one of the glass pendants on the merry-go-round, and the evening star twinkled like a friendly eye. She remembered what Leah had said about her lost child and how she imagined him looking down at her from the stars. Perhaps Owen and her ma were up there too. Effie felt a superstitious shiver run down her spine. What would Owen think if he knew that she had felt something awaken in her that she thought had gone to the grave with him? Would he ever forgive her if she allowed herself to love another man? She paused as she entered the circle of light from the camp fires and saw Gert sitting on the steps of her caravan.

'So you've met him then.'

Effie stared at her, thinking she must have misheard. 'I'm sorry, what did you say?'

'Beware, little one. The heart leads us down strange pathways, and you will soon have to choose which one to take. You will find love only to lose it again. I see treachery and dark water, mist and hidden danger.'

Chapter Six

Effie tried hard to put Gert's grim warning out of her mind, and for the most part she was successful. Her days were filled from the moment she awakened in the morning until late at night when she curled up on the bunk with Georgie in her arms. Each morning she helped Leah set up her stall while Georgie played with the children under Jessie's strict eye. Then it was time to practise the act with Arnoldo, but first Effie made sure that the interior of his caravan was clean and tidy. Having brought Arnoldo's home up to a reasonable standard of cleanliness it was just a matter of tidying up after him each day, and Effie found herself slipping into the role of confidante.

Arnoldo, it seemed, had fallen madly in love with Ethel, the bareback rider, but Elmo was fiercely protective of his sister, and did not consider the strong man to be good enough for her. Effie had tried several times to talk to the elusive Ethel, but she was shy and seemed to be very much under the influence of her brother, although he did occasionally allow her to assist Dr Destiny to peddle his pills and potions. Ethel was also called upon to help Jed when the occasion arose, and this was usually to calm a nervous patient or to spirit them away and help staunch the blood if the afflicted gums continued to haemorrhage. Effie had begun to suspect that Jed also harboured feelings for Ethel, and, as Arnoldo was also aware of this fact, she feared that the two strong men might resort to fisticuffs as they battled for the young lady's affections.

Despite all this heightened emotion, Effie considered that she had her own feelings under control. Her heart did a little skip and a jump every time she saw Frank, but although he was always nice to her, there was nothing in his manner to suggest that the attraction was mutual. She tried to convince herself that this was good, although deep down she was a little disappointed, but whatever her own personal feelings might be Effie remained focused on her main aim which was to find Tom. Arnoldo paid her a small wage for her part in the show but it was barely enough to feed herself and Georgie. To her chagrin, she was often forced to rely on the generosity of the other fairground folk who gave her meat for the pot, usually rabbit or pigeon that the younger boys went out on the common to snare. Effie's lack of anything decent to wear had been noticed by Laila, who came to the caravan one morning with a brightly coloured array of clothes which she said were out-moded. Effie would be doing her a favour if she took them off her hands as they were taking up room in her van and she needed the space. It was all said with such a charming smile and the kindliest of intentions that Effie could not refuse. In fact she was delighted to have something clean and pretty to wear, even if the garments were a little flamboyant for her taste.

At the end of a fortnight there was still no sign of Toby or Tom. The fair was being packed up ready to leave the next day, but without a horse Effie had no way of moving her caravan. She sought out Frank senior and found him busy taking the merry-go-round apart. 'Mr Tinsley, may I have a word with you?'

He looked down at her from the top of the canopy. 'What can I do for you, Miss Effie?'

'The first thing is that I don't have a horse to pull my van, and secondly, I've never handled the reins before.'

He climbed down to stand beside her. 'The two-headed bitch took a couple of our best horses when she ran off with the lizard man, but that's hardly your fault. We always keep some spare nags so that's not a problem, and I'll get Frank junior to show you how to harness the beast. He can drive you tomorrow and teach you how to handle the reins. It's not difficult, and you seem like a bright girl, you'll soon learn.'

He went back to his work and Effie could see that it was useless to protest, and she had no valid excuse for refusing Frank junior's help. The thought of spending time alone with him was exciting, but admitting her attraction for another man so soon after Owen's death made her feel guilty. Gert's grim warning was never far from her mind and that only added to her dilemma.

'Stuff and nonsense,' she murmured as she walked back to her van. 'You're just being foolish, Effie Grey.' She smiled as she saw Georgie and some of the children playing ring-a-roses under Jessie's watchful eye, and seeing his happy face made Effie even more conscious of how their lives had changed for the better. Even so, she could not forget that the *Margaret* should have been Georgie's birthright. She did not care for herself but she minded very much for her son, and for Owen also. Not for the first time, she was thankful that he could not see how his father had treated them. She went inside the van to finish making everything secure for the journey to their next camp on Wanstead Flats where there was an annual summer fair. Effie had asked

Zilla if she thought that Toby might be there, and she had nodded emphatically. Toby Tapper, she had said, was never one to miss a good business opportunity. Effie could only hope that Zilla was right as she packed the pieces of china that Leah had given her by way of payment for helping on the stall. She wrapped them in newspaper and stowed them away so that they would not get broken as the cart rattled over rutted tracks. Having satisfied herself that she could do no more that afternoon, she went outside to sit on the steps and enjoy a brief respite.

She leaned back against the door, closing her eyes and welcoming the soft caress of the sunshine. There would be one show tonight and then she had been advised to get a good night's sleep as they would leave early in the morning. Tomorrow she might see Toby and she prayed that Tom would be with him.

'You look so peaceful that it's a shame to disturb you.'

Effie opened her eyes and found herself looking up into Frank's handsome face. She knew that she was blushing but she hoped that he would mistake it for a healthy flush brought about by exposure to the sun. 'Good evening, Frank.'

He put one booted foot on the bottom step,

leaning forward so that his face was close to hers. She could smell the male scent of him and the salty tang of clean sweat. She smiled shyly. 'Did your pa send you?'

He held out his hand. 'He did, my dear. I'm to find you a good strong horse and show you how to deal with him. Tomorrow I'm to drive you to Wanstead and I'll teach you how to handle the reins. We'll have a very pleasant journey, Miss Effie.'

'If we're to be travelling companions I think you could call me Effie.'

'Effie it is then.' He took her by the hand. 'Come, we'll choose a nice quiet animal that won't give you any cause for alarm. You aren't frightened of horses are you?'

She allowed him to help her to her feet. 'No, certainly not. I used to groom Champion and sometimes I led him along the towpath, when Owen was alive.'

Frank met her gaze with a sympathetic smile. 'Your late husband?'

'Yes. Owen died of consumption before Georgie was born.'

'And you lived on a narrowboat. I've always thought that that must be a nice peaceful way of life. Quite different from the hectic way we live.' He squeezed her hand and his eyes caressed her face. 'We'll have plenty of time to talk tomorrow. I'd like to hear every detail of your past, Effie. I'm looking forward to our time together.'

All next day the cavalcade of caravans, carts and wagons plied its way along the dusty road which crossed the marshes and skirted the deep green depths of Epping Forest. It was late evening by the time Frank drew the horse to a halt, and he leapt from his seat to unharness the tired animal and allow it to join the others as they slaked their thirst in the nearby pond. Having consumed a bowl of bread and milk purchased from a farm along the way, Georgie had been asleep for the last couple of miles and he lay in Effie's arms, the picture of contentment. She raised herself with difficulty, realising with a feeling of pride that her small son had put on weight since leaving the *Margaret*, and she was certain that he had grown at least an inch. She carried him into the van and laid him on the bunk, tucking a blanket around him and dropping a kiss on his cheek. Having satisfied herself that he was safe and unlikely to awaken until morning, Effie climbed down the wooden steps and stretched her cramped limbs. All around her was a hive of activity as the men began to unload the wagons and set up the stalls while the women set about making camp, lighting fires and preparing the evening meal. Set free after a long day of enforced inactivity, the older children shrieked joyfully as they raced about.

Spirals of smoke began to drift upwards into an opal sky, and the aroma of cooking mingled with the scent of woodsmoke. Effie set about building the fire as Leah had shown her. Orange tongues of flame licked around the kindling and Effie added more wood. Satisfied that it was burning well she reached for the wooden pail, intent on fetching water, but a strong male hand covered hers and she looked up into Frank's engaging smile.

'Allow me, Effie.'

Pride would not allow her to accept without a protest, however mild. 'It's all right, Frank. I can manage on my own, ta.'

'I'm sure you can, but you must be tired and you don't want the boy to wake up and find himself all alone.'

It was the most persuasive argument that he could have chosen and Effie gave in without any further objections. She watched him stride off towards the pond and her heart went out to him. It was a long time since a man had given her his undivided attention and for the most part Frank had been the perfect travelling companion. She had found herself telling him about the hardships of the workhouse, of her time working as a barmaid for Ben Hawkins and her brief marriage to Owen. She glossed over the treatment she had received from Jacob, but she told him about Tom's plight and her desperate attempts to find him. She ended with the hope that he was safe with Toby. Frank had listened attentively until then, but at the mention of Toby's name his manner had altered and he had turned to her with a scowl marring his good looks.

'You should not have anything to do with a man like Tapper. He's a didicoi and a cheat.'

'That's not true. Toby has been a good friend to me.'

'Don't ever put your trust in a man like him. He's bad news, Effie. Very bad news.'

'I think I might know him a bit better than you, Frank,' Effie had said defensively. 'And I'm getting a bit tired of everyone warning me about Toby.' She had realised that he was about to argue and she managed to change the subject, but his words still rankled.

Even now, as she threw a log on the fire and waited for him to return with the water, she was still a little angry with him. But perhaps Frank was simply jealous? The thought warmed her chilled heart, although she could not quite forget the steel in his eyes or the harsh tone of his voice as he had spoken of Toby.

Effie sighed heavily as she started peeling potatoes to put in the pot. She had a small supply of carrots, onions and cabbage, bought from a stallholder in one of the many market gardens through which they had passed. There was no meat for the stew but she had flour and lard which she intended to form into dough and bake in the hot wood ash. Zilla had shown her how to make this unleavened bread and it served to fill an empty belly, even if it could not compare with a loaf hot from a baker's oven.

Frank returned moments later and set the bucket down on the ground. 'I'll get back to my own van now then, Effie. Have you every-thing you need for tonight?'

Looking up into his liquid brown eyes, Effie forgot that they had ever had a disagreement and she smiled. 'Won't you stay and have supper with me, Frank? It seems the least I can do after you've been so good to me.'

He knelt down by her side, taking the paring knife and the half-peeled potato from her hand. 'I'd be pleased to, my dear. I hear from Zilla that you're a very good cook and my old folks won't mind if I miss a meal with them. It will mean all the more for Pa, who has an appetite like a horse.'

The supper of boiled vegetables flavoured with wild garlic and mopped up with the smoky-tasting, slightly burnt bread might not have been food for the gods, but seated close to Frank with the sun sinking slowly behind a curtain of violet and crimson clouds, Effie felt as though she was in a delightful dream. She could feel the warmth from his body and as he reached out to place his wooden bowl on the grass she saw the muscles ripple in his sun-tanned forearm, bare to the elbow where he had rolled up his shirtsleeves. As he turned to her with a smile, she allowed her eyes to travel down the strong column of his throat to where the open neck of his shirt revealed a tantalising hint of golden flesh, warmed by the sun like a ripe peach.

She raised her eyes to his face and almost drowned in the depths of his ardent gaze. His arms enfolded her and she abandoned herself to the moment, parting her lips and sighing as she returned his passionate embrace.

It was over so suddenly that she opened her eyes, blinking into the darkness that seemed to have embraced the encampment like a velvet blanket. In the glow of the camp fire she saw Frank rise to his feet. He bent down to brush a lock of hair back from her forehead and his lips grazed her cheek. 'Goodnight, Effie, my love.'

Despite the heat from the fire and the warmth of the evening, Effie shivered. She felt cold suddenly and very much alone. She leapt to her feet and caught his hand as he was about to walk away. 'Frank?'

He glanced down at her hand clutching his arm and he frowned. 'I'm sorry, my dear. I should not have kissed you. It was a mistake.'

The whole day seemed to flash before Effie's eyes; they had been so close, as if they had known each other for years instead of days. Surely he could not have kissed her with such tenderness if he had not felt something for her? 'A mistake, Frank? I don't understand . . .'

He unclasped her fingers, one by one, but he did not look her in the eyes. 'I like you very much, but I have an understanding with someone else.'

'You are in love with another woman?'

A wry smile twisted Frank's lips. 'I didn't say that, Effie. We fairground folk marry within our own circle. It makes sense and marriages are arranged by our families long before we are old enough to make a choice for ourselves.'

'But that is dreadful,' Effie exclaimed, shocked to the core. 'Who is this woman? It isn't Ethel, is it?'

'It isn't Ethel. The young lady in question travels with another fair. We are going to be married when we meet up at Lammas.'

'But that is only a few weeks away.' Effie

133

controlled her raging emotions with a determined effort. 'I wish you every happiness then, Frank.'

She turned away so that he would not see the hurt and chagrin in her eyes but he caught her by the shoulders and twisted her round to face him. 'I am sorry, Effie. I didn't mean to hurt you and I didn't intend to fall in love with you, but it happened all the same.'

'You – you love me?' Effie raised her startled gaze to look him in the eyes. 'You say that you love me, Frank?'

'From the first moment I saw you, but I thought I could control my feelings and I find that I can't. I never meant to hurt you or to give you false hope.'

His last words stung her like a whiplash and she broke free from his grasp, backing away from him. 'False hope? You make it sound as though I am desperate. I loved my husband, and this was just a moment of – of silliness. It was nothing, Frank. I am not hurt and I wish you well, but I won't be here to dance at your wedding. I will leave the fair as soon as I get word of my brother.'

Frank bowed his head. 'If it could be any other way, Effie.'

'Go back to your van, please. It's been a long day and I'm very tired.' She did not watch as Frank walked away, but turned her attention to dousing the fire and making it safe for the night. She was so absorbed in her task that she did not hear the soft footfalls on the springy turf and she turned with a start at the sound of Leah's gruff voice.

'I could have told you it would end in tears, girl.'

Effie turned to face her. 'I hardly know him, so no harm done.'

'You like him though, Effie. I can see it in your eyes, and Frank wants you; that's clear for anyone to see.' Leah knocked her clay pipe on the heel of her boot, sending a shower of ash into the embers of the fire. 'He's spoken for, but I think he must have told you that.'

Effie nodded her head. 'He did, and I understand. It was just a little flirting, nothing more.'

'I hope so, for both your sakes, but be careful, Effie. Passion is an unruly monster when it's unleashed.' With a hearty slap on Effie's shoulder, Leah strode off to join Zilla who was reclining on a pile of cushions by their camp fire.

Effie sighed as she saw them embrace and then settle down side by side like an old married couple. A hazy mist hung over the water and darkness was consuming the camp, layer by layer. The babble of voices was gradually fading away as more and more people retired to bed, either in their vans or outside under the stars. A gentle breeze rustled through the reeds and moths fluttered drunkenly in the light of oils lamps hanging from the caravans. Effie wrapped her arms around her thin body and closed her eyes, reliving the tender embrace she had shared with Frank. Old desires which she had thought long dead had been stirred and flooded her with longing for a man's arms to hold her close. She realised now how much she missed caresses and whispered words of love culminating in the joyous union of two bodies and souls. She had loved Owen with all her heart but she was young and healthy and the thought of living alone for the rest of her life was daunting to say the least.

She made her way slowly up the steps of her van, determined to put all such thoughts behind her. She had something infinitely more precious than a fleeting dalliance with Frank Tinsley, and she closed the door, shutting out the rest of the world as she prepared to sleep close to her son, Owen's child, the only person in her life who mattered apart from Tom. She would devote herself to raising Georgie to be a healthy, happy boy and she would find Tom if the search took her to the ends of the earth. They would be together as a family and no one else mattered. She could only hope and pray that they would be reunited soon.

* * *

Each day, Effie looked in vain for Toby amongst the crowds that thronged the fairground. However much effort she put into avoiding Frank it was almost impossible to keep out of his way altogether. If their paths crossed, she would greet him cordially, but when their eyes met she could see that it was just as hard for him as it was for her. They were drawn together as if by some mystical power and she always knew when his eyes were upon her; she could feel him willing her to look his way and she was powerless to resist the compulsion. Even Ethel, who Zilla said was not the sharpest knife in the box, realised that there was something going on between Effie and Frank and she did not hesitate to say so.

'You want to watch him,' Ethel whispered as she and Effie waited to go into the ring one evening towards the end of their time in Wanstead. 'He's spoken for, you know.'

'I'm aware of that,' Effie said stiffly.

Ethel tossed her dark curls. 'No offence meant, I'm sure, but he's a good-looking cove and I wouldn't blame you if you was flattered by his attentions. I'm no stranger to having men fall at me feet, so I know how you must feel.'

Relieved to be able to change the subject, Effie smiled. 'It must be hard for you, knowing that you must break one man's heart in order to make another happy.'

Ethel's painted lips drooped into a pout. 'I suppose you mean Arnoldo, the great soft thing.'

'And Jed,' Effie prompted. 'I believe that he has his eye on you too.'

A round of applause signalled the end of Elmo's act and Brag, seeming to know that it was his turn next, jerked his head back and snorted. Ethel tightened the reins with a practised hand. 'Stop that, Brag. If you're a naughty boy you shan't have your sugar lump treat.'

'Does he really understand what you say?' Effie asked curiously as Brag stopped prancing and nuzzled Ethel's small hand.

'Of course he does. Horses are so much more sensible than men,' Ethel said in a loud voice as Elmo strode past them reeking of raw alcohol and singed hair.

'Get on and do your act,' he muttered, frowning at his sister. 'And no larking about afterwards. I want you where I can keep an eye on you – you Jezebel.'

With a self-conscious giggle, Ethel leapt nimbly onto Brag's back and urged him into a trot.

'She's very young, Elmo,' Effie said gently. 'And very pretty too; you can't blame the men for fancying her.'

'I blame her for encouraging them, and you can mind your own business, missy. In my opinion you're no better than she is.'

Elmo strode off leaving Effie staring after him. So everyone in the fairground was talking about her and Frank. She had not thought it had gone so far, but in such a small community she had already learned that gossip was the main source of entertainment. She turned her head as she felt someone enter the tent and come to a halt at her side, but it was only Arnoldo and he was not looking at her. His gaze was fixed on Ethel as she rode round the ring with her arms outstretched and a wide smile on her face.

'She's an angel,' he breathed. 'Just look at her, Effie. Have you ever seen her like before?'

Effie watched Ethel as she knelt on Brag's wide back revealing frilly drawers and a great deal of bare leg; then, with more determination than grace, she clambered to her feet before sliding to a sitting position with her legs wide apart, which exacted a grunt of sympathy from the audience followed by a standing ovation. Effie had seen it all before and really it was not terribly clever, but it was obviously quite new to the audience and they loved it, calling for more. Ethel did another circuit of the ring, blowing kisses to the men which caused Arnoldo to bristle with indignation.

'Just look at them yokels leering at her,' he groaned. 'I'd like to go out there and smack them in the teeth, and for tuppence, by golly, I will.'

He made as if to carry out his threat, but Effie caught him by the arm. 'No, Arnoldo. It's just an act on Ethel's part and the men don't mean any harm. They are just showing their appreciation of a lovely and talented girl. You can't blame them for that.'

She stared up at Arnoldo but he was so tense that she could see the veins standing out in his neck and forehead. He shook his head, unable to speak, and she could feel the emotions raging inside his bosom. Effie squeezed his hand. 'Look, she's coming now and she looks so pleased with herself. Don't spoil it. Anyway, we're on now.' She gave him a gentle push and Arnoldo said nothing as Ethel rode past them giving him the brightest of smiles. He hunched his shoulders and waited for Frank to announce them. Effie followed him into the ring, avoiding Frank's eyes, which she knew followed her during the act. She hoped that Arnoldo was not too upset to concentrate on catching her after he had tossed her so easily into the air, but he appeared to have his emotions under control as they performed to the crowd.

Their long hours of practice paid off and

the act went smoothly, exhorting gasps of admiration from the audience and cries of 'Bravo' when they took their final bow. Effie followed Arnoldo out of the ring trying hard not to look at Frank, but somehow he managed to bar her way just long enough to entreat her to meet him after the show. She shook her head, but he repeated his request, telling her to meet him where the animals were left to graze overnight. 'It's urgent, Effie. We're moving on soon. I must speak to you alone.'

She looked up and was lost in the depths of eyes that sparkled like vintage sherry wine when he smiled, but were darkened now with emotion. The audience were becoming restive and beginning to demand the next act. Margery the Midget sent them meaningful looks as she waited to go on with her husband, Johann the knife-thrower, who spoke very little English but was pointing one of his stilettos at Frank in a rather menacing manner. 'Very well, Frank,' Effie said reluctantly. 'I'll be there.' She hurried out of the tent, leaving Frank to appease Johann and Margery and to announce their act, which was the finale.

Effie returned to her caravan to reassure herself that Georgie was sleeping soundly. She found Jessie sitting outside on the steps telling a story to her younger brothers, and judging by the looks on the boys' faces it was not a tale for the highly strung or over-sensitive child. They jumped and almost fell off the steps as Effie came round the corner of the van, but Jessie was unrepentant. 'They're a couple of big babies, ain't they, Effie?' she said with a throaty chuckle.

Effie was not so sure, but she managed a smile. 'I hope they don't have nightmares.'

'Oh, no. They're used to my tales, ain't you, boys?'

The brothers nodded their heads vigorously. 'Tell us what happened next, Jess,' the elder of the two pleaded. 'We'll go to bed then and I won't piss meself like I did the other night.'

'I should hope not, young Mickey,' Jessie said sternly. 'I ain't washing your blankets if you does. Now where was I?'

Effie peered into the van and saw the outline of Georgie's head on the pillow. He was sound asleep despite the noise outside. She put her hand in her pocket and took out a penny which she handed to Jessie. 'Will you stay and keep an eye on Georgie for a little while longer? I'll give you another halfpenny when I come back.'

'That's all right,' Jessie said calmly. 'I ain't got nothing to do but look after the nippers.' She cocked her head, staring at Effie like a curious robin. 'Are you meeting a bloke then?'

Effie felt the colour rise to her cheeks and was grateful for the gathering dusk to hide her blushes. 'No, of course not. I just have some business to discuss. I won't be long.' She hurried off before Jessie could ask any further leading questions. Threading her way between the caravans, she headed for the patch of scrub where the horses were tethered and Charlie the capybara dozed in a pen made from hurdles. Her heart was thudding against her ribs as she looked for Frank, and when she saw a male figure emerge from between a group of grazing animals she hurried towards him.

'Frank?'

He stopped, setting down the saddle he carried and pushing his cap to the back of his head. She could not see him clearly but she realised with a start that it was not Frank. She hesitated, poised ready to run. 'I'm sorry, I made a mistake. I thought you were someone else.'

For a moment he remained motionless, and although she could not make out his features clearly in the gathering darkness she knew that he was staring at her and she was suddenly afraid. She glanced anxiously over her shoulder hoping to see Frank's familiar figure striding to her rescue but there was no one in sight. She was alone, with the wide expanse of the flats on two sides, the pond on the other and about a hundred yards or so of open ground to cover before she reached the safety of the encampment. She backed away as the man began to advance slowly towards her.

'Who are you?' she whispered. 'What are you doing here? If you're stealing horses I have only to call out and the men will come running.'

He quickened his pace and Effie panicked. She started to run but she could hear his footsteps pounding on the dry earth behind her, and she knew she was being outpaced. She did not see the tussock of grass that tripped her up and sent her sprawling headlong on the ground, knocking the breath from her body. She lay there, gasping for breath and unable to move as the man caught up with her and pulled her to her feet.

Chapter Seven

'Effie! I thought it was you but you're the last person I expected to run into on Wanstead Flats.'

'Toby.' Effie uttered his name on a sob but it was from relief that she was crying, and she leaned her head against his shoulder. 'I've been hoping and praying that you would come.'

'What a welcome,' Toby said, taking her by the shoulders and peering into her face. 'But what are you doing here? Have you run away to join the fair?'

She clutched his lapels, pulling his head down so that his face was close to hers. 'Where is Tom? Please tell me that he found you.'

'Effie, ducks, I haven't seen young Tom since the last time we met at the Prince of Wales tavern.' Gently disengaging her fingers, he hooked his arm around her shoulders. 'You're shivering, girl. What's been going on? What brought you to this place?'

'So you don't know where Tom is then?'

He slipped off his jacket and wrapped it

around her shoulders. 'I think you'd best start at the beginning and tell me everything. I can't help you unless I know what's troubling you.'

She tried to speak but her teeth were chattering uncontrollably and it was not the cool breeze from the marshes that chilled her to the bone. She had placed so much faith in Tom being safe in Toby's care. The shock of discovering that he knew nothing of her brother's whereabouts was almost too much to bear.

'Come and sit down,' Toby said gently. 'Take it slow and start at the beginning.'

She opened her mouth to speak but was forestalled by a shout from Frank and the sound of footsteps pounding on the hard-baked ground. She turned her head, and saw him racing towards them.

'Leave her alone.' He gave Toby a shove that sent him staggering backwards.

'No!' Effie cried, finding her voice. 'Stop this, right now.'

Frank peered anxiously into her face. 'Are you all right? Did he hurt you?'

'He's my friend, Frank.' Effie clutched his arm to prevent him taking another swing at Toby, who had regained his balance and had his hands fisted, preparing to fight back.

'Try that again, mister, and see what you get,' Toby said, squaring up.

'Tapper!' Frank almost spat the word, curling

his lip. 'I might have guessed it was you. You never could keep your hands off a pretty woman, especially one who's spoken for.'

Effie uttered a squeak of protest. 'That's not true, Frank. You shouldn't say things like that.'

He cupped her face in his hands, looking deeply into her eyes. 'It could be true, Effie, my sweet. If I can break the wretched pledge that binds me to a woman I barely know and do not love, then I will be free to court you properly, like the lady you are.'

'Sounds like a rum do to me,' Toby snorted. 'I dunno what's been going on here, but I wouldn't trust a cove who spoke so easily of breaking his promise to someone simply because he's met a better prospect.'

Effie turned on him, her pent-up emotions bubbling over like an unwatched pot left to simmer on the fire. 'This has nothing to do with you, Toby. And you, Frank, you're going too fast. We hardly know each other.'

He laid his hand on her shoulder. 'I thought we came out here to discuss our future, girl. Are you denying your feelings for me?'

'Yes. No. I don't know,' Effie cried passionately. 'I can't think about us at this moment, Frank. I have to talk to Toby about my brother. I have to find Tom.'

Frank dropped his arm to his side and his expression was lost in the deepening shadows.

'It would seem that I was mistaken in you, Effie. I thought you had fallen in love with me as I have with you.'

'Look, cully,' Toby said pleasantly. 'Can't you see you're upsetting her? This ain't the time or place for romance, especially when you can see that Effie's got other things on her mind.'

She felt Frank's body tense and she laid her hand on his sleeve. 'Please, Frank. This is very important to me. I need to speak to Toby. He's the only person I know who might be able to find Tom.'

'I suppose you've decided to join us so that you can get rid of your dodgy old nags. Well I'm not having it, Tapper. We don't want the police sniffing round looking for stolen animals.'

'I don't indulge in that trade, mate.'

Toby spoke in an even tone but Effie knew him well enough to see that he was struggling to keep his temper. She glanced up at Frank. As the clouds parted a shaft of moonlight lit his face, revealing a martial gleam in his eyes.

'Is that so?' he said with a scornful curl of his lips. 'Well, I recall a certain stallion with a white blaze blacked out with boot polish. The brute had won quite a few races and had been put out to stud. The owner was pleased to offer a fat reward, and the police were even

148

keener to get their hands on a certain horse trader by the name of Tapper.'

'A misunderstanding,' Toby said airily. 'Could have happened to anyone, and it was all sorted out in no time at all. You're just trying to paint a dark picture of me, Tinsley, but it won't work with Effie because we know each other too well.'

Frank took a step towards him but Effie thrust herself between them. 'Stop it, both of you. You're behaving like schoolboys.' She raised her hand to touch Frank's cheek. 'There's no need to worry. Just give me some time to talk to Toby. After all, finding him was the reason for my joining up with the fair.'

'All right,' Frank said grudgingly. 'I'll leave you two to talk, but I'll be keeping my eye on you, Tapper. If there's any hint of trouble I'll turn you over to the johndarms.' With one last threatening glance in Toby's direction, he turned on his heel and strode back towards the camp.

'Well,' Toby said, grinning. 'Seems you've made a conquest there, Effie.'

'And it's obvious to me that there's more between you two than trouble with the police,' Effie said, angling her head. 'He seems to hate you, Toby.'

'He don't like being crossed, that's all. But more important now is for you to tell me what happened to make Tom run away, and why you left the *Margaret* for this sort of life. It's not for the likes of you, Effie.'

She linked her arm with his. 'Come to my van and we'll talk over a cup of tea. Young Jessie is looking after Georgie, but I can't leave her for too long. She's only a nipper and she must be in need of her bed.'

Later, sitting inside the caravan with Georgie sleeping soundly, Effie recounted everything that had happened since she parted with Tom on the fateful day when the Salters were hired to crew the *Margaret*. Toby listened attentively and when she finished speaking he ran his hand through his tumbled mass of dark curly hair. 'Well, that's some tale, girl. I've been out in the wilds of the Essex countryside doing a bit of dealing at horse fairs, and it's unlikely that young Tom could have caught up with me since he was on foot. He could be anywhere, and that's the truth of the matter.'

Effie's breath hitched in her throat. 'He might have been forced back into the work-house, or he could have starved to death on the highway.'

'Don't get yourself into a state. He's a bright boy, and I'm sure he's got the sense to keep away from danger of all sorts.'

'He's only thirteen, Toby. He's just a child.'

150

'I was on the road at that age, and look at me now.' Toby beat his breast with his fists and his dazzling blue eyes danced with merriment. 'Well, maybe I ain't the best of examples, but I'll wager that young Tom is doing all right, and we'll soon find him.'

'You'll help me then?' Effie held her breath; she had known that he would but she wanted to hear it again from his own lips.

'I'll do my damnedest, ducks.' The smile faded from his eyes and he leaned towards her. 'Just tell me one thing, Effie. Are you serious about Frank Tinsley?'

It was such a direct question that it caught her off guard. It was one that she had been asking herself and she simply did not know the answer. She supposed that she was in love with Frank, but her reaction to his charms might simply have been the desire to belong and to feel beloved again. Looking into Toby's eyes, she was even more uncertain of her feelings and she shook her head. 'I don't know, and that's the honest truth. Anyway, what is it to you?'

'Well,' Toby said slowly, as if picking his words with care. 'It might have some bearing on what we do next.'

'I don't understand.'

'I'm not suggesting that you leave the fair immediately, but it would be easier if there were two of us looking for young Tom. Would you want to leave your new life and travel like a gypsy?' He stood up and went to the open door, staring out into the darkness. 'From what you've told me, you've found friends here and you can support yourself and young Georgie. Then there's Frank, the bloke you might or might not have fallen in love with. Would you want to give all this up?' He turned his head to give her a searching look. 'I only ask because it's something you will have to consider, should the need arise.'

'Apart from my son, there's nothing more important to me than Tom,' Effie said, clasping her hands and holding them to her breast. 'All I want is to make a home for us so that we can live together. We'll never be separated again or be forced to return to the workhouse. I'll do anything I can to keep us out of that fearful place.'

'I have my answer,' Toby said seriously. 'Now I'd best leave and let you get a good night's sleep.'

Effie jumped to her feet. 'But what are you going to do?'

'I dunno yet. I'll sleep on it and tell you in the morning.'

He stepped outside and she watched him until his tall figure was enveloped by the darkness. She closed the door wondering if she ought to have offered him a bed for the night, and a smile curved her lips as she imagined the inevitable gossip that would fly round the camp following such an action. But the thought of Frank's reaction to such a titbit of news sent a chill down her spine. Frank was a complication that she could neither have foreseen nor imagined. She made herself ready for bed, putting him resolutely out of her mind. Tomorrow she must decide whether to leave the fair and accompany Toby in the hope of finding Tom, or to remain where she was and suffer the torment of loving a man who was promised to another.

The next day dawned warm and sunny with the promise of intense heat later on. The ground was baked hard beneath her feet as Effie made her way to Arnoldo's van. Flies swarmed over scraps of food thrown out for the dogs that were kept to guard the caravans left unoccupied while their owners worked their stalls, and the valuable horses put out to graze on common land. There was no sign of Toby, but as she paused to pass the time of day with Leah, who was setting up her stall, Effie caught sight of Frank leaning against one of the painted horses on the merry-go-round. He spotted her and waved, his handsome features suffused with a smile that made her heart do a somersault inside her breast.

'Forget him,' Leah said sternly. 'He'll break your heart.'

Effie dragged her gaze away from the man who looked to her like a sun god with his bare-chested masculinity and chestnut hair gleaming with golden tints. She avoided meeting Leah's gaze as she shook her head. 'It's not like that.'

'I'm glad to hear it,' Leah said, sounding unconvinced. 'He's not for you, ducks. And I don't think this life is for you either.'

This made Effie look up, startled. 'Why do you say that?'

'Because it's true. Fairground folk are born to the life. They take a partner from another world at their peril and it rarely works. Frank's future was mapped out for him from the day he was born, and one day he'll be head man, just like his pa. He needs a woman who under-stands the way of things, or else it will bring misery to both.'

Effie could find no answer to this and she merely nodded her head and moved on hastily. She entered Arnoldo's caravan without knocking and found him curled up on his bunk like an overgrown child. His pale eyelashes were wet with tears and he raised his head only to drop back against the pillows with a deep sigh.

'What's the matter, Arnoldo?' Effie approached him cautiously. 'Are you ill?'

'Sick at heart, little one.'

'It's Ethel, isn't it?'

'I love her,' Arnoldo said, his voice breaking
on a sob.

'Then tell her so.'

'I c-can't. She doesn't care for me. She's in
love with that bloody blacksmith.'

Folding her arms across her chest, Effie
shook her head. 'What sort of talk is that for
a grown man? How do you know what she
feels? Have you asked her?'

'Elmo hates me. And he's quite right. I'm
not good enough for his sister. I may be strong
in the body but I'm a coward, afraid of my
own shadow.'

Effie moved swiftly towards the bunk, and
before Arnoldo could stop her she pulled the
coverlet off him. 'Get up and prove him
wrong. Go out there and sweep Ethel off her
feet.'

He curled up in a tight ball, eyeing her nervously. 'Don't strike me, Effie.'

'I'm not going to hit you, you silly man. I'm
less than half your size and you toss me
around in the act, so why should you fear me,
or anyone else for that matter?'

Arnoldo buried his face in the pillow with
a loud groan. Effie couldn't make out his

words but she guessed that it was an admission of defeat, and taking him by the shoulders she shook him. It took a considerable effort, and she only succeeded in creasing his grubby nightshirt, but it seemed to have the desired effect as he hauled himself into a sitting position. 'Why do you bother with me, Effie? You must think me a poor sort of fellow.'

Embarrassed by her boldness, she took a step away from his bed. 'I'm sorry I had to do that, but you must stop being such a baby. You are a fine figure of a man, and you are a kind and gentle person. Any girl would be proud to have you as a suitor, but you must stop feeling sorry for yourself. Get up. Put your clothes on and go to Ethel. Tell her how you feel and allow her to choose between you and Jed, and that foreign chap, Fernando, who keeps making eyes at her.'

'I'm old enough to be her father,' Arnoldo whispered, wiping his eyes on his sleeve. 'She'll think I'm just a silly old fool. It must seem ridiculous for a man of my age to be thinking he stood a chance with such a lovely young thing.'

Effie picked up his shirt and trousers which had been discarded in a heap on the floor and she tossed them at him. 'You know what they say, Arnoldo. Faint heart never won fair maid.

If you don't do this you'll regret it for the rest of your life.'

'And if she rejects me?'

'You will be no worse off than you are now, and I'm sure there are other women who would think themselves lucky to have attracted the attention of a man like you. I've seen the way the females in the audience look at you when we perform. You could take your pick.'

He snatched up his trousers and thrust his feet into them. 'If you put it like that, perhaps it's worth a try.'

Averting her eyes, Effie backed out of the van. 'I'll wait outside.' She stepped out into the sunshine, blinking as the bright light hurt her eyes. In between the parked caravans she could see Ethel practising her equestrian act. Brag cantered round in a wide circle as she attempted to stand on his back. Picking up her skirts, Effie ran towards them. 'Ethel, stop. I must speak to you.'

Pink-cheeked with heat and exertion, Ethel slid to a sitting position, pulling on the reins until Brag came to a halt beside Effie. 'What's up?'

Effie glanced over her shoulder, but there was no sign of Arnoldo. She hoped he was still getting ready to make his declaration of love and devotion, and had not simply given up. 'Please get down. There's something I have to ask you.'

Ethel leapt to the ground. 'Well, what is it?'

'Are you in love with anyone, Ethel?' It was a direct question, but Effie knew she had no time to lose.

Ethel's blue eyes opened wide and her soft lips formed a perfect circle as she appeared to consider her answer. She shrugged her shoulders. 'I might be, but I don't see it's got anything to do with you.'

'I know it must seem very rude and quite unforgiveable, but this is very important to someone who is your devoted admirer. He has loved you from afar for quite a long time.'

'Really?' Ethel said, smiling coyly. 'Who can you mean?'

'Don't play games,' Effie said severely. 'You know very well who it is, and the poor man is at this moment trying to pluck up courage to speak to you. I'm not saying anything more, but I beg you to be kind to him. If you can't find it in your heart to love him, please let him down gently.'

'It's not that easy,' Ethel murmured with tears welling in her eyes and sparkling on the ends of her long lashes. 'Elmo won't allow me to have gentlemen friends. He says I am too young and too scatterbrained to choose for myself.'

Effie glanced over her shoulder and saw Arnoldo standing at the top of the caravan steps. He was fingering his cravat nervously as he stared in their direction. She seized Ethel's hand and squeezed it. 'You know who I mean. I'm not talking about Jed or Fernando, but a good honest man who loves you with all his being.'

'I know,' Ethel said, fixing her gaze on Arnoldo as he walked slowly towards them. 'I think I love him too, but Elmo forbids me to have anything to do with him.'

'Be brave. Follow your heart. If you care for Arnoldo he will look after you and your brother will have no say in the matter. This is your chance to stand on your own two feet and not be cowed by Elmo. Your future happiness may depend on what you say now, so good luck.' She gave Ethel a gentle push in Arnoldo's direction. 'I'll take Brag and make sure he's safely tethered.' She took the halter and walked away before Ethel had a chance to protest, but curiosity got the better of her and she paused, looking back in time to see Arnoldo go down on one knee in front of Ethel.

Brag jerked his head as if to remind Effie that he was eager to get back to the patch of grass where he had been grazing, and she patted his neck. 'You're quite right, Brag. They should be left alone to sort things out between them.'

The horse whickered softly, as if in agreement with her, but as she was leading him back towards the edge of the encampment Effie saw Fernando approaching with Charlie on a lead as if he were walking a large dog. Fernando doffed his wide-brimmed hat and gave her a courtly bow.

'Good morning,' Effie said hastily as he was about to walk past. She did not want him interrupting the tender scene between Arnoldo and Ethel.

Fernando hesitated, staring at her with a questioning look in his dark eyes. 'It is a good morning, yes.'

He seemed about to move on again, but Effie bent down to stroke Charlie. 'He is a fine animal.'

Fernando smiled and twirled his waxed moustache. 'You like animals, I think.'

Effie didn't quite like the way he was eyeing her up and down. He was undoubtedly a handsome fellow but he was obviously well aware of the fact. She suspected that many of the female punters paid their halfpenny more in the hope of receiving a smile from him than a desire to see a large and extremely docile rodent.

'You're quite right,' she said coolly. 'I love all animals.'

'We must share a glass of wine together one evening,' Fernando said, putting a wealth of meaning into the invitation.

Effie had not intended to divert his attention by flirting with him, but it seemed that Fernando needed very little encouragement. She managed a half-hearted smile. 'Perhaps, but I must go now. I have to get back to my child.'

'Ah, yes. There is nothing so stirring to the heart as to see a beautiful woman with her infant.' He crossed his hands over his heart. 'I shall come to your fire tonight when all is quiet. We will sit beneath the stars and talk about life.'

'Is this fellow bothering you, Effie?'

She turned to see Toby standing behind her. 'We were just passing the time of day.'

'Your rat looks a bit hot, mate. I should get it out of the sun if I was you,' Toby said, addressing himself to Fernando.

'Charlie is a capybara, not a rat.' Fernando's golden earring glinted in the sunlight as he tossed his head. 'I should call you out for that insult, but I am a man of peace.' Taking Effie's hand, he raised it to his lips. 'We will continue our conversation another time, my lady. Come, Charlie.' He strode away with Charlie breaking into a trot at his side.

Effie breathed a sigh of relief. 'Thanks, Toby. You came just in time.'

'This ain't the place for you, Effie,' Toby said, frowning. 'These fairground people are a rum lot. I'm used to dealing with them but it's not the life for a girl like you.'

Effie met his anxious gaze with a smile. 'They've been very kind to me, and I don't know what I would have done if they hadn't taken us in.' She walked on, leading Brag towards the pond where the other horses were grazing.

Toby fell into step beside her. 'What happens when we find Tom? Do you want him to lead this sort of life?'

'It's been good enough for you.'

'That's not the point. I was raised by gypsies, but you weren't.'

'I don't know what I was born to do, Toby. What I do know is that I'm never going back to the workhouse and neither is Tom. I have to find employment somewhere and it was pure chance that led me to the fair. It's not a bad way to live.'

Toby shrugged his shoulders. 'Young Georgie should inherit his grandpa's business. Are you just going to let those people take it from him?'

'What am I supposed to do? My father-in-law hates me, and he's under the influence of that villain Salter and his wife. They'll rob him of everything, and there will be nothing left for Georgie to inherit. I've put it all behind me, Toby. It was another life and I'm making the best of what I've got now.'

They had reached a spot close to where the horses grazed and she tethered Brag to a spindly tree.

'We'll find Tom,' Toby said slowly. 'I've got a day's trading here, but when I've done I'll be moving on.'

'I've been racking my brains trying to imagine where he would go,' Effie said, frowning. 'When he couldn't find you at the tavern he must have headed off somewhere. What would you do if you were thirteen and looking for someone like yourself?'

Toby took off his cap, running his hand through his hair. 'I'd go to fairgrounds and markets where horse dealers meet and trade. But I haven't seen hide nor hair of the boy.'

'Perhaps he just went to the wrong places. I know that Tom wouldn't give up. He'll still be searching for you.'

'Or for you.' Toby grasped her hand. 'If he couldn't find me, perhaps he decided to look for you instead.'

Effie stared at him, struggling to come to terms with the thought that Tom might have done something as rash as braving her father-in-law and Salter. 'No,' she said slowly. 'He wouldn't do that. Would he?'

'He's a boy, Effie. He had no money and nowhere else to go. I think Tom would have been more worried about you and Georgie than himself. It's possible he would track along the towpath, looking for the *Margaret*.'

'Salter will kill him,' Effie whispered. 'He's a bad man and his wife is no better. I saw them dragging my pa-in-law back onto the barge, dead drunk. Sal Salter wanted to toss him overboard but her husband shut her up in case I overheard them, which I did. Who knows, they might have done for the old man already, and Tom too.' Her voice broke on a sob and Toby put his arms around her, stroking her hair and holding her close.

'We won't let that happen, Effie. I'll find a way, I promise you.'

She drew away from him, wiping her eyes on the back of her hand. 'I'm sorry. I didn't mean to cry all over you. It's just so – horrible. I can't bear to think of Tom all alone and in danger.'

Toby regarded her steadily, and, for once, there was no smile lingering in his eyes. 'Leave it to me.' He turned on his heel and strode back into the fairground.

Effie watched him go with a heavy heart. She seemed to have been living in a dream since she joined the fair. She had thought that everything would come right simply by hoping and praying, but now she realised that she

164

must face reality. There would be no happy ending if Tom confronted the Salters in his search for her. She hurried back to her van, intent on finding Georgie and holding him in her arms as if she could never let him go. She had lost Owen and Tom might have been taken from her. She would keep Georgie safe at all costs.

Jessie looked up in surprise as Effie burst into the caravan. 'I thought you was helping Leah on her stall,' Jessie said, continuing to spoon bread and milk into Georgie's eager mouth. 'Have you forgotten something?'

Effie attempted a smile but her throat was tight with unshed tears of relief. 'No. I just wanted to make sure that Georgie was behaving himself.' Georgie gave her a milky grin and opened his mouth wider, like a baby bird demanding more food.

'He's a little angel, that's what he is,' Jessie said happily. 'If only my brothers were half as good as little Georgie, I'd have a much easier job, I can tell you.'

Effie acknowledged this accolade to her son with a brief nod of her head as she struggled to control her emotions. She had panicked needlessly, but the relief of stepping into a scene of such normality was almost overpowering. 'I'll be back after the first show, Jessie.'

'We might come and watch,' Jessie said, wiping Georgie's mouth with her apron. 'It's one way to keep the nippers quiet, if I can smuggle them in under the canvas.'

Effie slipped out of the caravan safe in the knowledge that Georgie was in good hands. Jessie might only be a child but she was probably more reliable than many girls twice her age. Effie was about to make her way to Leah's stall when Gert hailed her. 'Come here for a moment, Effie.'

She approached the caravan where Gert was perched on the steps, smoking a clay pipe. 'Did you want me, Gert?'

'I see trouble in the smoke,' Gert said tersely. 'Laila saw it in the crystal, and now I see it in the smoke. I see money changing hands and there's someone close to you who's in danger. Do you understand what I'm saying?'

The blood thundered in Effie's ears, drowning out the sounds of the children playing and the music from the merry-go-round. She closed her eyes, picturing Tom's face.

'Don't pay no mind to him who wants you when he has no right.' Gert said softly. 'You know what you must do, so don't delay.'

At a loss for words, Effie raised her hand in acknowledgement of Gert's warning. She felt as though she had turned to stone, but somehow she managed to put one foot in front of the other as she went in search of Toby. She found him haggling over money with a rotund man wearing a mustard-yellow check suit and a bowler hat.

'Toby, I must speak to you.'

The fat man took off his hat and wiped the sweat from his brow. 'Go away, little lady. This is business.'

Toby put his arm around Effie's shoulders. 'No. You stay, Effie.'

'You're not making a friend here, mate,' the man snarled. 'You'll pay the extra or I'll take the mare back.'

'We had a deal,' Toby said, shaking his head. 'You agreed the sum and we shook hands on it.'

'Please come away,' Effie said, eyeing the angry man warily.

He shook his fist at her. 'Keep out of this, missis.'

'Give us a moment, cully,' Toby said affably. He lowered his voice. 'What's up, Effie?'

She glanced nervously at the fat man who was mopping his brow with a crimson silk handkerchief. 'Can we talk in private, Toby?'

'I've seen you, missis,' the man said, pushing his face close to Effie's. 'I've seen you in the ring being tossed about and showing your drawers to all and sundry. You live in one of them painted vans like the other sluts. There's a name for women like you. Now clear off before—' His last words were lost as Toby took a swing at him, catching him on the jaw and sending him sprawling on the ground.

A crowd materialised as if from nowhere, calling for a fight, but at that moment Frank came striding up and grabbed Toby by the collar. 'What the hell d'you think you're doing, Tapper?'

'Leave him alone,' Effie cried. 'It's not his fault.'

Frank turned an angry face to her. 'Go away. This has nothing to do with you.'

Toby struggled free. 'It has everything to do with her. That man insulted Effie. I'll not stand for it.'

'You won't stand for it? Effie belongs to me. She'll have nothing to do with you.' Frank lashed out with his fist, striking Toby on the side of his head. The blow sent him staggering into the fat man who had scrambled to his feet, only to be knocked down again like a skittle. He bounced back up, roaring with rage, but was shoved out of the way by Barney, the man who operated the swingboats. It seemed to Effie then that every man in the fairground joined in the fight. Fists flew, punches landed. Blood spurted from squashed noses and cut lips. Women screamed and others egged the men on.

'Stop it,' Effie cried. 'Stop it at once.' She attempted to throw herself between Frank and Toby who had each other by the throat, but as she leapt she caught a fist between the eyes and spiralled into darkness.

Chapter Eight

'Wake up, Effie.'

She opened her eyes to find something cold and wet running down her face. With difficulty, she focused her gaze on Leah's lean face. Effie blinked and attempted to sit up, but found herself thrust back until her head rested once again on Zilla's lap.

'Take it slow, ducks,' Leah said, mopping Effie's brow with a wet sponge.

'Is it over?' Effie whispered. 'What happened between Frank and Toby?'

'I dunno, but I expect they're getting a roasting from Frank senior. He wasn't too pleased to find that sort of ruckus going on,' Zilla said, stroking the hair back from Effie's damp forehead. 'It ain't good for business.'

'How's the head?' Leah demanded gruffly. 'You was hit hard.'

'It hurts,' Effie said, squinting up at the patch of blue sky above her head. It occurred to her suddenly that they were not in the place where the fight had occurred. 'How did I get here?' In her befuddled mind it seemed to her that she had been transported by magic to the ground outside the show tent.

'Arnoldo picked you up like a rag doll. You might have been trampled underfoot if he hadn't stepped in,' Leah said grimly.

'When men get it into their heads to fight, there's no stopping them,' Zilla added sagely. 'You were foolish to try to intervene, but I thought you were very brave.'

Effie held her hand out to Leah. 'Help me up, please. I'm quite all right now and I must find Toby and sort things out with Frank.' Despite her brave words, Effie soon realised that she had been too optimistic, for as she attempted to stand the sky and grass seemed to change places in a whirl of green and blue. She leaned against Leah's shoulder for a moment until the world righted itself. She took a deep breath and she straightened up, brushing the dust from her crumpled skirts. 'I'm fine now.'

'You won't be if you go chasing after Frank and the gypsy,' Leah muttered.

'Leah's right, ducks,' Zilla said, rising to her feet in a swirl of hoops and petticoats. 'Let the horse trader go on his way. His sort is nothing but trouble to a girl like you.'

'You don't understand,' Effie murmured. 'It wasn't Toby's fault.'

Leah and Zilla exchanged meaningful glances.

'It's worse than we thought,' Leah said gruffly. 'She's been bewitched by his Romany arts.'

'That's nonsense,' Effie cried angrily.

'You'd best forget the gypsy.' Leah shook her finger at her, scowling.

'Stay here where we can keep an eye on you and the boy,' Zilla pleaded. 'You've got friends in the fairground, Effie. Don't go with the horse trader.'

'You don't know what you're saying. I'm not running off with Toby. He's helping me find my brother. We think Tom might be in danger.'

Leah took her pipe and tobacco pouch from her pocket. 'That's different. But think carefully before you leave us, Effie. Let Tapper search for the boy.'

For a moment Effie was tempted to agree with Leah. It would be so easy to allow matters to take their course, but Gert's warning was still uppermost in her mind. She could not bear to think of Tom alone, hungry and possibly in danger. 'I don't want to leave you, but I know what I have to do.' She threw her arms around Leah and gave her a hug. 'You two are the best friends anyone could have, and I love you both.' She turned to Zilla, planting a kiss on her whiskery cheek. 'Goodbye, and thank you for everything.'

172

With tears in her eyes she parted from them despite their entreaties for her to stay. Closing her ears to their pleas, Effie returned to the scene of the fight in the hope of finding Frank and Toby.

The crowd had dispersed, and the only evidence that remained of the fracas was the splintered remnants of the sweet stall. Arnoldo was hefting planks of wood back into place as easily as if they had been matchsticks, while Ethel and Myrtle scrabbled about in the grass like a pair of demented chickens attempting to retrieve the toffee apples and sweets that the local children had somehow missed.

Ethel looked up and smiled. 'Where are you off to in such a hurry, Effie?'

'It's complicated,' Effie said, unwilling to waste any more time with explanations.

'She said yes,' Arnoldo announced proudly as he set the trestles back in place. 'I'm the happiest man on earth.'

'Oh, you do exaggerate, Arnie,' Ethel said, blushing. 'He was ever so brave, Effie. Did you see my Arnie break up the fight? He's a real hero.'

'She didn't see nothing, you silly tart.' Myrtle rose to her feet, staggering beneath the weight of an apron filled with sweets and toffee apples. 'She had a bang on the napper that would have felled an ox. Got a headache, love?'

'I'm all right, ta,' Effie said, forcing her lips into a smile. 'Congratulations, Arnie, and you too, Ethel; I'm sure you'll be very happy.'

'You ain't running away, are you, Effie?' Ethel asked anxiously. 'You must stay to dance at our wedding.'

'You can't go now,' Arnoldo added, abandoning the planks and moving to Ethel's side. He raised her to her feet, dusting her down like a mother with a child that had tumbled over in the playground. 'There's the act, Effie. You're the best assistant I've ever had.'

She smiled despite the pain in her head. 'You've got the perfect partner standing by your side, Arnoldo. I'm surprised you never asked Ethel to do it in the first place.'

'I dunno why I didn't think of it before.' He picked Ethel up and twirled her over his head, catching her in his arms as she fell. 'Will you, my duck? Will you give up helping Dr Destiny and that blooming blacksmith, and be my partner in work as well as in life?'

Effie didn't wait to hear Ethel's answer. She took the opportunity to slip away and went in search of Frank, but no one had seen him since the fight, although Jed suggested that she try Frank senior's caravan where Mrs Tinsley was probably patching her son up, scolding him and fussing over him in turns. Effie decided reluctantly that it would be best to avoid confrontation with Frank's over-protective parents. Her heart might feel as though it were breaking at the thought of leaving Frank, but a small worm of doubt had wriggled into her mind. She had seen a different side to him when he started the fight, and she had not liked the way he had spoken of her as a mere chattel that belonged exclusively to him. Perhaps it would be better for all concerned if she slipped away with Toby.

Almost without thinking she had made her way back to her caravan. Outside in the hot summer sunshine, the children were playing on the hard-baked turf and Georgie was amongst them, making as much noise as his companions. Not wanting to spoil his fun, Effie left him to his game. She went inside the van to pack up their belongings and she was in the middle of wrapping her precious china fairings when Toby arrived. He was dirty and dishevelled with a split lip and the beginnings of a black eye.

'You're hurt,' Effie said anxiously. 'Let me bathe that cut lip for you, and perhaps Gert will make up something for your poor eye. If not we could buy something from Dr Destiny.'

'I'm all right, but how are you? You should

never come between two blokes fighting, Effie.'

'I'm fine now. I'll be ready in two ticks.'

Toby stared meaningfully at the pile of objects laid out on her bunk. 'I'm sorry, but you'll have to leave all that behind.'

She stared at him blankly. 'I don't understand.'

'We have to travel light. You can't bring anything that won't fit into a saddlebag.'

'But these are my things, Toby.' Effie glanced round the cosy interior of the van which had become home. 'I knew I couldn't take the caravan as it was loaned to me, but these things were presents from my friends. They mean a lot to me.'

Toby took the china shepherdess from her hand and set it back on the shelf. 'I'm sure the fairground folk will look after them for you, Effie. When everything is settled you'll be able to collect your belongings.'

Effie sat down suddenly as the full impact of leaving hit her. 'But I won't, will I? If I leave with you now Frank will think . . .' She hesitated, unable to continue.

'I know what he thinks of me,' Toby said gently. 'But I haven't got evil designs on you. Forget him, Effie. He's not good enough for you, girl.'

She smiled ruefully. 'That's funny. They all say the same thing about you.'

'And they're right,' he said, chuckling. 'I'm a bad lot and don't pretend to be anything else, unlike Frank Tinsley.' He held his hand up as Effie opened her mouth to protest. 'But we'll say no more about him. Pack just what's necessary and we'll be off.'

'I ought to say goodbye to Gert and Annie,' Effie murmured. 'They've been good to me, and I must tell Jessie that we're leaving.'

Toby shook his head. 'There's no time for that, Effie. Tinsley wants me out of here and we've got a long ride ahead of us.'

Effie emptied the sack and began repacking it with a change of clothes for herself and Georgie. 'Where will we go?'

'We'll start at the Prince of Wales. I'm working on the notion that Tom will think that you're still on the *Margaret*, and Ben will know when she passed through Limehouse Cut and which way she was headed. Once we find out which direction they were travelling in we can follow the towpath. The lock keepers along the way will be able to tell us if they've seen Tom.'

'You make it sound so easy, but we have to find somewhere to stay for the night, and Georgie is just a baby. We can't sleep rough.'

'I'll look after you both. There's no need to worry, love. I've got money enough to keep

177

us going until the next horse fair, and hopefully we'll have found young Tom well before then. You'll have to trust me, Effie.'

'I do, Toby, and I've got the money I took from Jacob.' She slid her hand beneath one of the bunks where she had hidden the leather pouch, but her searching fingers found nothing. She went down on her hands and knees, peering into the empty space with a groan. 'Oh, Toby. It's gone. Someone's stolen my money. It's all I have in the world.'

'There's no time to worry about that now. Come on, Effie.'

She sat back on her haunches, unable to believe that anyone in the fairground would have perpetrated such a crime. 'Who would have done such a thing?'

He helped her to her feet. 'I don't know, but we can't hang about here. It could have been anyone.'

'No one here would have stolen it,' Effie cried passionately. 'They're my friends.'

'We made one enemy today. I thought he'd been seen off the grounds by Arnoldo, but maybe he came back.'

'Who?' Effie demanded, clutching his arm. 'Who do you mean?'

'That bloke who tried to cheat me over the price of the mare. I should have known better than to have dealings with Slippery Sid.

He's well known from Bow to Bermondsey and he'll be long gone by now. I'm sorry, Effie.'

She stared at him, barely able to take in the enormity of what had occurred. She had been counting on Jacob's money to keep them from the workhouse and now it was gone.

Toby brushed a lock of hair from her forehead and he frowned. 'That's a nasty bump you took.'

She brushed his hand away. 'That money was our future. It would have rented us a lovely little house and kept us in food until I had found work. Now it's all gone.'

'It was tainted money if it came from the old miser.' Toby slipped his arm around her shoulders. 'You're white as a ghost, Effie. Are you certain you're well enough to travel?'

'Gert warned me but I didn't listen. If I'd only hidden it somewhere safer.'

Toby took the sack from her hands. 'Come on, girl. It ain't the end of the world. I'll look after you and Georgie.' He took her by the hand and led her out of the van and down the steps.

Effie paused, taking one last look at the caravan. It had only been their home for a short time, and it had proved to be a haven from the troubles that had beset them, but it was time to go. Finding Tom was more important than anything. She took a deep breath and called to Georgie, bending down and holding out her arms as he ran to her with his small face wreathed in smiles. She snatched him up, cuddling him to her breast. Toby was right; money was unimportant when compared to caring for her loved ones. She kissed him on the tip of his small nose. 'We're going to have a big adventure, darling.'

'Gee-gee,' Georgie said, pointing to the bay gelding waiting patiently with its companion, a grey mare, which Effie knew was Toby's pride and joy.

Her heart swelled with pride. 'That's right, darling. You remember Champion, don't you?'

'He's a bright boy, Effie.' Taking Georgie from her and sitting him on the caravan steps, Toby tossed her up onto the saddle. 'We'll make a horseman of him yet, but I'm afraid you'll have to sit astride, my lady, since I don't possess a side-saddle.'

'I wouldn't know how to sit on one anyway. Whenever I rode Champion it was like this, only bareback. A saddle is a luxury.'

Toby grinned as he picked up Georgie and handed him to his mother. 'You won't be saying that after a day's riding, Effie.'

Toby's words proved to be prophetic. By the evening, Effie was exhausted and saddle-sore.

The heat of the day had cooled gradually but now, as the summer dusk swallowed the vast expanse of Hackney Marshes, they were pestered by biting insects and a damp mist curled up from the boggy ground. Georgie had long since fallen asleep, and Toby had taken him for the last few miles when he became too heavy for Effie to hold. As the sun plummeted beneath the horizon, strange lights floated above the marsh, and the air was filled with noxious smells as gas bubbled up between the tussocks of grass and sedge. Frogs croaked in an eerie chorus, and the marsh seemed to breathe as the mud cooled with soft sighing sounds.

'What are those lights?' Effie whispered as they rode side by side along a narrow track which she would never have known existed if Toby had not been familiar with the route. 'They look like ghostly spirits hovering and beckoning us to follow.'

'They call it will-o'-the-wisp.'

'Is it supposed to be a fairy or a spirit?'

Toby chuckled. 'Nothing so romantic; it's caused by marsh gas, and those who follow its eerie dance get sucked into the bog and drowned. Don't be tempted to stray from the path.'

She glanced round, peering into the gathering gloom with a shudder. 'This place looks like the end of the earth. How far must we go before we can stop for the night?'

'Not far now.'

Effie stared at his profile as he rode beside her, and it was as if she were seeing him for the first time. His straight nose and high cheekbones were complemented by a firm jawline and a determined chin, but there was a delicacy about his features that gave him a boyish charm. It was little wonder that women found him irresistible, she thought, as she observed how gently he held her son, and how easily Georgie's curly head rested on Toby's shoulder. She shivered as a cool breeze blew in from the east. She was cold now, but earlier in the day she had been drenched in sweat. Despite the wide-brimmed felt hat that Toby had given her, she could feel her skin aflame with sunburn, and she was so hungry that her stomach felt as though it was eating itself. They had stopped by the wayside at noon and purchased milk from a farm together with a freshly baked loaf and strong cheese that had taken the skin off the inside of Effie's mouth. But that was many hours ago, and although Toby had filled a leather flask with water they had had nothing to eat since their picnic at the roadside.

'See that light in the distance?' Toby said, breaking the silence that stretched between them like an invisible cord.

Effie strained her eyes to see the pinprick of a glow that might have been a star it seemed so far away. 'I think so.'

'It's Marsh House. My mother worked there as a girl, and I was born within its crumbling walls.'

A shudder ran down Effie's spine. 'It doesn't sound very welcoming. Will they let us stay for the night?'

'The housekeeper makes money on the side by taking in travellers who would otherwise be stranded overnight on the marshes. Desperate people will pay almost anything for the privilege of sleeping in the barn, or on the kitchen floor.'

Effie said nothing. She was so tired that she would willingly have slept anywhere providing it was warm and dry. Toby urged his horse into a brisk trot and Effie followed suit. The sooner they reached Marsh House, the better.

But when they arrived at their destination she was not so sure. It was almost dark and the Elizabethan manor house was silhouetted against the residual glow in the western sky. To Effie's tired eyes it looked more like a ruin than a habitable home. The roof was bowed and the ground littered with fallen tiles and the odd chimney pot that had crashed to earth and splintered into shards. The garden appeared to be a tangle of overgrown bushes and brambles, and as Toby guided his horse round the back of the building to the stable yard the dereliction became more apparent. A light filtering through a ground floor window revealed mossy cobblestones and stable doors hanging by single hinges, creaking and groaning in the cold wind from the marsh.

A flickering beam of light from a lantern preceded an aged retainer as he hobbled across the yard to take the horses into the stables. A few words from Toby brought a semblance of a smile to the man's lips, and he grunted a reply in a cracked voice so deep and low that Effie could not make out the words.

With the saddlebags looped over his shoulder, Toby headed for the back door of the house. 'Come on, Effie.'

She followed him slowly, her cramped muscles protesting with every step, and Georgie's sleepy head bumping up and down against her shoulder. It appeared that no one had bothered to lock the door as Toby walked into the scullery without knocking. Effie thought that the occupants were either supremely confident in their isolation, or else there was nothing of value to steal. She wrinkled her nose at the smell emanating from the drain in the stone sink, and the buckets of slops left to ferment on the flagstone floor.

Toby led the way down a narrow passage to the kitchen. The heat from the range enveloped Effie like a warm cloak, and the light from the fire cast a friendly glow on what was otherwise a scene of total chaos. Candle stubs wallowing in pools of melted wax were stuck to every available spare inch of tabletop or shelving that was not hidden beneath a jumble of pots, pans, dirty crockery, old boots and dog leads, rotting vegetable matter and mouldy loaves. The floor was thick with mud so that it was impossible to tell whether flagstones or floorboards lay beneath the piles of old grain sacks and bundles of kindling.

'You wouldn't describe it as homely, would you?' Toby said in a low voice, pointing at an elderly woman who was dozing in a rocking chair by the fire. 'That is the housekeeper I mentioned earlier.' He cleared his throat noisily. 'Ho there, Mrs Halfpenny.'

The woman raised her head and pushed her mobcap back from her eyes, peering at them with a disgruntled look on her lined face. 'Is that you again, Toby Tapper?'

'It is I, Mrs Halfpenny.'

'And who's that with you? If that's a kid she's holding, I don't like children. I don't want it in the house.'

Toby made his way to her side, which Effie observed was more like wading through a rubbish heap than simply crossing from one end of a room to the other. He stood before the irate housekeeper, and taking a package from his pocket he pressed it into her hand. 'That should sweeten your temper, my old duck.'

Mrs Halfpenny ripped the brown paper open and held the brown powder to her nose, sniffing it with an appreciative grin. 'That's more like it. What d'you want, you rogue?'

'A bed for myself and my travelling companions, and something to eat.' Toby glanced at the detritus on the table and frowned. 'Well, perhaps some eggs if the hens haven't stopped laying, and some milk for the little one.'

'Show me your money and I'll think about it.' Mrs Halfpenny held out her hand.

Toby took some coins from his pocket and placed a silver threepenny bit on her palm.

'Not enough, cully.'

He added a penny, but she shook her head. 'Sixpence and not a penny less.'

'You are an old robber. We could stay at an inn for less.'

Mrs Halfpenny put her head on one side, staring up at him with a sly expression in her beady eyes. 'But you don't have to please the master as I do. He's never been the same since he took to the drink and opium, and sometimes it's hard to know how to deal with his fits of madness. There's not many as would put up with him, I can tell you that for nothing.'

'You're a saint, I'm sure,' Toby said, placing two more pennies in her hand. 'I want a proper bed for Mrs Grey and her son, but I can sleep anywhere.'

'I can let you have the Blue Room, but there's only one bed and you'll have to make your own arrangements.' Mrs Halfpenny darted a sly look at Effie. 'I'm sure she won't say no, if pressed.'

'There are plenty of rooms,' Toby protested. 'I can remember almost exactly how many beds my mother had to make each day.'

'And she slept in a fair number of them,' Mrs Halfpenny said, cackling with mirthless laughter. 'Well, she ain't here to wash the bedlinen now, young Toby. In fact there ain't any to spare because I sold it all to pay me wages.'

'But there are beds . . .' Toby faltered as Mrs Halfpenny shook her head.

'No. I sold 'em too. There's not a stick of furniture left in most of the upstairs rooms, and it weren't all sent to auction for my benefit. The master's mind is wandering and he don't know what day of the week it is. He's gone through his money and allowed the farm to go to ruin. I've had to trade furniture for food and drink, so don't look down your nose at me, young man.' She rose to her feet and hobbled across the room to peer at Effie. 'You dress like a gypsy and you might be a pretty girl when your face goes back to normal, but take my tip and be on your way as soon as it gets light. This ain't no place for the likes of you and an innocent child.'

'A bed for the night will be more than welcome,' Effie said with an effort. 'We are very tired, ma'am.'

'I can see that you ain't no common slut. Where did he come across you, I'd like to know?'

'Mrs Halfpenny,' Toby said sternly. 'That's none of your business. We'd like something to eat now, if you please.'

'You know where the henhouse is, and there's milk in the dairy if it ain't curdled. Old Jeffries gets a bucketful from the farm across the marsh every morning when his rheumatics don't get the better of him.'

Georgie chose this moment to wake up and he began to snivel. Effie cast an agonised glance at Toby and he nodded his head. 'Don't worry. I'll see what I can do. I could find my way blindfold round this old place.' He picked up a jug, sniffed it and pulled a face. 'Is there a clean pot or pan in the house, Mrs Halfpenny?'

'Don't you be so cheeky,' she snapped, bridling. 'You ain't too big to warrant a clip round the lug.'

'I'll be as quick as I can,' Toby said, addressing his remark to Effie as he left the room.

'He was a young limb and he ain't changed very much now he's a grown man.' Mrs Halfpenny resumed her seat and took a hefty pinch of the brown powder from the packet that he had given her. She sneezed and wiped her nose on her stained pinafore. 'That's proper snuff. Not like the sweepings off the floor that Jeffries gets for me in town.'

Georgie rubbed his eyes and began to bawl in earnest. Effie paced up and down, rocking her son in her arms. 'There, there, darling. We'll have supper soon and then Mama will put you to bed.'

'Shut him up,' Mrs Halfpenny grumbled. 'I can't hear meself think.'

'He's had a long day, and he's hungry.' Effie brushed the damp curls back from Georgie's forehead. He was flushed and she could feel the heat emanating from his small body. She prayed silently that it was just a touch of the sun and not one of the dreaded childhood ailments that seemed to be consuming his small body.

'Give him a potato to chew on then. There's some in one of them sacks, though don't ask me which one.' Mrs Halfpenny slipped the packet of snuff into her apron pocket and reached for a stone bottle placed strategically on the floor at her side. She took a swig with apparent enjoyment and sighed. 'That's real Hollands, that is. None of your cheap booze for Nellie Halfpenny.'

Effie did her best to comfort an increasingly irritable Georgie, pacing the floor with him until Toby returned some minutes later with a jug of milk and four eggs.

'I'm going to me bed,' Mrs Halfpenny announced. She drained the last of the gin and rose unsteadily to her feet. 'Sort yourselves out, but don't make a noise. The master is a light sleeper and I don't want him wandering about in the middle of the night.' She staggered from the kitchen leaving a trail of gin fumes and body odour in her wake.

Toby picked up an empty wicker log basket, and with one sweep of his arm sent the dirty crockery, remnants of past meals and vegetable peelings tumbling into its capacious depths. 'That's the only way to deal with a mess like that,' he said, putting the rubbish outside the door. 'If you can find some clean cups and plates, I'll see to the food.'

'I'll scream if a rat jumps out at me. Goodness knows what's lurking inside the cupboards if the mess outside is anything to go by.' Effie settled Georgie on her hip while she explored the kitchen, peering nervously into cupboards and drawers. She found some clean, if dusty, cups and plates in the dresser, and a reasonably fresh loaf of bread on the larder shelf. She wrinkled her nose at the rancid stench emanating from a lump of mouldy cheese, and a tub of lard studded with what she thought at first were currants and on closer inspection turned out to be dead flies. She closed the door on such abominations and sat Georgie down in the rocking chair, where he flopped listlessly like a rag doll. 'I hope he's not sickening for something,' she said anxiously as she poured warm milk onto some crumbled bread.

'He's caught the sun and he must be worn out,' Toby said soothingly. 'All he needs is some food and a good night's sleep.'

Effie was not convinced, but she was relieved when Georgie took a little of the bread and milk, although he fell asleep after a few mouthfuls.

Toby took a caddy from the mantelshelf and spooned tea leaves into a brown china teapot. 'Nothing changes here,' he said, adding boiling water. 'Everything is kept in exactly the same place as when I was a nipper.' He set the pot on the hob to brew and turned his attention to toasting the bread and scrambling the eggs.

Effie watched him with a degree of

surprise. This was a side of Toby Tapper that she could never have imagined, and quite different from the image he assumed as a womanising scallywag and dealer in horses of uncertain origin. Her curiosity was aroused as she realised how little she knew of him and how much of his character she had taken at face value. 'How long did you live in this house, Toby?'

'Like I said before, I was born here, and I was only seven when Ma died. She nursed the master through a bout of smallpox, but she caught it herself and was dead within days. He survived but the illness seemed to send the old man a bit mad, and he sent me to live with my mother's people. They were good to me in their fashion, but I was not one of them. My mixed blood went against me as much with the Roma as with the gorgios.'

Effie was quick to note the pain behind his words and her heart went out to him. 'Poor little boy, you must have been very unhappy.'

'Not a bit of it.' Toby's insouciant smile banished the wistful look and he set the plates of food on the table. 'Come and eat while it's hot.' He poured the tea and handed a cup to Effie. 'You must be tired, Effie. I'll show you your room when you've finished your meal.'

'Where will you sleep?'

'Don't worry, Effie. I'll take the chair by the range.' His lips twitched and his eyes twinkled merrily. 'You're in no danger from me.'

She was too tired to think of a suitable response. She had never thought of Toby in a romantic light, but his cheerful words did nothing for her self-confidence. She knew she must look a sight with her bruised face, tangled hair and travel-stained clothes, but she found herself wondering how Frank would have behaved in a similar situation. She had done her best to put him out of her mind, but the knowledge that they had parted for good was weighing her down so that she felt close to despair. She had never thought to love again, but now it seemed that she was doomed to lose the men closest to her heart. Sadness and loneliness threatened to engulf her. She would have welcomed a loving hug from a man's arms, even if it was Toby who held her and told her that everything would be all right in the end. She raised her eyes and realised with a jolt of surprise that he was staring at her intently. 'What's the matter?' she demanded anxiously. 'Why are you looking at me like that?'

'You were thinking of him, weren't you?'

'No, I was not.' She took a mouthful of toast and chewed it, but her throat was so tight that she found it almost impossible to swallow.

She gulped and took a sip of tea. 'I'm tired, that's all.'

'Of course you are.' Toby's expression lightened. 'Eat up and we'll get you both to bed. Things will look better in the morning, I promise you.'

The Blue Room proved to be large and sparsely furnished. In the flickering light of a candle, Effie could see a chest of drawers standing on the bare boards beneath the mullioned window. There was a washstand with nothing but rings in the dust to show that it had once boasted a jug and basin, and she noted that there were no towels hanging from the rail. There was also a marked absence of curtains hanging at the window or from the tester on the large four-poster bed that dominated the room.

'Nellie seems to have been extremely thorough when it came to selling off Mr Westlake's possessions,' Toby said, placing the candlestick on the washstand. 'I suppose the furniture will be the next to go to the auction rooms.'

Effie lifted the bedcovers with a sigh of relief. 'At least she's left the bedding. We'll be comfortable enough tonight, Toby.' She laid Georgie on the pillow without waking him. 'It may be wishful thinking, but he seems to be a little cooler now.'

'I'm sure he'll be fine in the morning,' Toby said, patting her gently on the shoulder. 'I'm going downstairs, but I'd advise you to lock the door when I've gone.'

'Goodnight, Toby. Thank you for everything.'

'Get some sleep, Effie. We'll leave first thing in the morning.'

She followed him to the door but when she went to lock it she discovered that the key was missing. She was too exhausted to worry about such a triviality and she lay down beside Georgie, pulling the bedcovers up to her chin. She was certain that the bedding was damp, but she had kept her clothes on. Tomorrow they would leave this horrible old house and be on their way to find Tom. She closed her eyes and slipped into a deep sleep, but vivid dreams disturbed her slumbers. She was out on the marsh, following the fairy lights into a cold, thick mist. She could not see and she was sinking into the boggy ground. She could not move. She was shivering and ice-cold. She opened her eyes and in the half-light she found herself gazing into the pockmarked face of a man with a mane of black hair and wild blue eyes. He smelled as if he had not washed for a year at least, and his breath stank of stale brandy and a substance that she did not recognise. His hands were tugging at the bedclothes and the weight of his body made it impossible for her to move. She opened her mouth and screamed.

Chapter Nine

'Mirella, don't be frightened. You've come back to me, my darling, and you've brought the boy.'

Effie's heart was beating a tattoo against her ribs. She realised that this madman must be Mr Westlake, the master of the house. She was terrified and yet she felt pity for the tortured soul who gazed at her with such passion. 'I am not Mirella,' she whispered. 'My name is Effie. Your housekeeper allowed us to stay for one night.'

'I am not mad, Mirella. She says I am out of my mind, but she is wrong. They are all trying to get my money and my land. You must help me, my love.'

Effie edged up the bed until she was in a sitting position. 'I will help you,' she said, forcing herself to remain calm. 'But first you must allow me to get out of bed.'

'I could slip in beside you,' Mr Westlake said, reaching out to cup her breast with one hand while he tugged at the cord of his robe with the other. 'We will keep each other warm as we did in the old days, my love.'

Effie pushed his hand away and she snatched Georgie up in her arms, but her fear for her own safety was forgotten when she realised that her small son was burning up with fever. She called his name but he did not open his eyes. She kicked the bedclothes off with all her strength, sending her would-be seducer tumbling onto the floor. 'Get off me, you horrible man. Can't you see that my baby is sick?' With Georgie in her arms she tried to escape but Mr Westlake caught her by the wrist.

'Run away, would you, lady? This is no time to play games. I've fallen for your wiles too often, Mirella.' He scrambled to his feet, but in doing so he loosened his hold and Effie kicked out at him, catching the side of his head with her bare foot. She ran for the door but he was close on her heels. She was sobbing uncontrollably with Georgie clutched to her breast when the door opened and Nellie Halfpenny erupted into the room, followed by Toby.

'What are you doing here, master?' Nellie stood, arms akimbo, glaring at her employer who had fallen to his knees, bowing his head and clutching his arms around his body.

'She's tormenting me again, Nellie. The harlot has returned to tease the life out of me.'

Toby slipped his arm around Effie's shoulders. 'Are you all right? Did he hurt you?'

She was trembling from head to foot but she managed to shake her head. 'N-no. I'm fine, but Georgie is ill. He's burning up with a fever and I don't know what's wrong with him.'

Nellie took off her shawl and wrapped it around her master's thin shoulders. 'Look at you, Mr Westlake, wandering about in your nightshirt. What will the young lady think?'

He shot a sly glance at Effie. 'It wouldn't be the first time, would it, my love? Don't play the innocent, Mirella.'

'Take him to his room, Nellie,' Toby said angrily. 'Give him something to calm his nerves.'

'Come with me, Master Seymour.' Nellie helped him to his feet, speaking in the gentle tone she might have used to a small child. 'Let me take you to your room and I'll give you some medicine to make you feel better.'

'Very well,' Seymour said reluctantly. 'I am a little tired.'

'And you must rest now.' Nellie led him towards the door. 'Don't worry, ducks,' she murmured in Effie's ear. 'He's harmless but he gets a bit confused at times. Best keep out of his way.'

'What did you say, Nellie?' Seymour demanded. 'Don't talk about me behind my back.' He shook off her restraining hand and,

199

holding himself erect, he marched out of the room without a backward glance.

Toby closed the door. 'You'd best put the boy back to bed, and I'll go for the doctor.'

Georgie had gone limp in her arms and Effie laid him on the pillows. 'He's got a rash,' she said anxiously as she examined his chest. 'I think it's measles.'

'That's all the more reason for me to ride out and fetch a physician.'

'Don't leave me in this awful place, Toby. Mr Westlake scares me and Mrs Halfpenny made it clear that she doesn't want us here. Couldn't we take Georgie back to Bow? I'm sure Ben would take us in for a night or two at least. I could work in the bar to pay for the room and board.'

Toby shook his head. 'The journey would only make his condition worse, and Maggie Hawkins wouldn't allow you anywhere near her children for fear of them catching the disease. I'm afraid you'll have to stay here until Georgie is well again.'

'It killed many young ones in the work-house,' Effie whispered. 'Georgie might die.'

'Not if I have anything to do with it, girl. I'll be back in no time at all.'

There was little that Effie could do other than wait for Toby to return with the doctor. She ventured down to the kitchen while

Georgie slept, returning quickly with a jug of water and a piece of cloth with which she bathed his head and fevered limbs. He tossed and turned on the pillows and when he opened his eyes briefly he did not seem to recognise her. Effie knelt by the bedside and prayed for his recovery. Death had robbed her of those she loved most in the world, and the dark days spent in the workhouse had left their imprint on her forever. She found it almost impossible to believe in a loving and forgiving god. She had seen very little mercy or genuine charity shown to the poor and needy, but she was willing to promise anything to a higher power that would spare her son. She buried her face in her hands, murmuring the prayers that she had been taught in the workhouse chapel.

'Much good that'll do you.'

Effie had not heard the door open and she was startled by the sound of Nellie's voice and the thud as she set a tray down on the washstand.

'I've brought you a cup of tea and a bit of bread and dripping. You got to keep your strength up.'

This unexpected act of kindness came as a shock after Nellie's less than enthusiastic reception the previous evening. Effie rose to her feet with a gallant attempt at a smile.

'Thank you. That was a kind thought and I'm sorry to be so much trouble to you, especially after what happened last night. Is Mr Westlake feeling better today?'

'He's sleeping off a dose of laudanum. He won't bother you again.'

'He called me Mirella,' Effie said, treading delicately in case she upset the fiery little woman who appeared to be devoted to her master. 'He must have mistaken me for someone he was very fond of. Who was Mirella?'

'She was Toby's mother, and this was her room.' Nellie said tersely. 'And before you go prying into things that don't concern you, I can tell you that there was talk at the time, but it was idle gossip. The master was devoted to his wife and Marsh House was a different place to what it is today.'

'Mrs Westlake is dead?'

'The poor lady was ill for many years. She suffered from a wasting disease that left her weak and crippled. It must be twenty-five years since she died.'

A whimper from Georgie momentarily distracted Effie, and she picked him up. He quietened instantly and she rocked him gently in her arms. Nellie was about to leave the room but Effie was still curious. 'Toby said that his mother worked here as a maid, and yet this was her room. Isn't it a bit odd?'

'Mirella Tapper descended on us like a wild March wind,' Nellie said, pursing her lips. 'She was a gypsy girl who had run away from an arranged marriage, or so she said.'

'And she was beautiful?'

'Oh yes, she had looks and she could charm the birds out of the trees if she put her mind to it. She could sing like a lark and she brought springtime into a winter house. It weren't surprising that the poor mistress took a fancy to her, and Mirella was the only servant she would tolerate to tend to her personal needs.'

'And Mr Westlake liked her too.'

Nellie cackled with laughter. 'That's one way of putting it. The master was bewitched from the first moment young Mirella danced into our lives. It was like having a creature of the forest captured and tamed after a fashion, but there was always the wild gypsy streak in her that could not be denied.'

'So who was Toby's father?' Effie had to ask the question, but she could see from Nellie's taut expression that she was not going to get a satisfactory answer.

'There's only one person who knows the answer to that, and she's been dead these past eighteen years.'

'I still don't understand why Mr Westlake

thought I was Mirella. I don't think anyone would describe me as a wild gypsy girl.'

'Maybe not, but you're pretty in the same way that she was. You look as though a puff of wind would carry you away, and I reckon those big blue eyes of yours have turned a few heads.'

'I was happily married,' Effie said hastily. 'I loved my husband and it broke my heart when he died, but at least I have Georgie to remind me of him.' She laid him back on the bed. 'The thought of losing him is terrifying. I can't imagine my life without him.'

Nellie thrust a cup of tea into her hands. 'No need to talk like that. He's a sturdy little fellow and no mistake. Drink this and have a bite to eat, but don't think I'm going to wait on you hand and foot because I ain't. I got enough to do keeping me eye on the master without acting like a lady's maid.'

Effie took a sip of the hot, sweet tea. 'Thank you, Mrs Halfpenny.'

'There's some of her old clothes in that chest of drawers if you need 'em, and I suppose you'd better call me Nellie, seeing as how you're staying awhile.'

'You're very kind, Nellie.'

'Well, I am too. I'm me own worst enemy with me big soft heart and kindly nature.' Nellie marched to the door. 'And as soon as the young 'un is on the mend, you can repay me by doing a bit of spring cleaning, and there's a pile of dirty washing to launder.' She whisked out of the room, closing the door behind her.

Effie drank the tea, but with the memory of the pan of lard dotted with dead flies still fresh in her mind she could not touch the bread and dripping. She spent the rest of the morning tending to her sick child. She held his small hand and stroked his forehead as she sang the lullabies that had sent him happily off to sleep when he was a baby. The sound of her voice seemed to calm him, and when she could sing no more she made up stories about anything that came into her head. There was no clock in the room and the only way she had of telling the time was by the height of the sun in the sky. She judged that it was about noon when Nellie brought her another cup of tea and a plate of bread and butter.

'I was taking food up to the master,' she said with a twitch of her shoulders, as if daring Effie to accuse her of another kind deed. 'I don't want you fainting from lack of nourishment so that I have to look after the nipper. I can't abide kids, as I've told you before.' She leaned over the bed. 'Is he any better?'

'He's no worse, but thank you for asking.'

Nellie tossed her head. 'I was just being

polite. He'll soon be up and about and poking his sticky fingers into everything.' She went to retrieve the breakfast tray. 'I dunno what's keeping young Toby and the doctor. It ain't that far to his house, unless he was called out and Toby had to go searching for him.' She snatched up the tray and left the room, grumbling beneath her breath.

Effie was not fooled for a moment. She had begun to realise that Nellie Halfpenny was not nearly as unfeeling as she made herself out to be. Beneath that steely exterior, Effie was beginning to believe that there really was a soft heart. She eyed the food warily and was going to push the plate away when she realised that she was extremely hungry. The aroma of freshly made bread was too tempting to resist, and when she took a tentative bite she found that it tasted as good as it looked and smelt. She ate hungrily, and having drunk the tea she began to feel stronger and more positive. Georgie was still feverish, but at least he seemed to be no worse.

There was little she could do other than to settle down and wait for Toby to return with the doctor. It was mid-afternoon when he burst into the room and Effie leapt to her feet. 'Where is the doctor?' she asked anxiously when she realised that there was no one following him. 'Is he coming?'

Toby shook his head. 'I'm sorry, Effie. I've spent the day chasing him from one place to another and finally caught up with him at a difficult confinement. He said that there is very little he can do for a case of measles, but he'll look in when the woman is delivered of her child.'

Effie sank down on the bed. 'It could be too late then. I don't know what to do.'

'Don't give up so easily.' He put his hand in his pocket and took out a small green bottle, which he placed in her hand. 'I knew that there were gypsies camped on the edge of Epping Forest, and when the doctor wouldn't come immediately I decided to pay my family a long overdue visit.'

'What is this?' Effie demanded, holding the bottle up to the light.

'My grandmother is a wise woman. She makes medicines for humans and animals using herbs that she picks in the fields and forests. I've seen her pills and potions work miracles.'

'I don't know,' Effie said, shaking her head. 'I'm not sure I believe in magic.'

Toby took the bottle from her and drew the cork. 'Give the boy a couple of drops at a time mixed with a little water. She said that it would bring the fever down and make him more comfortable. Come on, Effie. It's worth a try, isn't it?'

She sniffed the mixture suspiciously, and she glanced down at her sick child. She had watched Owen breathe his last and she did not intend to see Georgie slip away before his time. 'Pass me the jug of water and a spoon, please, Toby.'

He smiled. 'Wise choice, Effie. We'll soon have young Georgie up and about again.'

By evening there was a slight improvement in Georgie's condition. Effie had not left his bedside other than to go down to the outside privy when she needed to relieve herself. Toby had remained long enough to eat a hasty meal, and leaving his horse to rest, he had saddled the mare that Effie had ridden the day before and set off for Old Ford lock where he intended to ask the lock keeper if the *Margaret* had passed that way recently.

Effie waited anxiously for his return, alternately sitting on the bed and watching Georgie or pacing over to the window which overlooked the tangled garden at the front of the house and the road beyond. It was dark by the time Toby returned, and having recognised his firm tread, Effie ran to open the door. She could see lines of fatigue around the corners of his eyes and he was coated in dust from head to foot. He glanced past her at the tiny figure in the bed. 'Has the doctor been?'

Effie shook her head. 'No, but the medicine seems to be working. He's much quieter than he was this morning and he feels cooler to the touch.'

'That's good,' he said tiredly.

'Did you find anything out at the lock?'

He shook his head. 'The lock keeper hadn't seen them for weeks and no sign of Tom either. I'm sorry, Effie.'

Swallowing the bitter pill of disappointment, she laid her hand on his arm. 'It's not your fault, Toby. You did your best and I'm truly grateful.'

'I'll pay a visit to the tavern in the morning. I'm sure that Ben will have some news for me. I won't give up until I find him, I promise you that.'

'I just wish that I could come with you.'

A frown creased Toby's brow. 'The old devil hasn't been bothering you again, has he?'

'No. Nellie saw to that. She's not a bad old thing when you get to know her. In fact she's been quite kind and considerate today.'

'Nevertheless, I'll sleep up here tonight,' Toby said firmly. 'I'll take the floor so there's no need for you to worry.'

Effie smiled up at him. 'I trust you completely, Toby.'

'Damnation. I must be losing my touch.'

His expression was so comical that it made Effie laugh. 'You are such a fool.'

He bent down to brush her cheek with a kiss. 'Now I am a comic turn. You'll ruin my reputation as a libertine and seducer of pretty women.'

She tossed her head. 'I never believed it anyway. I think that the girls chased after you, and your reputation is quite unjustified.'

'Damn it, Effie. Can't you leave a fellow with a scrap of vanity?' He pulled a face as he walked towards the door. 'I'm going to stick my head under the pump in the stable yard and get rid of some of this Essex dust before it chokes me.'

Effie smiled to herself as she slipped into bed beside Georgie. In spite of everything, she thought how lucky she was to have found a friend like Toby. She could not think of many young men who would behave as valiantly, or with such chivalry, as the man who was labelled a didicoi and a horse thief by those who did not know him well. After a while she heard the soft thud of his stockinged feet as he returned to the room and the rustling of blankets as he made his bed on the floor. She closed her eyes and relaxed, safe in the knowledge that with Toby to protect her she could sleep easily.

*   *   *

The following day Georgie continued to improve. The doctor came eventually, and after a cursory examination he declared that the patient was over the worst. There had been no need to drag him out into the wilds of Hackney Marshes to see a child who was obviously on the road to recovery, he told them crossly. Having been charged a shilling for the privilege of being scolded for wasting the doctor's valuable time, Effie had keep a rein on her temper as she saw him out of the house. She longed to tell him that it was the gypsy's medicine that had cured her son, but she held her tongue. She was well aware that the general population were suspicious of travellers, and that included fairground folk and boat people as well as the Romany. She could tell by his superior attitude that he had taken her at face value, assuming that her gaudy patchwork skirt and low-cut blouse, given to her by Laila, had marked her out as one of them. She supposed that she could hardly blame him as the master of the house had jumped to a similar conclusion. Out of politeness, she held the doctor's bag for him while he mounted his horse.

'I would advise you to keep the curtains drawn in the boy's room,' he said, gruffly. 'The child should be kept in the dark for at least a week to protect his eyes.' Taking the bag from her hands he dug his heels into the horse's flanks and rode off at a steady trot.

'That was a waste of a shilling,' Effie muttered, addressing his retreating figure. If he had not been in such a hurry to get the examination over and done with, and had paid more attention to the sparse condition of the sick room than to her manner of dress, he might have noticed that there were no curtains at the windows to draw. She took a deep breath of the fresh breeze skimming the farmland east of the marsh. She could smell the honey scent of clover and new-mown hay mingled with the summer perfume of roses and honeysuckle from the overgrown manor garden. Overhead a skylark warbled its melodious song and the drone of bees was like sweet music to her ears. After the stench of the city with its constant din of traffic and the noise and hullabaloo of the fairground, it was a relief to be once again in the quiet of the countryside. Here she had time to think and feel whole again, just as she had in the early days of her marriage. She smiled as she remembered how she had stood at Owen's side while he steered the *Margaret* along the waterways leaving the smoke and dust of the East End far behind them. She lifted her face to feel the caress of the sun and she stretched her arms out wide. It was wonderful to be outdoors, but she had left Georgie sleeping and she must be at his side when he awakened.

She walked back along the garden path, treading carefully so that she did not trip over broken roof tiles or get her skirt snagged on the brambles that rampaged around the house in wild profusion. Now that she could see it clearly in broad daylight, she observed that the half-timbered building was almost completely blanketed by ivy and briar roses. Crazy paving paths were half hidden by carpets of moss, while daisies and dandelions struggled for existence with tall grasses. It was difficult to imagine how the garden would have looked had any effort been made to prevent it from reverting to wilderness. Similarly with the house, Effie thought, as she entered the wainscoted hallway. The floor tiles were scuffed and dulled by many layers of dirt, and the oak staircase leading up to the first floor would have benefited from a thorough dusting and the application of beeswax polish. As Effie ascended the stairs, she trailed her hand along the banister. If she were the proud possessor of a home like this she would never allow it to fall into such disrepair and decay. She paused to straighten a portrait of a young man that hung askew and was in danger of crashing to the ground. She was about to walk on but she paused to look again at the eyes which seemed to follow her as she moved. Despite the dirt that muted the colours so that everything looked beige or brown, she was aware that the eyes were a singular shade of blue. The brass plate was inscribed *A Portrait of Seymour Westlake, Esquire, 1845*. It was not surprising, she thought, that the gossips pointed their fingers at Mr Westlake, accusing him of being Toby's father. She wondered if Toby had ever stood before the painting and seen the likeness to himself. Or perhaps she was just being fanciful and had fallen under the spell of the old house which seemed to sleep, like the beautiful princess in the fairy story, awaiting a kiss from the handsome prince to awaken her.

Startled out of her reverie by the sonorous tones of the long-case clock in the hall striking twelve, she hurried back to the Blue Room and found that Georgie was awake and staring at the patterns on the wall where the sun shone through the windows. She laid her hand on his brow and realised that his flushed cheeks owed more to the rash than to a high fever.

'Mama,' Georgie said, smiling. 'Mama.'

Effie picked up the green medicine bottle and kissed it. 'Thank you, Grandmother Tapper,' she said out loud. 'Thank you for my son's life.' She scooped Georgie up in her arms and cuddled him. 'My darling boy, nothing matters as long as you are safe and well.'

With Georgie still poorly but out of imminent danger, Effie spent the rest of the day keeping him amused, venturing down to the kitchen to fetch food and drink only when absolutely necessary. She could hear Seymour roaming about in his room and his bell was constantly ringing. The sound echoed throughout the house and sometimes Nellie responded to it but more often than not she allowed it to ring unheeded. Effie was beginning to feel sorry for the man who was locked up from morning until night, and sedated by large doses of laudanum when he became too much of a nuisance. No wonder he was going out of his mind. She decided to speak to Toby about it when he returned, but although she waited until late in the evening there was no sign of him, and she began to worry.

Georgie had taken a little food during the day and a cup of milk before he fell asleep while listening to one of his favourite fairy stories. Effie felt weak with relief as she crept out of the room taking care not to waken him. He was over the worst and she had no doubt he would make a full recovery. She found Nellie in her usual seat by the kitchen range with her feet up on a wooden milking stool and the bottle of Hollands at her side. She

215

opened her eyes as Effie entered the room. 'What's the matter?' she asked in a gin-soaked voice. 'What's up?'

'Toby hasn't returned,' Effie said anxiously. 'I'm worried.'

Nellie took a pinch of snuff from the poke in her lap and inhaled it with a satisfied sigh. 'You can't keep a man like Toby tied to your apron strings. He's a rover and always will be.'

'I'm not making him do anything he doesn't want to,' Effie protested. 'He offered to go in search of my brother.'

Nellie pulled herself to a sitting position, eyeing Effie with a pitying smile. 'He's got more important things to do than waste his time looking for a runaway.'

'What do you mean by that?'

'Look, ducks, I've known him since he was a boy. He's here one minute and gone the next. That's the way gypsies are. He probably got in with a harlot who'll give him what all men want, or he's gone chasing off after some valuable horseflesh.'

Effie recognised a hint of the truth in Nellie's words. When she had first met Toby at the Prince of Wales tavern he had come and gone like the will-o'-the-wisp. He had been there one day and off on his travels the next. She had thought nothing of it then, but now when she needed him most it seemed quite likely that Toby had abandoned her. She sat down on the nearest chair as the full impact of her situation hit her. She was on her own with a sick child. She had little money and she was stuck in this remote, crumbling manor house with a drunken woman and a madman.

'That's the way it is,' Nellie said as if reading her mind. 'He'll come back in his own good time, or maybe not. Don't get involved with a gypsy man, ducks. You might as well try to harness the wind.'

'It isn't like that,' Effie murmured. 'I'm not in love with Toby. He's just a friend, but I thought I could rely on him, and now I don't know what to do.'

'Have a nip of Hollands,' Nellie said, offering her the bottle. 'It'll take your mind off your troubles.'

Effie shook her head. 'No, thank you. I need to keep a clear head in case Georgie needs me in the night.'

'Go to bed then and get some sleep. You look done in and you'll be no good to the boy if you fall sick.' Nellie took a swig from the bottle and smacked her lips. 'Don't fret about Toby. He'll come back when he's ready, and in the meantime you can stay here. To tell the truth, I quite like having someone other than the master to talk to. Sometimes I think I'll end up as mad as him.'

'You're very kind,' Effie said, rising to her feet. 'I don't know what I'd have done if you hadn't taken us in.'

'Don't talk soft. I'll get me tuppenny-worth out of you yet. Now that the boy is on the mend you can start on the kitchen tomorrow and we'll go on from there. There's enough work in this old ruin to keep you in vittles for a year or more.'

'Thank you, Nellie, but I don't intend to stay any longer than necessary. I have to find my brother, and as soon as Georgie is well enough I'll be on my way, with or without Toby.'

Nellie shook her head. 'I've known him go off for months on end, girl. I doubt if we'll see him again before Michaelmas or beyond. He's got too much of his mother in him for his own good.'

'And his father?' Effie left the question hovering in the air.

Nellie's face darkened. 'Even if I knew, I'd say mind your own business. That's what I'd say.'

Her question had obviously hit a raw spot, and although Effie could see that she was upsetting Nellie she was not going to give up so easily. 'I couldn't help noticing the likeness between Toby and the portrait of Mr Westlake—' She broke off as the Hollands bottle flew over the top of her head and landed on the table, smashing a pile of crockery.

'You're as bad as the rest of the gossipmongers round these parts,' Nellie cried angrily. 'Mr Westlake may be a bit eccentric these days, but he is a gentleman through and through. Mirella Tapper was anybody's, and the master wouldn't have lowered himself to have anything to do with a harlot like her.'

'I'm sorry,' Effie said, rising hastily to her feet. 'I didn't mean to upset you again, Nellie.'

'Get out of my sight.' Nellie seized the poker, wielding it above her head as if it were a broadsword. 'Get out before I clout you for saying such wicked things.'

Effie picked up her skirts and fled.

Chapter Ten

Effie had suffered a disturbed night. Georgie was wakeful and fractious, and even when he slept she had lain in bed worrying. In the creaking old house with the marsh winds sighing outside the windows like souls in distress, it was hard keep matters in proportion. She thought of her brother out there in the wide world, alone and defenceless. She could only hope that Toby had discovered the whereabouts of the *Margaret* and had gone in search of Tom, which would explain his continued absence. The picture of Toby's character as painted by Nellie was not an attractive one. Effie did not want to believe the worst of him but she could not quite put the niggling doubts from her mind, and her most pressing worry was for her brother's safety and well-being.

In the long wakeful hours she remembered happier times, recalling with a shiver of delight how Frank's kisses had made her feel young and alive again. Had be missed her and would he be content to let her slip away from him without putting up a fight? Was his loyalty to his family greater than his professed love for her? These were questions to which she had no answers, but her time spent with the fairground people was becoming distant and misty with a dreamlike quality, and she clung to it like a drowning woman. She would go back to them, she decided. When she had found Tom, they would seek out the fair and make a life for themselves amongst the travelling entertainers. They would be a family once again.

She yawned and sat up in bed, taking care not to disturb Georgie. The early summer dawn was alive with birdsong, and the sun slanted through the leaded lights creating diamond patterns on the floorboards. Effie slid off the bed and went to the window. She gazed out at the dew-covered marshland beyond the garden, and strained her eyes to peer along the track that led eventually to the main road, but there was no sign of a horse and rider. It was the start of what promised to be a glorious June day, but as far as she knew Toby had not returned. That could be a good sign, she thought, more in hope than with any conviction.

She dressed herself, and having checked to make sure that Georgie was still sound asleep, she hurried downstairs to the kitchen.

There was no sign of Nellie, which was something of a relief as Effie had been trying to think how best to apologise for upsetting her, although the question about Toby's parentage had been asked in all innocence. This was a strange house, she thought, as she searched the newly tidied cupboard for the sliver of soap she had discovered yesterday in what should have been a butter dish. She took a towel from the clothes horse and went outside to wash at the pump. The sun shone on the moss-covered cobblestones giving them the appearance of a croquet lawn rather than a working stable yard, and a door hanging on one hinge creaked as it swung to and fro in the gentle breeze. Taking a quick look round to make sure there was no one about, Effie stripped off her blouse and worked the pump handle. Water gushed into the stone trough below and she held her head under the ice-cold stream; it took her breath away, but was just what she needed to wash the away the imagined night terrors. She was drying her hair when Jeffries emerged from the tack room clutching an empty bucket.

'Good morning, ma'am.' He stood back and waited, staring down at his boots.

'Good morning, Mr Jeffries.' Effie covered her embarrassment by wrapping the damp towel around her shoulders. She stepped aside to allow him to fill his bucket.

'It's going to be a hot one today,' he said, keeping his gaze averted.

'I think you're right,' Effie said, hastily slipping her arms into her blouse and turning away to do up the buttons. 'Do you know if Toby returned last night, Mr Jeffries?'

'I don't think he did, ma'am. His horse isn't in the stables.'

A sudden thought crossed Effie's mind, or rather a suspicion that she hardly liked to put into words. 'And the mare?'

'She's ready for you to ride if you wants her saddled up, ma'am.'

'No, at least not today, thank you,' Effie said, breathing a sigh of relief. If Toby had been as untrustworthy as Nellie had made him out to be, he might have taken both horses and sold the mare for a tidy profit. There must, as she had thought, be another explanation for his continued absence. With a lighter heart, Effie made her way back to the kitchen. She had hoped to make a pot of tea and heat some milk for Georgie before Nellie was up and about, but as she entered the room she saw Nellie bending over the range, raking the embers into life. She turned at the sound of Effie's footsteps pitter-pattering across the tiled floor, and her expression was not welcoming.

Effie cleared her throat nervously. 'I want to apologise for what I said last night. I didn't mean to upset you.'

Nellie shrugged her shoulders and went back to poking the fire. 'Maybe I was a bit hasty, but I won't have a word said against the master.'

'No, of course not. I understand perfectly, and I won't mention it again.'

'The past is dead and buried,' Nellie said tersely. 'It looks as though you're here for some time to come and so you'd best begin earning your keep. You can start by cleaning in here and work your way through the house, room by room. But you can have breakfast first. I don't expect anyone to work on an empty stomach.'

'Thank you,' Effie said meekly. 'I'll do whatever you want, but Georgie is still quite poorly. I can't leave him on his own.'

'Then bring him down here. He can sit and watch his ma work, and you can keep an eye on him. That's what I had to do when my nippers was young.'

'You had children?'

A glimmer of amusement flickered across Nellie's thin features. 'I weren't always this old, and I was considered to be quite a catch when I was young. I could have taken my pick and my old man had to work hard to win my hand, but he was head gardener here and a handsome chap with winning ways. We had a cottage down by the marsh, but it's crumbled into a ruin now, more's the pity.'

Effie digested this piece of information in silence as she cut slices from yesterday's loaf.

'I gave birth to five beautiful babies,' Nellie continued sadly. 'All gone now.'

Perhaps that explained Nellie's dislike of children, Effie thought, sympathetically. 'You lost them all?'

'Two taken by diphtheria before they'd reached their first birthdays. Then my Annie died in childbirth when she was just sixteen and the baby too. Bertie married a girl from up North and moved away, and Sidney, my youngest, got caught stealing and was transported to the penal colony in Australia. I doubt if I'll ever see either of them again.'

Stricken with remorse for judging Nellie without any knowledge of her past, Effie laid a hand on her shoulder. 'I'm truly sorry that I spoke out of turn last night. You've been good to me, Nellie, and I won't forget it. Sit down and I'll make a pot of tea and some toast.'

Nellie shrugged her hand off. 'I don't need your pity, my girl.' She snatched a toasting fork from its hook on the wall. 'Stick the bread on here and put the kettle on. Like I said, the past is over and done with. We've got no choice but to get on with things. As for now, I'm gasping for a cup of tea. My mouth is so dry I can hardly speak.'

Effie cut a slice from the loaf and handed it to Nellie. 'I'll put the kettle on and then I'll go upstairs and fetch Georgie, if that's all right with you.'

'Do what you like. There's no hurry since it seems that you're going to be here for a long time.' Nellie glanced up at the ceiling as the sound of rhythmic thumping echoed round the room. 'That's the master wanting his breakfast. Go and see what he wants, Effie.'

'Perhaps you'd best go. I mean, he thinks I'm that other person.' Effie avoided mentioning Mirella by name in case she upset Nellie yet again.

'He'll have forgotten about that now. The master won't hurt you; he's as gentle as a lamb when the drink and drugs wear off.'

The thumping grew louder and more insistent and Nellie jumped to her feet, taking the kettle from Effie's hand. 'Damn it, girl. Anyone would think you was going to the gallows. Get on up them stairs and see what he wants for his breakfast. Tell him there's cold mutton and beer, or toast and coffee if he ain't feeling too well.'

Effie could see that any attempt to argue would be futile. She hurried upstairs, checking first on Georgie. Satisfied that he had not moved and was likely to sleep on for a while yet, she made her way along the landing to the room above the kitchen where Mr Westlake slept. Opening the door, she stepped into a room that took her breath away. She had seen something very similar in a book she had found on the shelves in the pub. Ben Hawkins was an avid reader, and he had allowed her to borrow books and read them at her leisure. The particular edition that had caught her eye was called *One Thousand and One Nights*. The tales were told by an Arabian princess named Scheherazade, and these had enthralled her as had the illustrated colour plates. Seymour Westlake's room could have come straight from the pages of that book. The ceiling was tented in crimson satin trimmed with gold braid. The walls were draped in rainbow-hued silk taffeta, and the bed was covered in quilted purple damask and half buried beneath tasselled cushions of all shapes and sizes. Oriental rugs were scattered about the floor and pierced metal lamps hung from the ceiling, casting a kaleidoscope of patterns on the walls and floor. The air was heavy with the scent of burning incense, which did not quite overcome the odour of a male body in desperate need of a bath.

Seymour was seated in the middle of all this faded, moth-eaten but still exotic splendour on a chair carved out of dark wood and inlaid with mother-of-pearl. He was wearing a flowing crimson velvet robe and his head was covered by a jewel-encrusted silk turban. He glared at her with no hint of recognition in his speedwell-blue eyes. 'Who the devil are you?'

'Effie Grey, sir.' She bobbed a curtsey. 'Mrs Halfpenny sent me to see what you want for your breakfast.'

He eyed her up and down. 'I don't know you, Effie Grey.'

'No, sir. I'm staying here for a while and helping with the cleaning.'

'I can't afford to pay for more servants. You'll have to leave immediately.'

'I'm not being paid, sir. And we don't eat much.'

'We?' Seymour said, raising his eyebrows. 'Are there more of you?'

'Just me and my son, Georgie. He's just a baby and he's been ill, which is why I can't leave right away, although I can assure you we'll be off as soon as he's well enough.'

Seymour raised his hand, closing his eyes. 'Stop chattering, woman. I really don't care.

Just fetch me a pot of coffee, and tell Nellie that I want to speak to her.'

'Yes, sir.' Effie backed towards the door, eyeing him warily. He seemed to be quite normal today, and nothing like the madman who attempted to get into her bed under the misconception that she was his long lost love.

'Go now,' he said without opening his eyes. 'Hurry.'

Effie left the room feeling dazed and slightly sick. The smell of the incense had been quite overpowering and there were overtones of odours that she could not identify. She returned to the kitchen to relay his request to Nellie, who appeared to have anticipated her master's request and had made the coffee. She placed a bone china cup and saucer on a tray. 'Was it just coffee he wanted?'

'Yes. That's all.'

'Take it up then. It won't walk upstairs on its own.'

'He wants to speak to you.'

'Tell him I'll come when I'm ready.' Nellie sat down in her chair and sipped a cup of tea. 'Well, what are you waiting for? He was all right, wasn't he?'

'He seemed quite normal, apart from that strange room. I've never seen anything like it, and the smell in there is very odd.'

'That would be the incense and opium,'

Nellie said in a matter-of-fact tone. 'The master travelled a great deal in his youth; he brought back many souvenirs from far countries.'

'But opium,' Effie said, shocked. 'That's bad.'

'It ain't good, but you've seen what he's like when he can't get any. Without it he acts like a lunatic. When he's got it he's almost normal again. I know which I prefer and the doctor says as his mind is wandering anyway, the opium does him no harm.'

Effie knew almost nothing about the drug, apart from the fact that there were places in the worst parts of the East End where men went to smoke opium and send themselves into oblivion. 'The doctor gives it to Mr Westlake?'

Nellie snorted and almost choked on a mouthful of tea. 'That's a laugh. Nothing in this life is for free, Effie. A country doctor don't earn much, and this one makes his money by charging a pretty penny for keeping the master and others supplied with their needs, whether it's opium or contraband spirits. Don't look so shocked, girl. It's the way of the world. Now take the coffee up to the master and then you can start on the cleaning. Like I said, nothing is for free. You'll start paying for your keep right now.'

*   *   *

All morning, Effie scrubbed and cleaned the kitchen. Before she could start she had to heft sackfuls of rotten vegetables, mouldy oats and flour crawling with weevils to a rubbish heap on the far side of the stable block. Bluebottles feasted and multiplied, turning a small mountain of waste into a moving mass of maggots. The stench was terrible but she did not tarry long enough to be sickened by the smell. She had had to leave Georgie in Nellie's care while she left the kitchen, but today he seemed a little better and in between naps he played with a small wooden horse that Nellie had unearthed from a cupboard somewhere in the depths of the house.

'My Bertie used to love that toy,' Nellie said, looking up and smiling as Effie entered the kitchen. 'I'd forgotten all about it until now.'

Georgie looked up at his mother and grinned. 'Gee-gee,' he said, holding the toy up for her inspection.

'Well, I never did,' Nellie said, gazing at him in wonderment. 'He spoke. There's a clever boy. You're all right, you are, Georgie Grey.'

'Gee-gee,' Georgie responded, chuckling.

Nellie leaned over and lifted him onto her lap. 'We'll soon have you running about again, young Georgie.' She looked over his head and smiled as she met Effie's anxious gaze. 'He's

231

over the worst, but he needs rest and quiet and good food. Do you know how to milk a goat?'

'No,' Effie said, horrified by the idea. 'I wouldn't know where to start.'

'Then you'd best learn. We've got a couple of goats and some kids. I'll show you what to do and then you can manage on your own. In fact, when you've finished the kitchen you could make a start on clearing out the dairy. We haven't had our own butter and cheese since the last maid left and I've a fancy for warm bread and goat's cheese for my supper.'

'Just a minute,' Effie protested. 'I can't do everything and I don't know how to make butter and cheese, even if I could learn to milk a goat.'

'But think what good it will do the boy. He'll get better all the sooner if he has good nourishing food.' Nellie dandled Georgie on her knee. 'Who's a fine boy then? You're just like my Bertie. He was a lovely baby and Nellie is going to make sure that you grow up big and strong, just like him.'

Effie felt a shiver run down her spine at Nellie's assumption that they were here for the foreseeable future. She was beginning to wonder if Nellie was not a little mad like her employer. Mr Westlake had appeared to be sane enough at breakfast time, but when she had taken him a cup of tea mid-morning she had found him lying in a stupor on his bed. Effie frowned as she watched Nellie plant a kiss on Georgie's head and set him back on the floor, smiling at him as if he were her own child. Alarm bells were ringing in Effie's brain. This really was a madhouse, and as soon as Georgie was fit enough to travel they would leave here with or without Toby, although she had not entirely given up hope. He might walk through the door at any moment; she prayed that he would.

The rest of the day passed without any word from Toby, and the next. A week went by and in that time Effie had learned how to milk a goat, although catching the nanny was more difficult than the actual milking. The billy goat proved to be a problem in that he seemed to resent her presence and tried to butt her out of the way when she approached the female. After a few painful encounters with the aggressive billy, Effie found a way to distract him with crusts of stale bread, and while he gobbled them up she was able to lure the nanny goat away to be milked. The dairy had been scrubbed clean and Effie churned some of the rich milk into butter, although there had not yet been enough to make cheese. She had also taken over the bread making, which was something she could do well having been taught to bake in the workhouse.

At the end of the second week at Marsh House, Effie had worked her way through all the rooms with the exception of the long disused attics. She had scrubbed floors, polished wainscoting, and dusted furniture. She had cleaned out grates in the dining hall, the morning parlour, the drawing room and the small study. She had taken threadbare carpets outside and hung them on a washing line, beating them until the dust fell in showers onto the ground below. Cleaning the seven main bedchambers had been easier as she was not allowed to enter Mr Westlake's room, and the one she shared with Georgie was the only bedroom left furnished. Nellie slept in a small room off the kitchen, and no one other than herself was allowed to step inside.

Nellie's attachment to Georgie was becoming more of a worry for Effie. He seemed to have taken the place of Nellie's children, and sometimes when she had been drinking heavily she even called him Bertie. Effie kept Georgie with her whenever possible, but it was obvious that Nellie's delusions were increasing with each passing day. As Georgie's health improved, Effie made her plan of escape. She intended to take Toby's mare in the dead of night when no one was about. She knew that Jeffries was hard of hearing, so there was little fear of waking him, but she had to wait until there was a full moon as it would be madness to attempt to cross the marsh in total darkness.

In the meantime, Effie tried to avoid Mr Westlake as much as possible. He only left his room on rare occasions and then usually at night. During the day he seemed to spend most of his time smoking a strange-looking pipe, an event that Effie had witnessed one day when she had taken him his midday meal. He had seen her incredulous look and had smiled. 'I don't suppose you've ever seen one of these contraptions, Effie?'

She set the tray of food down on a brass table in front of him. 'No, sir.'

He sucked on the pipe and the water bubbled as he inhaled the smoke. 'It's called a hookah, and it came from Morocco, where I spent several years in the British Embassy as a very junior clerk.' He exhaled smoke through his nostrils. 'I fell in love with that country, as you can see.' He waved his hand, encompassing the dramatic and exotic furnishings and fabrics. 'I was happy then, before I lost my beloved Mirella.' He leaned forward so that the light from a small oil lamp reflected the deep pockmarks on his face. 'This is my legacy of the disease that robbed me of my beautiful gypsy girl. When I slide into oblivion I am reunited with Mirella.' His smile faded and he glared at Effie. 'Go away, girl. I don't want anyone to pity me.'

Effie fled from the room, terrified by the sudden change in his demeanour. After that she was extra vigilant when she took him his food. Nellie admitted that the master suffered fits of deep depression when he refused to eat or drink anything other than wine or brandy. At these times she waited on him herself, refusing to allow Effie anywhere near his room. Effie could hear him pacing the floor when she was downstairs in the kitchen, and at night he roamed the house, opening and closing bedroom doors as if searching for someone or something. She had taken to sleeping with the washstand pushed against the door so that it jammed the handle and prevented anyone from entering. Sometimes she heard him moaning as if in pain, and at other times she heard him laughing, but it was a mirthless, hollow sound that made her shudder. Only once since their first encounter had Mr Westlake mistaken her for Mirella, and that had been one evening when she had taken him his evening meal. He had been drinking steadily all day, having had a keg of brandy delivered to the door by a pair of shifty-looking men who, Nellie had said with a chuckle, had managed to slip past the excise men, bringing contraband from France. As Effie put the tray on the table at his side, Mr Westlake reached out to grasp her wrist. 'Mirella, my love. Why do you leave me so long without your company? Have I done something to offend you?'

Terrified, Effie tried not to panic. Nellie had told her that if it ever happened again she should play along with him, pretending to be Mirella until she could slip away without upsetting him further. 'Don't anger the master,' Nellie had warned. 'Smile and make him think that you are who he wants you to be, then get away and come for me. I know how to handle him.'

'No, sir. Of course not,' Effie said, attempting a smile.

He pulled her onto his lap, stroking her hair, but as he twisted a flaxen curl around his finger his expression changed. He threw her to the floor. 'You are not Mirella. My love has hair the colour of a raven's wing. Who are you? Why do you come here to torment me?'

Effie scrambled to her feet. 'I'll get Mirella for you, sir. Be patient for a moment longer and I'll fetch her.' She ran from the room, and raced down the stairs as if the devil were after her. She burst into the kitchen and collapsed onto the nearest chair.

Nellie looked up with a startled expression on her lined face. 'What's happened now?'

'Mr Westlake is having one of his strange turns.'

Georgie had been sitting on Nellie's lap and his mouth drooped as he registered his mother's distress. Nellie set him down on the floor. 'I'll go to him,' she said briskly, rising to her feet. 'You'd best keep out of his way until this passes. He's always worse when there's a full moon.'

As she whisked out of the room, moving with uncharacteristic speed, Georgie toddled over to his mother, holding his arms out to her. 'Mama.'

Effie bent down to pick him up. 'It's all right, darling. Mama's here.' She closed her eyes as she held him close. 'It's a full moon tonight, Georgie. It's high time we left this madhouse.'

It seemed to Effie that she had done this before, only last time she was escaping from her father-in-law's clutches and now, in the dead of night, she was leaving Marsh House. She crept through the silent corridors and tiptoed down the stairs with Georgie in her arms. She paused as a floorboard creaked beneath her feet, holding her breath and praying that she had not disturbed Mr Westlake. She stood statue-still, but the only sound she could hear was the thumping of her heart and Georgie's soft breathing as he snuggled up to her and went back to sleep. She was trembling with relief as she slipped out through the scullery door and crossed the stable yard to the stall where the mare welcomed her with a soft whinny of pleasure. Effie had packed her few belongings in a saddlebag earlier that day and she set Georgie down in the straw while she saddled the horse. Jeffries slept above the tack room next door and she hoped that he was a heavy sleeper as she lifted Georgie onto the saddle and led the mare out into the yard. The thick coating of moss on the cobblestones muffled the sound of the horse's hooves and Effie concentrated on keeping Georgie from falling off as she walked the animal away from the house.

A full moon shone down from a cloudless sky and myriads of stars twinkled against a background of indigo velvet. The marsh was lit by a silver sheen and the track twisted into the distance like a glossy satin ribbon. Effie used the crumbling brick wall at the front of the house as a mounting block, and settled Georgie comfortably on her lap. Awakened from his slumbers he was still drowsy but the rhythm of the horse's steady gait soon lulled him back to sleep. Effie allowed the mare to walk on at her own pace. There was no hurry now. Even if their absence was noticed at daybreak, there was no one to chase after them. Glancing over her shoulder, Effie took one last look at Marsh House silhouetted against the flat skyline. It looked dark and foreboding, and not a little sad in its isolation. She could understand why Toby was reluctant to return to the place of his birth with all its painful memories, but she found it hard to believe that he had callously abandoned her. She had put her trust in him and it had apparently been misplaced. Her feelings were mixed as she rode towards the River Lea. Her plan was to cross the river at White Bridge and to take Temple Mill Road, which would lead her to the canal. She would be in familiar territory once she came to the towpath, and she could then make enquiries as to the whereabouts of the *Margaret*. It was a slim hope, but she tried to imagine what Tom would have done when he failed to find Toby, and each time she came to the same conclusion: Tom would try to find her.

She rode on for what seemed hours, half asleep herself, and allowing the mare to have her head. The damp air rose from the marshes and Effie wrapped her shawl around Georgie, but that left her shivering in the chill east wind that whipped across the flat land even in midsummer. The track seemed to go on forever and she was just beginning to think that they were lost and going round in circles when she saw a pinprick of light in the distance. At first she thought it was the infamous will-o'-the-wisp, but it proved to be constant and as she drew closer she realised it was a lantern hanging inside a farm outbuilding. The soft lowing of cattle made her want to shout for joy as she realised it was a milking parlour, and there were other human beings close at hand. If there was a farm it meant that she had reached the edge of the marsh and she was getting close to the river.

Wide awake now, she rode on with renewed enthusiasm. There was a soft shimmer of light to the west where the streetlights of east London sent up a warm glow, and the great bowl of the sky was cracked by a silver line to the east as dawn broke. It was a new day and Effie's spirits rose as she anticipated her reunion with Tom. She urged the mare to a trot and Georgie opened his eyes, smiling up at her as though it was quite normal to wake up on horseback. 'Gee-gee,' he murmured sleepily.

Effie dropped a kiss on his upturned face. The world was coming alive again and the early morning sun rose in a burst of scarlet and orange. Its rays warmed her chilled body and the mist curled away, dissipating into a clear sky so blue that it almost hurt her eyes to look up. She was excited now and even more so when they reached Temple Mills and the White Hart inn, where she dismounted and paid the stable boy a penny to feed and water the mare and give her a well-earned rub down. She took Georgie into the inn where the landlady fussed over him. She insisted on feeding him bread and milk while Effie breakfasted off freshly baked bread spread with lavish amounts of butter and washed down with hot coffee. It was obvious that not many travellers passed this way, and judging by the woman's open curiosity it was almost unheard of to find a young woman travelling alone with a small child. Effie parried the landlady's questions with a vague story of having become separated from the travelling fair, and saying that she was on her way to re-join them. This unlikely tale seemed to satisfy the woman who tut-tutted sympathetically and took Georgie off to change his soiled garments, replacing them with clothes outgrown by her own children. Effie's offer of payment was firmly rejected. 'I won't hear of it, my dear. I've had five of my own and it's nice to have a little one to fuss over.' She pressed a bundle into Effie's hand. 'Take these, ducks. I'd rather the sweet boy had them than some of the filthy little urchins that come across the river for nothing better than thieving and shouting abuse at their betters.'

Almost overwhelmed by this unexpected kindness, Effie thanked her profusely and insisted on paying for their food, but her kind host seemed unwilling to let them leave. Her thirst for information about the travelling way of life, and the world in general outside the narrow confines of her existence might have delayed their departure by hours, but politely and firmly Effie insisted that they must be on their way.

It was late afternoon and Effie had ridden along the towpath and seen many familiar faces along the way. She had not had the opportunity to question any of the narrow-boat people until she reached Lea Bridge lock, where the lock keeper gave her a cheery wave. 'Well then, it's good to see you again, young Effie. I heard that you'd left your pa-in-law, and I can't say I was surprised. What brings you back?'

'I'm looking for Tom,' Effie said breathlessly. 'Have you seen him recently?'

He shook his head. 'Can't say I have, but the *Margaret* went past this morning. They must be close by Old Ford lock now. You might catch up with them there.'

Effie could hardly believe her ears. She

could not believe it was this easy. 'I will, thank you,' she murmured, flicking the reins to encourage her tired mount to walk a mile or two further.

She found the narrowboat moored close to Old Ford lock, as predicted. It looked the same as when she had left, although perhaps the paintwork was a little shabbier and the gold lettering slightly more chipped. The deck was fully laden with bales of hay, and smoke wafted out of the chimney stack on the cabin. She dismounted, setting Georgie down on the ground and holding tightly on to his hand.

'Well, well, so you've decided to return to us.'

Effie spun round to find herself looking up into Salter's weathered face. His lips were curved into a grin but his eyes were hard and calculating.

'I haven't come to stay,' Effie said, clutching Georgie's hand a little tighter. 'I'm looking for my brother.'

'Young Tom?' Salter nodded his head. 'You've come to the right place. He's in with the old man.'

Effie stared at him in disbelief. It couldn't be this easy. 'He's really here?'

'Why don't you go and see for yourself?'

She lifted Georgie in her arms and stepped on board with no thought in her head other than to be reunited with Tom. She made her way to the cabin and opened the door but there was no one there. 'Where's Tom?' she demanded, turning to Salter. 'You lied to me. He's not here.'

'My mistake,' Salter said, giving her a shove that sent her stumbling into the cabin.

The door slammed and she heard the key turn in the lock.

Chapter Eleven

Effie set Georgie down and threw herself at the door, hammering on it with her fists. 'Let me out. Do you hear me, Salter?'

A deep chuckle was her only answer, and the sound of retreating footsteps. Georgie began to whimper and Effie picked him up again, giving him a reassuring cuddle. 'It's all right, sweetheart. Mama is just cross with that silly man.'

Georgie hiccuped and plugged his thumb into his mouth, gazing up at her with trusting eyes. Effie stroked his cheek and forced a smile. She was furious with herself for allowing Salter to trick her, but she had wanted desperately to believe that she had found Tom. There was nothing she could do other than sit and wait. She gazed at the once so familiar surroundings and saw that little had changed. Everything was in its place, but a film of dust covered the shelves and the stove had not been black-leaded for some time. The pots and pans looked as though they could do with a good wash and the brasses were dull and in need of a polish. The stale odour of tobacco smoke and neat spirits filled the air and ash flowed from the range onto the unwashed floorboards. Everything was the same and yet it felt unbearably different. She had come here as a new bride filled with hopes and dreams for the future, but the Salters had defiled the tiny cabin with their filth and corruption. The memories were bittersweet as she held Georgie closer to her heart, rocking him and singing his favourite nursery rhymes.

So much happiness and yet so much tragedy had occurred in this confined space, and now she was imprisoned by the man who had sought to ruin their lives. She wondered what had become of her father-in-law. Had the Salters carried out their threat to murder him? She doubted if they had the brains or the courage to do such a foul deed, and Jacob Grey was too well known on the waterways to be disposed of without causing suspicion, and the canal was too shallow to swallow up a dead body.

Effie was startled out of her grim musings by the sudden opening of the door. She leapt to her feet as Sal staggered into the cabin, supporting Jacob who was obviously drunk.

'So you've come crawling back.' Sal dumped Jacob on the bunk as if he were a sack of coal. 'See who's come to visit you, Jacob me old cock. It's that stuck-up daughter-in-law of yours and her brat, the one you wanted to keep close by you, for some reason best known to yourself.' She eyed Georgie with a curl of her lip. 'Nasty things, boys; they grow up to be rude and dirty. A good thrashing is what they need to teach 'em manners.'

Effie moved towards the doorway. 'Don't you dare lay a finger on my son.'

Sal threw back her head and laughed. 'Or you'll what? I could take you with one hand tied behind me back, missis. So don't act hoity-toity with me.'

'Stop shouting, woman,' Jacob muttered, slurring his words. He stared at Effie, focusing his eyes with an obvious effort. 'So she's come back to haunt me. I don't need another harpy to make me life a misery.'

Sal plumped down on the bunk and hooked her arm around his shoulders. 'I make you happy, Jacob, dear. You know I do, but she's a stuck-up cow and only here because she's brought the boy back to you.'

Jacob shook his head. 'Boy? What boy?'

Effie inched closer to the door. 'I'm going now, Father-in-law. I didn't want to come here but I'm looking for Tom. That man told me he was in here and then he locked me in.'

'She's trying to take your grandson away again,' Sal hissed, giving Jacob a sharp prod in the ribs. 'Is that what you want, old man? You was mad as fire when she took the brat. Are you going to let him go now?'

Jacob pushed her aside and staggered to his feet. 'No, I'm not. Owen's son belongs here on the *Margaret*.' He advanced on Effie. 'You can push off, but give me the boy.'

'I'd die first,' Effie cried passionately. 'You shan't have my son.' She ran from the cabin but was stopped by Salter's considerable bulk. He took her by the shoulders and propelled her back inside.

Sal lunged forward, catching Effie off balance, and she snatched Georgie from his mother's arms. 'Get rid of her, Salter. Toss her overboard if you have to.'

'No,' Effie screamed as Salter picked her up bodily. 'Give me back my baby.'

Georgie's distressed shrieks cut her like a knife as Salter carried her out on deck. She fought and struggled but he heaved her over the side into the River Lea. The shock of the cold water took her breath away and she found herself sinking into a tangle of weeds. Her voluminous skirts pulled her down and her boots filled with mud and water as she hit the bottom. She had never learned to swim but sheer instinct made her kick out and rise to the surface. The water was deeper here just outside the lock gates, especially at high tide, and she would have gone down again, but miraculously she was prevented from sinking. Some unseen force was dragging her towards the bank.

Dazed and coughing up filthy, brackish water, Effie was heaved out of the river by a pair of strong hands. She collapsed on the towpath and the same hands were slapping her on the back, encouraging her to clear her lungs of water and to take a breath of air.

'Are you all right?'

The anxious voice floating somewhere above her made Effie look up. She recognised the weathered face of Hoskins, the new lock keeper who had taken the job just before the Salters arrived on the scene. He disentangled the boat hook from her torn skirt with a rueful smile. 'Sorry, missis, but it was the only way to get you out afore you drownded.'

Effie struggled to her feet. 'My son,' she gasped, pointing at the *Margaret* on the far side of the canal. 'He's got Georgie.'

'There, there, ducks,' Hoskins said gently. 'Your nipper will be all right with his grandpa.'

'You don't understand,' Effie cried desperately. 'Those people with him are bad. The man threw me overboard.'

250

Hoskins shook his head. 'It's shock, missis. You must have tripped and fell in the water.'

Momentarily prevented from speaking by a bout of coughing, Effie fought to catch her breath. 'No, you don't understand. They're taking my baby.'

Hoskins slipped his arm around her shoulders. 'I heard as how you'd gone a bit funny in the head when your husband passed away. Come into the cottage and Mrs Hoskins will dry you off before you go back on board. I daresay a nice hot cup of tea would be just the ticket.'

Effie was too breathless to argue and her sodden clothes made it difficult to walk. She had no choice but to allow Hoskins to help her into the cottage. 'Mother,' he said, pushing Effie gently forward. 'You heard me speak of young Widow Grey from the *Margaret*. The poor girl fell in the canal and her mind is wandering. Look after her, ducks, while I go and tell old Jacob what's happened.'

'He threw me overboard,' Effie said in desperation. 'Why won't you believe me?'

Mrs Hoskins bustled forward, snatching a dry towel off the clothes horse in front of the fire and wrapping it around Effie's shoulders. 'There now, let's get you warm and dry and hear no more of that wild talk. I've got tea brewing in the pot and you can sit by the fire and drink it while my Jimmy sorts things out with Mr Grey.'

Effie's teeth were chattering so violently that she could not speak. She towelled her hair but her sodden clothes clung to her, making it impossible to dry herself. Mrs Hoskins poured tea into two china mugs, adding two generous spoonfuls of sugar and stirring the tea before handing it to Effie. 'Drink this, Mrs Grey. Have you a change of clothes on board the *Margaret*?'

The tea was hot and sweet and Effie could feel it warming her chilled bones. She shook her head. 'M-my clothes – s-saddle b-bag – horse.'

'Saddlebag? I see. Well Jimmy will find your horse and bring your things to you. Sit down, ducks. Warm yourself and drink your tea.' Mrs Hoskins hurried out of the cottage, calling for her husband.

Effie's legs were trembling and her knees gave way beneath her. Shock, distress and the inability to convince these kind people that something terrible had occurred made her too weak to stand. She sank down on the chair and sipped the tea. Her worst nightmare had come true. Her child was in the hands of the unscrupulous Salters and her drunken father-in-law. She did not think that Jacob would harm his grandson, but she was painfully aware that they were both in danger. She could hazard a guess that the Salters' plan was to encourage Jacob to drink himself into an early grave. Georgie would be safe until then, but if his grandfather was not there to protect him . . . She could not bear to think of the outcome.

She drank the last of the tea and made a determined effort to rise to her feet. She would go back on board the *Margaret*. With Hoskins and his wife as witnesses the Salters would not dare to keep Georgie from her. She tried to walk but the wet material clung to her legs, making each step an effort. She had almost reached the door when Mrs Hoskins returned with a worried look on her pleasant face. 'You shouldn't try to walk yet, my dear. Hoskins has found your horse and he's bringing her across. Let's get you changed into some dry clothes before you catch your death of cold.'

'I must go now,' Effie protested. 'My son is being held without my permission. He's just a baby. He'll be so frightened without me.'

'And you'll see him soon,' Mrs Hoskins said gently. 'Sit down, dear.'

'You don't understand,' Effie cried, pushing past her. She staggered out of the dim inter- ior of the cottage into brilliant sunlight. Shielding her eyes from the sun, she peered across to where the *Margaret* had been moored, but the berth was empty. She ran along the towpath, stumbling and tripping over her wet skirts as she saw the vessel gliding through the open tide gates. 'No,' she shouted. 'Come back.' She turned at the sound of a horse's hooves and saw Hoskins leading the mare towards her. 'They've gone, Mr Hoskins. They've taken my baby. Send someone for a constable.'

'I'm sure it's a mistake, ducks,' Jim said, handing her the reins. 'After all, the child is with his grandpa. He'll look after the boy.'

'You don't understand,' Effie sobbed. 'They've taken my baby from me. I must get him back.' Despite her wet clothes, she managed to clamber onto the mare's back, and she dug her heels into the animal's flanks. 'Giddy-up.'

The tired mare snorted in fright but lurched forward at a spanking trot, almost unseating Effie. She regained her seat with an effort and urged the mare to a canter. 'Stop,' she cried breathlessly as she drew nearer to Salter, who was leading Champion along the towpath on the opposite bank. 'Stop, please. Give me back my baby.'

'You're wasting your time, girlie,' Salter called over his shoulder. 'You can follow us all the way to Limehouse Basin but it won't do you no good.'

Effie drew the mare to a sudden halt. She looked down into the muddy waters of the canal, wondering how deep it was at this point. The *Margaret* was pulling away from her and she was desperate. She leaned forward to pat the mare's neck, whispering in her ear, 'Come on, you can do it.' She tugged at the reins in an attempt to make the horse enter the canal, but the animal reared on her hind legs, whinnying with fear. Effie struggled to regain control but the mare bucked and Effie went flying over her head.

Effie lay in a crumpled heap dazed, winded and fighting for breath. She tried to sit up but a searing pain in her left arm brought tears to her eyes.

'Are you all right, missis?' Jim Hoskins threw himself down on his knees at her side. 'You took a mighty tumble. Is anything broke?'

Unable to speak, Effie pointed to her left arm.

He examined it gently, shaking his head. 'I can't tell if it's busted or not. We'd best get you back to the cottage and I'll send for the sawbones.'

'N-no,' Effie gasped. 'Must go after them.'

'All in good time, ducks. But you ain't going nowhere in this state.' Jim rose to his feet. 'D'you think you can stand?'

She made an attempt to rise but each movement hurt, making her feel sick and dizzy.

Jim raised her to her feet, hooking her uninjured arm around his shoulders. 'We'll take it slow. One step at a time.'

'My horse,' Effie murmured anxiously.

'She's not going to wander far. I'll see to her later. We've got to sort you out first, young lady.'

With one arm hanging limply at her side, Effie was in too much pain to argue as they made their way slowly back to the lock keeper's cottage. Mrs Hoskins was waiting in the doorway and she ran towards them. 'Oh, you poor thing. You could have broken your neck.'

'I think her arm might be broken.' Jim handed Effie over to his wife. 'Take her indoors and look after her, Mother. I've got to get back to work but I'll send the boy to fetch the doctor.'

'Come inside, ducks, and we'll soon have you put to rights.' Mrs Hoskins hustled Effie into the cottage.

The heat of the kitchen almost took her breath away as Effie allowed herself to be guided to a rocking chair close to the range, and as if seeing it for the first time she took in the cosy interior of the cottage. A kettle simmering on the range puffed out clouds of steam and a large pan of savoury smelling stew bubbled away on the hob.

The aroma of freshly baked bread mingled with the scent of herbs drying in the chimney breast. 'I can't stay,' Effie protested dazedly. 'I have a change of clothes in my saddlebag, and if you could bind my arm I'm sure I could ride.'

'You're not going anywhere until the doctor has taken a look at that arm.'

'But you don't understand. They've kidnapped my baby. The Salters are bad people.'

Mrs Hoskins' eyes widened and she stared at Effie in disbelief. 'You poor soul. The fall has addled your wits and you don't know what you're saying. My Jimmy says that Salter and his wife have done a good job in caring for old Jacob since he took to drink. You've got it all wrong, dear. Rest awhile and perhaps the doctor can give you something to make you feel a bit better.'

'I need to leave now,' Effie said firmly. 'If you would be so kind as to fetch my saddlebag I could change my clothes and be on my way.'

'You're in no fit state to travel.' Mrs Hoskins wrapped a warm towel around Effie's shoulders. 'A cup of strong sweet tea is what you need.'

Frustrated and anxious, Effie realised that there was truth in her words however unwelcome. The pain in her arm had dulled to an ache as long as she kept it absolutely still. Her headache was improving slightly but the worst pain of all was in her heart. She had not been parted from Georgie for a single day since his birth and having him wrested from her was like losing a limb. She was consumed with terror at the thought of what might befall him on board the narrowboat. Sal Salter had all the maternal instincts of a cuckoo, and Salter would think nothing of beating a child, even one as young as Georgie. She did not think that her father-in-law would physically harm her son, but the Salters had Jacob in their power and from what she had seen, Effie could only guess that they kept him drunk and possibly drugged to suit their own ends. She was in a living, waking nightmare and she could do nothing about it.

She watched Mrs Hoskins as she bustled about making a fresh pot of tea, and it seemed to Effie that this was her answer to everything: a cup of tea could solve all the problems in the world. If only it were that simple. She closed her eyes as a wave of exhaustion washed over her. The night ride and lack of sleep made it impossible for her to keep awake and she found herself drifting off into an uneasy sleep.

* * *

'The doctor's coming, Mother.'

The sound of Jim's voice awakened Effie with a start. She sat upright, wincing as a shaft of pain seared through her left arm. Mrs Hoskins rose from the table where she had been shelling peas and she wiped her hands on her apron. 'About time too. I thought that boy had run off again.'

Jim shook his head. 'He's here now, and that's all that matters.' He ushered the doctor into the room. 'It's good of you to come so quickly, sir.'

'That's quite all right, Hoskins. I was in the neighbourhood when the boy caught up with me.' The young doctor approached Effie with a friendly smile. 'You must be the unlucky young woman who was thrown from her horse.'

Effie nodded her head. 'My arm, doctor. It hurts when I move it.'

'Does it indeed? Then I'd better take a look at it.' He examined the injured limb, noting Effie's reactions when the pain caused her to flinch and bite her lip.

'Is it broken?' she asked anxiously.

'No. I'd say it's just a bad sprain, but you should try not to use the arm for a few days at least.' He opened his bag and took out a square of calico, which he deftly folded into a sling.

'But I can't impose on Mr and Mrs Hoskins any longer than necessary, and I have to travel on to find my son.'

'The young woman thinks her baby has been kidnapped, doctor.' Mrs Hoskins drew him aside, speaking in a low voice. 'I think she may have hit her head when she fell off the horse.'

'Rest is the answer, Mrs Hoskins. Rest and quiet and a few drops of laudanum to be taken at night before retiring to bed.' He took a small brown bottle from his bag and placed it on the table. 'That will be one and six for my fee, a penny for the laudanum and twopence for the sling.'

Effie put her hand in her pocket and counted out the coins. It was, she thought, an exorbitant amount to charge for a brief consultation and a scrap of calico that couldn't have cost more than a halfpenny. 'I'm sorry to have put you to so much trouble, doctor.' She could tell by his rueful smile that she had hit a nerve, and she was ashamed to have spoken so sharply, but having to part with almost half the money she possessed in the whole world was as worrying as it was painful.

'We all have to make a living, ma'am.'

'And some of us profit from the misfortune of others.' Effie knew that she was being unreasonable, but they were all treating her as though the bump on her head had addled her brain. She could not tell these well-meaning strangers the true extent of her trials. She had lost Tom. Georgie had been wrenched from her arms, and Toby had seemingly deserted her. She could hardly be in a worse position.

'She's a bit shocked by the experience,' the doctor said, shaking his head. 'I know I'm leaving the poor lady in good hands. Good day, Mrs Hoskins.' He tipped his hat, turning to Jim with a tired smile.

'If you'd get the boy to fetch my horse, please?'

'Certainly, Doctor,' Jim said, following the doctor outside.

Effie attempted to rise to her feet but every muscle in her body protested and her arm hurt with even the slightest movement.

'You must do as the doctor says.' Mrs Hoskins went back to shelling peas at the table. 'We can put you up for a day or two, but you'll have to sleep on a truckle bed under the stairs. I'll only charge you for the food you eat and not a penny more.'

'You're very kind,' Effie murmured gratefully. 'I do appreciate it, but you must see that I can't stay. Georgie needs me and I must go to him.'

'You could catch up with them tomorrow

if you're feeling better, but your poor horse needs a rest too. You won't get far if the animal goes lame, now will you?'

Effie knew that everything Mrs Hoskins said was true, but commonsense flew out of the window when it came to a mother's anguish on being separated from her child. She could see Georgie's tear-stained face and his desperate sobs echoed in her head, but she realised that she would have to put her feelings aside for the moment. She must take the doctor's advice, however unwelcome. Tomorrow, when both she and the mare were rested, she would follow the *Margaret*. Quite how she would rescue Georgie she had no idea, but no one was going to keep her from her baby. She sat quite still, watching Mrs Hoskins as she finished shelling the peas and put them in a pan to cook. The stew simmering on the hob smelt appetising and Effie's stomach rumbled in anticipation of a tasty meal. It seemed callous to think of food in such extreme circumstances, but she knew she had to keep her strength up for the long ride next day.

Mrs Hoskins cut a hunk of bread from the loaf she had just taken from the oven and she ladled soup into a tin pannikin. 'For the boy,' she said tersely as she carried the food to the door. 'Boy.' She stepped outside. 'Boy, come and get your dinner.'

Effie heard the clatter of hobnails on the gravel path followed by a brief exchange of words that she could not quite make out, and she was suddenly curious. The boy seemed to be at the Hoskins' beck and call, but he was not allowed into the house to eat his meals. 'Is that your son?' she asked as Mrs Hoskins returned to her task of serving the midday meal.

'We was never blessed with children. He's a stray that Jim took in a couple of days ago. He gets fed in payment for helping work the lock gates and running errands, although I daresay he'll be off as soon as the spirit takes him. You can't rely on his sort.'

'What sort is that, Mrs Hoskins?'

'Didicoi, that's what he is, or maybe he's run away from the workhouse. You can't trust them no further than you can see them.'

Effie held her tongue with difficulty. She knew what it was like to suffer the stigma of having been in an institution, and she felt instantly sorry for the boy who was forced to accept grudgingly given charity.

'He sleeps in the pigsty,' Mrs Hoskins said, hacking slices off the loaf. 'He has plenty of clean straw and the old sow don't mind. They're company for each other.'

The remainder of the day passed in a haze. Mrs Hoskins had made up the truckle bed and insisted that Effie lay down to rest. Exhaustion combined with a dose of laudanum sent her drifting off into a dreamless oblivion.

When she awakened next morning the sun was already high in the sky and breakfast had been eaten and cleared away. Mrs Hoskins was scrubbing the floor with lye soap and hot water, sending wavelets rippling across the flagstones. Effie raised herself to a sitting position. She ran her hand through her hair and yawned. The headache had gone and she felt surprisingly refreshed; she had slept remarkably well even though the bed was hard and the straw-filled mattress prickly. An attempt to move her injured arm proved to be a mistake, but it was not quite as painful as it had been the previous day. She swung her legs over the side of the cot and stood up. 'Good morning, ma'am.'

'Mind how you step,' Mrs Hoskins warned. 'The floor's wet and slippery. We don't want you breaking a leg as well as an arm.'

Effie shifted from one foot to the other. 'Do you think I could have my saddlebag now, please? I need to change my clothes, and then I'll be on my way.'

'You can stay another day if you've a mind to. Tenpence should cover the cost of the vittles, and I'll say tuppence for the hay that Jim's fed your horse.'

'Yes, of course, but I really would like my things.'

Mrs Hoskins dropped the scrubbing brush into the bucket and scrambled to her feet. She made her way carefully across the wet floor to the open doorway. 'Boy,' she shouted. 'Fetch the saddlebag for the lady and bring it here.' She picked up the mop and began swishing it around to sop up the suds. 'I dunno how long Jim means to keep him on, but that boy is eating us out of house and home. He's nothing but a yard of skin wrapped round an empty belly and just about as useful.'

Effie padded over to the table and helped herself to a slice of bread and butter. She was going to be charged for the food so she might as well eat her fill before setting off. She had not thought how she would ride with one arm in a sling, but she was determined to leave as soon as possible, even if she had to lead the horse and walk all the way to Limehouse Basin.

'There's tea in the pot, but I expect it's stewed,' Mrs Hoskins said, wringing out the mop. 'Where is that boy? He'll get a clip round the ear if he don't get a move on.' She went to the door. 'Oh, there you are, boy. You took your time, I must say. Come in and give the young lady her things.'

'I had to chase the blooming horse halfway to Bow, missis,' the boy protested.

Effie froze at the sound of his voice. She turned slowly, hardly daring to breathe.

Chapter Twelve

'Here you are, missis.'

'Tom, is it really you?' She blinked hard to make sure that her eyes were not deceiving her. He was painfully thin and his skin was almost obliterated by a layer of dirt. His hair was a matted mass of dark curls spiked with pieces of bedding straw, but he was unmistakeably Tom.

'Effie.' He stood as if transfixed, staring at her in disbelief. 'No, it can't be. I'm dreaming. Pinch me, someone.'

'I'll pinch you,' Mrs Hoskins said, cuffing him round the head. 'Look what them dirty boots have done to my nice clean floor.'

'Ouch,' Tom clutched his hand to his head, but his gaze never wavered from his sister's face. 'Bloody hell, Effie. What have you done to yourself? Ouch, that hurt even more,' he cried as his employer clouted him for a second time.

'It was meant to,' she said angrily. 'I won't have that sort of language in my house.'

Tears streamed down Effie's face as she

held out her good arm. 'Tom, my dear, dear Tom. I've been out of my mind with worry about you and yet here you are. I can hardly believe it.'

He rushed to her and gave her a hug, which made her cry out with pain. He took a step backwards. 'I'm sorry. I didn't mean to hurt you, Effie. It's just that – well – I'm lost for words. How did you know where to find me?'

'I didn't,' Effie said, wiping her eyes on her sleeve. 'Toby was supposed to be looking for you, but he let me down.'

'No, he didn't. Toby found me, but I was sick with the measles and he took me to his people in the gypsy camp.'

'That proves I was right,' Mrs Hoskins said angrily. 'I don't hold with travellers.'

Effie placed her arm protectively around Tom's thin shoulders. 'You've no need to worry, Mrs Hoskins. We'll be moving on as soon as I've changed my clothes.'

'I think you'd best go straight away, missis. I don't want no gypsy coming to look for the boy and bringing his thieving didicoi ways here to a respectable house.'

'That's not fair,' Tom protested. 'You can't talk to my sister like that, you old hag.'

'Tom,' Effie said sternly. 'That's enough. Mrs Hoskins has been very kind to me, and she's entitled to her opinions, even if they are misjudged.'

'Just go and leave us in peace. You can pay what you owe and take some food for the road. I won't have anyone say that Janet Hoskins ain't a fair woman, nor a mean one.' She took a square of butter muslin from the table drawer and proceeded to wrap up what was left of the loaf and a chunk of cheese. 'Make yourself useful, boy. Go and bring the mare to the door so that your sister don't have far to walk.'

Tom shot her a resentful glance. 'I ain't going to thank you for taking me in. You got your money's worth out of me in kind, so I paid me way.' He turned to his sister and his small features relaxed into a fond smile. 'Get your shoes on, Effie. We're leaving.'

Half an hour later they had left the lock keeper's cottage behind and were on their way to London, following the route that the *Margaret* would have taken. The narrowboat had a good twenty-four hours' start, but Effie knew that the Salters would have tied up for the night somewhere along the route and she hoped to catch up with them before they reached Limehouse Basin. She rode the mare while Tom walked at her side. He had not spoken too much for the first mile or so, insisting that she told her story first, but now as they passed the London Water Works reservoir, Effie had brought him up to date and it was her turn to question him.

'So where have you been all this time?' she demanded. 'Where did you go after Salter threw you off the boat? How did you live without any money? Oh, Tom, I've been out of my mind with worry about you.'

He gave her a cheeky grin. 'Same old Effie, always worrying about other people.'

'You're my brother and I love you, of course I was worried about you.'

'I'm a man now, Effie. I was fine at first. I went looking for Toby but they hadn't seen him at the tavern, so I just kept on going. I slept rough and did a few odd jobs to earn money for food, or else I was paid in kind with a meal or a night's shelter in a barn. I went in search of the gypsy camp, but it was then I started to feel bad. I don't remember much else until I woke up in a caravan with some old woman looking down at me. I thought she was a witch.'

'Poor Tom. You must have been terrified.'

'I was ready to run I can tell you, but then the old girl give me a toothless grin and told me she was Toby's granny. He'd found me wandering about the countryside and taken me to the camp.'

'Thank God for that,' Effie said whole-heartedly. 'You might have died if he hadn't come across you. But where is he now and why did he leave you with the lock keeper?'

'We was on our way to the old house on the marsh where he'd left you and Georgie. We'd stopped at a pub for a bite to eat and Toby got into conversation with this cove he knew who gave him a tip-off about some horses that were coming up for sale at a fair on Hampstead Heath. Toby said it was a chance he couldn't afford to miss and he paid old Hoskins to take care of me while he was away. He said he'd come back soon and then he'd take me to you.'

'But he didn't return.'

Tom shook his head. 'No, but he must have had a good reason. Toby's a good 'un. He wouldn't let me down.'

'I trusted him to find you and bring you back to me, but he left you here and went off without giving me a second thought. I'll have a few words to say to Toby Tapper when I meet up with him again.'

Tom slanted a sideways look in her direction. 'Sounds as if you like him a bit yourself.'

'He's as unreliable as the weather,' Effie said, holding up her hand as drops of rain fell from the gathering clouds. 'Nellie was right. He's a charmer but he's fickle and he'll never change.'

'What now? How are we going to get Georgie back? You and me are no match for Salter and his slut wife.'

Effie shivered as the heavy shower soaked through her clothes and trickled down her neck. 'I don't know, but I'll think of something. I'm not leaving my baby with that dreadful woman for a minute longer than necessary. I'll get him back even if I have to sink the boat to do it.'

'Perhaps we'll meet up with Toby at the tavern,' Tom said hopefully. 'He'll know what to do.'

'Forget Toby. He's helped us all he can and now he's looking after himself. We're on our own, Tom.' She knew by his hurt expression that he did not believe her. He quite obviously hero-worshipped Toby, but she was certain now that his loyalty was misplaced. She had made the same mistake, and had relied too much on a man whose reputation was sadly tarnished. She had put her trust in Toby but he had abandoned them all while he went in search of a good deal.

'He'll come back. I know he will,' Tom said stubbornly.

'At least we're together again and that's the way it's going to stay. We'll rescue Georgie and then we'll go back to the fair. I'm sure they'll let us have use of the caravan and we can both work on the stalls.'

Tom wiped his wet hair back from his face, leaving a clean patch on his grimy skin. 'You can help the blacksmith when he's pulling teeth and I'll get a job as barker for the merry-go-round.'

'That's Frank's job,' Effie said, smiling.

Tom let out a whoop of laughter. 'You're sweet on Frank. I thought you was by the way you looked when you told me about him. So that's why you want to join the fair.'

'No, of course not. Frank is spoken for and I've got over that piece of silliness.'

'I'm glad to hear it. We don't want no more broken hearts. I'm the man of the family now and I'm going to look after you and Georgie.'

'Yes, Tom,' Effie said, hiding a smile. 'Would you like to hop up behind me? I'm sure the mare could carry both of us and we could move a bit faster.'

Tom needed no second bidding. He vaulted onto the horse's back and wrapped his arms around his sister's waist. 'She belongs to Toby and she's worth a lot of money. He'll be back if only to collect the mare. You'll see.'

They rode on, stopping at midday on a piece of waste ground between the soap works and lime kilns close to Five Bells Bridge. The rain had ceased and the sun forced its way through a bank of clouds. Steam rose from their clothes as they sat on the damp grass and ate the bread and cheese provided by Mrs Hoskins. The mare munched placidly on clumps of grass and after a brief rest they continued on their journey. It was early evening when they reached the Prince of Wales tavern, and Effie uttered a strangled cry of relief as she caught sight of the *Margaret* moored alongside with several other barges.

Toby fisted his hands. 'I'm going on board. I'll sort old Salter out.'

'You'll do no such thing. Help me down, and we'll tether the mare here with Champion and the other horses. We don't want Salter to see us.'

'He's probably in the pub anyway.'

His glum face brought a smile to Effie's lips. 'You'll get your chance to better him one day, Tom. But getting Georgie back is the most important thing now. I want you to take a look inside the pub and tell me if they are in the bar.'

'What if they spot me?'

'I hardly recognised you, Tom. You look like a street urchin.'

'You look a bit of a mess yourself,' Tom said, grinning. 'Stay here and wait until I come back.'

Chapter Thirteen

Effie watched her brother saunter off with his hands in his pockets, and in spite of everything, his cocky attitude made her smile. He seemed none the worse for his adventures. He had survived the twin ordeals of being abandoned and combating the dreaded disease that claimed so many young lives, and now he was prepared to take on Salter. She felt a rush of pride and admiration for his indomitable spirit, but her nerves were raw as she waited for him to reappear. She was within yards of her child and her instinct was to rush on board and demand his return, but she knew this could be a fatal mistake if the Salters were on board and not, as she hoped, drinking themselves into insensibility in the pub.

She paced up and down as she waited for Tom to return. Each time the pub door opened she paused, stepping into the shadow of the trees and hardly daring to breathe in case it was Salter or Sal who emerged on a waft of tobacco smoke and the smell of stale beer.

After what seemed like an eternity, Tom burst through the door and sprinted over to her.

'They're in the snug bar, both of them, but there's no sign of the old man. I went into all the public rooms and he wasn't there.'

'That means he's on his own. If we take him by surprise we can rescue my baby.'

Tom laid a hand on her arm as she was about to head for the barge. 'Wait, Effie. Stop and think. We'd do better to take the *Margaret* even if we have to put up with the old man.'

Effie stared at him blankly. All she could think of was being reunited with her beloved Georgie. 'Why would we want to rescue Mr Grey? He made our lives a misery and he stole my son.'

'Think about it, Effie. They want to be rid of the old devil and keep the boat. It's worth a small fortune and it belongs to you and Georgie. It's his birthright and they want to take it away from him. Are you going to let them do that?'

'No,' she said slowly. 'You're right, Tom. The *Margaret* should belong to Georgie. That's what Owen would have wanted.'

'Wait here while I fetch Champion and the mare. You can't do nothing with one arm in a sling, let alone fend off the old man if he decides to put up a fight. We'll be off before the Salters can down another pint or swig another tot of gin.' He ran towards the horses without waiting for a reply.

Effie knew that what he suggested was only commonsense, but it was a shock to find her little brother grown suddenly into a man and taking command of the situation. She waited for Tom to return and they made their way stealthily on board the boat. The nauseating smell of rancid fat, unwashed bodies and stale alcohol hit her forcibly as Tom opened the door. There was mess everywhere. Unwashed pots and pans littered the range and the small table where they ate their meals. Dirty clothes were flung about with careless abandon and ashes spilled out of the range, littering the floor.

Gazing anxiously around the small cabin, Effie's heart gave a convulsive leap when she saw Georgie curled up like a small puppy on the end of the nearest bunk. His golden curls were matted and unwashed and his pale cheeks were streaked where his tears had dried and made runnels in the dirt, but he slept peacefully enough with his thumb tucked firmly in his mouth. She took an instinctive step toward him, but Tom caught her by the arm, pointing to where Jacob lay flat on his back, snoring loudly. Tom pulled her gently aside and closed the door.

'What are you doing?' Effie hissed. 'I want my baby.'

'Keep your voice down and listen to me. I'm going to lead Champion and I want you to take the tiller. The old man is dead drunk and we don't want young Georgie waking up and raising the alarm with his bawling.'

Effie's mind had gone blank. Her arms ached to hold her baby and every instinct in her body told her to go to him. Tom nudged her in the ribs. 'Are you all right, Effie? Can you do this? We've got to get away before the Salters realise what's happening.'

She nodded mutely and, forcing her feet to move, she went swiftly to the stern of the vessel. She glanced nervously at the pub as she waited for the barge to glide over the water. Each time the door opened she held her breath, praying that it was not the Salters and sighing with relief when it was someone else. She could hear music and laughter and the babble of raised voices. She peered through the gathering twilight, straining her eyes for a signal from Tom. He seemed to be having difficulty with the mare as she whinnied with fright and skittered about nervously as the barge began to move forward. Champion's hooves clattered on the gravel path and the mare's frantic noise was attracting attention from the men who strolled out of the open pub door. The boat was not moving fast enough for Effie, and then there was a loud crump as the bows tipped the stern of the narrowboat moored in front of them. The boat juddered as if with shock and the sound echoed through the empty hold.

'Tom,' she screamed as the cabin door opened and Jacob lurched out on deck. 'Hurry.'

The *Margaret* was gaining momentum and Effie had to use all her skill and experience in order to steer the boat away from the barges moored ahead of them. Jacob was staggering towards her waving his fist and shouting drunkenly. 'What d'you think you're doing, you maniac?' he bawled at the top of his voice. 'Is that you at the tiller, Sal?'

'Father-in-law, it's me, Effie.'

Jacob stumbled to a halt. 'Who's that? Are you playing tricks on me again, Sal?'

Effie breathed a sigh of relief as the boat skimmed past the last moored craft and she set a straight course. It was almost completely dark now and she could only just make out the horses plodding slowly on ahead. She could not see Tom, but she knew he was out there on the towpath and she rejoiced in the fact that they were once again a team. She could have navigated this stretch of Limehouse Cut blindfold and she lashed the tiller, leaving her free to approach Jacob who was leaning over the side and retching.

'Are you ill?' she asked, her anger turning

to contempt for this wreck of a man who had once bullied her and made her life a misery.

'Who are you?' he murmured, peering up at her blankly. 'You ain't Sal. Where's that bugger Salter? You can tell him I ain't giving up and he hasn't done for me yet.'

'I'm Effie, your daughter-in-law. I've come to get my son.'

'Effie's gone,' Jacob said dully. 'I sent her packing but now I wish I'd kept her on. She weren't a bad girl, and she looked after the boy better than that doxy Sal.'

It was becoming clear to Effie that this was not simply the talk of a drunken man. Jacob's mind was obviously wandering. She led him back along the narrow deck to the cabin and pressed him gently onto his bunk, her compassion unwillingly aroused by his helplessness. 'Lie down and go back to sleep. The Salters won't trouble you again.'

He stared at her without any sign of recognition on his wizened features. He seemed to have aged greatly since Effie had last seen him and he was a mere shadow of his former self. She left him cowering beneath his blanket while she checked on Georgie, but he was still sleeping peacefully and she had not the heart to wake him even though her arms ached to hold him again. She longed to see him smile and to hear him call her Mama, but she knew that she must be patient just a little longer. He was safe and that was all that mattered. Dirt would wash away and he was too young to have much memory of what had occurred. He did not look as though he had been ill-treated and for that small mercy she was extremely grateful. She sat on the edge of the bunk, gently stroking his hair. 'My baby,' she crooned. 'You'll never know how much I've missed you.'

'I need a drink,' Jacob muttered. 'Get me some brandy, woman.'

Effie rose slowly to her feet. 'I am Effie Grey, your daughter-in-law. I'm Georgie's mother – you must remember me.'

'Brandy and some of that smoke that makes everything go away. For God's sake have pity on me, Sal.'

'I'm not Sal,' Effie said firmly. 'And I wouldn't know where to get opium even if I had a mind to. You'll not get any from me.'

Jacob held out his hand. 'I'm going off my head for want of it. Give me some, Sal. I'll do anything he wants, but give me what I crave.'

Effie was momentarily at a loss, and then she remembered the laudanum that the doctor had prescribed to relieve her pain. She put her hand in her pocket and took out the small brown glass bottle. A quick search of the cupboards produced a flask of brandy and she measured a tot into a tin cup, adding several drops of laudanum.

'Give it to me,' Jacob pleaded. 'I'm in agony. Help me.'

She held the cup to his lips and he gulped the liquid down in one swallow.

'More,' he murmured. 'Please.'

Effie could see his eyelids beginning to droop and she pressed him back against the pillow. 'You'll feel better in the morning, Pa. Sleep now.' She had only a few minutes to wait as the combined effect of brandy and laudanum worked quickly. She could tell from Jacob's emaciated frame that he had been starved of food. Perhaps he had given his share to Georgie? She would never know, but for all his faults she knew instinctively that Jacob would have tried to protect his grandson. She tiptoed out of the cabin, leaving the door ajar so that she could hear if Georgie awakened and cried. She hurried to the stern and took the tiller, using her uninjured hand. Leaning back against the bulkhead, she stared up at the night sky. The sliver of moon hung like a silver crescent amongst a diamond necklace of stars. The daytime stench from the manufactories on both sides of the cut was ever present but was diluted by a salt-laden breeze carried upriver on the incoming tide. She had no clear idea of where they were heading or what they were going to do, but escaping from the Salters was paramount. The *Margaret* slid through the water and there was silence, except for the distant clatter of the horses' hooves punctuated by the occasional screech of a barn owl and the bark of a dog fox calling to its mate.

Now that they were out of danger, even if temporarily, Effie began to relax and she had to fight to keep awake. They had passed beneath the bridge that carried the North London Railway over the cut, and the factories had made way for brickfields on the north side and the grounds of Manorfield House on the south bank. It was unlikely that the Salters would get this far in the dark, and it was important to rest now if they were to get an early start in the morning. Rising to her feet Effie put two fingers in her mouth and whistled. Almost immediately the narrowboat slid to a halt and Tom came running along the towpath.

'What's up, Effie?'

'We'll stop here for the night. I'm worn out and you must be too.'

'Where's the old man? I heard him bellowing at you and I was all set to come and toss the old devil overboard, but then he went quiet.'

'He was drunk and I gave him a dose of

283

laudanum, but I'm certain that the Salters have made him smoke opium, and he's very much the worse for it.'

'He was always so strict and he didn't hold with vices like drinking and smoking. I can't see how they managed to get him in such a state and so quickly.'

'I don't know either, but he's a sick man, Tom.'

'That's his stupid fault. Don't ask me to feel sorry for him. I say we ought to cut and run as soon as it gets light.'

'I'm so tired that I can't think straight. We'll talk about it in the morning.'

'Go to bed, Effie. I'll make fast and see to the horses.'

'Ta, Tom. It's wonderful to have you back safe and sound.'

'I'll look after you now,' Tom said stoutly. 'We'll be all right, you and me and Georgie. You'll see.'

Effie made her way to the cabin and took off her boots but she was too tired to bother with undressing. Her clothes were already crumpled and in desperate need of a wash and some repair, but this was her least concern. All she wanted to do was to lie down and take her baby son in her one good arm. She would hold him close and never let him out of her sight again.

* * *

Effie awakened to find Georgie stroking her face and planting sticky kisses on her cheeks as he tried to lift her sleepy eyelids with his chubby fingers. She hugged him to her and tears of joy trickled down her cheeks.

'Mama cry,' Georgie said, frowning.

'I missed you so much, and I'll never go away again,' Effie promised. 'Tom is here too.' She pointed to the ragged figure curled up on the opposite bunk. 'Go and wake him for me.' She lowered Georgie onto the floor and watched him toddle over to tug at Tom's coverlet.

She would have loved to lie there and simply revel in the fact that she had her family back, but she knew that they must lose no time in setting off again. She did not think that the Salters would give up easily. They had obviously set their sights on getting the *Margaret*, whatever the cost, and she wanted to put as much distance between them as possible. She sat up and reached for her boots, pulling them on with difficulty, but it was impossible to tie the laces with one hand. Tom could fasten them for her when he was fully awake, but she could see the first hint of daylight through the cabin window and there was no time to worry about small details. She rose to her feet, shaking the creases from her skirt. Her hair hung about her shoulders in a tangled mass and she knew she must look a sight. She was in dire need of a wash, but her personal discomfort was less important than the need to get the fire going in the range. They would not get far on empty stomachs and making breakfast was her first priority. Georgie had managed to climb up onto Tom's bunk and he was bouncing on him with gleeful shrieks and gurgles of laughter.

Effie smiled as she riddled the ashes in the grate, and despite her worries she felt almost ridiculously happy as she performed the mundane task of lighting a fire and preparing a meal. Sal Salter might be a slut but there was a plentiful supply of coal and kindling and a well-stocked store cupboard. Once the fire was going, Effie filled the kettle from the rain barrel on deck, and having found a small sack of oats she made a pan of porridge for their breakfast. She had come to the conclusion that they should avoid the Three Mills back river, as this would be the first place that the Salters would look, and that their safest course would be to follow the River Lea up country. With the oatmeal bubbling on the hob and a pot of tea brewing, Effie turned to Tom, who was bouncing Georgie up and down until he was almost hysterical with laughter. 'You'll make him sick if you carry on like that.'

'He's all right, aren't you, Georgie?' Tom said,

tossing him even higher. 'I'll swear he's grown an inch or two since I last saw him, and he's dirtier than a sweep's boy.'

Effie ladled porridge into three bowls. 'It's nothing that soap and water won't cure. You'd best eat up, Tom. I know you didn't get much sleep but I want to get going before the Salters come looking for us.'

Tom took the bowl, adding a generous helping of sugar. 'They lived well, I'll give them that.'

'Spent all my hard-earned money,' Jacob muttered, raising his head and then falling back against the pillow with a groan. 'My head aches something chronic.' He focused his eyes with difficulty, staring at them with a puzzled frown. 'Where are the others and how did you two come to be on board?'

Effie thrust a mug of tea into his hands. 'Drink this, Pa-in-law. I'm afraid the milk was sour but we'll get some as soon as we come to a farm.'

'Where's Sal and that swine Salter? Why aren't they here?'

Tom picked up his mug of tea and headed for the door. 'I'll leave you to it, Effie. I'll see to the horses and I'll give you a shout when we're ready to move on.'

'I'll be ready,' Effie said, wiping a dribble of porridge from Georgie's chin.

'What's going on?' Jacob demanded feebly. 'I feel bad. Give me the brandy bottle.'

Effie shook her head. 'I most certainly will not. You've been drinking too much, and it's done you no good.'

Jacob attempted to stand but he fell back on the bunk with a groan. 'Don't torment me, woman. Give me a drop now. There are devils with pickaxes hammering away inside me head.'

'Last night you were out of your mind, and it wasn't just the brandy that was making you act like a madman.'

'Remember who you're talking to, girl. I'm still the gaffer round here and don't you forget it.'

'Don't shout at me,' Effie said angrily as she saw Georgie's lips beginning to tremble. 'I'm surprised at you, Pa-in-law. You would never even go into a pub and now you can't live without a drink or a smoke of that evil thing that sends men insane.'

'Don't lecture me, girl. Where's Sal? She gives me what I want.' He peered at Effie, squinting as if the light from the open door hurt his eyes. 'Why are you here anyway? I thought I sent you packing.'

'I'm here for Georgie,' Effie said, biting back a sharp retort. 'You took him from me and that was unforgiveable.'

'I never did that. It was Salter who snatched the boy.'

'On your say-so,' Effie countered. 'I can't forgive you for what you did.'

'He's my grandson and he should be here with me.'

'No, Pa. Georgie is my son and Owen would turn in his grave if he knew what you'd done.'

Jacob's rheumy eyes filled with tears. 'I wanted the boy to inherit the business. I wanted him to take over where Owen left off.'

'But he's just a baby. It will be years before Georgie is old enough to work, and then he might not want to live this sort of life. I want better for him.'

'It was good enough for you when you caught my boy in your web. You didn't mind this sort of life then.'

'I would have done anything for Owen. I loved him and now I have to bring up his son as he would have wished. I don't want him mixing with the likes of the Salters.'

'You've got a mighty lot to say for yourself all of a sudden.'

'I kept silent too long, and you've been taken in by bad people who mean to steal the *Margaret* from you. They'll stop at nothing to get what they want.'

Jacob's hands shook so violently that he

slopped most of his tea on the floor. He slammed the mug down on the table and held his head in his hands. 'Stop tormenting me. Leave me alone. I can't think straight when you go on at me like that and the pain in my head is driving me mad.'

Taking pity on him, Effie added a few drops of laudanum to what was left of his tea. She held the mug to his lips. 'Drink this. It will make the pain go away.'

He gulped the liquid. 'Why are you helping me? You don't owe me anything.'

'I'm doing it for Owen and for Georgie. You are his grandpa, after all, and I believe you wanted to do your best by him, but you chose the wrong way to do it. Lie down now and rest.'

Jacob sank back on the bunk. 'They'll come after us. Salter has taken all my money but he wants the *Margaret*. She's all I have left in the world.'

'We'll put as much distance as we can between us and them.'

'Don't go to Three Mills,' Jacob murmured drowsily. 'That's where they'll expect to find us. Take the river and head north.'

'That's what I thought, Pa,' Effie said, pulling the coverlet up to his chin. 'Tom and I can handle the boat. Rest easy now.'

*   *   *

With Effie at the tiller and Tom leading Champion, they made good progress and were out of Limehouse Cut and navigating the River Lea before noon. They stopped once to buy milk and a sack of potatoes from a farm along the way, and the farmer's wife gave Tom permission to refill their water barrel from the stream that flowed through their field. Once again they started their slow progress northward with Effie at the tiller while Georgie played with his wooden bricks by her feet. The sun beat down on them from a clear sky, and, if it had not been for the fear of being pursued and the worry about Jacob's declining state of health, Effie thought that she could be happy to go on like this forever.

'Ahoy, there. Lock keeper.'

The sound of Tom's voice brought Effie back to earth and she realised that they had reached Old Ford locks, and she looked up, shielding her eyes against the sunlight as Jim Hoskins strolled over to open the massive gates. 'So you found the *Margaret* then?' he shouted, his voice barely audible above the groans of the creaking metal and the sound of rushing water.

'As you can see,' Tom called back.

Jim cupped his hands around his mouth. 'Come over here, boy. I've something to tell you.'

Effie was consumed with curiosity but she had to be content to wait until they were safely through the lock and out the other side. After a brief conversation with Jim, Tom leapt back on board and bounded over to her grinning from ear to ear. 'What did I tell you, Effie?'

She shook her head. 'I don't know, but it looks as though I'm about to find out.'

'I said he'd come back and you didn't believe me. I knew Toby was a good 'un.'

'What are you talking about? If you don't tell me what Mr Hoskins said I think I might scream.'

'He came back for me. Toby turned up here yesterday looking for me, as I knew he would. He told Hoskins that his business had taken him a bit longer than he thought.'

'So where is he now?'

'When Hoskins told him that we'd found each other, Toby went looking for us,' Tom said, beaming.

Effie frowned. 'If he'd followed the towpath he would have caught up with us by now.'

'You just want to believe the worst of him, don't you?' Tom cried angrily. 'He must have taken the Back River which would explain why he didn't come across us. He's probably making enquiries at the tavern even as we speak.'

'And by asking questions there he'll have

292

alerted the Salters to the fact that we came this way. We'd best leave now, Tom. Neither of us would stand a chance against the Salters, and Pa-in-law would do anything to get his hands on some of that evil substance they encouraged him to take.'

'Let's leave him then, Effie,' Tom said urgently. 'We could take Champion and the mare and ride to that place you spoke of in the middle of the marsh. Or we could join the fair as you said we would.'

It was a tempting idea and it made good sense, but Effie's conscience would not allow her to agree. 'Salter wants the *Margaret* and he'll stop at nothing to get it. We can't leave the old man to their mercy. He may be hateful, but he's Georgie's grandfather for all that.'

They travelled on despite Tom's reluctance to help the man who had caused them so much hardship, but no matter how persuasive his arguments, Effie was adamant that family must come first. She was determined to stay with Jacob until he regained his health and could see the Salters for what they were. When he was free of the twin demons of drink and drugs, she would leave him to manage his own life; until then he was her responsibility. She owed that much to Owen, and she was unshakeable in her resolve to do the right thing.

293

They continued northward, stopping only for brief spells to feed and water the horses and for Tom to rest and bathe his sore feet. Effie was horrified when she saw the state of his boots. The soles were worn through and his toes poked out through a gap in the uppers. They were past the point where a cobbler could repair them and Effie took Jacob's Sunday best boots from the cabin while he slept. Tom protested that he would rather suffer sore feet than wear anything belonging to Jacob, but Effie solved the predicament by tossing Tom's old boots into the canal, leaving him little choice other than walking barefoot. With a long day ahead of him, Tom reluctantly put on Jacob's boots and was forced to admit that they were a perfect fit.

'It's like wearing dead men's shoes,' he muttered, staring down at his feet.

Effie thrust a mug of tea in his hands and a bowl of warmed-up porridge left over from breakfast. 'Here, eat your dinner, and look after Georgie. I won't be more than a few minutes.'

'Porridge for dinner?' Tom stared at his plate in disgust.

'When I've got two hands to work with I can make bread, and until then you'll have to put up with porridge, and the same for supper unless you'd like to peel some taters. You need two hands for that as well.'

'I was better off living with the old sow,' Tom said, grinning. 'At least Ma Hoskins fed me well.'

Georgie picked up a potato and was about to sink his teeth into it when Effie swooped on him and took it away. He opened his mouth to bawl but Tom dipped his spoon into the porridge and fed it to Georgie. 'We'll share our dinner and then you can help me peel the spuds.' He glanced up at Effie with raised eyebrows. 'I hope you ain't going to fuss round the old man while I do woman's work.'

'If you must know, I'm going to get out of these filthy clothes,' Effie said, cuffing him playfully round the head. 'And I'm going to have a strip wash so don't come into the cabin until I say so.' She left them, safe in the knowledge that Georgie was in good hands.

Jacob was still sleeping with the help of another small dose of laudanum that he had begged for when his craving became too intense, and Effie was able to strip off her soiled garments without embarrassment. She put them in a bucket of water and lye soap to soak and set about washing herself. It was wonderful to feel clean again and she towelled her skin until it was tingling and pink. Earlier that morning she had been relieved to find

295

her old clothes undisturbed in a drawer beneath her bunk. They would have been little use to Sal even if she had found them as she was more than double Effie's size, but at least she had not thrown them out or pawned them.

Every movement was painful but Effie managed to struggle into clean undergarments topped with a white cotton blouse and a grey linsey-woolsey skirt. Fastening the buttons took time and patience, and she dragged a comb through her hair but she was beaten when it came to tying it back with a length of red ribbon. She went out to join Tom who was playing happily with Georgie.

'I need some help to tie my hair back, Tom.'

'What am I?' he demanded, chuckling. 'A blooming lady's maid?'

'Yes, and a very poor one you'd make too.' Effie thrust the ribbon into his hand. 'Do this for me and I'll take a turn at leading the horses while you rest your poor feet.'

Tom pulled a face. 'And play nursemaid to Georgie, I suppose. That's not much of a rest.'

'Woman's work is never done,' Effie said with mock severity. 'As a matter of fact, I thought he could ride on Champion's back, but you'll have to lift him up there for me.'

The afternoon passed pleasantly and Effie kept glancing at Georgie as he sat astride Champion's broad back with his little legs stuck out at right angles. She had not until now realised how much he had grown in the last two months, and, despite the upheavals that he had undergone in his short life, he seemed none the worse for his experiences. His happy smiles and chuckles were enough to gladden any mother's heart. The summer sun shone from a cloudless sky and the scent of clover sweetened the air. They had left the city streets and foul-smelling manufactories behind them and they passed through fields of ripening wheat and barley. The muddy water of the canal was dyed blue by the reflection of the sky and she had put all thoughts of the Salters out of her mind.

That evening, having moored in a quiet spot, Effie set about making their supper of boiled potatoes which they ate with slivers of melting cheese. When they had finished their meal, Tom took Georgie with him to settle the horses for the night, and Effie returned to the cabin to see if Jacob, who had refused all offers of food, had changed his mind about eating. She had a pan of oatmeal and water simmering on the hob in readiness for breakfast next morning, and she hoped he might take a little of the gruel, but Jacob would have none of it. He accepted a cup of sweet tea, querulously demanding brandy, which Effie ignored. He fell back against the pillows, weakened by a bout of coughing.

'I must speak to you, Pa,' Effie said softly. 'We're heading northward but we have no cargo. I need you to tell me what to do.'

'What do I care?' Jacob moaned. 'I'm not long for this world. Do as you please.'

Effie stared at him, shocked by this unexpected pronouncement. 'That's the laudanum talking,' she said briskly. 'You feel bad now but it will pass. I won't leave you while you're sick, but we have to find a cargo or there'll be no money for food or hay for the horse.'

Jacob's thin hand shot out and he gripped Effie's wrist with surprising strength. 'Take the boy. Get away from here before Salter catches up with us. He wants the *Margaret* so let him have it. I've fought my last battle and now I'm on me way out, Effie.'

A cold shiver ran down her spine as she looked into his eyes and realised that he was not rambling now. She could see a glimmer of his old self in the wreckage of a human being that had once been a proud and dominant man. 'You're not dying, Pa. I'll look after you until you are well again.'

'Why should you, girl? I've treated you and that brother of yours badly, and I've blamed you for Owen's death, but I know now I was wrong.' He pulled a rag from beneath his pillow and held it out for her to see the unmis-takeable dark red stains. 'I've known for months,' he murmured. 'It's over for me and for the *Margaret* too.'

Effie was only too familiar with the symp-toms of consumption and her breath hitched in her throat. 'I didn't know. I'm sorry.'

Jacob's eyes flashed with some of their old vigour. 'Why should you grieve for me? I've done nothing for you, and you are nothing to me. Owen was all I had and he's gone. You'll take the boy, but only because I can't look after him. Now give me brandy and laudanum and then leave me alone.'

Reluctantly, Effie went to the cupboard where she had hidden the brandy.

'Give me the bottle,' Jacob growled. 'Add all the laudanum. It's not going to make much difference to me now, Effie Grey. Put a sick man out of his misery forever.'

Effie stared at him in horror and disbelief. 'What are you saying, Pa?'

Jacob leaned over the edge of the bunk, holding out his clawed hand. 'Give it to me and the laudanum. It will all be over by morning and you'll be free.'

'No. I won't do it,' Effie cried passionately. 'I'll look after you. We're free of the Salters now. They would have caught up with us by now if they meant business. Tom and I can work the canal as we used to and we'll make a good living. You always intended that Georgie should follow in Owen's footsteps. I won't stop him, if that's what he decides to do.'

'You don't understand,' Jacob said, shaking his head. 'The drink and the opium had a price. They made sure that I couldn't do without them.'

'What are you saying, Pa?'

'In a moment of weakness, I signed the papers. The *Margaret* belongs to Salter, and you've stolen it from under his nose.' Another violent paroxysm of coughing caused Jacob to reach for the rag and hold it to his mouth. Blood trickled down his chin and he collapsed against the pillows gasping painfully for every breath.

Effie was too stunned to move or speak, but a hullabaloo outside made her leap to her feet.

'Effie, come quick. It's the law.'

Chapter Fourteen

Frightened shrieks from Georgie brought Effie to her senses. She tore out of the cabin to find Tom on deck with Georgie in his arms and two police constables standing on the towpath with Salter at their side.

'What's going on?' Effie demanded, with a defiant toss of her head.

'That's the bitch who stole my craft,' Salter roared. 'Arrest them all, Officer.'

The more senior police constable turned to Salter with the hint of a smile. 'Isn't the baby a bit young to be a felon, sir?'

Salter's face flushed brick-red. 'This isn't funny. I want you to arrest that woman and the boy for stealing this vessel which is legally mine.'

The younger policeman cleared his throat nervously. 'Excuse me, guv, but my pa is a lock keeper at Lea Bridge Dock. I believe the owner to be a certain Jacob Grey.'

'He was the owner,' Salter snapped. 'He signed it over to me all legal and above board. This is my vessel and she stole it.'

The senior constable eyed Effie severely. 'Is this true, ma'am?'

'Mr Grey is a sick man, Officer,' Effie said firmly. 'My pa-in-law would not have willingly given away the boat that has been his home and his livelihood for thirty years or more.'

Tom thrust a sobbing Georgie into Effie's arms and he leapt ashore, squaring up to Salter with his hands fisted. 'You're a liar and a bully. You want the old man's money and you'll stop at nothing to get it.'

'That's slander.' Salter grabbed Tom by the throat.

'And that's enough of that,' the senior officer said, dragging them apart. 'This is a matter to be sorted out by the magistrate in the morning.'

'I want you to arrest them,' Salter muttered. 'They'll be gone by daybreak if you let them go free.'

'I want a word with Mr Grey,' the constable said firmly. 'Don't worry, ma'am. I won't upset the old gentleman but I need a statement from him.'

Georgie buried his face in his mother's shoulder and Effie held him tightly. Just hours ago they had been laughing and enjoying their freedom, and now it seemed as though everything was going to be snatched from them. 'He's in the cabin, Officer. Please don't upset him any more than you have to.'

'I'll handle him gently, ma'am.' He stepped on board, pausing at the cabin door to address his subordinate. 'Keep an eye on those two, Morris. If they start anything – cuff them.'

Constable Morris leapt to attention. 'Right you are, guv.' He glanced nervously at Salter. 'You heard him, mate. I suggest you calm down and act sensibly.

Salter stuffed his hands in his pockets. 'You won't get away with this, missis,' he said, scowling. 'I've got written proof that the *Margaret* belongs to me, so you're wasting your time making sheep's eyes at the copper.'

Tom fisted his hands but Effie shook her head. 'Don't, Tom. He's just trying to start a fight. He'd love to see us locked up in a police cell.'

'That's right,' Salter sneered. 'You'll end up in jail if there's any justice.'

'You can all shut up,' Constable Morris said angrily. 'You heard what the guv said. I don't want to hear another word from any of you.'

They waited in silence, except for Georgie who snuffled and gave the occasional hiccup. Effie wished that the constable would hurry as her good arm was aching beneath Georgie's weight and she was beginning to feel sick with apprehension. Whatever happened they were in a parlous state. She had not realised until last night that Jacob's illness was not caused by drink or even the drug that temporarily

303

robbed him of his wits. She knew that he had always suffered from a weak chest, but she had never heard him complain or even hint that he might have contracted the disease that had killed his wife and son. Effie shifted from foot to foot as they waited for the constable to reappear. The summer dusk was closing in on the Hackney Cut, leaving just a pearly glimmer in the west where the sun had plummeted beneath the horizon in a fireball of crimson and gold.

Tom climbed back on board. 'Let me take him, Effie,' he whispered, holding his arms out to relieve her of her heavy child. 'He's almost asleep anyway.'

Reluctantly, and only because her arm was now numb and she was in danger of dropping him, Effie handed Georgie to her brother. She turned at the creak of the cabin door as it opened and the constable stepped out onto the deck. His expression was grave.

'I've spoken to Mr Grey, and I've decided to leave his daughter-in-law and her brother on board for tonight.' He raised his hand for silence as Salter began to protest. 'The old gentleman is very sick, and I don't want to distress him any more than necessary. You will all report to the magistrate's court in the morning and there the matter will be settled one way or another.'

'Hold on, mate,' Salter said, scowling. 'These people are trespassing on my property. What's to stop them taking off in the middle of the night?'

'They can't get far. I'll alert the lock keeper at Lea Bridge and should they be foolish enough to try to make a run for it, he'll refuse to open the gates.'

'I'm not leaving this spot,' Salter said, folding his arms across his chest. 'I'm staying where I can keep an eye on these two.'

'A young woman, a boy and a baby ain't my idea of a ferocious gang, mister,' Constable Morris said scornfully. 'You heard the guv; no one is going anywhere tonight. I suggest you get on home and leave these people in peace.'

Salter looked as though he was about to argue, but the constable fingered his truncheon in a manner that suggested he was quite prepared to use it should the necessity arise.

'I ain't going far,' Salter muttered. 'I'm watching you two, so don't try nothing funny.'

'And don't you,' Tom countered. 'You heard what the copper said. It'll be sorted out by the beak tomorrow, and it ain't up to you.'

'That's enough,' Effie said, laying her hand on his shoulder. 'Let's get some sleep.'

The police officers strode off along the towpath, but Salter stationed himself on the ground, squatting down and wrapping his arms around his knees as if he intended to keep watch all night.

'I'll kip on deck,' Tom said stubbornly. 'I don't trust him.'

'I think we'll all sleep on deck,' Effie said, eyeing Salter anxiously. 'Mr Grey needs absolute quiet and I don't want Georgie to see him in such a state. I'll fetch pillows and blankets. It's a warm night and there's a clear sky, so I don't think it will rain.'

'Just let him try something,' Tom muttered, glaring at Salter. 'I've been waiting for a chance to get my own back on the old devil.'

'Take Georgie to the stern and don't even look at Salter. He's spoiling for a fight and you're half his size; you'd end up in the cut with your throat slit.' Effie waited to make sure that Tom obeyed her instructions. Satisfied that he had done as he was told, she went into the cabin to check on Jacob. The brandy bottle was empty and he lay flat on his back, pale and still like a marble statue. His breathing was stertorous but at least he was not in pain and would hopefully sleep through the night. All her bitter feelings and anger towards the man who had made her life a misery seemed petty and of little importance now. Jacob Grey would soon join his beloved Margaret and their son, and she could only hope that when the end came it would be mercifully swift and painless. She made a bundle of their blankets and pillows and she was about to extinguish the flame in the oil lamp, but she changed her mind and left it burning. If Jacob were taken ill in the night she would need to reach him quickly, and it would be easier if the cabin was not in complete darkness. She turned the wick down and went outside, closing the door behind her.

Salter was in the same position on the towpath and she could feel his eyes upon her as she made her way to the stern.

'Make the most of it,' he shouted. 'This is the last night you'll ever spend on my boat.'

Ignoring his taunts, she went to join Tom who was cradling Georgie in his arms. They made themselves as comfortable as possible, wrapped in blankets against the damp chill that rose from the water even though it was a warm night. Effie closed her eyes but Salter's words played on her mind. If the magistrate ruled in his favour they would once again be homeless, with the added burden of a mortally sick man. The prospect was frankly terrifying.

She was dreaming. It was hot and the sun was beating down mercilessly. She was back in the fairground and she could hear the barkers shouting, but there was panic in their voices. Something was wrong. She could smell woodsmoke but it was not the pleasant aroma of camp fires; there was a hint of hot tar and blistering paintwork.

'Fire!'

Effie opened her eyes and saw flames shooting up from the cabin roof. The first streaks of light split the dark sky but the orange glow of the fire turned night into day. Tom was already on his feet and Georgie sat up, rubbing his eyes as he stared in amazement at the inferno.

'Fire! Effie, the boat is on fire.' Tom snatched Georgie from her side clutching him tightly in his arms. 'Get up. There's nothing we can do.'

Dazed and only half awake, Effie could see the outline of Salter's large frame as he attempted to douse the flames that engulfed the cabin with buckets of water that he hefted from the canal.

'Where is Pa-in-law?' Effie cried as the enormity of the situation hit her like a hammer blow. 'He's in the cabin, Tom. We must get him out.'

Tom climbed onto the towpath with Georgie safely tucked under one arm. 'Come on, Effie. There's nothing you can do.'

'I can't leave him to burn to death.' Effie had to shout to make herself heard above the roaring of the flames and the crackling, splintering sound of the wooden vessel going up in smoke.

Tom reached down and seized her hand, dragging her onto the canal bank with a super-human effort. 'It's too late. He wouldn't have stood a chance.'

'The oil lamp,' Effie murmured. 'I left it burning in case he needed me in the night. He must have knocked it over. It's all my fault.'

'It weren't an accident.' Jacob's breathless whisper behind them sounded like a voice from the dead.

Effie spun round expecting to see a ghost but Jacob emerged from a cloud of smoke, coughing and retching but very much alive. She threw her arms around him, all animosity forgotten. 'What happened?'

'I done it on purpose,' Jacob wheezed. 'I wasn't going to let that bugger take my Margaret away from me. She's going out in a blaze of glory is my old girl.' He covered his mouth with his hands as a spasm of coughing rendered him speechless. He swayed on his feet and Effie's efforts to support him were in vain. He collapsed onto the towpath strug-gling for each painful breath.

'Help me,' Salter bellowed. 'Don't just bloody stand there, boy.'

'I wouldn't spit on you if you was on fire,

Salter.' Tom swung Georgie onto his shoulders. 'That's what happens to bad boys, Georgie.'

'Hot,' Georgie cried gleefully. 'Fire.'

'Take him away from here,' Effie cried anxiously. 'The fire is spreading.'

Tom eyed her doubtfully. 'I can't leave you.'

'And I can't walk away from a dying man,' Effie said gently. 'I've seen it before, Tom. Owen was like this at the end and it's not pretty. I don't want Georgie to see his grandpa breathe his last. The Lea Bridge lock isn't too far off. Take the mare and ride to the keeper's cottage. Ask them to send for a doctor, although I doubt if anything can be done.'

'Never mind the old fool,' Salter shouted. 'I need help.'

Tom turned his back on Salter and the burning narrowboat. He hesitated for a moment but a pleading look from Effie seemed to convince him. 'All right. I'll go, but I'll be back as soon as I've seen Georgie safe.' He strode off along the towpath to where the horses were tethered.

Satisfied that her son and brother were out of harm's way, Effie went down on her knees beside Jacob. She could tell by his ashen colour and the amount of blood that had come from his last fit of coughing that the end was near. She slipped her left arm out of the sling and found to her relief that she could move it without too much pain. She raised Jacob's head gently in an attempt to ease his laboured breathing. 'Was it an accident, Pa?'

'He would have taken my Margaret. I couldn't lose her twice.'

'I understand.' There was nothing she could say that would ease the situation or comfort the dying man. Effie stroked his forehead and held his hand. The heat was intense and the smoke threatened to choke her, but she could not leave him to die alone. Salter fought on, heaving buckets of water over the side in a vain attempt to quench the raging inferno, but eventually he had to abandon his efforts and leap to safety. He backed away, shielding his face with his arm. 'Move, you silly bitch.' He roared. 'You'll roast if you stay there.' He retreated into the smoke and Effie was left alone with her father-in-law.

'I – I'm s-sorry, girl.'

The words were so faint that Effie was not certain whether she imagined them. Jacob's eyes were open but the rattle in his chest could have been his last breath or simply the struggle to stay alive. The towpath was illuminated by a fiery glow and smoke billowed up into the pale green dawn sky. She felt the heat searing her skin but she could not move. She was trapped in a fiery hell with a dying man. She was finding it difficult to breathe. Her lungs were filling with noxious fumes and she felt faint. There was a sudden whoosh as flames engulfed the *Margaret*'s deck and the hull above the waterline, and Effie felt herself lifted off the ground. She thought vaguely this must be what it was like to die and that her end had come.

When she came to she found herself hanging upside down over the saddle of a cantering horse. The breath was being pummelled from her lungs with every bucketing movement. The stench of the fire was replaced by the comforting smell of horseflesh and leather. The next thing she knew she was lying on a patch of damp grass with water being splashed on her face. Her attempt to sit up was foiled by a pair of strong hands and the sound of a familiar voice. 'It's all right, Effie. You're safe now.'

'Toby?' She focused her eyes with difficulty. She was neither dead nor dreaming. She was staring up into Toby Tapper's anxious face. 'It is you.'

'It most certainly is, my dear girl. You've led me a merry dance, I must say.'

This casual remark brought Effie back to reality with a jerk and she sat up. 'Don't you dare speak to me of merry dances. You abandoned me and Georgie in that awful place. Where were you when I needed you?'

'I'll explain later, but if you're feeling better I think we'd best move on.' Toby stood up, brushing the mud off his knees. 'Can you stand, or must I lift you?'

Effie allowed him to help her to her feet. 'Mr Grey,' she said weakly. 'I was with him and I could see that he was dying.'

'He's gone, Effie. I could see that even as I snatched you from the jaws of death. Don't I get a kiss for saving your life?'

'That's not funny.' Effie slapped his hand away. 'You're a rogue and a scoundrel. You left me and my boy to the mercy of that madman in Marsh House while you went off trading horses. You've neither conscience nor a sense of responsibility.'

'Guilty as charged, although I think you exaggerate.'

'I do not. You promised to find Tom and bring him back to me and you let me down.'

'I know it and I admit that I'm past redemption. I'll explain everything later but Tom and Georgie are waiting for us at the lock keeper's cottage, and I suggest we make haste to join them.'

Effie's breath hitched in her throat. 'You've seen them. Are they all right?'

Toby whistled for his horse and the chestnut gelding trotted obediently to his side. 'Both are well and anxious about you.'

Effie glanced over her shoulder expecting to see Jacob's body sprawled on the towpath, but it was concealed by a veil of smoke. 'I can't just leave him lying there. It wouldn't be right.'

'We can't take him with us, Effie. Best leave it to the police.'

'I can't do that. He's Georgie's grandfather when all is said and done. Owen would never forgive me if I abandoned the old man now.'

Toby thrust the reins at her. 'Hold my horse.'

'What are you going to do?'

'Just wait there.' Toby strode off into the swirling smoke and disappeared from sight. Minutes later Effie heard the clatter of hooves and he reappeared, leading Champion with Jacob's corpse draped over the animal's back.

'It's disrespectful,' Effie murmured, swallowing a sob. 'He looks like a sack of coal.'

'It can't be helped,' Toby said with a sympathetic smile. 'It's not very dignified but I can't see any other way.' Before Effie had a chance to protest he tossed her onto the saddle and vaulted up behind her. With Champion's halter in his hand, Toby urged his mount forward. 'We need to get away before the police start asking awkward questions. Tom told me that Salter was out for revenge, so we haven't much time to lose.'

'Where are we going?' Effie demanded. 'We should take Mr Grey to an undertaker.'

'Not a chance,' Toby said, shaking his head. 'Stop worrying, and leave it to me. I've got a lot to make up for. Hold your breath, Effie; we're going through the smoke.'

An hour later the small procession was wending its way across Hackney Marsh with Toby and Effie at its head. Champion plodded along behind them with Jacob's body wrapped in an old bed sheet purchased from Mrs Hoskins. With Jim's help, Toby had draped the corpse over the saddle, securing it with a length of rope. Effie protested that it made the dead man look like a bundle of dirty washing, but the only response she received was a sympathetic grunt from Toby and Jim had urged them to be on their way before Salter arrived with the police. They had set off immediately with Tom and Georgie bringing up the rear.

'I can guess where you're taking us,' Effie said as they headed deeper into the marshes. 'I don't want to go back there, Toby.'

His arms tightened almost imperceptibly around her waist. 'We've no choice. The police would have no reason to look for us at Marsh House, and where else could we turn up with a dead man in tow and the police on our tail?'

Put like that there was little that Effie

could say. 'I suppose we must, but I won't stay a moment longer than necessary.'

'I don't understand why you ran away in the first place. Did you fall out with Nellie?'

'You promised to return,' Effie said bitterly. 'You said you would find Tom and bring him to me.'

'I did find him and I left him with Jim while I went about my business.'

'But you knew that I was worried sick. Why didn't you bring him straight to me?'

'I had the chance of a deal that was too good to miss, and then I heard that my grandmother had died. She was the last of my Romany family and I had to go to her funeral. I owed her that at least.'

'I'm sorry,' Effie murmured. 'Her medicine made Georgie well again, and I never had the chance to thank her.'

Toby was silent for a moment and Effie felt his muscles tense as he struggled with his emotions. Until now she had thought him superficial and incapable of deep feeling, and his genuine grief came as a surprise. He cleared his throat as if embarrassed to admit that he was mourning the death of his grandmother. 'You haven't answered my question,' he said with an obvious attempt at bringing the conversation back to safer ground. 'Why did you leave Marsh House in such a hurry?'

'It was Mr Westlake. Nellie made me wait on him. I think she knew what would happen.'

'Seymour is a drunkard and his mind wanders, but I can't believe he would do anything to harm you.'

'You know very well that he tried to get into bed with me. He thought I was Mirella.'

'I told Nellie to take care of you and make certain that he was locked in his room at night.'

'She did neither of those things. She made me take food to his room. Sometimes he was quite sensible and at other times when he was obviously under the influence of that terrible drug he thought I was Mirella. I don't think he's a wicked man, Toby, but he is confused and very unhappy.'

'I don't know why.' Toby's voice throbbed with suppressed anger. 'He has the manor house and more money than he could spend in a lifetime. He was quick enough to throw me out when my mother died.'

'Do you really not know, or don't you want to admit the truth?'

'What truth? You're rambling, girl. It must be the shock of what's just happened.'

'I'm perfectly clear in my head. I think that Mr Westlake and Mirella were lovers and that he is your father.'

'That's nonsense. My father was a gardener

who was sent packing as soon as the master found out that my mother was in the family way.'

'I don't know much about these matters,' Effie said, choosing her words carefully. 'But it was said in the workhouse that the woman always suffered in such circumstances. She was the one who was sent off without a character and left to fend for herself and her child, not the man.'

'What are you saying? What has that to do with my mother?'

'She was allowed to stay on at Marsh House after you were born, and you were both treated well. She was close to Mr Westlake after his wife died and she nursed him through the illness that scarred him for life. I believe that he's never got over her death.'

'If that was so, why did he send me away after Ma died?'

'I don't know, but maybe he was ashamed to have fathered you out of wedlock, or perhaps the mere sight of you reminded him of the love he had lost.'

'That is all supposition on your part, Effie. He is nothing to me.'

'And yet you return to Marsh House again and again. Why do you do that, Toby? What draws you to that sad and lonely place?'

He threw back his head and laughed. 'What

a wonderful imagination you have, Effie. You could write stories for magazines and get paid for your flights of fancy.'

'What's the joke?' Tom called from behind them. 'Are we nearly there yet? I'm blooming starving and so is Georgie.'

'It won't be long now,' Toby shouted, digging his heels into the horse's flanks. 'Trot on.'

It was raining by the time they reached Marsh House. A mist had crept over the marshes, blotting out the horizon, and the rain sizzled and steamed as it hit the dried mud on the track. It was a bleak sight that met their eyes and an even gloomier welcome as they rode into the stable yard. Jeffries hobbled out of the tack room. 'I thought we'd got rid of you for good,' he said, addressing Toby as he lifted Effie from the saddle.

'It's nice to see you again too, old man,' Toby said cheerfully. 'Take the horses and give them a rub down.' He moved swiftly to take Champion's halter. 'Except this one. I'll see to him.'

'What's that you've got there?' Jeffries demanded, squinting short-sightedly at the bundle on Champion's back. The outline of a body was clearly visible beneath the wet calico. 'What've you got there, master?'

Toby turned to Effie. 'Take the boys into the house. We'll see to everything out here.'

'What are you going to do?'

'I know where there is a patch of soft ground. He'll lie easily there.'

'You can't just plant him like a tree. We must say some prayers and give him a decent burial.'

'All right. Anything you like, but go indoors and get out of those wet clothes.'

'What shall I tell Nellie?'

'Tell her the truth. You can trust her to keep her mouth shut.' Toby turned to Jeffries who was standing in the pouring rain, gaping at the ill-disguised cadaver. 'See to the horses first, Jeffries, and then we'll need shovels and spades.'

A shout from Tom brought Effie to her senses and she took Georgie from his arms. 'Come with me, Tom,' she said, heading for the scullery door.

'What is this place?' he said, hurrying after her. 'I've never seen anything like it.'

'It's the saddest house in the world.' Effie thrust the door open and stepped inside. 'And I hoped never to see it again.'

In the kitchen, Nellie was seated in her usual chair by the fire. She looked up, taking in their bedraggled state with a resigned sigh. 'So you've come back. I thought we'd seen the last of you, Effie Grey.'

'I'm sorry for leaving without telling you,' Effie began, but Nellie raised her hand.

'I don't want to know the details. You're here now and I suppose it was young Toby who brought you. That boy turns up like a bad penny.' She glared at Tom. 'And that must be the brother you kept on about. He looks old enough to take care of hisself.'

Tom shook the rain from his hair and wiped his sleeve across his wet face. 'You was good to my sister, missis. I thank you for that, and we're only passing through. We won't trouble you for long.'

Nellie rose to her feet. 'Ho, it speaks. Well, I like the cut of your jib, boy. You don't look like one of the rapscallions that torment old folks and steal the food from under their noses.'

'I should think not,' Effie said indignantly. 'Tom is a good boy and he's been brought up to respect his elders.'

'Hoity-toity as usual,' Nellie muttered. 'Nothing's changed. Anyway, best get out of them wet things. Give me the baby and I'll look after him while you go upstairs to change. Your room is just as you left it and Mirella's old clothes are still in the chest of drawers.'

Effie held on to Georgie, shaking her head. 'It's all right, thank you, Nellie. I can manage.'

'But you haven't brought any clothes for

the poor little mite, I can see that. I've still got some of Bertie's things in my trunk. I hadn't the heart to throw them out and now they'll come in useful again. You really should take better care of him, missis. He's a poppet.'

As if responding to this flattery, Georgie held his arms out to Nellie.

'See,' Nellie said triumphantly. 'He remembers me.' She prised him from his mother's arms, hugging him to her flat breast. 'Who's a lovely little fellow then? Who is Nellie's best boy?'

Georgie tugged at her mobcap, pulling it down over one eye. 'Hungry,' he said.

Nellie set him down on her chair. 'And you shall have some of Nellie's freshly baked bread with lots of butter and some strawberry jam. There was a good crop this year even though the plants are choked with weeds.' She turned to Effie and Tom who were staring at her as if in a trance. 'I daresay I can find some of Bertie's old clothes for you, young man. I kept everything of his in the hope that he would return one day with his nippers, but it never came about. Wait here a minute.' She left them staring after her as she hurried into the room, which was little more than a cupboard, where she slept and stored her possessions. She returned almost immediately with an armful of garments which she thrust at Effie. 'They're a bit moth-eaten and shabby, but they're dry and I'm sure you'll find something there to fit the boy. I'll see to little Georgie.'

'You're very kind,' Effie murmured. 'I'll go and change, but what about the master? Is he well?' She did not know how else to put such a delicate question, but Nellie seemed to understand her meaning.

'He's been better, but he's had to do without his smoke. The excise men caught up with them as they smuggled the stuff upriver. He went through a bad patch, but he's getting over it. He won't bother you.'

Leaving Georgie with Nellie, Effie led Tom through the house to the staircase. He paused, looking round him in awe. 'What a place, Effie. I'd no idea you'd been living in a mansion.'

She mounted the stairs. 'I cleaned every room in this place, but I couldn't wait to get away from here.'

Tom followed her, stopping to stare at the portraits and then taking two steps at a time in order to catch up with her. 'I wouldn't say no to having a house like this. It's really grand and I bet it's haunted.'

'I think the ghosts are more like memories from the past, and they're not happy ones.' Effie hurried past Mr Westlake's room and breathed a sigh of relief when she opened the door of her old bedchamber. Her clothes clung damply to her body and she shivered although the room was warm. While Tom rifled through the pile of old clothes, Effie went to the chest of drawers and selected a blouse and skirt that had belonged to Mirella. Toby might choose to deny the past, but it was obvious to Effie that the illicit love affair between the master and his gypsy maid-servant had been both intense and long lasting. Separated by death, Mr Westlake was in love with her ghost. Reluctantly, Effie changed out of her wet clothes and dressed in Mirella's faded finery.

Tom had found a pair of breeches and a shirt that were worn and patched but fitted reasonably well. He wrinkled his nose. 'They stink of lavender,' he grumbled. 'And they itch.'

Effie opened the door. 'Never mind that now. I'll see to our laundry when I've got a moment. Come on, Tom. I don't want to leave Georgie alone with Nellie for long. She gets funny ideas and convinces herself that he's her long lost Bertie.'

'This is a madhouse,' Tom muttered, following her out onto the landing. 'But I wouldn't mind stopping here for a while. I might see the ghost.'

Effie came to a sudden halt as Mr Westlake's door opened and he emerged, resplendent in his crimson and gold robes with a tasselled velvet cap on his head and his long, dark hair flowing around his shoulders. 'Mirella, my darling. You've come back to me.'

Chapter Fifteen

Effie stood her ground, determined to put matters right there and then. She faced up to Seymour, looking him in the eye with an unflinching gaze. 'I am not Mirella. I am Effie Grey.'

His smile faded. 'Effie Grey,' he repeated dazedly. 'Do I know you?'

'Yes, sir. I've been here before and you made the same mistake then. I am not the person you think I am.'

'What's going on, Effie?' Tom demanded, clutching her arm. 'Who is this old cove?'

'This is Mr Westlake. He owns Marsh House and he mistook me for a lady he knew a long time ago.'

'You are not Mirella,' Seymour said, frowning. 'I know that now.' His face crumpled and he bowed his head. 'She was taken from me.'

Casting a warning glance at Tom, Effie moved swiftly to Seymour's side. She took him by the arm and led him back to his room. 'Sit down, sir,' she said, helping him to a chair.

'Mirella died years ago, but her son lives and he is here now.'

'Her son?'

'Your son too, I think,' Effie said gently. 'Will you see him, Mr Westlake? Will you tell him the truth about his birth? As I see it, you are both alone in the world which is madness when you have each other.'

'My son?' Seymour raised his head. 'I did have a son, but he went away a long time ago.'

'You sent him away when he was just a boy, but something draws him back to Marsh House. I beg you to see him, sir.'

'Effie, come away,' Tom called nervously from the doorway. 'The old bloke is clearly off his head.'

Seymour rubbed his hand across his brow. 'Did you come here to torment me, Effie Grey?'

'No, sir. This is the last place I would come to willingly, but Toby brought me here with my baby son and my brother Tom.' She indicated Tom who was hopping from one foot to the other in a state of agitation.

'Why come to this sad place? It's fit only for ghosts and memories of the past.'

'You're right, Mr Westlake. There is something else and we need your help.'

'My help? I can do nothing for anyone, least of all myself.'

327

'I'm asking your permission to bury my father-in-law on your land. It's a long story but he took sick and died.'

This bizarre statement had the desired effect. Seymour was suddenly alert and interested. 'You want to bury a corpse on my land?'

Effie rose to her feet. 'Yes, sir. As I said, it's a long story.'

'And one I want to hear,' Seymour said eagerly. 'Sit down and tell me this extraordinary tale.' He waved his hand at Tom. 'Boy, go to the kitchen and ask Nellie to bring up a tray of tea for Effie and a jug of ale for myself.'

'Effie?' Tom shuffled a few steps closer to her, eyeing Seymour as though he were a wild animal about to pounce on its prey. 'I don't want to leave you with him.'

'It's all right, Tom. I'll be quite safe with Mr Westlake, and I'm going to tell him everything.'

'Fetch the ale, boy,' Seymour said impatiently. 'My throat is dry as tinder and I've a craving for brandy, but there is none in the house.'

Tom left the room encouraged by a nod from Effie. She turned to Seymour with an attempt at a smile. 'Ale is better for you, sir.'

'My supplier ran into a spot of bother,' Seymour said, tapping his finger on the side of his nose. 'Excise men, you know. But Nellie makes a tolerable drop of beer, and I'm told it's better for my constitution, although it doesn't blot out the painful memories like opium and a fine cognac.'

'And it doesn't addle your brain,' Effie said, pulling up a footstool and sitting by his side. 'You are not an old man, Mr Westlake, but you're wasting your life away shut up in this room. You have so much more than most people and yet you wallow in self-pity. Do you think you are the only person in the world who has lost a loved one?' She realised that she was pushing him to the limit, but she could not stop herself. All her pent-up feelings had bubbled to the surface and now her anger was directed at Seymour Westlake. 'You were born into wealth and privilege but you've let it all go to ruin. There are people who would give anything to have what you have.'

'I expect you're right, but why are you so angry with me, Miss Grey? What has my sad life got to do with you anyway?'

'It's Mrs Grey,' Effie said, forcing herself to keep calm. 'I'm a widow and my husband died of consumption before our son was born. My little boy will never know his father, but you with all your money and education have abandoned your son.' She stopped, biting her lip, knowing that she had said too much. She waited for a tirade from Seymour but he was silent for a moment, staring at her thoughtfully.

He reached out and touched her hand. 'Tell me your story, Scheherazade. I'm sober for once and I'm listening.'

Half an hour later, Effie returned to the kitchen feeling drained and exhausted after reliving her past in order to satisfy Seymour's curiosity.

Toby and Tom were sitting at the table eating bread and cheese washed down with tankards of ale, and Nellie was seated by the range feeding Georgie with bread and milk.

'There's tea in the pot,' Nellie said, eyeing Effie with a tilt of her head. 'You took your time.'

'Mr Westlake wanted to know all about us,' Effie said tiredly. 'He seems a lot better in himself now.'

Nellie spooned food into Georgie's open mouth. 'He'll fall into his old ways again. Someone will come knocking on the door in the dead of night offering cheap brandy and opium, and the master will be off again on one of his wild flights of fancy.'

Effie helped herself to a cup of tea. 'I don't think you should sit back and do nothing about it.' She took a seat at the table next to Tom. 'I'm sorry, I shouldn't have said that. It's really none of my business.'

'You're right there, missis. What the master does has nothing to do with you.' Nellie set Georgie down on the floor as he clamoured to be with his mother and he toddled over to Effie.

'That's a bit harsh, Nellie old girl,' Toby said mildly. 'Effie's speaking the plain truth.'

Effie turned to him eagerly. 'Why don't you go upstairs and see him, Toby? I think he's lonely and maybe some young company would make him feel happier. Maybe you could persuade him to join us for supper?'

Toby rose to his feet. 'You won't catch me out like that, Effie. I see through your little game, and it won't work. The man upstairs is not my father.' He tapped Tom on the shoulder. 'Come on, we've got work to do. The dead won't bury themselves.' He cast a questioning look at Effie. 'I take it there were no objections.'

She shook her head. 'No, he was very good about it after I had explained the circumstances.'

'Right, then there's no time to lose.' Toby beckoned to Tom. 'There's a reasonably clear patch in the orchard, and the rain has stopped so we'll start digging there. Come on, old chap, we've a lot of soil to shift.'

Tom drained his tankard of ale and grabbed a hunk of bread and cheese. 'Ta, Nellie,' he said, grinning. 'You're a toff.' He hurried off in pursuit of Toby.

'He's a young limb if ever I saw one,' Nellie said, chuckling. 'He reminds me of my Sidney when he was a nipper. He had the cheek of the devil, but it landed him in trouble and now he's in Australia for life, so maybe it ain't a good comparison.'

Effie absorbed this remark in silence as she sipped her tea. It had not occurred to her until this moment that Tom's lively and adventurous nature might lead him astray. She would have to watch him carefully in future and guide him along the winding path to manhood. She had two boys to nurture and raise to be good citizens. It was not going to be easy.

'You ought to eat something,' Nellie said severely. 'You look peaky, although it's hardly surprising after what you've been through. Why don't you have a lie down? I'll look after Georgie.'

There was nothing that Effie would have liked more than to sink into a soft feather bed and sleep for hours, but she resisted the temptation. Once again, Nellie's obvious fondness for Georgie was making her apprehensive. Marsh House seemed to cast a spell over its inhabitants, locking them in the past and never allowing them to move on. 'Thank you,' she said with an effort. 'But I'd rather keep busy. If it's all the same to you, I'll take Georgie and show him the goats and hens. I could do the milking if you haven't already done it.'

'I won't say no to that, but you ain't going nowhere until you've had a bite to eat.'

Outside in the yard Georgie chased the hens and sent them flapping and clucking in protest. The more they fluttered about the faster his little legs went, and his shouts of laughter brought a smile to Effie's lips. Effie filled a rush basket with eggs and took them into the dairy, returning with a wooden pail and a milking stool. With Georgie trotting along beside her she went to the overgrown kitchen garden where the goats had demolished just about every plant in sight. She chased the nanny and caught her eventually, despite Georgie's attempts to help which consisted of getting underfoot and taking a few tumbles, which he seemed to think were all part of the game as he struggled to his feet, unscathed and chuckling.

At midday the sun was high in the sky when Effie took bread, cheese and a flagon of ale to the spot where Toby, Tom and Jeffries were digging the grave. Tom had discarded his shirt and Toby was also stripped to the waist. Sweat glistened on his muscular torso and his curly hair clung damply to his brow. He rested on the pick handle, wiping the back of his hand across his forehead. 'You're a sight for sore eyes, Effie,' he said, smiling.

She tried not to look too pleased at the compliment, but she could feel the blood rushing to her cheeks all the same. 'I've brought you some food,' she said, placing the basket in the shade of a gnarled apple tree.

'Good, I'm starving.' Tom flopped down on the grass and helped himself to bread and cheese.

'Leave some for us old 'uns,' Jeffries muttered. 'Digging graves ain't the work of a stable man.'

'It's not my line of work either,' Toby said easily. 'The clay is hard as iron.' He took the flagon from Effie and drank deeply. He passed it to Jeffries. 'If I'd known that Nellie could brew beer like that I'd have come more often.'

Effie peered into the shallow trench. 'It's not very deep. How long will it take you to finish it?'

'We should get it done before sunset.' Toby reached for his shirt which he had slung over a tree branch. He slipped it on. 'Apologies for my state of undress, Mrs Grey, but it's hot work.'

She knew that he was teasing her, but Effie

averted her eyes. Her feelings for Frank had awakened emotions and desires that she had thought were dead and buried with her late husband. It was a shock to realise that her young body responded to Toby in the same way, and she could not bring herself to look him in the face. 'I'll leave you to eat your meal,' she murmured.

'Bring us some more ale, Effie,' Tom urged, holding the empty flagon upside down to emphasise his need. 'Digging in this heat is thirsty work.'

'I think you've had enough of that strong brew. You can fill it with water from the pump and wash some of that dust off you at the same time.' Effie tried to sound severe but Tom had a way of making her laugh. In his tipsy state, with dirt smeared all over his skinny torso and a wide grin on his face, he had even brought a smile to Jeffries' lugubrious features.

Toby was openly amused. 'Do as your sister says. I don't want you falling into the grave dead drunk. If you do, Jeffries and I might decide to bury you instead.'

Tom looked as though he would like to argue, but he stuck his tongue out instead, and retreated hastily in the direction of the stable yard, swinging the flagon at his side and whistling a defiant tune.

'That boy will either end up a rich man or a jailbird,' Toby said, chuckling. 'He needs a firm hand.'

'I can manage him,' Effie said firmly. 'I won't allow Tom or Georgie to fall foul of the law.'

'The boys need a father. It's hard for a young chap to grow up without a man's influence.'

Effie shot him a glance beneath her lashes and she realised to her surprise that, for once, he was deadly serious. 'You did,' she said softly.

'And look at me now. I'm a case in point, aren't I, Jeffries? You've known me since I was a nipper; what d'you think?'

Jeffries swallowed a mouthful of bread and cheese. 'You're a chip off the old block, master. I'll say no more.'

Toby frowned. 'You knew my father, but you won't speak to me of him. Why?'

'That's for me to know and you to find out, if you've a mind to know the truth,' Jeffries said mysteriously. He leaned back against the tree trunk, closing his eyes. 'I'm going to have forty winks. I can't work on a full belly. Give me half an hour and I'll be ready to start again.'

'You do know,' Effie said gently. 'You know, but you won't admit it, and neither will he. When are you two going to face the truth?'

Toby's expression was not encouraging.

336

He met her questioning look with a blank stare. 'You've got it all wrong, Effie. You're making up fantasies in your head, and I want you to stop. That wreck of a man in the house is nothing to me, and I am nothing to him.' He threw off his shirt and seized the pickaxe, attacking the ground with renewed vigour.

Effie walked slowly back to the house, her tired mind in turmoil. Perhaps she had it all wrong. Maybe she just wanted a happy outcome for Toby and the master of the house who was scarred both physically and mentally by a long lost love.

The grave was dug by sunset. Effie's concern that Owen's father was to be buried in un-consecrated ground without the benefit of a clergyman to say prayers for his soul was overridden by the need to inter his corpse before putrefaction set in. Champion had been harnessed to the farm cart and Tom led the horse to the edge of the orchard with Effie holding Georgie's hand, followed at a respectful distance by the others. The air was pleasantly cool and filled with birdsong. The tangled branches of the apple trees were heavy with unripe fruit, and the grass around their roots was cropped to velvet smoothness by the sheep that roamed freely. The sky to the west was streaked with livid gashes of purple, orange and scarlet and overhead was an infinite arc of pale turquoise. As Toby and Jeffries lowered Jacob's body into the dark maw of the grave, Effie looked upwards, hoping that his soul was reunited with those whom he loved the most. She could not grieve for a man who had shown her little kindness in life, but she could give him the respect due to a father-in-law. She looked round at the bent heads and solemn faces and she was lost for words. Toby met her eyes with a questioning glance, but all she could do was shake her head.

The silence was broken by the sound of approaching footsteps, and glancing over her shoulder Effie was both startled and amazed to see Seymour Westlake striding towards them. His long robes flowed out behind him and his head was bare. There was something majestic and almost biblical about him; he might, she thought, have been Moses about to part the Red Sea. He stopped at the foot of the grave and in his hand he held a leather-bound Bible.

'Would you like me to say a few words, Effie?'

She nodded her head. 'Thank you, Mr Westlake.'

In a well-modulated voice, Seymour read a passage from the Bible, followed by a simple prayer. There was a moment of silence when he finished speaking, and it seemed to Effie that even the birds had stopped singing in deference to the occasion. A murmur from Georgie brought her to her senses and she tossed a handful of dry earth onto the body, which was bound tightly in a winding sheet. There could be no coffin for Jacob Grey, but at least he had had a burial ceremony of sorts. Georgie tugged at her hand and she picked him up, wondering at his resilience. He seemed perfectly happy and had taken everything in his stride so far; but how much a child of twenty months understood of the situation she had no way of knowing.

'So this is Georgie,' Seymour said, smiling. 'He's a fine boy.'

'Thank you, sir.' Effie shifted Georgie to a more comfortable position on her hip. She felt slightly at a loss in the strangeness of the situation and the deepening twilight. Seymour seemed to sense it too as he gazed thoughtfully into the lengthening shadows that turned the fruit trees into ghostly shapes. 'I haven't been out of the house for years,' he said more to himself than to anyone else. 'I'd forgotten how pleasant a summer evening could be. It's a long time since I smelt the salt tang of the sea brought upriver by the tide and felt the warmth of the earth beneath my feet. I didn't realise how much I missed all this.'

'Why don't you join us for supper, Mr Westlake?' Effie asked impulsively. She could see by the look he gave her that Toby did not appreciate her boldness, but she was determined to bring father and son together. Standing side by side the likeness between them had been startling. The clean cut of the jaw, the high forehead and the thick tangle of dark hair were clearly passed down from father to son. Their eyes were almost exactly the same shade of periwinkle blue and they were both as stubborn as mules. She held her breath, waiting for his answer, but it was Nellie who broke the tension. She had been silent during the whole proceedings but now she nudged Seymour in the ribs with a cheerful grin. 'Aw, c'mon, master. Join us in the kitchen for a slice of game pie and a tankard of ale. Jeffries has been out shooting wildfowl and the snares have caught some fine rabbits. We'll feast like royalty tonight.'

Seymour hesitated and then shook his head. 'I think not, Nellie. I've had enough excitement for one day, and I'm tired. I'll take dinner in my room as usual.'

Effie cast a pleading look at Toby. 'Won't you try to persuade him?'

'Mr Westlake is master in his own house,' Toby said stiffly. 'I still have work to do.'

He inclined his head in Seymour's direction. 'If you'll excuse me, sir?'

'Of course, you must do what is necessary. I'll say goodbye, Tapper. I assume you'll be on your way now.'

Effie could have cried with frustration when Toby nodded his head and turned his back on them, picking up a spade and tossing soil into the grave. She wanted to bang their heads together in order to make them see sense, but Seymour was already striding off in the direction of the house.

'Come on, ducks,' Nellie said briskly. 'You won't get them together not even if you was to tie them back to back and leave them for a month of Sundays.'

'You know, don't you?' Effie fell into step beside her as they returned to the house. 'You've always known.'

'Of course,' Nellie said with a careless shrug of her shoulders. 'I've worked here since I was a girl of eleven. Servants always know what's going on above stairs, and I worked alongside Mirella. She was a wild one, but I'll say this for her, she might have been free with her favours before she took up with the master, but she never looked at another man after they got together. She was true to him and there's no doubt in my mind who was Toby's pa. I think the master knows it too, but he couldn't bear to be reminded of her, and it's no use having a son and heir born the wrong side of the blanket. He sent the boy away, and he's too proud to admit that he was in the wrong.'

Later that evening Georgie and Tom were in bed. Nellie had also retired for the night and was in her cupboard-like room off the kitchen with the door firmly closed. Effie sat in the chair by the range, grateful for its warmth as the darkness enveloped the old house and a cool wind from the marshes sighed around its walls like a lost soul. Toby had gone to the stables to check on the horses, and she waited patiently for his return. He had said that he intended to leave first thing in the morning, and she needed to speak to him before he disappeared from their lives yet again. She needed to find out where the fair might be found and that was something only Toby would know for certain. It was a slim chance and she doubted whether Frank senior would take her back, but it was worth a try and the alternative was homelessness or, horror of horrors, the workhouse. She would have to convince him that there was not and never could be anything between herself and Frank, but she was willing to go down on her knees and beg if it was the only way to put a roof over their heads and provide food for the table.

She did not have long to wait. Toby strolled into the room, but he came to a sudden halt when he saw her.

'Effie! I thought you'd gone to bed.'

'I wanted to talk to you, Toby.'

'If it's about the old man . . .'

'No,' she said hastily. 'I've said my piece and the rest is up to you.'

'Then what is it that's so urgent it couldn't wait until morning?'

'I need to ask you a favour.'

'Go on. What can I do for you, Mrs Grey?'

'Now you're laughing at me, and that's not fair.'

'I'm sorry. I didn't mean to tease you. You've had a rough time, and I should be more sympathetic.'

Effie felt her throat unaccountably tighten, but she was determined not to allow emotion to cloud her judgement. 'I wanted to ask if I might borrow the mare for a while longer. I want to leave here tomorrow and go in search of the fair.'

Toby's smile faded into a frown. 'You mean to go back to Frank Tinsley, despite everything you know about him?'

'I was happy with the fairground people,' Effie said, staring down at her tightly clasped hands. 'The caravan was home and I had work. I could support myself and Georgie, and I'm sure that Mr Tinsley could find something for Tom to do. We would have a life, Toby.'

'You would have heartbreak. Frank is promised to a girl from another travelling family. His father wouldn't allow him to break with tradition, and you would end up as his mistress.'

'That's a horrible thing to say. It's insulting to me and Frank. He's not like that.'

'If you believe that you're a fool,' Toby said angrily.

'I have friends amongst the fairground folk; good people who made me feel that I belonged. Where else am I to go, Toby? I have a child to consider and Tom, who needs a proper home and a way to earn his living.'

Toby paced the floor, running his fingers through his hair so that it curled wildly around his head. 'What will you do if they don't want you? Have you thought about that? With a baby and a young boy in tow you would be forced back into the workhouse.'

Effie sprang to her feet. 'Never,' she cried passionately. 'I'll never set foot in that place again. I don't care what I do but I'll keep my son and Tom out of the workhouse, even if I have to scrub floors or sell bootlaces on street corners.'

'And that's just what you will end up

doing.' Toby came to a halt in front of her and he grasped her hands. 'I feel responsible for you and your little family, Effie. I won't stand by and see you ruin yourself, and there's still Salter. Have you forgotten him?'

She shook her head. 'No, I'll never forget that man, but what would he want with us now?'

'Revenge, my love. And there's something that he wanted which Mr Grey intended to give you and Georgie. Salter would sell his own mother for less.' Toby released her hands and went to fetch his jacket from a peg behind the door. He put his hand in his pocket and pulled out a leather pouch. 'When I went through the old man's clothes I found this on him. I think he intended to give it to you.'

Effie took it gingerly, feeling the soft leather with her fingers. 'It feels like something metal. Is it money?'

'Look inside.'

Effie untied the cord and tipped the contents onto the table. A gold half-hunter watch and some sovereigns rolled out onto the scrubbed deal. 'I never saw this,' she murmured, holding up the watch. 'And there must be seven or eight sovereigns here.'

'It's yours, Effie. It won't make you rich, but you can live for a year or more on that much money. It will give you time to look around and decide what is best for you and the boys.'

'I could rent the caravan,' Effie said, breathing a sigh of relief. 'I can go back to the fairground with money in my pocket and start all over again.'

Toby's smile froze and he stared at her in disbelief. 'You still intend to do that, after everything I've said?'

'I know you mean well, but you've got it all wrong as far as Frank is concerned. He told me everything. It was all a big mistake and he won't make things difficult for me. I trust him, Toby.'

'Good God, girl. Have you lost your wits?'

His shocked expression brought a smile to Effie's lips. 'I think I may have, but I know what I must do and I need the mare. Please will you lend her to me, just until I get back on my feet again?'

'You are a stubborn woman, Effie Grey.'

'That's rich, coming from a man who refuses to acknowledge his own father.' Effie met his angry gaze with a lift of her chin. She had left the fair without giving Frank a chance to apologise or to explain himself. She had been so intent on finding Tom that she had allowed Toby to convince her of Frank's duplicity. She knew there could be nothing romantic between them but that did not mean she had to cut Frank out of her life altogether. Maybe, in the fullness of time, his fiancée might change her mind and release him from the promise that locked them into a loveless match.

Effie laid her hand on Toby's arm, regretting her hasty words. 'I'm sorry, I shouldn't have said that, even if it is true. I know you are only trying to help me, and you've been a true friend in all my troubles. I don't know why you are so good to me, but please let me do this my way.'

His expression softened and he covered her hand with his. 'I didn't want to tell you this, Effie. I've done my best to keep it from you, but Frank is married. He wed the girl that his family wanted him to marry.'

Effie snatched her hand away. 'You're lying. You're just saying that to make me change my mind.'

'No, my pet. I swear it's true. I traded some horses in Waltham Abbey last week. The fair was there and the wedding party was in full swing. Frank married his sweetheart.'

Chapter Sixteen

The news that Frank had married had dealt Effie a bitter blow. She had been furious with Toby for keeping the truth from her, although in her heart she knew she was being unfair and he was not the one to blame. She had stormed out of the kitchen and had spent a sleepless night, tossing and turning in the bed she shared with Georgie. Tom's snores had echoed round the room as he lay on the palliasse where Toby had once slept.

Next morning, Toby was gone. Nellie showed no sign of surprise when she discovered that he had left, taking the mare as well as his own horse. That was the way he did things, she told Effie. He came and went as the spirit moved him, but he would turn up again sooner or later, drawn back to his birthplace by invisible silken cords that could not be broken. Effie had been left in a quandary, not knowing what to do for the best. She had money now; not a fortune, but enough to keep them for a year if she was thrifty, but they only had Champion as a means of transport and nowhere to go.

She kept putting off the inevitable, making excuses for not moving on, and as the days went by Tom struck up an unlikely friendship with Jeffries. He worked alongside the old man, helping him in his vain attempts to keep Marsh House from falling into an even worse state of decay. They cleared the overgrown vegetable garden where they discovered raspberry canes bearing fruit beneath a tangle of wild convolvulus, and late strawberries hidden from the birds by a mat of brambles. They dug the soil in readiness for planting winter cabbage and potatoes.

Nellie seemed to have come to terms with the fact that Georgie was not her long lost Bertie, and was only too pleased to keep an eye on him when Effie was busy. The summer days passed pleasantly and Effie slipped comfortably into the daily routine of cleaning, doing the laundry and cooking their meals. Georgie had no fear of the animals and he loved to help her when she fed the hens and milked the goats. He grew chubby and healthy on the good food that Effie cooked in the now spotlessly clean kitchen, and his fair skin glowed with a healthy tan. When the housework was done, Effie enjoyed the peace and quiet of the dairy where she made butter and cheese. Nellie proved to be adept at brewing ale, and she was only too happy to pass her skill on to Effie.

Using part of the dairy as a makeshift brew-house, Effie and Nellie worked hard to keep Seymour supplied with a less harmful alter-native to the brandy and opium for which his body constantly craved. At night, they could hear him pacing the floor above them when the torments grew too much for him to bear. He cried out for relief and flew into rages, throwing things at Nellie when she took him his food, but gradually these fits grew less frequent and he became, as she said, more like his old self. He ventured out into the grounds on sunny days, taking long walks and scaring the occasional traveller by his strange and exotic appearance. He seemed to take pleasure in gaining a reputation as an eccentric rather than a madman, and he would sit in the kitchen and recount his experiences with relish and a wry sense of humour. Effie was begin-ning to quite like the master of Marsh House, and, to her intense relief, he seemed to have forgotten that he had ever mistaken her for his beloved Mirella.

She knew that they must leave Marsh House eventually, but each day there was something urgent that needed to be attended to: the cheese had to be salted, or the excess of goat's milk churned into butter, and then the ale might be ready to be strained into wooden kegs. Effie was kept busy from dawn to dusk.

One day in late July Tom found a beehive almost hidden by nettles at the far side of the orchard. He consulted Jeffries who had vague memories as to how the former beekeeper used to scrape off the wax to get at the delicious honeycomb and they feasted on bread and honey that day and the next. There was enough left for Tom and Jeffries to take into Clapton with the eggs and cheese surplus to their needs, which they sold at market. They came home that evening with fresh supplies of lard, flour, tea, sugar and candles, and the essential ingredient for Nellie's ale, a sack of dried hops. That afternoon Effie made pastry and they had rabbit pie for supper. She decided to postpone their departure for a while longer.

A blazing July gave way to an even hotter August and the fields across the River Lea were golden with ripening wheat. There had been no sign of Toby for weeks and Effie wished that she had not been so hard on him. He had, after all, only been the bringer of bad tidings; it was Frank who had led her to believe that he loved her, and she was the fool who had fallen for his lies. She told herself that she was not putting off their departure in the hope that Toby would return. It did not matter to her if she never saw him again, but he had been good to them, and she was desperate to apologise for her apparent ingratitude. Sometimes in the evening, when her work was done and Georgie was safely tucked up in bed, Effie took a stroll along the track at the edge of the marsh. Across the flat landscape to the west she could make out the pall of smoke that hung in a permanent cloud over the city, and if the wind was from the west she could smell the stench emanating from the manufactories and the gas and chemical works. If the breeze wafted across the marshes she could smell clover, tinged with marsh gas and the earthy aroma of mud. She could see for miles although there was little to view other than marsh and sky, and her eyes constantly scanned the horizon for the sign of a traveller on horseback. The evenings were almost imperceptibly drawing in and summer was fading away. Swallows were gathering as they prepared to migrate for the winter, and Toby had not come home.

The longer they remained in Marsh House the more Effie became aware of Seymour Westlake's straitened circumstances. The empty rooms echoing with the slightest sound were a testament to Nellie's attempts to raise cash, in order to satiate her master's desire for brandy

352

and opium. His supply might have dried up and he was stumbling along the road to recovery, but there was still the need to obtain money for essentials. The occasional glut of eggs, butter and cheese had kept them going throughout the summer, but Effie knew that life would not be as easy during a long and harsh winter. She had offered Nellie money for their keep, and it had been gratefully accepted, but the sovereigns would not last forever, and Effie realised that the time had come for them to move on.

It was a golden September with just a hint of autumn in the air. The branches on the apple trees sagged almost to the ground beneath the weight of the crop, and the hedgerows were studded with jewel-like blackberries. Effie and Georgie went out picking and returned with rush baskets brimming with ripe berries.

Nellie threw up her hands and laughed at the sight of Georgie's purple lips and fingers. 'I can see someone's put more in his belly than in his basket.' She picked him up and carried him protesting into the scullery.

Effie could hear the splashing of water and Georgie's protests as he was scrubbed clean. She set the baskets on the table. 'We'll have blackberry and apple pie for supper.'

Georgie scuttled back into the kitchen

followed by Nellie, wiping her hands on her apron. 'That's one of the master's favourites. I can't remember the last time I made a fruit pie. There didn't seem much point when the master had no appetite and it was only me and Jeffries to feed.'

Effie emptied the contents of one of the baskets into a pan. 'There are plenty here. We could make jam with the rest.'

'Or wine,' Nellie said, licking her lips. 'A drop of blackberry wine would go down a treat on a cold winter's day.'

Effie handed the empty basket to Georgie. 'Take this to Tom and ask him to fill it with apples from the store, there's a good boy.'

'Tom,' Georgie cried gleefully. 'Find Tom.'

'That's right, darling,' Effie said proudly. 'Go and find Tom. He's outside in the yard. I saw him a minute ago through the window.' She watched him toddle off carrying the basket which was almost as big as him. 'He's growing up so fast.'

Nellie popped a berry into her mouth. 'Hmmm, these are just right. What shall it be? Jam or wine?'

Effie hesitated. It was now or never. She had to make the decision and break the news to Nellie. 'I've got something to tell you.'

'That sounds serious.' Nellie flopped down on the nearest chair. 'What is it? Have we run out of sugar or have the mice eaten all the flour?'

'You've been so kind to us, and I want you to know how much I appreciate you taking us in when we had nowhere else to go, but the time has come to move on.'

What?' Nellie stared at her open-mouthed. 'No. You're joking. Why would you want to do a silly thing like that? Has him upstairs been upsetting you again?'

'No. Mr Westlake has been a perfect gentleman and he's doing really well now. I'm glad that he's getting better.'

'Then what is it? You're not going to chase after that good-for-nothing son of his, are you?'

Effie shook her head. 'No, it's nothing like that. We can't stay here forever.'

'I don't see why not,' Nellie said angrily. 'It's not like he's asked you to go, and you've earned your keep as well as paying for it.'

'The money won't last long, Nellie. I have to think of Tom and Georgie. We have to build a life for ourselves, and we don't belong here.'

'Stuff and nonsense,' Nellie cried, rising to her feet. 'I've never heard such rubbish. Why, you three are like family now. You've brought this old ruin back to life. You can't leave us.'

Effie hurried round the table to hug Nellie. 'Don't get upset. It's for the best and you know it. Tom needs to find paid work and I have to support my son.'

'Haven't you been happy here? I know I ain't always the easiest person to get on with and neither is the master. Old Jeffries is a bit of a moaner, but he don't mean it. Stay here, Effie. Don't leave us.'

'I have been happy here, but I've got to think of the future. I want a proper home for Georgie and Tom.'

Nellie went to sit in her chair by the range. She pulled her apron over her head, rocking to and fro in the chair. 'And this is a madhouse. Why don't you say it?'

'It's not that,' Effie said gently. 'But we don't belong here. Mr Westlake might remarry one day.'

'Never!'

'Never is a long time. He's not an old man and he's lonely.'

Nellie peeped out from beneath the folds of the apron. 'You could marry him and then the house would be yours. You'd be made for life.'

Effie threw back her head and laughed. 'I don't think so, Nellie. If I marry again it will be for love, but I don't expect to find that again, so I'll stay as I am and devote myself to my son.'

'Yes, and he'll grow up and leave you,'

Nellie said darkly. 'Don't go, Effie. Please say you'll stay.'

Nellie was not the only one who was against their leaving. Jeffries spoke up for once in his life, making an impassioned plea for Effie to change her mind. Tom was doubtful about the move at first, but when he saw it as an adventure and considered the possibilities as to his future he changed his mind and wholeheartedly supported Effie's decision.

Unable to dissuade Effie from her purpose, Nellie went to her master, and when Mr Westlake appeared in the kitchen Effie thought she was going to have to do battle with him also, but he said he understood her feelings and applauded her courage. 'A young woman like you shouldn't be buried alive in this sad house,' he said seriously. 'There is more to life than trying to keep the marsh from swallowing up this old ruin, and myself along with it.'

'No, master,' Nellie cried passionately. 'Don't say such things. We rub along well enough, with or without young Effie.'

'You are a treasure beyond the price of rubies,' Seymour said, smiling. 'But we must not allow Effie to bury herself here for our selfish sakes. She has a life to lead and she must follow her heart.' He turned to Tom, who

357

had been shuffling awkwardly from one foot to the other. 'Go to the stables, boy. Somewhere amongst the rack and ruin you should find an old dog cart. It might have rotted away, but perhaps you and Jeffries could make it roadworthy. It will be my gift to you all to make up for the work you have done on my property.'

Effie opened her mouth to thank him, but he held up his hand. 'I have come to myself in the past few months, Effie. I have seen the improvements and I'm ashamed that I allowed the place to get in such a state. It's too late now to bring prosperity back to Marsh House, but you have the will and the energy to go out into the world and succeed. I wish you well, my dear.'

He turned to go but Effie ran after him. 'Sir, you don't have to live like this. If you would just acknowledge your son . . .'

Seymour's brows drew together in an ominous frown. 'Say no more on the matter, Mrs Grey. I have no son.' He strode out of the kitchen, slamming the door behind him.

The ancient dog cart was found beneath a pile of sacks and rusty garden tools. Although Jeffries made it plain that he disapproved of their plan to leave, he became engrossed in the restoration of the vehicle, telling Tom and

Effie stories of the old days when Toby and his mother used to go about the countryside, visiting friends or going to market.

'Of course,' he said gravely, 'the master couldn't be seen out with a servant girl, but sometimes he'd take the reins and they'd go off for a picnic somewhere quiet where the gossips wouldn't see them.' He stroked the wooden seat, shaking his head. 'Not that it would have mattered to the mistress; she was past caring about things like that.'

Effie stopped scraping off the flaking paint-work to stare at him. 'The mistress, Jeffries? I thought she must have died before Toby was born.'

He shook his head. 'She might as well have been dead, missis. She were a delicate slip of a thing when the master married her. She took sick soon after the honeymoon and she got worse with each passing day. She lost the use of her legs and had to be pushed round in one of them Bath chairs.'

'Poor lady,' Effie said sincerely. 'How sad.'

'It were, missis. She was a gentle soul and never said a cross word. She spent her last few years bedridden and just faded away gradual like. She died a few months before smallpox almost took the master's life.'

'And killed Mirella,' Effie murmured, half to herself.

'They're both buried in the orchard, close by where we put the old man. I seen the master walking there at dusk, when he thinks no one is about. I say it's no wonder he took to the drink.'

Effie put down the metal scraper. 'I don't think I can do any more today. It's time I started making supper.'

'Stop talking about people dying,' Tom said impatiently. 'Tell me about the time you got lost in the marsh, Jeffries, and would have drowned but for the will-o'-the-wisp leading you to safety.'

Effie left them to get on with their work. She could hear Jeffries' voice droning on as he recounted lurid tales of the past, but it was the star-crossed lovers who occupied her mind as she crossed the stable yard and went into the house. Nellie never talked about the late Mrs Westlake, but her long debilitating illness and slow death would explain why Seymour had never been able to make an honest woman of Mirella. Effie's heart ached for all three of them in their hopeless triangle of love. She shivered. The autumn nights were slowly drawing in and winter would be upon them all too soon. She was determined to be settled in a home of their own before the bad weather made life even more difficult.

*   *   *

The dog cart was repaired and it was packed in readiness for their departure. It was early morning and a fine mist blanketed the marshes. A heavy dew lay on the ground like hoar frost and there was a definite chill in the air. Tom went out to the stables to put Champion between the shafts and Effie was upstairs in her bedchamber, making certain that she had left nothing behind. She went to the window, peering out into the swirling mist. The sky and marsh were the same uniform shade of pearl grey and there was no sign as yet that the sun would break through and burn off the mist. She was about to turn away when she saw a movement out of the corner of her eye. The breath hitched in her throat as she made out a man's shape emerging from the fog. For a wild moment she thought it was Toby coming home and she lifted her hand to wave to him, but then she realised that he would not be travelling on foot and when a second figure staggered out of the mist she realised her mistake. A woman was traipsing after the man and Effie let out a horrified cry. She ran from the room and almost fell down the stairs in her haste. She arrived in the kitchen breathless and hardly able to frame the words.

'Salter,' she gasped. 'Salter and his wife – they're here, Nellie.'

Georgie's lips trembled at the sound of his mother's raised voice and Nellie snatched him up in her arms. 'Let them come,' she said angrily. 'I'll sort them out for you.'

'No,' Effie shook her head vehemently. 'They mustn't find us here. I don't know how they've found us, but I want you to tell them that you know nothing. You've never seen us.' She snatched her cloak and bonnet from the peg behind the door and Georgie's little jacket and cap that had once belonged to Bertie.

'What are you going to do?' Nellie demanded anxiously.

'We're leaving right away.' Effie crossed the floor to take Georgie from her arms. 'Please, Nellie. Do me this last favour. Keep them here as long as you can. Offer them a cup of tea or anything that will delay them. They're on foot and they'll never catch up with us in the dog cart. We must go now while it's too foggy for them to see us.'

A loud hammering on the front door made them both jump and Georgie began to whimper. Effie cuddled him to her. 'Hush, darling. We're playing a game of hide and seek.'

'They'll have the door down in a minute,' Nellie said angrily. 'I'll give them a piece of my mind.' She strode out of the kitchen and her footsteps echoed off the flagstones in the passage.

Effie hesitated by the open door, straining her ears to hear what they were saying.

'What d'you want?' Nellie demanded.

'We're looking for a woman with a baby and a young boy.'

The sound of Salter's gruff voice made Effie shudder.

'You've got the wrong house,' Nellie answered crossly.

'We've been told they're here.' Sal's voice had a wheedling tone. 'You wouldn't want to be harbouring felons, I'm sure, missis.'

'I ain't harbouring nobody. Clear off.'

'She stole money,' Salter roared. 'And a gold watch that was left to me all legal and above board. I got the old man's will to prove it.'

Effie clapped her hand over her mouth to stop herself from crying out. She was angry now and her first instinct was to go out and face the Salters, but Georgie was obviously terrified and any minute he might open his mouth and yell. Hoping that Nellie would keep them occupied long enough for them to get away, Effie hitched her son over her shoulder and tore out of the house. Tom was in the stable yard with Champion harnessed to the cart and Jeffries making last minute checks as to the roadworthiness of the vehicle.

'They're here, Tom,' Effie said breathlessly.

'Salter and Sal are at the front door. We must leave now.'

'Hold on, missis,' Jeffries protested. 'I ain't checked everything yet.'

'We can't waste another minute. It will have to do.' Effie handed Georgie to Tom while she climbed up onto the driver's seat. She held out her arms. 'Come along, poppet. We're going for a drive with Tom. Won't that be fun?'

Tom lifted Georgie onto her lap and leapt up onto the cart, taking the reins. 'Goodbye, Jeffries, old chap. I'll come back and see you often, I promise.'

'You'll forget,' Jeffries said morosely. 'Once you've gone on your way you'll put us out of your mind.'

'You don't know me very well if you think that.' Tom flicked the reins and Champion moved forward. 'I'll be back before you know it. Just make sure those people don't follow us.'

'Go slowly until we're out of earshot,' Effie whispered. 'Once we're on our way they won't be able to do anything about it. Let's hope the mist doesn't lift until we're out of sight.

'Where are we going?'

'Head for the city. We need to disappear and we're too easy to spot in the country. I think we should head for Ben Hawkins' pub. We can put up for the night there and maybe

Ben can help us find somewhere cheap to rent. He knows everyone in Bow.'

Tom shot her a curious look. 'Isn't that a bit dangerous? Won't that be the first place that Salter will look for us?'

'There's no reason for him to follow the canal now that the *Margaret* is gone, and we have to sleep somewhere. To be honest, Tom, I can't think of anywhere else to go and Ben is a friend.'

'Mrs Hawkins ain't a friend,' Tom said glumly. 'She's an old besom.'

'I'll make certain that I avoid her at all costs, but Betty was kind to us last time we were there. I feel in need of seeing some familiar faces.'

Tom grinned and nudged her in the ribs. 'I suppose you want me to go by way of Bow Common, just in case the fair happens to be there.'

'The thought hadn't crossed my mind.' Effie turned her attention to Georgie who was fidgeting on her lap. 'Sit still, there's a good boy. We've a long way to go yet.'

The mist cleared as they left the marsh, and the ride was smoother now that they had left the rutted track and were driving on metalled roads. After weeks in the depths of the country it seemed strange to be back in the hurly-burly of city life. Horse-drawn vehicles clogged the streets and people bustled about their daily business. Smoke belched from factory chimneys and the once familiar stench of chemicals, tar, varnish and fumes from the gasworks came as a shock after the clean air they had grown accustomed to breathe without coughing and choking. The soot-blackened buildings looked grim even in the golden September sunlight, and Effie could only be thankful that it was a fine day. Had it been raining or foggy she thought she might have turned tail and returned to Marsh House.

After several stops along the way to eat and allow Champion to rest it was early evening by the time they reached the tavern. The horse was showing signs of age. Effie did not know exactly how old he was, but she knew that he had been working the canals for many years. He had cast a shoe halfway and they had had to find a farrier to replace it, which had taken up even more time. There had been no sign of the fair when they passed through Bow Common, and Effie was not sure whether to be relieved or saddened. A part of her wanted to see Frank again. She wanted him to tell her that it was all a mistake and he had walked away from the arranged marriage. But she knew in her heart that Toby had told her the truth, and to meet Frank face to face would only open up old wounds. He was lost to her forever and there was nothing she could do about it.

The bar was crowded with workmen slaking their thirst after a long day's toil in the factories. Ben was behind the bar and his face split into a wide grin when he saw Effie. He finished serving a customer and came round the corner of the bar to greet them.

'Where've you been all this time?' He slapped Tom on the back, ruffled Georgie's blond curls and kissed Effie on the cheek. His smile faded. 'That bloke Salter was looking for you. It's a few weeks ago now and I couldn't tell him what I didn't know, but he'd been asking questions all round the pub.'

'He found us,' Tom said, puffing out his chest. 'But he didn't catch us. We was too smart for Salter and his missis.'

Ben regarded him with a frown. 'Don't you be too cocksure, young 'un. He was in here spouting off that you'd burnt the boat and taken a watch or something that was rightly his. He's a nasty piece of work and out for trouble.'

'We won't be staying long,' Effie said hastily. 'Could you give us a bed for tonight, Ben? I can pay.'

He shook his head. 'I'm sorry, love. We're full up with commercial travellers, and even if we wasn't, I don't think the missis would appreciate me giving you a room. You know how it is.'

'It was just a thought. We'll find a lodging house somewhere round here.' She glanced down at Georgie as he tugged at her hand.

'Hungry, Mama.'

Ben's taut features dissolved into a grin. 'He's coming on, Effie. He was just toddling when I last saw you. Now he can speak up for hisself.' He lifted Georgie onto his shoulders. 'You're a fine fellow and we can't let you go hungry. We'll see what Betty has for you.' He headed for the kitchen, beckoning to Effie and Tom. 'Come on, you two. I won't let you leave without a bite to eat, and Betty might know of a place you can stay until you find something more permanent.'

Betty's face lit up when she saw Georgie. She stopped what she was doing and hurried forward with her arms outstretched. 'Why, here's my lovely boy. How you've grown, young Georgie.' She took him from Ben and sat him down on the table. 'You look as though a slice of cake would go down well, young man.' She cut a wedge of chocolate cake and he bit into it with a beatific smile on his face.

'I've got to get back to the bar,' Ben said, glancing anxiously over his shoulder as if he expected to see his wife standing behind him. 'I'll leave them in your capable hands, Betty.

Give them what they want to eat and no charge.'

'I should think not, master,' Betty said, pursing her lips. 'After all the work Effie done for you in the past she deserves a free meal.' She ruffled Tom's hair. 'I don't know about this one, though. As I recall he weren't the most reliable pot boy.'

'I've changed,' Tom said stoutly. 'I'm a good worker now, ain't I, Effie?'

'When you want to be,' she said, smiling. 'But we can pay, Ben. I don't want charity.'

'Sit down and eat. Talk later.' Betty took a pie from the oven and served two generous portions. 'It's beef and ale; the best in the house.'

Tom grabbed his plate and sat down, tucking in with relish. Effie was more eager to speak to Ben than she was hungry and she took him aside. 'I need to find somewhere cheap to rent. I thought you might be able to help.'

'I'll do anything I can, but I'm sorry to see you in this plight, Effie. I heard that the old man died when the barge went up in flames.'

'He was a sick man, although I think the Salters might have quickened his end.'

'It's a bad business, Effie. What will you do now?'

'I need work and I want to make a home

for us so that we don't have to keep moving from place to place.'

Ben scratched his head. 'Things ain't easy. The railways have taken a lot of the trade from the canals and I don't need any help in the bar.'

'I wasn't asking you for work. I know Mrs Hawkins wouldn't put up with having us around, but I'll do anything to earn a respectable living. At the moment the most important thing is to find somewhere to live.'

Betty pushed a plate towards Effie. 'I shan't tell you again, Effie Grey. Sit down and eat. You can put up at my place tonight, although you'll have to share a bed with my three girls and young Tom can sleep with the boys.'

Tom looked up with a mischievous grin. 'How about I share a bed with the girls and Effie can sort herself out?'

Betty cuffed him round the head. 'That's enough of that talk, young man. Any more like that and you'll sleep in the cellar with the rats and mice.'

'Ben.' Maggie Hawkins entered the kitchen, arms akimbo, glaring at Effie. 'I might have guessed you'd turn up again. What is she doing in my kitchen?'

'They're just passing through, my love,' Ben said nervously.

'And eating our vittles by the look of it. We're not running a home for paupers.'

Effie put her hand in her pocket and took out a shilling, tossing it onto the table. 'That should cover the cost of the meal, Mrs Hawkins. We'll be gone as soon as we've eaten and we won't trouble you again.'

'No, really,' Ben protested. 'There's no need for payment, Effie. I'm sure we can treat our old friends to a bit of supper without breaking the bank.'

'You'd take the food from our infants' mouths and feed it to the poor if I let you.' Maggie gave Effie a look that would have curdled cream. 'I expect you to be gone by the time I come back.' She marched out of the kitchen with an impatient twitch of her thin shoulders.

'She don't mean half of what she says, Effie,' Ben said apologetically. 'She gets tired of a night after a long day looking after five little ones. I'd best get back to the bar.'

'I'm sorry, Ben,' Effie murmured. 'I didn't mean to cause trouble.'

He hesitated in the doorway. 'It's not your fault. I'd like to help but you can see how it is. If there's anything I can do . . .'

Effie thought of Champion, the faithful animal who had worked tirelessly pulling the narrowboat in all weathers for so many years. She knew that she would not be able to keep him now, but he was getting towards the end of his working life and she could not bear to think of him going to the knacker's yard. 'There is something,' she said tentatively. 'Could you look after Champion for me? Just until I can find someone who will let him live out the rest of his days at pasture.'

'Gladly. I could use a docile animal to pull the trap when Mrs Hawkins takes the nippers out to visit their granny. My horse is fine with me but he's a bit temperamental when my wife takes the reins.'

'Thank you, Ben. I'm in your debt,' Effie said, blowing him a kiss as he hurried from the room.

'I'm on his horse's side,' Tom muttered. 'I'd bite the old hag if she took a whip to me.'

'I brought up ten nippers,' Betty said, 'and I worked here until I was fit to drop, but I never spoke to my old man like that. He'd have taken his belt to me if I had.'

'She's a mean old crow,' Tom said cheerily. 'Can I have some more pie, please, Betty?'

Betty piled his plate with food. 'You've paid for it, so you shall have it.' She turned to Effie with a frown. 'I know you're worried, love, but you must eat something.'

Effie sank down on the chair, staring at the rapidly cooling meal. 'I should never have come here, Betty. We could end up in the workhouse again if things go wrong.'

'There, there, love. Don't lose heart,' Betty said hastily. 'I'm sure it won't come to that.'

Effie looked up, meeting Betty's anxious gaze with a stubborn lift of her chin. 'I'll do anything to keep us from that dreadful place. I won't let Salter see me beaten. I won't give in.'

Chapter Seventeen

Betty's tiny terraced house in Phoebe Street overlooked the chemical works. The fumes from the factory had rotted the outside paint-work and eaten into the curtain material so that they hung in tatters at the windows. The whitewashed walls of the kitchen were yellowed by steam and grease from the range, and the ceiling was coated in a tarry mixture of tobacco smoke and soot. Betty's husband, Fred, was employed in the factory as were their three elder sons, and they enjoyed a pipe of baccy after supper, sitting with their feet as close to the grate as they could get without setting the soles of their boots on fire.

Two of the daughters were in service and living away from home, and two of the three remaining sisters worked in the market gardens on Bow Common, bringing home little in the way of pay but a plentiful supply of vegetables deemed unfit for sale. The third daughter stayed at home to look after the two youngest boys who were not yet old enough to attend the board school. With most of the family in full-time employment, the Crooke family were comparatively well off. They had adequate food and clothing and none of the children went barefoot. Fred Crooke was a silent, stolid and dependable sort of man, who said very little but seemed amiable enough, and did not complain when his wife brought three strangers into their home.

Effie was grateful for their hospitality but she felt that she was imposing on the family's good nature. As it was, the house seemed to be bursting at the seams, and the sleeping arrangements were cramped and uncomfortable. In the small back bedroom, the three sisters shared a double bed, with the two youngest boys sleeping top to toe in a truckle bed beneath the window. Effie and Georgie shared a straw palliasse on the floor, and Tom was relegated to the downstairs parlour where the older Crooke brothers laid their heads for the night. On their first morning in Phoebe Street Tom appeared tousled-headed and bleary-eyed at breakfast. He confided to Effie later that he had barely slept a wink, having been kept awake at first by the brothers smoking cigarettes and chatting about the events of the day, which excluded him entirely, and then, when they finally settled down for the night, two of them snored so loudly that it was like trying to sleep in a farmyard filled with pigs.

Later that morning Effie left Georgie playing happily with the youngest Crooke boys while she went out looking for a suitable place to rent. Tom went with her, studying advertisements in shop windows in the hope of finding work, but all the vacancies seemed to be for able-bodied men and there was nothing suitable for a boy of his age.

They scoured the streets of Bow all day but the premises they saw were either too expensive or too appalling even to consider. There were attics with leaking roofs housing poverty-stricken families and rats in equal proportions, or cellars stinking worse than sewers with ten or twenty people to a room. Effie and Tom were used to the confined conditions on the narrowboat and the caravan, but they found the way people lived in this part of the city was too dreadful to contemplate. They returned to Phoebe Street tired and dispirited.

Betty was sympathetic but unsurprised by their failure to find somewhere suitable to live. As to work, she shrugged her shoulders. There were many unemployed, especially amongst the very young and those advanced in years. Beggars on street corners and in shop doorways were a common sight and the soup kitchens did a roaring trade. She assured Effie that they were welcome to stay as long as necessary and were not putting the Crooke family out in the least. After a few days in the Crooke household Effie realised that Betty had been speaking the truth. The more the merrier was her favourite saying when the house was crammed to bursting point with friends and family. People seemed to gravitate to Betty and her stoical husband. There was always a fire burning and a kettle simmering on the range. Cups of tea and slices of Betty's famous cake were dispensed with open-handed hospitality and no one was turned away from the door of number fifteen Phoebe Street.

The days turned into weeks and a balmy September gave way to a chilly October with rain and gales sweeping the streets almost clean, but not quite. Tom earned a little as a crossing sweeper and Effie did her best to help Betty in the house, although she spent most of the day tramping the streets in the hope of finding a home they could afford on the dwindling amount of money left in her purse.

Georgie's second birthday came round all too quickly in late November and Betty baked him a chocolate cake. The Crooke children made paper hats from old newspapers and Effie bought him a warm jacket from a dolly shop. It was slightly too big but Betty said cheerfully that he would soon grow into it. The cuffs were a little frayed but Effie stitched them so neatly that the garment looked almost like new. Tom had spent some of his earnings on a tin monkey that climbed a pole when its strings were pulled. He had found it at the bottom of a box filled with junk in the pawnshop in Limehouse, and the other children eyed it enviously. After supper, which had to be taken in shifts as there was only room for six people to sit at the table at any one time and even then it was a bit of a squash, the women washed the pots and pans in the scullery and the men sat round the fire smoking their pipes and roll-up cigarettes.

'That was a good meal, Betty love,' Fred said, patting his stomach. 'Boiled mutton is my favourite dinner.'

She smiled, dropping a kiss on his bald pate as she walked past his chair. 'I know that, ducks. It was a bit of an extravagance, but it's the nipper's second birthday and we all deserve a treat.'

'A pint of ale would go down nicely,' Fred said, receiving a grunt of assent from his sons.

'And I'd say you was welcome to go to the pub and down a couple,' Betty said, shaking her head. 'But we're saving up for our Elsie's wedding in January. We've got to send her off in style.'

This statement brought another murmur of agreement from the brothers and their father. Effie had been wiping Georgie's sticky hands and face with a damp cloth during this conversation and she was struck again by a feeling of guilt. She paid her way, but she still felt beholden to the family who had taken her in, and there was still no sign of either work or a house they could afford to rent. It was then that an idea came to her in a flash of inspiration. She smiled to herself and she kissed Georgie's rosy cheek as she set him down on the floor. She knew exactly how she would repay the Crookes' kindness.

Next day she wrapped her shawl around her head and shoulders against the bitter wind blowing in from the east. She knew the streets well by now and she made her way across Bow Common Bridge to the market in Randall Street, where she found costermongers vying for position in front of the more fashionable lock-up shops in the covered marketplace. What might be bad for trade for the shopkeepers proved to be a boon to someone with only a little money to spare and Effie returned to Phoebe Street laden with parcels. With a project in mind, she felt her spirits rise. Ignoring the inquisitive questions from Bella, the youngest Crooke girl, Effie went outside to the washhouse and filled the copper with water from the pump. She lit a fire and stood back to wait for the water to reach the correct heat, which Nellie had told her was when she could see her face reflected on the still surface as if she were looking into a mirror. She had been an apt pupil in the art of brewing and had taken Nellie's teaching very much to heart. When she was satisfied that the time was right, she drew off the water and added malted barley, stirring vigorously. She had begun her first brew of ale since she left Marsh House and she hoped it would be ready in time for Christmas and the feast that she knew Betty was planning to give her family.

It was impossible to keep such a project secret. The smell of the malted barley alone was enough to have the Crooke men sniffing the air like hungry hounds. One by one they ventured into the washhouse, eager to find out what Effie was preparing that smelt so appetising. She had many hands willing to help her strain the liquid into a washtub, and they stood back watching with interest as she added sugar, yeast and dried hops. Everyone wanted a stir and things were getting a bit out of hand in the tiny outhouse with everyone talking at once. Effie was relieved when Fred opened the door and demanded to know what was going on. His craggy features broke into a delighted smile when she told him her plan and he shooed his family out into the yard.

'Is it too soon to have a taste, Effie?' he asked eagerly.

'Much too soon, Mr Crooke, but it will be ready in time for Christmas.'

He patted her on the shoulder. 'We'll have the best time ever.' He shuffled out of the steam-filled building and Effie found herself alone for once. She smiled, shaking her head. She loved the noisy, boisterous family who had made them feel that they belonged, but recently she had become aware that the eldest son, Harry, was paying far more attention to her than he did to his sisters. The girls had commented on it too, and although Effie liked Harry well enough there was nothing about him that made her pulses race or caused her heart to miss a beat when he came through the door. In short, she knew that their time in Phoebe Street must come to an end soon. She did not want to cause upset amongst the family that she had come to love and think of as her own, but it was now imperative to find somewhere else to live. She made up her mind to go out next day and accept the first dwelling that was reasonably habitable and also affordable.

Large snowflakes tumbled like goosedown from a solid mat of grey clouds as Effie and

Tom trudged along Bow Common Lane. It was mid-afternoon but soon it would be dark and the snow was settling on the rooftops and pavements in a thick white blanket. The streets had never looked so clean, but Effie knew that would all change in minutes, and the snow would turn to blackened slush when the men poured out of the factories and the gas works. Smoke and steam belched out in equal amounts, curling up to be absorbed in the clouds and turned into icy flakes that were sent fluttering back to earth like scraps of freezing lace.

'Let's go home,' Tom muttered through the folds of his muffler. 'My boots leak and my feet are blooming freezing.'

Effie nodded her head. The air was so cold that it hurt to breathe and snowflakes clung to her eyelashes making it difficult to see. 'I don't think we can do any more today. The last place we saw was a midden. I wouldn't put a pig in a place like that.'

Tom shot her a sideways glance. 'It ain't so bad living in Phoebe Street. At least we get fed properly and old Fred's a decent enough chap. If I can put up with Harry ribbing me all the time, I don't see why you can't encourage him a bit. It's obvious he's sweet on you.'

'I know, but I don't feel the same way about

him. It's going to upset Betty if she thinks I've been encouraging her son, especially when I haven't done a thing to make him like me.'

'You don't have to, Effie. The blokes take one look at you and they're smitten. I wish I had that effect on girls.'

'You're too young to think about things like that,' Effie said, chuckling in spite of the bitter cold and the fact that she had lost all feeling in her fingers and toes. 'Fred will come after you with a cudgel if you make eyes at young Agnes. I know you fancy her so don't deny it.'

'I like her a lot and she's going to get me a job in the market garden when they start hiring again, only there's nothing doing until they start planting in the spring.'

Effie stopped, holding her side as a painful stitch made her gasp with pain. 'Wait a moment, Tom. I need to catch my breath.'

'The snow is getting thicker by the minute,' he said, drawing her into the comparative shelter of a doorway. 'At least we haven't got far to go now.'

'I just need a moment,' Effie said breathlessly.

'I'm starving. I wonder what Betty's got for our supper tonight.' Tom leaned his shoulders against the door, but it opened suddenly pitching him backwards into a narrow hallway.

'Are you all right, Tom?' Effie peered into the darkness, but all she could see were Tom's legs thrashing about as he scrambled to his feet.

'Bloody hell. I wasn't expecting that.'

'The door wasn't shut properly,' Effie said, too shaken to upbraid him for swearing. 'Are you hurt?'

'Only me pride.' Tom rubbed his backside with a rueful grin. 'This place stinks.'

'And we're trespassing,' Effie said, tugging at his arm. 'Let's go before someone catches us.'

He pulled away from her. 'If they couldn't be bothered to lock up, they can't be too worried about their property. I'm going to have a nose around.'

'No, Tom. You can't,' Effie protested, but too late. Tom had disappeared down the dark passage into the bowels of the house. She hesitated, wrinkling her nose. The smell was nauseating and being next door to the gas works did not improve things. The stench of coal gas together with other noxious odours was suffocating. When Tom ignored her cries, she ventured a little further into the house. She found him in the front room. 'Tom, come away. This isn't right.'

He was standing in the middle of the floor staring at the chaotic jumble of old furniture, empty bottles and tin cans, yellowed newspapers and bundles of rags. Cold white light filtered in through the grimy window-panes and cinders tumbled out of the grate, filling the hearth with ash. 'It looks as though tramps have been living here,' Tom said slowly. 'I don't think it can belong to anyone in particular or they wouldn't have let it get into this state.'

Effie jumped as a piece of plaster fell from the ceiling, narrowly missing her head. 'Someone owns it. Every square inch of London belongs to someone.'

'I'm going to have a look round.'

She opened her mouth to protest but he had gone and the door swung drunkenly on a broken hinge. Effie hurried after him. She did not want to be left alone in such a place. It felt eerie, as though somebody had died in that room and might come back to haunt them at any moment. She felt the hairs on the back of her neck stand on end. 'Tom, come back.'

She heard him clattering about in the back room which turned out to be a kitchen of sorts with a rusty old range and a door leading into a back yard that looked out over the snow-covered expanse of Bow Common. Memories of the fair came flooding back as Effie stood in the doorway. It had been summer then, only six months ago but it seemed like a lifetime. She felt a shaft of pain cut through her as she recalled the first time she had seen Frank. He had looked so handsome and carefree with his tanned complexion and open countenance. It had been easy to believe him when he said he loved her, but she had to accept that it was all over now and fading into memory as if it had been a dream.

'Look, Effie,' Tom shouted, stamping about in the snow. 'It's got a pump and a privy. It only needs a bit of elbow grease and it would make a fine home. I think it could be ours if we find out who owns it and offer them a decent rent. They might pay us to live here and tidy it up. What d'you think?'

Dazedly, Effie shook her head. 'You're mad. It's beyond repair. I expect the floors upstairs are rotten and the ceiling will fall in at any moment.'

Tom pushed past her, stamping the snow off his boots as he entered the kitchen. 'I'm going upstairs. You stay down here and if I fall through the floor you can pick me up.'

'No, don't go up there. Someone might be asleep in one of the rooms. You could be attacked by the lunatic who lives here.'

'Poppycock,' Tom snorted. 'I'm not afraid.' He bounded out through the door and his footsteps reverberated throughout the house as he took the stairs two at a time.

Effie went to the foot of the stairs, waiting

anxiously. 'Tom, can you hear me? Is every-thing all right?'

He leaned over the banisters. 'Come up and see. There's no one here, and judging by the cobwebs it's been empty for years. Come on up, Effie. It's fine.'

Against her better judgement, Effie allowed curiosity to win and she climbed the stairs, pulling a face as her boots crunched the cara-paces of dead cockroaches and spiders' webs caught in her hair.

'Come into the back bedroom,' Tom called excitedly. 'It looks out over the common. It's like being back in the country.'

She crossed the narrow landing and found herself in a small room festooned with cobwebs and smelling strongly of mice. Tom had his back to her as he stared out of the window. He turned his head at the sound of her footsteps and even in the dim light she could see that he was smiling. 'Take a look for yourself, Effie. This is the place for us. The market garden is on the other side of the common and it would be just the thing if I could get a job there. You'd be able to stay at home and look after Georgie and we'll be a proper family again. Never mind Toby Tapper. We don't need him. I can take care of you both.'

Effie heard the wistful note in her brother's

voice and it cut her to the quick. Until now she had not given a thought to how Tom might have felt when Toby failed to return. She had never considered that he might be genuinely fond of the gypsy horse trader who came and went as he pleased. She experienced a rush of anger towards Toby that shocked her with its intensity, and she moved swiftly to Tom's side, slipping her arm around his thin shoulders. 'We are a family, Tom. You and me and Georgie, but Toby will turn up one day. He always does.'

Tom's downcast expression melted into a smile. 'And this is just the place he might come to. When the fair comes back, Toby will be out there selling his old nags. Come the spring we'll see him again, I know we will.'

Effie gave him a hug. 'Of course we will. Let's go take a look at the front room. If we're going to rent this old wreck of a house I need to see where I'm to sleep.'

'I'll make it nice for you,' Tom said, bounding on ahead of her like an eager puppy. 'There's a bed in here, Effie,' he shouted gleefully. 'And it ain't half bad. A new feather mattress and you'll be sleeping like the queen.'

Effie examined the room with a critical eye. The ceiling plaster was cracked and the wallpaper was peeling off, but it was a reasonable size and there was enough room for a truckle bed for Georgie in spite of the iron bedstead that took up half the floor space.

'It will clean up a treat,' Tom said enthusiastically. 'We could get Betty's girls to help.'

His eagerness made Effie smile. 'I'm sure Agnes would do anything you asked her to.'

Tom's cheeks flushed scarlet. 'We're just friends.'

Effie gave him a hug. 'Of course you are. Let's go before someone walks in and tells us that it's all a dream and they want us out of their house.'

'It won't happen like that. I've got a good feeling about this place, Effie. It was meant to be, that's what Nellie would have said.'

So many people and so many different places in such a short time; the memories crowded into Effie's head as they tramped home through the deepening snow. The faces of Nellie, Seymour Westlake and old Jeffries flitted through her mind together with Zilla and Leah, Arnoldo and Ethel, Laila and Dr Destiny, and Frank, of course, but the one person who linked them all was Toby. Effie struggled with her feelings as the snow blinded her and the cold air felt like ice in her lungs. Whenever there had been trouble in the past, Toby had seemed to appear like the genie from the lamp in the story of Aladdin. She clutched her shawl around her, bending her head against the bitter wind, and she smiled to herself as she pictured Seymour in his exotic room rubbing one of the brass oil lamps to conjure up the son he refused to acknowledge. She felt a tug somewhere deep inside her at business left only half done. She wished that she could have united father and son as each one seemed in equal need of the other.

'Come on, Effie. Best foot forward,' Tom bellowed in her ear. 'I want my supper, and I can't wait to tell everyone we've found our new home.'

'That'll be Albert Place,' Fred said, taking his pipe from his mouth. 'Next to the gas works.'

Betty stopped ladling stew into bowls for a moment. 'It's been empty for years.'

'I know who owned it,' Agnes said importantly. 'It was a mad old man who worked in the market garden. They say he died there and no one found him for days. It weren't until the flies was thick over the windows and round the door that the police ventured inside. They found his rotted corpse sitting in the chair with a month-old newspaper still clutched in his hands.'

Bella let out a muffled scream and Betty brandished the soup ladle at her daughter. 'That's enough of that talk, Agnes Crooke.

You're old enough to know better than to scare the young 'uns.'

Agnes shot a sideways glance at Tom and they dissolved into a fit of giggles.

'He weren't mad,' Fred said, relighting his pipe with a spill from the fire. 'He was old and lonely, young Agnes, and I'll thank you not to spread tales like that.'

'Sorry, Pa.' Agnes hung her head, receiving a sympathetic pat on the shoulder from Tom.

'Do you know if it's up for rent, Mr Crooke?' Effie asked, trying not to sound too eager although her heart was beating fast in anticipation of his answer.

'I believe the terrace is owned by some bigwig up West. They don't notice when the rent isn't paid. I daresay it wouldn't keep the toffs in cigars for a day.' Fred stopped to puff at his pipe while the family waited patiently for him to finish his pronouncement. 'Anyway,' he said after a moment's reflection. 'the whole terrace is due to be torn down some time in the future, so they probably don't think it's worth letting the place.'

'It's been used by tramps and dossers for the past year,' Betty said, shaking her head. 'It'll be in a terrible state.' She angled her head, giving Effie a searching look. 'But if your

391

heart's set on it, my girl, then we'll see what can be done. You need a place of your own.'

Having spent a rumbustious Christmas in Phoebe Street enlivened by the consumption of Effie's home-brewed ale, the entire Crooke family helped Effie and Tom move into their new home. It had been scrubbed from top to bottom and Harry had patched up the fallen plaster while his brothers sanded down the paintwork and applied a fresh coat. Agnes and her sisters scrubbed floors and washed windows while Betty attacked the rusty range with a wire brush and grim determination to get it going as soon as possible. Betty could not work without her cup of strong, sweet tea and it was important to have some form of heating in the house as the temperature outside was still below freezing and the snow showers continued to fall.

On Boxing Day, the Crookes marched in procession from Phoebe Street to Albert Place, each one bringing something that would help Effie set up home. Fred and Harry hefted a deal table that had been purchased from a second-hand furniture dealer in Limehouse for seven and six, and that included three ill-matched kitchen chairs which were slung over the older boys' backs. The girls brought pots and pans that Betty had unearthed from a forgotten cupboard in the pub, and had been donated willingly by Ben, and the smaller children were the bearers of rush baskets filled with necessary provisions.

That evening, when they were finally alone in their new home, Effie and Tom sat on either side of the range toasting their bare toes in front of the fire. Georgie was asleep upstairs on the truckle bed also found in the second-hand shop, and a flock mattress donated by Betty together with some blankets and a pillow.

'This is the life,' Tom said happily. 'I never thought we'd have a proper house all to ourselves.'

'You don't remember the home we had before we went into the workhouse, but it was just like this. We were a happy family until that awful day.'

'I'm glad I don't remember it then. It would have made things worse. But we're all right now, ain't we, Effie?'

She had not the heart to tell him that their money had dwindled down to a few pounds which would not keep them for long. The worst of the winter was to come and coal was expensive. She made a brave attempt at a smile. 'Of course we are. We'll both find work and then we'll live like lords.' She put her hand in her pocket to reassure herself that

Jacob's gold watch had not been lost in the move. The precious metal warmed at the touch of her fingers and the ticking of the mechanism was like a beating heart. If all else failed she might be forced to pawn it, but this was Georgie's sole inheritance from his grandfather. It was little enough when all was said and done, but at least she had kept it from Salter's grasping hands. She rose to her feet and went to the cupboard where Agnes had put the odd assortment of cups, bowls and plates that had also come from the pub, courtesy of Ben Hawkins. On the top shelf Effie found an empty tin that had once contained butterscotch. She laid the watch in it and closed the lid. It would be safe there, she thought, putting it back in its place.

'It's for Georgie,' she said in response to Tom's questioning glance. 'It's the only thing he will have that belonged to his grandfather. It will be Georgie's only link to his pa, and it would be a black day if I was forced to part with it.'

'We'll manage,' Tom said stoutly. 'I'll find work soon and so will you.' He stretched his arms above his head and yawned. 'Is there any of Betty's meat pie left? I'm hungry.'

Next morning, Effie could hardly believe it when she awakened to a silent house. After the constant chatter and sounds of everyday life in the crowded home in Phoebe Street, it seemed like paradise to open her eyes and find that she and Georgie had a room to themselves. There was no one shouting at the boys to get out of bed or the sound of the girls' raised voices as they squabbled over their clothes, hair ribbons and whose turn it was to make the bed or tidy their room. There was no smell of tobacco smoke wafting up from below or of sweaty male bodies, but conversely there was no aroma of hot tea and buttered toast, and now that she was wide awake she realised that they were well and truly on their own. She had paid a month's rent in advance and Georgie needed new shoes. She must look for work and hope to find it soon.

They tramped the snow-covered streets together, Tom with Georgie perched on his shoulders and Effie holding her skirts above her ankles as her boots sank into the thick snow. While she knocked on doors or enquired at factory gates, Tom looked after Georgie. When it was Tom's turn to seek employment, Effie allowed Georgie to play in the snow, but she regretted having shown him how to make snowballs as he proved to be adept at throwing and she found herself being bombarded mercilessly by a gleeful two-year-old. Despite the fun in the snow, neither Effie nor Tom had any luck in finding work. They returned home briefly at midday to snatch a meal of bread and margarine washed down with tea, and having dried their boots by the fire, they set off again in the afternoon. No matter how many places they tried, there was no work to be had for a boy and a slight young woman who were both deemed unsuitable for factory labour. Untrained in anything other than working the canals, serving behind a bar or assisting the Great Arnoldo in his strong man act, Effie was close to tears when the final door slammed in her face. It was dark and they had tried the varnish works, the bone factory, the metropolitan alum works and the tar factory, all without success. They were close to Bow Common Bridge and Tom suggested that they pay a call on Ben Hawkins. Recalling her last brush with Maggie, Effie was reluctant, but the factory gates had opened spilling men and women out onto the pavements as they rushed homewards. George began to whimper as they were pushed and jostled and Effie lifted him onto Tom's shoulders, the decision taken out of her hands.

Ben greeted them enthusiastically, calming Effie's worries about upsetting his wife with the news that Mrs Hawkins had gone to visit her sick mother and was not expected back for an hour or more. He drew a pint of small beer for Tom, a glass of port for Effie and lemonade for Georgie. 'Now then,' Ben said, leaning his elbows on the bar counter. 'I hear that you've set up home. Betty keeps me up to date.'

'She's been a marvel,' Effie said sincerely. 'But we need to find work, Ben. We've been out since first thing this morning and tried just about everywhere.'

His good-natured face crumpled into a frown. 'I'd take you on here like a shot, Effie, but the wife wouldn't stand for it. She's taken against you for no good reason other than your pretty face, and it would be more than my life is worth to give you work. It's a crying shame, because you drew the punters in like bees round a honey pot.'

'And that's the trouble,' Tom said, winking. 'My sister has all the blokes running after her.'

Effie felt the blood rush to her cheeks. 'That's not funny, Tom.'

'He's right,' Ben said, nodding his head in agreement. 'You're a fine-looking woman, Effie. Your pretty face works for you and it works against you.'

'You could go on the stage,' Tom said, grinning. 'Only you can't sing and you've got two left feet.' He dodged Effie's hand as she went to cuff him round the head, but in doing so he knocked his tankard over and

397

the beer spilled in a cascade over her blouse and skirt.

'You're soaked to the skin,' Ben said sympathetically. 'Betty's in the kitchen. Go through, Effie.'

Tom scooped Georgie up in his arms. 'You stay with me, young man. Give your ma a bit of peace and quiet for a change.'

Effie did not stop to argue. She went through to the kitchen, leaving a trail of beer in her wake. Betty took one look at her dishevelled state and threw up her hands. 'Lord, girl, you smell like a brewery. Take them wet things off.'

'I can't walk about half naked,' Effie protested. 'What if Mrs Hawkins comes home early?'

'She won't, and you can't go traipsing about London like that. You'll catch your death of cold if you go out in that state. Now take everything off that's wet and I'll fetch a towel.' Without waiting for an answer Betty hurried from the kitchen.

Effie was cold and wet and the smell of ale was making her feel queasy. Glancing nervously over her shoulder to make certain that there was no one about, she took off her clothes and hung them over a chair near the range. She moved closer to the fire, shivering and holding her hands out to the blaze, but the sound of footsteps in the stable yard made her turn with a start. She stared helplessly at the outer door as it opened and a tall man strode into the kitchen, shaking snow off his caped greatcoat and stamping his boots on the floor. He took off his hat sending a shower of ice crystals into the air. 'By God. It's you, Effie, and you're half naked.'

Chapter Eighteen

He was standing in the shadows outside the pool of light created by the fire and the oil lamp hanging above the kitchen table, but Effie would have known him anywhere. It was as if the genie had suddenly appeared without being summoned. A jumble of emotions left her confused and not a little embarrassed to be caught in a state of undress. She crossed her arms over her breasts, which were partly exposed above the tight confines of her stays. 'Toby. What are you doing here?'

He tossed his hat onto a chair. 'I might ask the same of you.' He shrugged off his great-coat and wrapped it around her shoulders. 'Why are you standing half naked in Ben Hawkins' kitchen?'

'I don't think that's any of your business,' Effie said, clutching the garment around her shivering body. It was still warm and it hung to the floor in heavy folds enveloping her like a hug. 'You can't just walk in and out of our lives and expect to pick up where we left off.'

'I went to Marsh House but Nellie told me

you'd moved on. I thought that Ben might have seen you, although I didn't realise quite how much of you was on view.' Toby's lips twitched and his eyes twinkled. 'I assume that the good Mrs Hawkins is not at home.'

'Don't be ridiculous. There's a perfectly simple explanation.'

He folded his arms across his chest, angling his head. 'I doubt if the excellent Maggie would see it that way.'

'Stop teasing me. You know it's not like that. Tom accidentally spilt beer all over me and Betty has gone to fetch a towel. Are you satisfied now?'

'Completely. I never doubted your innocence, Mrs Grey.'

His mock serious expression elicited an unwilling giggle from Effie. She had been feeling tense and agitated after the frustrations of the day, but in happier times Toby had always known how to make her laugh. She realised with a jolt of surprise that she had missed his company, but she was not going to let him get off so easily. 'I think you owe me an explanation, Toby Tapper. You left without a word and you took the mare, even though I'd asked you if I might keep her for a while.'

He shrugged his shoulders. 'And where would you have gone if I had done as you asked? You'd have chased after Frank and found him to be a happy bridegroom with a doting young wife.'

The truth of this statement hurt and she reacted angrily. 'If I had chosen to return to the fair it would have been my business. You waltz in and out of our lives as and when you please and then you have the nerve to tell me what to do.'

'I've tried to take care of you and the boys.'

'If you think that abandoning us in that sad house on the marshes was looking after us, I'm afraid you're sadly mistaken.'

'I'm not used to taking responsibility for anyone other than myself, I admit that, but I knew you would be safe and well cared for.'

The teasing look had gone from his eyes and Effie knew that her angry words had hit a raw spot. She pursued her advantage ruthlessly. 'You ran away, and you keep running from the truth, just as Mr Westlake does. You are so obviously father and son and yet neither of you will admit it. Do you know what I think, Toby?'

'No, but I'm sure you're going to tell me.'

'Yes, I am. It's time someone told you a few home truths. I think that Mr Westlake loved your mother very deeply and is too frightened to let himself love again. He has closed

402

his heart to emotion and taken refuge in drink and drugs.'

'That may be true of the old man, but it has nothing to do with me.'

Forgetting that she had next to nothing on beneath his heavy coat, Effie let it fall to the ground as she moved towards him with outstretched arms. 'It has everything to do with you, Toby. You were just a child when your mother died and he sent you away. I think you are equally afraid to risk loving someone again as you loved her. She wouldn't have wanted you to live like that.'

Toby grasped her hands, looking deeply into her eyes. 'You don't know me, Effie. I left that poor little broken-hearted boy behind many years ago. I'm not the sort of fellow you should associate with. I've left a string of unhappy love affairs behind me.'

'That's as maybe, but I don't think they meant anything to you.' She drew one hand free from his grasp and laid it on his chest. She could feel his heart beating in time with her own. She met his intense gaze and experienced a surge of sympathy for the abandoned child she saw behind his carefree façade. 'You need each other,' she whispered softly. 'The house on the marsh calls you back again and again. Go home, Toby. Give him a chance to explain his motives for sending

403

you away. Get to know your father before it's too late.'

He was silent for a long moment but Effie held his gaze, stubbornly refusing to release him. She raised her hand and touched his cheek. 'You are a good man, Toby. For all your faults you are the best friend I ever had.'

His eyes darkened and he drew her into an embrace, kissing her softly so that her lips parted in a sigh. 'Effie, you witch. You've cast a spell binding me to you so that I can never break free.' He breathed the words into her hair, holding her so close that she could feel the warmth of his flesh beneath his thin cotton shirt. She made a vain attempt to pull away but his mouth was on hers, seeking, demanding, and robbing her of free will. She slid her arms around his neck, losing herself in his fierce embrace.

'Good Lord give me strength.' Betty's shocked voice from the doorway made them draw apart.

'Good day to you, Mrs Crooke.' Toby released Effie, placing himself resolutely between them in an attempt to shield Effie from Betty's shocked gaze.

'What's going on?' Betty demanded. 'Effie, have you lost your mind? You ought to know better than to act like a loose woman, and in my kitchen too.'

'That's not fair,' Effie protested. 'It was just a kiss.'

'It looked like more than that from where I'm standing.' Betty pushed Toby aside and she thrust a bundle of dry clothes into Effie's hands. 'Make yourself decent, and you, Toby Tapper, can go outside and wait in the yard until I call you in, although I don't know what you're doing in my kitchen in the first place.'

'Why, I came looking for you, Betty my love,' Toby said with a disarming smile.

She shooed him out of the door. 'Get on with you, you libertine.'

'It wasn't what you think,' Effie said earnestly, as Betty turned on her with a worried frown. 'It was just a little kiss in the heat of the moment. It meant nothing.'

Betty shook her head. 'It's never nothing with a man like him. He's a philanderer, Effie. I've known Toby for years and he's kissed and run a dozen times or more, and that's the ones I know about. Don't let his handsome looks and sweet words fool you into believing him.'

Effie turned away to hide her blushes. She might try to convince herself that it had been a casual embrace but the intensity of feeling that had passed between them could not be written off so easily. She covered her confusion by examining the garments that Betty had given her, holding up a dress of fine grey merino that looked almost new. 'Whose is this, Betty? It's not hers, is it?'

'Well it ain't mine and that's for certain,' Betty said, moving to the table where she had been preparing meat for the pot. 'It is one of hers but she took a dislike to it although she'd only worn it the once. She said it made her skin look sallow and she put it out with the other things to be given to the poor.'

Effie slipped the gown over her head. Her heartbeats had almost returned to normal and she managed a wry smile. 'I think I qualify then. We've little money left, and if I don't find work soon we won't be able to pay the rent, let alone eat.'

'Don't do nothing silly,' Betty said, jerking her head in the direction of the outer door. 'Don't let him lead you astray.'

'I don't know what you mean,' Effie protested, although she had a fair idea and it was too embarrassing to acknowledge. 'I told you, there's nothing between me and Toby. It was a mistake.'

'And it might have led to a bigger one if I hadn't come in when I did. You'll find there's plenty of blokes who'll try to get their feet under your table, and they won't all have honourable intentions.'

'Betty, please. I think I can take care of myself.'

'You've never lived on your own until now and I'm telling you for nothing, it's not easy bringing up a youngster without a man to protect you.'

'I've got Tom.'

'And he's just a boy. I'm not joking, Effie. There's men who will take whatever they can get, and if you let them have their way it's you who'll be left with more mouths to feed, if you get my meaning.'

Effie was spared from answering by Toby. He put his head round the door, giving Betty his most appealing smile. 'Is it safe to come in now, Betty my duck?'

'Yes, come in, young man. I have a few words to say to you.'

Effie snatched up the bundle containing her wet clothes. 'I think I'd best be going now, Betty.'

'I'm coming with you.' Toby moved swiftly to Betty's side and kissed her on the cheek. 'The lecture will have to wait, but don't worry, my intentions are totally dishonourable.' Laughing, he dodged her hand as she went to cuff him round the ear.

'They'd better not be,' she retorted. 'If you step out of line I'll set my boys on you.'

'I'm going,' Effie said, making for the door. 'I'll see you again soon, Betty, and thanks for the gown and shawl.'

'Maybe you'd best go out the back way,'

Betty suggested. 'We don't want you to bump into her ladyship when you're wearing one of her cast-offs.'

'I've stabled my horse here for the night,' Toby said, slipping on his greatcoat. 'I'll go and see Ben about a room for myself and I'll bring Tom and Georgie round to the stable yard. We'll meet you there, Effie, and I'll see you safely home.'

With a fire burning merrily in the range and candles on the table, the small kitchen took on a homely atmosphere as they prepared to sit down to a meal of eel pie and mash, purchased by Toby who had invited himself to supper. Georgie's head kept lolling sideways as he sat at the table, fighting to keep awake, after consuming a bowl of bread and milk. Finally Effie carried him upstairs and put him to bed. She bent down to kiss him goodnight, but he was already asleep. She tucked him in and tiptoed from the room, closing the door softly behind her.

Downstairs Toby and Tom were sitting at the table waiting for her, their food as yet untouched.

Toby leapt to his feet and pulled out a chair. 'Sit down, my lady. Dinner is served.'

'And I'm blooming starving,' Tom said, attacking his meal with relish.

Effie experienced a frisson of excitement fizzing through her veins as Toby's hand grazed her shoulder, whether by chance or deliberately she had no idea, but either way the effect was startling. Her lips still tingled at the memory of his kiss and she met his gaze with a shy smile as he took his seat at the table. There was no hint of mockery or teasing in his eyes and they reflected the candlelight with a warm glow that melted her heart.

'Eat up before it gets cold,' she said, making an effort to sound normal although her heart was beating like a hammer against her ribs. She looked away, dazed and unsure of what had just passed between them. It must be hunger, she told herself as she attempted to eat, but it seemed that her appetite had disappeared together with commonsense and good judgement.

Toby reached out and laid his hand over hers as it rested on the table. 'This is the best eel pie in town,' he said softly. 'Don't let it go to waste.'

Her hand seemed to have a life of its own as her fingers curled around his. 'I – I'm not as hungry as I thought I was,' she murmured, losing herself in the depths of his gaze. She realised dimly that he had long, thick eyelashes that would have been the envy of any girl, and that tiny laughter lines radiated from the corners of his eyes. He raised her hand to his lips and kissed it. The tingling sensation went straight to her heart, making her gasp, but she drew her hand away quickly when Tom looked up from his plate, staring at them as if they had gone mad.

'What's up with you two?' He eyed Effie's full plate, licking his lips. 'If you don't want your grub, I'll have it.'

Effie forked up a piece of pie. 'Eat yours first, greedy boy,' she said, hoping he had not noticed the slight tremor in her voice. She put the food in her mouth but it stuck in her throat when she attempted to swallow. She took a sip of tea, trying not to look at Toby even though she could feel his eyes upon her.

'It's snowing again,' Tom said, glancing out of the window at the white flakes hurling themselves at the glass panes.

'I booked in at the pub,' Toby said casually. 'But perhaps you could put me up for the night. I can sleep on the floor; I'm used to roughing it.'

Effie shot him a sideways glance beneath her lashes. 'You're welcome to stay, but we've only one chair in the front parlour. We haven't managed to furnish the house properly.'

'He can have my bed,' Tom said through a mouthful of pie. 'I don't mind dossing down on the floor. It wouldn't be the first time.'

'Thanks, Tom, but the chair in the parlour will suit me fine. I'll be on my way in the morning.'

Effie's breath hitched in her throat. 'You're leaving so soon?'

'I thought that was what you wanted, since I let you down so badly.'

'You know you did. You left us at Marsh House without a second thought.' She rose to her feet, unable to trust herself if she stayed to argue the point. 'I'll fetch some blankets and a pillow, but I'm afraid there's not enough coal to light a fire in the front room.'

'Can I finish up your supper now?' Tom demanded.

'Eat it if you like. It would choke me.' Effie left the room heading blindly for the stairs, her emotions jumbled into a confusing tumult. The memory of that kiss was still uppermost in her mind, but it was her reaction to it that shocked her to the core. Toby caught up with her before she had a chance to mount the staircase and seized her in his arms. This time his kiss was neither gentle nor tender. His hands raked through her hair, sending pins flying in all directions, and he pressed her against the wall kissing her with a passion that made her weak at the knees. She knew she ought to resist. Betty's warning rang in her ears but Effie was deaf to everything but the pounding of the blood racing through her veins. She had never been kissed like this before; neither Owen nor Frank had excited her to the point where she was ready to abandon everything to the moment. There was something feral and primeval in their mutual need for each other.

Toby lifted her off her feet and carried her upstairs. 'Which room?' His voice was thick with desire and his breathing was ragged as he hesitated on the tiny landing. She clung to him, inhaling the scent of him until she was dizzy with longing. 'The front room,' she murmured, rubbing her cheek against his. He pushed the door open with his shoulder and laid her on the bed. The room was bathed in a white light reflected from the snow outside and warmed by the golden glow of a gas lamp a little further along the street. Effie stared up at him and she could see her face mirrored in his eyes. She knew that she ought to send him away, but a power stronger than herself had taken her over, body and soul. She reached up and drew his head down so that their lips met. 'Don't go,' she whispered. 'Don't leave me again so soon.'

He stared down at her, stroking her tumbled hair back from her forehead, and then very slowly he straightened up, taking a step away from the bed. 'I can't do this, Effie.'

Shocked, hurt and mortified, Effie snapped into a sitting position. 'What's wrong?'

His whole body was tense and she could see a pulse throbbing at his temple. 'This isn't what I want with you, my love.'

She stared up at him as if he had spoken in a foreign tongue. 'You don't want me.'

'Of course I want you, you sweet idiot.' He perched on the edge of the bed, taking her hand and holding it to his chest. 'I've loved you for as long as I can remember, Effie, but there was always someone else.'

She could feel the erratic beating of his heart through her fingertips, but nothing he said seemed to make sense. 'I don't understand. You never said anything.'

'When I met you first you were engaged to Owen, and then you were a heartbroken widow. I wanted to take care of you, but then you met Frank and I thought I'd lost you forever.'

'Oh, Toby.' Effie leaned forward to wrap her arms around him, but there was no passion in the embrace. 'I didn't know.'

He drew away from her, kissing her lightly on the cheek. 'But you cared what happened to me and my wretched father, if that's what he truly is. I need to find out who I am, and I want to hear it from his lips.'

'You must go home and sort it out, Toby. Only you can do that, but it doesn't make any difference to me. I don't care if you are a horse trader or the son of Seymour Westlake. You are you, and I – I love you.'

A wry smile hovered on his lips. 'I've waited for years to hear you say that, but I'm not going to take advantage of you. I love you with all my heart, Effie, and I'm going to prove that I'm worthy of you.'

'That's nonsense, Toby.'

He rose to his feet, and his gaze was focused on Georgie sleeping peacefully in his cot. 'We're going to do this the right way. I want to spend the rest of my life with you, Effie. I want to bring up Owen's child as my own, and I want us to be a proper family. A boy needs a father and a mother.'

Slowly she was beginning to understand. 'You want to marry me?'

A tender smile curved his lips. 'I'm supposed to ask you that, but yes, my love. I want you for my wife, more than I've ever wanted anything.'

She slid off the bed and stood before him, close enough to feel the warmth of his body, but without touching. The magic was still there and the desire bubbling beneath the surface; she could see it burning in his eyes and feel it within her soul; it would only take a small flame to consume them both. 'Then you must do what you have to do.'

'It means that I will have to leave you yet again. Tomorrow I'll make my way to Marsh House and have it out with the old man once and for all.'

'This time you go with my blessing, and you take my heart with you.' She stood on tiptoe to brush his lips with a kiss. 'Next time we are alone together will be different, but I am yours already.'

His eyes darkened. 'We'd best get back to young Tom before we do something we'll both regret.'

'I've only one blanket I can give you,' Effie said, putting a safe distance between them by going to the cupboard where she kept her small store of linen. 'And an old cushion for a pillow.'

'I think I'd best risk the snow and return to the pub. I'm not used to acting like a gentleman, and I don't trust myself to do the right thing twice in one night.'

Toby had left a gold sovereign to help eke out the family's dwindling supply of money and allow them to buy fuel and food to combat the bitter cold. Effie had watched him walk away into the night with feelings of regret and happiness in equal parts. She understood now why his past actions had disturbed and angered her, but to admit that she loved him was a strange new emotion and she kept her feelings to herself. Tom was too young to understand, or so she thought, and the only person in whom she could confide was Betty, but the bad weather made venturing out difficult and downright dangerous. In the days that followed, Effie hugged her secret to herself, revelling in the memory of passion reawakened. Despite the lack of money and seeming impossibility of finding work, she kept her spirits up with dreams of Toby's return and a spring wedding. She found plenty to keep her busy in the house, cleaning and black-leading the range while Georgie played with a wooden Noah's Ark, an old toy that had belonged to the Crooke children and had been given to him as a Christmas present. Tom went out daily, trudging through the snow in search of work but returning each evening tired, cold and hungry, and unsuccessful.

Each time she heard the muffled clip-clopping of horses' hooves, Effie ran into the front parlour to peer out of the window in the hope of seeing Toby's familiar figure, but the days passed with no sign of him. At first she blamed the weather, but as the snow melted and the roads cleared she could no longer make that an excuse. Her feelings of euphoria dissolved into anxiety and then doubts crept into her mind. Had he regretted his impulsive words? Had he been carried away by lust and then assuaged his guilt by telling her that he loved her? How many women had suffered the same way at his hands in the past? Betty had warned her and she was being proved right. Effie struggled alone with her sense of betrayal and grief. Once again she seemed to have loved and lost but the pain was still the same, and grew sharper with every passing day as her hopes of happiness faded into misty memories.

February brought rain and March was heralded by strong winds. Their money had all but run out when Agnes came to the door one blustery afternoon, bursting with good news. She had persuaded her employer to interview Tom for a job in the market garden where they had begun planting seeds under the cover of glass. He went off with a grin on his face. Watching from the window, Effie could not help feeling a little envious of their innocent young love as they walked along the street hand in hand. She had tried to put Toby from her thoughts, blackening his character in her mind in an attempt to ease the suffering he had caused her by his apparent desertion, but deep down she knew that there must be a good reason for his continued absence. Anything could have happened to him and there was no way of finding out.

Gripped by the sudden need to get out of

the house, she hurried into the kitchen and dressed Georgie in his jacket, which was already too small for him. He would need new clothes soon and unless she could find work he would have to go barefoot. She put on her bonnet and shawl and taking Georgie by the hand she went out into the street. The wind rampaged over the cobblestones, picking up bits of straw and scraps of paper and whirling them round in crazy eddies before depositing them in shop doorways, or winding them like rosettes around the wheels of costermongers' barrows. Men clutched at their hats and Georgie laughed out loud to see a portly man chasing his bowler as it bounced along the pavement.

Effie had no clear idea where she was going, but she stopped to read advertisements in shop windows and salvaged a newspaper that had been caught by the wind and was flapping around like a wounded seagull. She paused to study the positions vacant page, but there was, as she had feared, nothing suitable for a mother with a young child to care for. The domestic posts involved living in, and she did not possess the qualifications required to become a teacher or to work in an office. She spent the afternoon visiting the factories that bordered Limehouse Cut but the answer at the gatehouses was the same as before.

No vacancies. The line of shabbily dressed men queuing to hear the same words depressed her even more.

The sun was struggling out between cast-iron clouds and there was the scent of rain in the air. Against her better judgement, Effie decided to cross the bridge and visit Betty in the pub kitchen. She had seen her only once since Toby's departure, but on that occasion she had taken care not to mention his name, keeping the conversation to enquiries about the Crooke family and listening to Betty's grumbles about Mrs Hawkins, whose temperament did not mellow with age.

As Effie entered the stable yard she saw Ben walking towards her. He greeted her with a warm smile. 'You're quite a stranger these days.'

'I know. It's not from choice, Ben. I don't want to upset Mrs Hawkins.'

He frowned, shaking his head. 'I know, and I'm sorry too. How are you managing?'

'Tom has gone to see about a job in the market garden. I keep looking.' She glanced over his shoulder as Bart, the potman, rolled an empty barrel over the cobblestones.

'What shall I do with this 'un, master? It don't belong to the brewery so the drayman says. It's a stray that got here somehow and they don't want it.'

Effie stared at the barrel and an idea flashed

into her head, almost blinding her with its brilliance. 'Can I have it, Ben?'

He scratched his head, staring at her with a puzzled frown. 'What on earth would you do with an empty beer barrel?'

'Keep things in it. Store potatoes or use it as a stool. I could find a dozen uses, but only if you don't need it.'

'It's yours. We've got enough rubbish stacked up in the yard and I'd only get coppers for it as firewood.'

'Thank you, Ben. I'll send Tom round to collect it.'

'I'll drop it off. I'll be passing that way with the cart later today. I've put your old horse to good use. He pays his way does old Champion.'

'Gee-gee,' Georgie cried, pointing to the open stable door. 'Champing.'

'It's Champion, darling,' Effie said fondly. 'You're a clever boy to remember him.'

'He's a fine chap,' Ben said, lifting Georgie in his arms. 'I'll take him to see the horse while you go and have a natter with Betty. I expect that's why you came.'

'Of course,' Effie said, smiling. 'I want to catch up on all the gossip.'

'She'll tell you that villain Salter's been back. I'm just warning you to steer clear of him, Effie. He's a real nasty piece of work.'

Effie felt a cold chill run down her spine. 'He's nothing to do with me.'

'Maybe not, but he's still ranting on about the *Margaret*. He says you stole the old man's watch or something like that, although of course no one round here takes any notice of him.'

'It belongs to Georgie,' Effie said indignantly. 'The Salters encouraged Mr Grey to drink and to smoke opium because they wanted everything that was his. They were the ruin of the old man.'

'We all know that, but he's taken his spite out on our friend Toby Tapper.'

Fear stabbed Effie like a dagger in her heart. 'Toby?'

'Salter accused him of setting fire to the narrowboat. The police caught him on Marsh Road over a month ago. Toby was tried at the County Court and found guilty of arson. He was taken straight to the house of detention in Clerkenwell.'

Chapter Nineteen

'Are you all right, Effie?' Ben asked anxiously. 'You're white as a sheet.'

'No, I mean, yes. It was a shock. I didn't know.' Effie found herself gabbling incoherently. She had been thinking of every possibility that could have kept Toby from her, but this was the last thing she had expected.

'It was in the newspaper, but in such small print that I would have missed it myself if it hadn't been for the missis. She took pleasure in pointing it out to me. She never liked Toby.'

She doesn't like anyone apart from herself, Effie thought bitterly. It was typical of Ben's wife to spot the piece and gloat over the bad news.

'You're upset,' Ben said sympathetically. 'Go inside and Betty will make you a cup of tea. Tell her that I said she was to put a drop of brandy in it – purely medicinal, of course.'

'I–I'm fine, really,' Effie lied. 'But a cup of tea would go down nicely.'

He patted her on the shoulder. 'Of course it would. Go on in and I'll take young Georgie to visit Champion.' He walked off towards the stable bumping Georgie up and down on his shoulders and making him crow with laughter.

Moving like an automaton, Effie entered the kitchen.

'So you've heard the news then?' Betty rushed over to give her a hug. 'I've only just found out myself or I would have come straight round to tell you.'

'It's awful, Betty, and it's all a pack of lies. Mr Grey set fire to the barge, not Toby.'

'Sit down and I'll make us a pot of tea,' Betty said, pushing her gently towards a chair. 'A blind man could see that there was something going on between you and Toby. He's been sweet on you for years.'

'Was it so obvious? I didn't know.'

'As plain as the nose on your face, girl. But you was took up with your husband at the start and then that fairground fellah, whatever his name was.'

Effie frowned. 'You've changed your tune a bit. Last time I was here you were warning me not to have anything to do with Toby because he was a philanderer.'

'A person can be wrong.' Betty turned her back on Effie, busying herself by making the tea.

'There's something you're not telling me,'

Effie said anxiously. 'What is it, Betty? What more do you know?'

'Sal Salter was in the bar last night, three sheets to the wind as they say. She told anyone who would listen that Salter had stood up in court and said you was Toby's accomplice, and that you'd both planned to finish the old man off and burn the *Margaret* so that you could claim the insurance.'

Effie's hand flew to her mouth. 'That's a wicked lie.'

'Of course it is, but the magistrate couldn't know that.'

'There was no insurance,' Effie murmured dazedly. 'Mr Grey said it was a waste of good money. No one would have gained from destroying the *Margaret*.'

'They wouldn't know that either. Anyway, Sal was crowing because Toby took the blame for the whole thing.'

'But he didn't do anything wrong.'

'Oh, he denied it all, but only after he'd sworn on the Bible that you was innocent of any wrongdoing and that you did your best to save the old man. It seems that the beak believed that part but he sentenced Toby anyway.'

Effie leapt to her feet, pacing the room. 'Why didn't they call me as a witness? Why wasn't I told that Toby had been arrested?'

'I dunno, love. Just be thankful that you wasn't dragged through the courts. I take back everything I ever said about young Toby Tapper. He acted like a real gent, and it's a crying shame that he's gone down for something he didn't do.' Betty took the teapot to the table and poured two cups of tea, adding a generous amount of sugar to the one she pushed towards Effie. 'Sit down and drink this. You won't do no good by getting yourself in a state.'

'What shall I do, Betty? I can't let Toby go to jail for a crime he didn't commit. What if I go to the police and tell them it was Mr Grey who set the barge on fire?'

'They'd think you was lying to protect your man. I think they'd say it was an open and shut case.'

After a sleepless night, Effie left Georgie with Tom and made her way to the courthouse in Bow Road where a bespectacled clerk echoed Betty's words. 'It's an open and shut case, miss,' he said gravely. The words would be engraved on her heart, Effie thought, as she made her way slowly home.

Tom's eyes widened with shock when she told him that there was nothing they could do to help Toby. 'But there must be, Effie,' he protested. 'Can't he appeal against the sentence?'

425

Effie shook her head. 'That would take money. We can't afford to pay the rent next week let alone find the money for a solicitor.'

'I wish I had Salter here this minute,' Tom said, fisting his hands. 'I'd give him what for.'

'He said he'd get even with me and he has.' Effie sat down at the kitchen table, staring into the fire.

'I start work tomorrow,' Tom said stoutly. 'I won't bring home much but it will help.'

Effie flashed him a grateful smile. 'What would I do without you, Tom?'

He puffed out his chest but his reply was drowned by the sound of someone banging on the front door. 'I'll go,' he said, sprinting out into the narrow hallway with Georgie toddling after him.

Effie recognised Ben's deep voice and she rose unsteadily to her feet, but she heard the front door close almost immediately followed by the echoing rumble of the beer barrel being rolled over bare boards.

'What's this for?' Tom demanded as he pushed it into the room. 'What use is an empty keg?'

'I was going to brew beer and sell it outside the factories when the men knocked off work.' Effie sat down again, glaring at the barrel as if it were to blame for the bad news she had received in the stable yard.

'That's a cracking idea if ever I heard one.' Tom's face shone with enthusiasm. 'I've got the rest of the day free. Tell me what you need and I'll go out and get it.'

'Georgie needs new shoes. I've saved just enough to get him some from the dolly shop. I can't afford to buy the things I need to make beer.'

'Come on, Effie. Don't give up. What would Toby say if he was here?' Tom pulled her gently to her feet. 'You won't help him by sitting there doing nothing.'

'It's not just that. We need every penny we've got for food and we'll have to use your wages to pay the rent.'

Tom angled his head. 'There's always the gold watch. I could take it to the pop shop and pawn it. That would keep us until you've got your brew ready.'

'It's Georgie's inheritance,' Effie protested. 'I can't let it go just like that.'

'We'll get it back when you sell your first brew. There might even be enough left for the omnibus fare to Clerkenwell. You could go and visit Toby in jail.'

Effie looked down at Georgie who had returned to his toy and was marching the wooden animals into the ark, two by two. Tom's words had struck home and she felt a glimmer of hope. 'You're right,' she murmured. 'Stay here with Georgie while I go to the pawnbroker. He might think it odd if a boy of your age turned up with an expensive gold watch.' She forced her lips into a smile. 'I don't want to see you locked up in jail alongside Toby.'

Three weeks later on a bright sunny April afternoon the rainclouds had been chased away by a frisky breeze. Reflecting the colour of the sky, Limehouse Cut flowed through the city like a blue satin ribbon. With the sun warm on her back Effie trundled her wooden barrow through the streets to wait outside the factory gates. The cart was a new acquisition. Tom had found the wheels on the canal bank and had enlisted Harry Crooke's help in the construction of the contraption, which had to be strong enough to transport the heavy keg. Harry had been only too pleased to come round each day after work, and they had turned the back yard into a carpenter's workshop. Effie had kept them supplied with copious amounts of tea, and when the light faded making it too dark to continue Harry had come indoors to sit by the fire and chat. He was as enthusiastic about the prospect of home-brewed ale as Tom, and they were eager to sample the results of Effie's labours. She had turned the front parlour into a brewery and the whole house reeked of malt, yeast and hops.

The gold half-hunter watch had fetched a reasonable amount at the pawnbroker's but nothing like its real value. Effie had spent it wisely and had bought two more second-hand barrels and two dozen pint mugs which now dangled from hooks on the cart. She was nervous as she waited for the factory hooter to sound signalling the end of the shift. Would the men simply barge past her without stopping to refresh themselves with a pint of ale? Would they like her home brew or would they compare it unfavourably with the beer they could get in the pubs? She had feared that Ben might take exception to her selling beer in the street, but he had said it was unlikely to affect his trade since his customers were mainly bargees or people from the south side of the cut. He had given her another barrel and a dozen half-pint tin mugs that were only slightly dented.

Effie shifted from one foot to the other as the steam whistles hooted a cacophony of sound, followed by the clatter of hobnail boots on concrete and cobblestones. The gates of the chemical works shrieked on their hinges as the gatekeeper swung them open. Effie stood aside as a stream of grime-encrusted men trampled the ground like a herd of stampeding cattle.

'Slake your thirst, gents,' Effie shouted in an effort to make herself heard above the din. 'Home-brewed ale, a penny a pint. The best in Bow.'

Harry Crooke was the first to stop. 'I'll try a pint, young lady,' he said, taking off his cap with a flourish. He held his hand out and took a mug from Effie, sipping its contents with an exaggerated smacking of his lips. 'Excellent ale.'

Another man, equally dirty, stopped to give Effie a penny in exchange for a drink. Within minutes she was surrounded by eager customers holding out their money and clamouring for a pint. It was all she could do to wash and dry the mugs in an effort to keep up with demand, but the men did not seem to be too worried about cleanliness and they held out empty mugs they had taken from their mates, impatient to taste Effie's brew. By the time the crowd had dispersed, she had an empty five gallon barrel and forty pennies in her purse. Exhausted but exhilarated, she trundled the cart homeward with the coppers clinking together like sweet music to her ears. As she reached the corner of Devons Road and Bow Common Lane she saw Harry leaning against a lamppost. He fell into step beside her. 'You done well, Effie.'

'You started them off,' Effie said modestly.

'I think I owe you a free pint or two for helping Tom with the cart.'

He puffed out his chest and his saunter turned into a swagger. 'I'm your man, girl. Anything you want doing just send for Harry Crooke.'

'You've done enough already. I don't know what I would have done without the Crooke family.'

'I'd do a lot more for you, if you'd let me,' Harry said earnestly. 'What do you say to an evening out, Effie? How about a visit to a music hall and a dish of jellied eels or a fish supper? My treat, of course.'

Effie stopped, drawing the cart to a sudden halt that caused the mugs and glasses to clink together as if in a toast. 'I don't think that would be such a good idea, Harry.'

He stared at her blankly. 'Why not? You're a free woman and I'm an unattached man. What's to stop us getting together? I mean no disrespect, Effie. I can assure you that my intentions are strictly honourable.'

'Oh, Harry, I know they are. I didn't mean to insult you, it's just that there's someone else.'

'What? D'you mean to say you've been stringing me along?'

'Most certainly not. How dare you say such a thing?'

431

Harry's open countenance was suffused by a deep flush. His ears shone pink in the rays of the setting sun. 'You led me to believe that there was a chance for me, Effie. All that tea and sweet smiles and you was just leading me on.'

'I was not. It was you who got the wrong end of the stick. I was just being myself.'

'And it's you I care for,' Harry muttered, staring down at his boots. 'You must have realised that I had feelings for you. I thought women knew that sort of thing.'

'I thought you were just being kind. I know you like Tom and I thought you were his friend as well as mine. I'm sorry, I really am.'

'There's plenty of girls who would give their eye teeth for an evening out with a chap like me.'

'Of course there are, Harry. You're a splendid fellow and I'm very fond of you.'

'Not fond enough, it seems. I still think you was leading me on, and I thought better of you, Effie Grey.' With a dispirited hunch of his shoulders, Harry turned on his heel and strode off towards Phoebe Street leaving Effie staring after him.

Suddenly the pennies in her purse did not seem quite so important, and as the sun plummeted below the city skyline Effie pushed her barrow homeward. She should have seen this

432

situation coming and put a stop to it from the outset but she had been too busy with her brewing and her thoughts had been elsewhere. Not an hour passed when she did not think of Toby incarcerated in the house of detention, awaiting removal to a prison where he would work out the rest of his sentence. She had planned all along to spend some of her earnings on an omnibus trip to Clerkenwell in the hope of being allowed to see him; now she had the money and tomorrow was going to be the day. She quickened her pace with renewed energy and hope in her heart.

A week later, Effie stood outside the forbidding walls of Clerkenwell prison with Georgie in her arms. She had saved up her money for the omnibus journey from Bow and it had taken the best part of the morning. Georgie had been excited at first as if they were on a pleasure trip, but after the second change of vehicle, which had involved waiting in the pouring rain, he had become subdued and had fallen asleep in his mother's arms during the final leg of their journey. A watery sun illuminated the grey stones of the prison walls but did little to cheer the dismal scene. Effie experienced a feeling of dread as she approached the gatekeeper's lodge. She tugged at the bell pull and the sound reverberated around an inner courtyard. A face appeared at the grille. 'Yes?'

'I want to see my husband,' Effie said, hitching Georgie a little higher on her shoulder so that the turnkey could see him better. 'I'm Mrs Tapper and my husband is Toby Tapper.' It was a desperate lie but she had banked on the fact that a young wife might be allowed visiting privileges whereas a mere friend would be turned away.

'It ain't visiting time.'

'When is it allowed?'

'That depends.'

Effie slipped her hand in her pocket and produced a silver sixpence. The man shook his head. 'Don't take bribes, missis.'

Effie replaced the sixpence with a shilling. 'That's all I got, mister. I'm a poor woman left to fend for herself by an unjust sentence.'

'They all says that.'

'Please, mister. Have pity on a poor woman and her child. My boy hasn't seen his pa for weeks.'

'He's lucky if he knows who his dad is,' the turnkey muttered, snatching the coin from her hand.

The door opened and Effie entered the grim building. The walls seemed to shriek despair as she followed the turnkey across the forecourt, passing beneath a high arch into a deserted inner yard. Pale faces stared down from narrow windows and it seemed to Effie that the place housed ghosts of men rather than flesh and blood mortals. They entered a sullen-looking building that stank of human excrement and filth. Rats scurried along the walls, glaring at them with diamond-chip eyes. Hands reached out through iron bars and voices pleaded for help. Georgie began to whimper and hid his head against Effie's shoulder as they passed deeper into the building, each long corridor more horrendous than the last.

The turnkey stopped, produced a bunch of iron keys and unlocked a door. 'Five minutes only,' he said, stepping aside.

The cell was small and only dimly lit by a barred window set high up in the wall. She hardly recognised the unshaven, tousled-haired man who leapt to his feet, staring at her as if he had seen a ghost. 'Effie, my love. Is it really you?'

'Toby.' Her voice broke on a sob.

'Toby,' Georgie repeated, holding out his arms.

His unquestioning acceptance of Toby's dishevelled state seemed to break the tension. Smiling, Toby ruffled Georgie's hair. 'I've missed you, little fellow.'

Effie set her son gently down on the only

chair in the cell. 'This is a dreadful place. I can't bear to see you here, Toby.' She would have walked into his arms, but he laid his hands on her shoulders, holding her away from him with a rueful grimace.

'Don't get too near me, darling. I'm alive with fleas and lice, and I must smell like the Thames mud at low water.'

His wry expression brought a reluctant smile to Effie's lips although her eyes were moist with tears. 'I don't care. I'm just glad to see you. It was worth a shilling,' she added in an attempt at levity. She could see that Toby was battling with his emotions and she could not bear to see him in such a weakened state.

He brushed his hand across his eyes, making an obvious effort to appear calm. 'The old devil took money from you?'

'I expect he does it to everyone. I said I was your wife.'

'You are the wife of my heart, Effie,' he said softly. 'But you are young and you are free. I'm going to be in prison for a long time and you must make a life for yourself and Georgie without me.'

'Never,' Effie cried passionately. 'Don't talk like that. What has this place done to you to make you give up so easily?'

'Salter was convincing. The judge believed him and there was nothing I could say to change his mind. If Mr Grey had lived it would have been a different matter, but there was no one to speak up for me. My gypsy blood alone makes me guilty in the eyes of some people.'

'That is so unfair. I won't let you be punished for something you didn't do.'

'Listen to me, my love. There is nothing you can do that will get me out of this place. Your word alone won't carry any weight and you are the only living witness to what happened that day.'

'I'll get a brief, Toby. A good solicitor will put in an appeal and get you off. The law must be on the side of an innocent man.'

'I wish I could believe that, but more important to me now is how you are faring. How have you managed these last few weeks?'

'Time's up.' The turnkey threw the door open and stood with his arms folded across his chest. 'You've had your bob's worth, lady. Now take yourself off.'

Effie stood on tiptoe to kiss Toby on the lips. 'I will get you out of here, Toby. Don't give up hope.'

The turnkey took a menacing step towards them. 'Do I have to throw you and the brat out, lady?'

Effie snatched Georgie up in her arms and backed out of the cell. 'Trust me,' she called as the cell door slammed, the sound echoing off the stone walls like the tolling of a death knell. She followed the turnkey in a daze. The place where Toby was incarcerated was far worse than she could have imagined. She felt as though her heart had been torn from her breast and locked in the cell with him.

'I don't see a wedding band,' the turnkey said conversationally as he led her across the courtyard. 'Jumped over the broomstick, did you? Ain't that what you didicoi people do?'

His sarcastic words and curled lip brought her back to the present with a jolt. 'No such thing,' she retorted angrily. 'I had to pawn my wedding ring to pay a bloodsucker like you.'

He unlocked the outer door. 'Don't bother coming back, lady. Your man won't be here long. He'll be sent to Millbank soon, or somewhere worse.'

Effie marched past him without dignifying his cruel jibe with an answer. Outside the prison she took a deep breath. The stench of the city streets was like fresh country air compared with the stink of despair and corruption within the prison walls.

'I don't know what to do,' Effie said, shaking her head.

'Have another cup of tea, ducks,' Betty suggested, casting an anxious glance at Ben who was hovering beside Effie with a concerned look on his face.

'Or maybe a drop of brandy,' he suggested lamely.

'You're both very kind, and I shouldn't have come here to bother you with my troubles.' Effie rose from the chair by the kitchen table but was pushed gently back onto her seat by Betty.

'Of course you should, love. We're your friends and we'd do anything to help, wouldn't we, Ben?'

He nodded his head emphatically. 'Yes, you know we would, Effie. But I think you've got to accept the fact that young Toby won't get out of jail before his sentence is up. Are you prepared to wait for him?'

'Forever and a day.' Effie looked up into his good-natured face with an attempt at a smile. 'You've been a true friend, Ben.'

His cheeks flushed a dull brick red and he cleared his throat. 'You've had a rough time of it, Effie. I wish I could do more.'

'And so do I,' Betty said, refilling Effie's cup with tea. 'If there's anything I can do, anything at all, just say the word. The whole Crooke family are behind you, love.'

'I think I've upset Harry, and it was the last thing I meant to do.'

Betty pulled a face. 'He's just a boy at heart.

He'll get over it and be soft on another pretty face before you can say Jack Robinson.'

Effie sipped her tea and as if by some divine intervention an idea came to her in a flash. 'Would you look after Georgie for a day or two, Betty?'

'Yes, of course I would. The girls love him and he's a good little chap. But what are you going to do?'

'Yes, what's going on in that pretty head?' Ben demanded. 'You're not planning anything silly, are you?'

'No, not at all. I wonder I didn't think of it in the first instance. I'm going to Marsh House to put Toby's case to his father.'

'His father?' Ben exclaimed, frowning. 'That's a new one on me.'

'He never mentioned his pa,' Betty added, her eyes gleaming at the prospect of a tasty morsel of gossip. 'Who is he?'

'That's what I'm going to find out once and for all,' Effie said, helping Georgie onto her lap as he clamoured for her attention. 'Will you be a good boy and stay with Betty and the girls for a little while, darling? Mama has to go away for a day or two but I promise I'll come back very soon.'

Georgie wrapped a lock of her hair around his small fist and grinned up at her. 'Betty,' he said happily. 'Aggie and Bella.'

'That's settled then.' Effie dropped a kiss on his curly head. 'All I need now is a horse. Could I borrow Champion tomorrow, Ben?'

March House shimmered in the sunshine after a heavy shower. Raindrops hung like jewels from the brambles and the branches of the trees that were just bursting into leaf. Steam rose from Effie's damp skirts and Champion's wet pelt, and the marsh and damp hedgerows smelt like Christmas pudding. Effie had the strangest feeling of coming home, an emotion that she pushed to the back of her mind. She was on a mission that had everything to do with Toby and related to herself only in the fact that she needed him and wanted him by her side.

Champion seemed to know his way and he ambled into the stable yard, whinnying when he spotted Jeffries standing by the pump.

'Good Lord, missis. What brings you here? I thought you'd gone back to the city.'

Effie slid from the saddle, handing him the reins. 'I came to see the master. Do you know where I might find him?'

'He'll be in the walled garden, I daresay. That's where he spends most of his days now that the spring sowing is finished.'

Effie stared at him in surprise. 'Mr Westlake has turned farmer?'

'Aye, that's about the nub of it, missis. You started him off, it seems, and he's trying to set the old place to rights.'

'I'm glad to hear it, but perhaps I'd better see Nellie first.'

'You'll find the old besom in the kitchen. *She* don't change.'

Jeffries led Champion into the stables, leaving Effie alone in the yard. She found it hard to believe that Seymour Westlake would be getting his hands dirty, and she wondered if the old groom's mind had begun to wander. She made her way to the kitchen to seek confirmation from Nellie.

'Why, just look what the cat's dragged in,' Nellie exclaimed with a wide smile that belied her sarcastic words. 'Where's the little lamb? Where's my boy?' She craned her neck as if expecting to see Georgie following his mother into the room.

'Georgie is being well cared for by friends.'

Nellie's mouth drooped and the light went out of her eyes. 'Why didn't you bring him with you? He'll forget old Nellie if you keep him from me.'

'Next time I come I promise I'll bring him with me, but this is an emergency. I've come to speak urgently with the master. Jeffries tells me that he's been working the farm.'

'What's up?' Nellie demanded. 'You can tell me.'

A wave of tiredness washed over Effie and she sat down at the table with a sigh. She had left Bow at daybreak and had not stopped to eat or drink. She was saddle-sore and weary. 'It's a long story.'

Nellie went to the range and picked up the kettle. 'A cup of tea is what you need, and something to fill your belly. You're as thin as a rake, Effie. You haven't been looking after yourself properly.'

Tired as she was, Effie realised that she would have to tell Nellie everything before she was allowed out of the kitchen, and she resigned herself to drinking copious cups of tea and forcing down generous slices of seed cake. It was a good half an hour before she escaped from Nellie's barrage of questions and made her way to the walled garden. The sun was brilliant now, shining from a sky which was the colour of a robin's egg. The scent of freshly dug earth and warm grass enveloped her as she entered the walled garden.

She saw Seymour digging a patch at the far end. His shirt sleeves were rolled up to the elbows and his flowing robes had been discarded for more conventional breeches and boots. His hair had been cut short and it rioted around his head in dark glossy curls. He was so absorbed in his work that he did not appear to have heard her soft footsteps on the wet grass. 'Mr Westlake? It's me, Effie.'

He turned his head and his similarity to Toby struck her forcibly. He had abandoned his exotic apparel and was dressed in ordinary garments, which made the likeness more startling, even allowing for the terrible pockmarks that marred his otherwise handsome countenance. Seen in this light there could be no denying Toby's paternity. She approached him cautiously, with memories of his former mental state uppermost in her mind. 'Mr Westlake, I must talk to you urgently.'

He stuck his spade into the ground, straightening up and wiping the sweat from his brow with the back of his hand. 'Effie. This is an unexpected pleasure.'

'I'll come straight to the point, sir. It's Toby. He's been sent to prison for a crime he didn't commit.'

Seymour eyed her warily. 'I'm sorry to hear that, but what has it got to do with me.'

'Everything, sir. Please don't play games with me. I know that Toby is your son; it would be obvious to anyone with half an eye. I'm begging you to help him.'

'What is he supposed to have done?'

She took a deep breath and once again went through the whole sorry tale. Seymour listened with an impassive look on his face. 'Well now,' he said slowly when she came to the end of her narrative. 'It does sound as though the boy has been unfairly condemned, but I don't see what I can do about it.'

'Will you stand by and do nothing while your own flesh and blood rots in that dreadful place? I believe he is going to be transferred to Millbank which is even worse than the house of detention, and that is terrible. I've seen it with my own eyes.'

'You are in love with him.' It was a statement rather than a question. Seymour's gaze never wavered from her face.

Effie swallowed hard to prevent herself from bursting into tears. 'Yes, I love him. He's a good man.'

'Then it's unlikely that I'm his father,' Seymour said with a harsh laugh. 'I can't help you, my dear. I have squandered my fortune and, as you see, I am reduced to working the soil like a common labourer.'

His attitude infuriated Effie. 'There's nothing wrong with honest work. I brew ale and sell it from a cart outside the factories in the East End. That's how I support myself and my son. My young brother works long hours for very little pay in a market garden and you live in this beautiful house with all this land that belongs to you.' She encompassed the estate with a wide sweep of her arms. 'And you expect me to feel sorry for you?'

Seymour picked up his spade. 'I expect nothing. Go away and leave me alone.'

'But he's your son,' Effie cried in desperation. 'I would give my life for my child. Why do you keep up this pretence?'

'Every time I looked at the boy I saw a likeness to his mother; he had lived and she had died. I had lost the love of my life and yet I survived, a worthless soul, scarred on the inside as well as outwardly. I had no love left to give to my son, nor for myself. Now leave me. I have nothing further to say.'

'You've said enough,' Effie said gently. 'You've admitted that you are Toby's father. I will go, but I leave the rest to your conscience. Toby might die in that dreadful place and then you will have lost your last link with Mirella. I can understand your love for her because that is what I feel for Toby. I am truly sorry for you, sir.'

She did not wait for a response – turning on her heel, she walked slowly from the walled garden, closing the gate behind her. She did not return immediately to the kitchen, but made her way to the orchard where the first signs of tight pink-tipped blossoms were budding on the apple trees. Standing by Jacob's grave, she bowed her head. 'If only you could speak, Pa-in-law,' she murmured. 'You alone know the truth about the fire on board the *Margaret*.' She closed her eyes, listening to the spring chorus of birdsong and the rustling of the breeze in the branches above her head. Was it her imagination, or did she hear a whispered answer to her question? It seemed to repeat over and over again, 'Salter knows, Salter knows.'

The words were so clear that she opened her eyes with a start, looking about her to see if there was someone hiding behind the gnarled trunks of the trees, but she was totally alone. She walked slowly back towards the house. Of course Salter knew, as did his hateful wife, but the chances of their admitting perjury before a magistrate were so slim as to be negligible. On the other hand, Seymour had refused to help and she was desperate. Salter would have his price. All she had to do was to discover what he wanted in return for an admission in court that he had been mistaken. It seemed no less impossible than persuading Toby's father to do the right thing by his son. Her heart felt like a lead weight inside her chest. She had come with high hopes, but Seymour's point-blank refusal had brought them crashing down around her head. What sort of man would allow his only son to rot in jail?

Chapter Twenty

Effie stayed long enough to share Nellie's midday meal of soup and bread, and she rode back to Bow late in the afternoon. She delivered the tired horse back to Ben's stable, but she had not the heart to call in at the kitchen and tell Betty her depressing news. She arrived home just in time to relieve Tom of the chore of pushing the barrow through the streets to stand outside the Imperial Tar Works, where as usual she sold every last drop of the ale. She was exhausted both mentally and physically, but too numbed to feel her aching limbs and weary bones.

Having collected Georgie from Phoebe Street, Effie gave him a ride home perched on top of the empty barrel, and on the way she bought fish and chips for their supper. Tom had built up the fire in the range and in between mouthfuls of food Effie told him of Mr Westlake's refusal to help.

'What will you do?' Tom asked, taking a chip and feeding it to Georgie. 'We haven't got anything that would tempt Salter to admit that he was lying. Don't forget that he tried to drag you into it. He's a stink-pot, Effie.'

'I don't know what we've done to make him hate us,' Effie said sadly. 'But maybe Sal has a better side to her nature if only I could dig deep enough to find it.'

'She can't testify against her old man. I heard that somewhere and I think it's true.'

'Then I must find some other way, but I'm not giving up and I won't rest until Toby is a free man.' Effie pushed her plate away, her appetite gone. 'You can finish this if you want. I'm going to get another brew going. Money talks and if all else fails I might be able to bribe Salter to tell the truth.'

Effie worked ceaselessly. She became a familiar sight pushing her barrow through the streets in all weathers. No matter how tired she was or if she was soaked to the skin by the pouring rain, she waited outside the factory gates for the flood of thirsty men eager to sup a pint or two of ale. She saved every penny she could spare after taking out their day to day living expenses, and at the end of the first month she redeemed the gold watch from the pawn-broker. She had intended to hide it in the house, but with the theft of her money still fresh in her mind, she decided it was too valuable an item to be kept at home. She took it to the bank and deposited it to be kept in a strong box until Georgie was twenty-one and old enough to claim his inheritance. She stowed the remainder of her profits in a leather pouch and hid it beneath a loose floorboard in her bedroom.

In the evenings when Georgie was tucked up in bed and Tom had gone out walking with Agnes, Effie sat down to write long letters to Toby. She posted them in the hope of receiving a reply but none came. She had no way of knowing whether he received the correspondence, but she comforted herself with the hope that he had, and that her words made his life a little easier. She was painfully aware that loss of freedom to a man who valued it so highly must be a constant torture. He would be like a wild linnet trapped and kept in a cage through no fault of its own. She longed to see him and to feel his arms around her. There was so much left unsaid between them, and there was the unfinished business between father and son that must be rectified if either of them were to live in peace.

Effie had received only a basic education in the workhouse, but she poured her heart and soul into her writing. If her spelling was a little erratic and her grammar less than perfect, she made up for her lack of literary expertise with words that expressed her hopes, her desires and above all the love for Toby that had grown slowly but surely like a tender green plant in springtime.

Even allowing for the gaping hole in her heart, Effie found some consolation in work and the friendship of the Crooke family. There was always a stream of visitors to the small house in Albert Place. Betty called in when she could snatch a free moment from working at the pub or caring for her large family, and she was always ready to lend a sympathetic ear. Ben visited as often as he dared without incurring the wrath of his wife, and he kept Effie supplied with oak barrels that had reached the end of their usefulness to the brewery. Whereas another publican might have resented Effie's success in selling ale, Ben actively encouraged her, and he was always on hand to offer advice when needed.

The lure of a good pint of beer might have had something to do with Effie's popularity with the male Crookes who came regularly to spend an evening by her fireside, and the girls were always eager to look after Georgie when she went out on her rounds. With her small son well cared for, Effie had taken to going out at midday as well as in the evenings, and that meant more beer had to be brewed. The front room was packed with barrels of beer in all stages of fermentation, and the copper in the washhouse was constantly heating water in order to mash the malted barley. Effie had become adept at brewing and could have gone through the process in her sleep. She had grown accustomed to the smell of malt, yeast and hops that permeated the house and clung to her hair and clothes. She taught Tom the rudiments of the craft, but although he did his best to help her it was obvious to Effie that his real interests lay elsewhere. He toiled for long hours in the market garden and seemed to thrive on hard labour and the outdoor life. Effie was unsure whether his commitment to his job was due to the fact that he worked alongside Agnes each day, or whether the call of the land had stirred in his blood when he had helped Jeffries resurrect the vegetable garden during their time at Marsh House. Whatever the source of his newfound enthusiasm she was happy to see him growing into a strong and healthy young man with a purpose in life and the ambition to do well. He might be her brother, but she felt more like a mother to him, and it was a mother's heart that swelled with love and pride to see the childish attachment between Tom and Agnes gradually maturing into something that might one day blossom into a lasting relationship. That, of course, was a long way off but Effie was determined to give her small family all the love and security that had been denied to them in the past, and a future free from poverty and the terrifying shadow of the workhouse.

The harsh winter had melted into a capricious spring, and with the passing of May summer arrived at long last. Effie had finished her chores for the day. She had taken three shillings and fourpence that morning and another three and four during her evening round of the factories. There was enough money in the rusty toffee tin to pay the rent and keep them in food, candles and coal for the next week at least, and her savings in the leather pouch were growing by the day, although, being realistic, Effie knew that it would take many months and possibly years to save enough to pay the fees of a good solicitor. She had stowed the coins in her secret cache beneath the floorboards and she was enjoying a cup of tea while Georgie played outside in the yard. She was standing by the window, watching him as he chased the red rubber ball she had bought from a market stall, when Tom arrived home bursting with the news that the fair had arrived on Bow Common. His eyes shone with excitement as he described the stalls and attractions like the merry-go-round and the swingboats. Effie was amused by his enthusiasm but she was suddenly nervous. She had put the past firmly behind her and that included Frank. The thought of seeing him again was unsettling.

Tom gobbled his supper, earning a stern rebuke from Effie. He washed the bread and cheese down with a draught of small beer, wiping his mouth on the back of his hand. 'I'm going to call for Agnes and take her to the fair. Why don't you come, Effie? You could do with a night out.'

'And who will look after my boy?' she demanded, reaching over to wipe dribbles of milk from Georgie's chin. He could feed himself now, but the result was usually messy.

'Bring him too,' Tom said, rising from the table. 'Don't be a misery. You won't help Toby by turning into a nun.' He strolled over to the mantelshelf and studied his reflection in the fly-blown mirror.

Effie said nothing as she watched Tom preening himself like a young peacock, attempting to smooth his unruly hair into submission with his hands, and scowling at his reflection when the curls bounced back like watch springs. She was hurt by his thoughtless words but she knew that they were not meant unkindly. He abandoned his attempts to tame his locks and snatched up the jacket that he had thrown carelessly over the back of his chair. 'I won't be late back,' he said, heading for the door. 'I can't wait to see all those folks you told me about and I bet they'd like to see you again too. You will come, won't you, Effie? Say you will.'

His persistence made her smile. 'I'll think about it. Go on and have a good time with Agnes.'

He grinned and blew her a kiss. 'I'll see you there. No excuses, Effie. Toby wouldn't want to think of you pining away and working yourself to the bone.'

After he had gone and the dishes were washed and stacked away in the cupboard, Effie put Georgie to bed. She sat down at the table with a sheet of paper in front of her and a pen clasped between her fingers, but she could hear strains of music from the fairground filtering through the open window. She could smell hot toffee and potatoes roasted over glowing embers in a brazier. The scent of woodsmoke from camp fires was in the air, and Effie felt the indefinable hint of excitement that seemed to travel with the fair, luring punters in to spend their hard-earned money. The summer evening was balmy and Effie was restless. She could think of nothing to write, and although her feelings for Toby were unchanged she was suddenly desperate for company. She went upstairs to her bedroom where Georgie slept like a rosy-cheeked angel.

She covered him with a thin blanket and dropped a kiss on his tumbled curls. Closing the door softly behind her, she went downstairs and out into the street.

Her neighbour, a hard-working widow who took in washing in order to raise her six children, was standing on the doorstep chatting to a friend. She glanced at Effie with a nod and a smile. 'Evening, Effie. Got any ale to spare?'

'I hear as how you're doing the brewery out of business,' the other woman said with a toothless grin.

Effie shrugged her shoulders and smiled. 'Not quite, but I might be able to spare a pint or two if your eldest could keep an eye on my boy for an hour, Mary.'

'I'll send her round right away. She's just put the youngest to bed and I'm sure she'll be happy to oblige.'

Effie went back into the house, filled a quart jug with ale and locked the front parlour door just in case any of the Smith brood decided to help themselves. Minutes later, when young Dotty Smith was settled in the kitchen with a slice of cake and a glass of lemonade, Effie put on her bonnet and shawl and set off for the fairground.

It was all so familiar and yet it seemed strange to be back amongst the people who had taken her in just a year ago. In some ways it was as if she had never left, and yet she felt like a total stranger. There were some new faces behind the stalls and there were others that she recognised instantly: Myrtle with her tray of glistening toffee apples, Johann, the knife-thrower and husband of Margery the midget, and Dr Destiny who had already set up his stall and was proclaiming the benefits of his new miracle cure to a fascinated audience. Effie made her way to the fairings stall and was greeted by a loud bellow from Leah, who abandoned her post to give Effie a hug that very nearly winded her.

'Where did you spring from, Effie?' Leah boomed. 'More to the point, why did you leave us in the first place?' She turned round to beckon to Zilla, who was about to enter the tent marked in bold print SEE THE BEARDED LADY, one penny. 'Come here, old girl. Look who it is.'

Zilla ambled over to them and kissed Effie on both cheeks. Her beard scratched Effie's skin but she was too pleased to see her old friends to complain. 'It's good to see you both again.'

'It was all that fellah's fault, wasn't it?' Zilla said, shaking her fist in the general direction of the roundabout. 'Frank junior has a lot to answer for.'

'He's a bloke,' Leah said darkly. 'They're all the same.' She peered at Effie as if attempting to read her thoughts. 'You look pale and thin. You ain't sick, are you?'

Effie shook her head. 'I'm well, thank you, and very pleased to see you two.'

'That don't explain why you took off like a scared rabbit,' Leah said.

'I didn't mean to leave in such a hurry. It was a misunderstanding between Frank and me.'

'And the gypsy horse trader,' Zilla said shrewdly. 'I think he had a lot to do with it too.'

'It's a long story, but I'm doing well now. I brew beer and sell it from a barrow.'

Zilla's eyes widened in surprise. 'Well I never did.'

'So where is Toby Tapper, then?' Leah demanded. 'And where's our little angel? Where is Georgie?'

'He's asleep at home. I've rented a house just over there.' Effie pointed in the vague direction of Albert Place. 'As to Toby, well that again is a long story.'

Before either Leah or Zilla could pursue the matter further, Frank Tinsley senior strode over to them. 'Ain't you supposed to be in your tent, Zilla? You won't collect no pennies standing out here gossiping.

Nor you, Leah. You've got a customer waiting to buy something from your stall.' He turned to Effie and his forehead knotted into a frown. 'So you've turned up again, have you? Keep away from my boy, that's all I have to say to you, Effie Grey. He's married now and got a nipper on the way. He don't need you unsettling him.'

'Hold on, Frank,' Leah said gruffly. 'That ain't fair. Effie's got as much right to visit the fair as anyone.'

'I don't say she ain't, but I've said me piece and I meant it. Now get back to work or you'll find your stall given over to someone who is willing to put in the time.' With a last threatening glance at Effie, Frank senior strode off towards the show tent.

'I'm sorry,' Effie said, biting her lip. 'I didn't mean to get you into trouble.'

Zilla tugged nervously at her beard. 'I'd best get back to work.'

'Pay him no mind,' Leah muttered. 'He's a bully and his son is no better. If I want to chat to Effie then I'm bloody well going to chat to Effie.'

'I tell you what,' Effie said hastily. 'My house is number three Albert Place. If you can get away tomorrow morning we can have a cup of tea and a natter. I'll tell you everything then.'

Zilla backed towards her tent, keeping a wary eye on Frank. 'That will be lovely.'

'We'll see you tomorrow then.' Leah turned to the customer who was examining a pair of china dogs. 'Can I help you, ducks?'

Effie left them, her feelings bruised by Frank senior's harsh words. She had no intention of seeking out his son, nor did she want to see him. Whatever feelings she might have harboured for him in the past were dead and gone and she decided to head for home. She caught sight of Tom and Agnes in one of the swingboats and it was obvious that they were having a marvellous time. That was just as it should be, she thought wistfully as she threaded her way through the eager crowds that had descended upon Bow Common. She dodged behind a booth in order to avoid Ethel and Elmo who were hurrying on their way to the show tent, the spangles on their costumes glinting in the light from the naphtha flares which were bursting into life as the sun went down. Effie would have liked to stop and talk to Ethel, but she did not want to cause any further trouble with the fairground boss. She hurried round the corner of the booth and walked slap into Frank junior. For a moment they stared at each other in total silence. Effie was the first to recover and she attempted to sidestep him. 'I'm sorry, I didn't mean to . . .'

He caught her by the arm. 'Effie, for God's sake don't run away again.'

She raised her eyes to meet his anguished gaze and her heart missed a beat. This was the man she had thought she loved, and yet he looked different somehow. There were deep furrows on his forehead and lines from his nose to his mouth that she had not noticed before. 'Let me go, Frank. I shouldn't have come.'

'But you are here now. Please don't go until I've had a chance to put things right with you.'

'How can you do that, Frank? You're married and that's an end to it.'

His fingers tightened around her arm and his eyes were hard as agates. 'I told you at the start that my marriage was arranged long before I met you. It was a matter of honour.'

'I understand. Now please let me go.'

'You don't understand at all. I've thought about you every minute of every day since you took off with that didicoi horse trader. Did he marry you? Or did he abandon you after he'd had his way with you?'

Effie wrenched her arm free. Her fingers itched to slap his face, but she controlled the urge with difficulty. 'It wasn't like that.'

'I'm sorry. I don't know what I'm saying. I still love you, Effie.'

She shook her head. 'You wouldn't have let

me go if you had truly loved me, Frank. I did care for you, very much, but that was a long time ago.'

'It seems like a lifetime, but I haven't changed.'

'It's all over between us, and I hear that you're going to be a father. You've got responsibilities now, and a wife who needs you.' Effie started to walk away but Frank followed her.

'I can't let you go like this. You must give me a chance to explain properly.'

'No, Frank. There's nothing you can say that will make any difference. Go back to your wife and leave me alone.' Squaring her shoulders, Effie hurried off without a backwards glance. Meeting Frank again had disturbed her and brought back memories of their brief romance, but the old feelings were like shadows now; shades of a past that was dead and gone. For good or ill, her future was with Toby. If she had had any doubts before, they had vanished forever. She quickened her pace as she walked past the beer tent. The smell of ale was so familiar that she barely noticed it, and judging by the pitch of the men's voices they had imbibed freely. A man lurched out, staggering and swaying on his feet, almost knocking her down as he barged into her. She leapt out of his way, but he turned on her with a ferocious snarl. 'It's you, you little trull.

I might have known that you'd turn up sooner or later.'

'Salter,' Effie gasped. 'Get out of my way.'

'Hoity-toity as ever.' He grabbed her by the shoulders, shaking her until her teeth rattled. 'I've been waiting for a chance to get me hands on you, lady.'

Terrified but with anger overriding fear, Effie pushed him away. 'Don't touch me, you brute. You're the reason that Toby is in jail. You're a liar, Salter, and a villain.'

'And you're a little whore, ready to drop your drawers for any man willing to pay the price.'

'You are disgusting, and it's you who should be in prison, not Toby.'

'I didn't kill the old man. He died of drink and drugs and he set fire to the barge so that I wouldn't get what he'd promised me. He signed the vessel over to me and then he set it afire. I've lost my living because of that old fool.'

'I heard that.' Frank had appeared as if from nowhere and he stepped forward, placing himself bodily between Effie and Salter. 'And my mate Jed heard it too.' He jerked his head in the direction of the blacksmith, who stood behind him with his muscular arms folded across his broad chest. Frank glanced anxiously at Effie. 'Are you all right, love? Did he hurt you?'

Effie realised that she was trembling from head to foot, but she was unharmed and she could not believe her luck. Salter had just admitted everything in front of witnesses. 'I'm not hurt, Frank. But you heard what he said.'

'I did indeed,' he said angrily. 'And I know Salter of old. He worked for us once as a labourer and caused no end of trouble. My old man had to sack him, but there were several unexplained fires after that. We never proved it but we all knew who had started them.'

'That's a slanderous lie,' Salter growled. 'I'll get you for that, Frank Tinsley.'

'I'll see you in jail first,' Frank retorted. 'Now clear off, or d'you want Jed to help you on your way?'

The blacksmith rolled up his sleeves, exposing muscular arms covered in tattoos and fists like York hams. 'Let me have him, Frank.'

Salter backed away, his eyes showing the whites like a rabid dog's. 'Touch me and I'll have the law on you.'

'Yes, fetch a constable if you dare,' Frank taunted. 'It seems you've condemned your-self out of your own mouth. I'll stand witness against you any time, Salter.'

Uttering a stream of epithets, Salter shambled off.

Effie cast an anxious glance at Frank, and then at Jed. 'You both heard what he said?'

'I'd like to mash him to pulp.' Jed flexed his fingers. 'Shall I go after him and give him what for, Frank?'

'No, save it for later. We'll let him sweat for a bit.'

'I'll get back to my stand then,' Jed said, tipping his cap to Effie. 'If you ever need a job, I could do with an assistant when I pulls teeth. None of the girls here has the stomach for it since Ethel left me for Arnoldo.'

'Thanks, I'll think about it.' Effie managed a smile although inwardly she was still quaking after her brush with Salter. She waited until Jed was out of earshot before tackling Frank. She laid a tentative hand on his sleeve. 'You did hear everything, didn't you, Frank?'

'I did.'

She breathed a sigh of relief. A ton weight seemed to have been lifted from her shoulders. 'Oh, Frank, you don't know what that means to me. It may not have made much sense, but if you repeat what you heard in court it ought to be enough to clear Toby of all charges. I just need to find the money to hire a good brief and Toby will be a free man.'

Frank's expression hardened. 'So that's it.'

'I'm just asking you to help an innocent man.'

'You're in love with the didicoi.'

'Yes, it's true, and I'm not ashamed to admit it, Frank.'

He curled his lip. 'You felt the same way about me not so long ago.'

'I thought I was in love with you, but looking back I think it was just gratitude I felt.'

'You can't write off what we had so easily, Effie. Deep down I think you still have feelings for me. You're just put out because I married Moll, but it was a business arrangement. Can't you see that?'

Effie backed away from him. 'Things have changed. Everything is different now. All I'm asking is for you to repeat what you just heard in court.'

'I've got work to do. We'll talk about it tomorrow.'

'You will do it though, won't you, Frank?'

'I said we'll talk about it tomorrow. Tell me where you live and I'll be there as soon as I can.'

The glint in his eyes and the hard line of his lips spoke volumes and Effie felt a shiver run down her spine. This was not the Frank she had thought she knew and loved. The man who eyed her so coolly was a stranger, but he and Jed were her only hope. 'I'll come to you,' she said warily. 'Tomorrow just before midday when things are quiet, I'll meet you behind the show tent.' She turned on her heel and walked away before he could pursue the matter further.

Effie had barely finished her chores when a loud banging on the doorknocker announced the arrival of Leah and Zilla. They breezed into the house followed by Margery, Myrtle, Gert, Laila and Annie, with Jessie squeezing past them so that she could be the first to reach Georgie. 'Georgie Porgie, pudding and pie,' she crooned. 'Kissed the girls and made them cry.' She gave him a smacking kiss and laughed when he rubbed his cheek, pulling a face. She picked him up and twirled him round.

'Less of that,' Annie warned. 'Sit down and play with him nicely, there's a good girl.'

Within minutes, the kitchen seemed to be bursting at the seams with chatter and laughter. There was a warm fug thick with smoke from Leah's pipe and the cigarettes that Margery rolled and lit with a spill from the fire. Effie was kept busy making copious pots of tea and handing out slices of the seed cake she had baked the previous evening in an attempt to keep her hands occupied. She had been shaken after her encounter with Salter and disturbed by her meeting with Frank.

Baking a cake had taken her mind off the turmoil in her breast, and as she watched everyone munching happily on the product of her labours she felt that she was truly amongst friends.

When the initial excitement had died down, Effie invited her guests to take a look around the house. They explored the tiny back yard, peeping into the privy and congratulating Effie on having all the modern conveniences. They took turns to examine the copper in the washhouse, and having exhausted the exterior they trooped upstairs to view the two bedrooms. They returned to the kitchen exclaiming over the size of the accommodation compared to the living space in their caravans. They were suitably impressed by everything they saw, complimenting Effie on the way she had turned a wreck of a house into a comfortable home.

Fairly bursting with pride, Effie took them into the front parlour to demonstrate the different stages of brewing. Everyone, with the exception of the children, tasted a sample of Effie's beer and the pitch of their voices seemed to rise an octave as their tongues were loosened by the strong ale.

Finally, when they were settled once again in the kitchen, Effie allowed herself to be cajoled into relating her exploits since she left the fair. There were oohs and aahs as she told them about her search for Tom and how she found him working for the lock keeper at Old Ford lock. Her voice broke as she described Jacob's untimely death and the fire that turned the narrowboat into a burnt-out hulk. She went on to tell them about her arrival at Marsh House and her meeting with its eccentric owner. She held her audience spellbound and reaching for their hankies as she regaled them with the story of his tragic love affair with the beautiful Mirella; of his subsequent heartbreak and his refusal to acknowledge his illegitimate son. She finished with a brief mention of last night's encounter with Salter, and her hope that the conversation overheard by Frank and Jed would bring the man to justice and ensure Toby's release from jail.

Leah finished off the pint of ale that she had chosen instead of tea, wiping the foam off her mouth with her sleeve. 'By golly, I never heard such a tale.'

'I remember Salter,' Zilla said, shaking cake crumbs off her beard. 'He was a bad lot if ever there was one.'

'And his wife was no better than she should be,' added Margery. 'No man was safe when Sal Salter was around. She made eyes at my Johann, but he wasn't having any of it. If he had I'd have thrown the knives at him instead of the other way round.'

This made everyone laugh and broke the tension. The sound of the factory hooters filtering through the open window reminded everyone of the time, and the party broke up with hugs and kisses all round. Effie promised to visit the fair as often as she could before they packed up at the end of the week, and Georgie burst into tears when Jessie eventually tore herself away from him. She gave him an affectionate hug. 'Come and play with us, nipper. We'll have a lark while your ma sits and natters with the old 'uns.' For which piece of cheek she received a cuff round the ear from her mother.

'Manners, Jessie,' Annie said sternly.

'It were the monkey on me shoulder made me do it, Ma,' Jessie said with a pert grin. She angled her head, sending a pleading look to Effie. 'Let me take Georgie for an hour or two, missis. I've really missed him.'

Effie hesitated, wary of allowing her son out of her sight, but swayed by the fact that it would help not to have him with her when she went to meet Frank.

'I'll keep an eye on him,' Gert said. 'Jessie's a good girl, she won't let no harm come to the little chap.'

'Do you want to go with Jessie?' Effie asked

anxiously, but the smile on Georgie's face was answer enough as he reached up to hold Jessie's hand. 'Bye-bye, Mama,' he chortled.

She blew him a kiss, watching misty-eyed as he danced off hand in hand with his friend.

Laila shot her an understanding glance. 'He'll be all right with Annie's nippers. You don't have to worry about the boy.' She hesitated, waiting until the others were out of earshot. 'But you must take care, Effie. I can see danger looming. Things won't go smoothly for you and your man. You must be careful of someone you once thought meant a lot to you. He means you harm and you can't trust him.'

'Who is this person?' Effie asked nervously, although she could hazard a shrewd guess as to Laila's answer.

'His face is in shadow,' Laila said, closing her eyes. 'But his intentions are evil. Beware of the man with the charming smile. I can't say more than that.' She sashayed down the street with the silver coins on the hem of her skirt tinkling a merry tune, and the bangles on her wrists jingling like sleigh bells.

Effie closed the door, leaning against it with her heart beating nineteen to the dozen. She was already late for her appointment with Frank, but Laila's warning had made her even more nervous than she had been before.

A sudden crashing on the doorknocker made

her jump. She opened the door and was dazzled by the hot June sun blazing from a cloudless sky. She could just make out the outline of a tall man whose face was in shadow, and for a moment she did not recognise him.

Chapter Twenty-One

'Are you going to keep me standing on the pavement, Effie?'

'How did you know where I lived?' Effie demanded, barring his entry. 'I said I'd meet you behind the show tent.'

'I wasn't sure you'd come so I followed the women. They weren't exactly secretive about their intention to visit you.'

'Come in, Frank,' she said reluctantly.

He strolled past her, looking around with a calculating eye. 'Nice little place you've got here. It's a step up from a caravan.'

Tight-lipped, Effie led the way down the narrow hall to the kitchen. The air was still heavy with the smell of tobacco smoke, cheap perfume, beer and hot tea. She went to the window and flung it open.

'A glass of beer wouldn't go amiss, Effie. I hear you make the best brew in Bow.'

She turned her head to look at him and was momentarily dazzled by his charming smile. This was the Frank that she had fallen in love with, but she realised now that his appeal was superficial. Beneath the charisma there lurked a hard-headed businessman who thought that money and power could buy love. In the tight-knit world of the fairground the Tinsleys were kings, but outside their realm they were little better than costermongers, selling the excitement of the fairground and trading in dreams.

'You're welcome to try some,' she said, slipping past him. 'Sit down and I'll bring you a pint.' She went into the front parlour and drew a tankard of ale from a barrel. She turned to leave the room and found Frank standing in the doorway, eyeing her speculatively. 'What is it?' she demanded nervously. 'Why do you look at me like that, Frank?'

The muscles of his face relaxed into a smile as he took the tankard from her. 'I was just thinking what an enterprising little thing you are, Effie Grey. And if anything you've grown prettier since I last saw you. It doesn't seem fair for one woman to have so many attributes.'

Effie felt the blood rush to her cheeks. She knew that he was deliberately flattering her but his words made her feel warm inside. 'That's pure blarney. I think you must be part Irish.'

'It's not a crime to admire a beautiful woman.'

'Stop flirting with me. It won't work.'

His expression altered subtly but the smile remained as if painted on his handsome features. 'It's good to see you again, my pet. I can't tell you how much I've missed you.'

'Tell me why you came. I know you want something from me in return for speaking up for Toby, but you must understand that there can never be anything between us now.'

He put his drink down without tasting it, and he took her by the shoulders, gazing deeply into her eyes. 'I want you, my dove. No beating about the bush. I want you as I've never wanted any woman in my life.'

His strength of will almost overpowered her, but Laila's words of warning rang in her ears. 'Let me go, Frank.'

'Stop playing games with me, Effie. You're no shrinking violet; neither are you an innocent virgin. I'm trading your favours for my word in the witness box, my angel. It's as simple as that.'

His mask had slipped and she found herself looking into the eyes of a ruthless man. She was suddenly afraid, but she was not going to let him see her fear. 'I don't need to bargain with you. Jed heard what Salter said. His evidence would be as good as yours.'

'And Jed works for me. He'll follow my lead, so don't try to play one off against the other.'

'I wouldn't have believed this of you. I thought you were a decent man, Frank Tinsley, but I see now how wrong I was.' Effie struggled to free herself from his grasp but he tightened his hold on her shoulders, digging his fingers into her soft flesh.

'I get what I want any way I can. You'll warm my bed until I tire of you. Refuse my offer and your gypsy lover can rot in jail for all I care.'

'Take your hands off me, Frank. You can't make me do this.'

'Can I not?'

'I want nothing to do with you. You're a brute and I hate you.'

'That will make it even more exciting.' He pulled her to him and took her mouth in a brutal kiss that bruised her lips and outraged her senses. With a swift movement he slipped one arm around her, ripping her blouse open from neck to waist with his free hand. His fingers probed the soft mounds of her breasts, seeking out and teasing her nipples. She fought to catch her breath, kicking out with her feet as his lips raked the slim column of her neck, his teeth nipping at her flesh as his mouth closed over her left nipple. It was a violation too far and Effie brought up her knee, catching him hard in the groin. With a howl of pain he released her and she fell against the wall, bruising her shoulders, but she felt no pain. Anger roiled inside her and she pushed him as hard as she could. Losing his balance he stumbled and fell to the floor.

'Get out of my house,' she cried, struggling to control the bubble of hysteria that threatened to overwhelm her. 'I'd rather die than give myself to a brute like you.'

Slowly, Frank rose to his feet. His face had paled alarmingly and he was in obvious pain. 'You bitch,' he hissed. 'Don't think you've heard the last of this, Effie Grey.' He seized the tankard, and downed the ale in several greedy gulps.

Effie backed away from him. 'You're no better than Salter. I can't think what I ever saw in you. I pity your poor wife.'

'I will have you, and it will be all the sweeter to hear you begging for more.'

'Get out. Leave me alone or I swear I'll go to your father and tell him what you've done.'

He threw back his head and laughed. 'He wouldn't believe a trull like you. He blames you for turning my head with your cunning ways. As for my wife, she'd wring your neck and throw you to the dogs. My Moll is a hard woman, not a soft simpering city girl.' He wrenched the door open. 'Your lover can spend the rest of his life in jail for all I care. You know where to find me if you change your mind.'

Effie managed to control her emotions until she heard the front door close behind him. She sank slowly to the floor, burying her face in her arms, and wept, but as the initial shock began to ebb away on a tide of tears, it was replaced by cold diamond-hard anger. She scrambled to her feet and made her way outside to the yard. Stripping off her clothes she worked the pump handle, allowing the ice-cold water to flow over her body in a cleansing stream. The sun was a flaming ball of fire, high in the cloudless sky. Steam rose from her naked limbs as she shook the water out of her eyes and wrung droplets from her wet hair. She snatched up her discarded garments, tossing them into the washhouse as she hurried indoors. She raced upstairs intent on changing into clothes that had not come into contact with any part of Frank's anatomy.

As she tamed her wildly curling damp hair into a chignon at the back of her neck she vowed never to allow Frank to get the better of her again. Whereas once she had longed for his caresses, now just the thought of his hands on her flesh made her feel physically sick. She secured her hair with a final pin, studying her reflection in the mirror above the mantelshelf. A livid bruise on her neck bore testament to the violence of his assault and she pulled her collar up to hide it. Frank Tinsley had much to answer for, but he would never get the better of her. She would not beg and she would never give in to him.

Satisfied that she looked presentable, she forced herself to go out on her rounds. No matter what her inner turmoil, life had to go on and she needed the money. If her hands shook a little as she poured beer for the thirsty factory workers from the Metropolitan Alum Works, they did not seem to notice. She sold out within minutes, pocketing another three shillings and fourpence. The hot summer weather was proving to be a marvellous boost for trade, and she pushed her cart home with a determined set to her jaw. No one, least of all Frank, was going to prevent her from securing Toby's early release and a full pardon.

Despite Frank's confidence that Jed would be easy to intimidate, Effie had more faith in the blacksmith. She did not believe that he would allow Frank to bully him into withholding his evidence, and after she had collected Georgie from the fairground she went to look for him. The agonised howls of a man having a tooth pulled led her straight to the blacksmith's stand. She arrived as the sufferer staggered out of the chair holding a hand-kerchief to his bleeding mouth. He was helped to the ground by a group of anxious relations and half carried towards the beer tent.

'Next,' Jed roared, but the queue of patients had dwindled away and Effie found herself standing alone on the crushed turf.

Jed wiped his bloody hands on his canvas apron, adding to the impressive array of gory stains already in place. 'Oh, it's you, Effie. What's up, ducks? Do you want a tooth pulled or have you come about the job? I still can't find an assistant like my Ethel.'

'Can I have a word in private?' Effie climbed onto the platform, dragging a reluctant Georgie by the hand. He clung to her skirts, peering nervously at Jed.

'Don't worry, nipper,' Jed boomed in his deep bass tones. 'I don't eat little boys.'

Effie glanced at the merry-go-round, praying silently that she would not see Frank or his father. Luckily, it was not Frank but a young boy who moved nimbly between the gallopers as he took the pennies from children and adults alike. She greeted Jed with a smile. 'About yesterday, when you overhead Salter talking to me. Do you remember what he said?'

Jed scratched his head, thinking hard before he answered. 'Aye, I think I do.'

'Has Frank said anything to you about it, Jed?'

'Not that I recall. What's up, Effie?'

'I need your help.'

'Speak up then, girl. I'm always ready to help a mate.'

Lowering her voice, Effie explained everything to him in the simplest possible terms. She waited for his response hardly daring to breathe.

Jed thought long and hard before slowly shaking his head. 'No, I daresn't, Effie. I'd like to help you and I got nothing against young Toby, but if Frank boots me out I'll have nowhere to go and my family will starve.'

'But you're a farrier by trade. You could set up anywhere.'

He shook his head. 'Times is hard in the country. Folk are flocking to the cities looking for work in the factories. I can't risk it, girl. I'm sorry.' He turned his attention to a woman who was struggling to hold a screaming child. 'Can I help you, missis?'

'It's my Solly, mister. He's got a rotten tooth.'

'I'll have it out in a trice, ma'am. Step this way.'

Effie picked Georgie up and descended the steps hastily. She did not want him to witness a tooth pulling, and to pacify his protests she purchased a toffee apple from Myrtle. The day that had begun so well had turned into a nightmare and when she saw Sal Salter barring her way, she knew that it was about to get worse.

'I've been waiting for you, Effie Grey.' Sal stood with her arms akimbo and her face flushed brick red, whether from drink or rage Effie could not tell, and she did not want to get close enough to find out.

'Let me pass,' she said coldly. 'I've nothing to say to you, Mrs Salter.'

'Don't get on your high horse with me, girl. I got something to say to you and it won't wait.'

'Then say it and let me get on my way.'

'You're a cool piece, I'll give you that, but you'll laugh on the other side of your face when I've finished with you.'

'Haven't you and your husband done enough to my family?' Effie demanded angrily. 'Leave me alone. I don't want anything to do with you.'

'I'm not playing games. Salter told me what happened last night and what he let slip in front of witnesses. If you try to use that against him it'll be the worse for you and for your family.' Sal ruffled Georgie's hair but the smile on her lips was anything but kindly. 'Accidents happen to little 'uns,' she added in a low voice. 'The canal is deep enough to drown a child.

They often topple in when they're not being watched.'

Effie shivered in spite of the heat, but she was not going to let Sal smell her fear. She snatched Georgie up in her arms, holding him as if she would never let him go. 'You're evil, Sal. You'll burn in hell for certain.'

'I expect I will, dearie, but you'll be there first, and that brat of yours.' Sal turned on her heel and walked away.

Effie struggled alone with her fears and worries. She dared not tell Tom in case he did something silly. He might think he was a man but he was no match for either of the Salters when it came to strength or cunning. There was no one in whom Effie could confide and there was nobody she could think of who could help with her predicament. She could not tell Betty what Sal had said as she knew that the whole Crooke family would be rallied in an attempt to get the better of the Salters and that would end badly. Gang warfare was prevalent in the East End and Effie was certain that Salter could raise a small army of villains to support him if need be. She did not want to place Fred or his sons in danger and for the same reason she did not go to Ben. The dead houses on the banks of the Thames were filled with corpses fished out of the river, and not all of them were suicides. But it was the threat to Georgie that terrified her most and she hardly dared let him out of her sight. She abandoned her midday round of the factories and only left the house at night when she was certain that Tom was there to watch over her son.

She barely slept at night for worrying and she had even stopped writing to Toby. In her present agitated state she was afraid that she would let something slip and he would read between the lines and realise that something was terribly wrong. She would have given anything to see him again, but even if she had had the opportunity to visit the prison she could not have burdened him with the problems that beset her now. To know that she was being propositioned by Frank and threatened by the Salters would only add to his frustration and increase his suffering. She hoped he would understand if she ever had a chance to explain, but she was beginning to think that she would never see him again. Once or twice, in the dead of night, she had considered giving in to Frank's outrageous demands, but the thought of being intimate with him was nauseating, and in the cold light of dawn she had abandoned the idea.

She had kept away from the fairground even though she would have loved to see more of her old friends, and at long last the fair was due to pack up and leave next day. To her intense relief Frank had left her alone, and she hoped that the departure of the travelling people would bring an end to the threat from the Salters. With just hours to go before the fair moved on to its next destination, she had gone out on her rounds. Having sold the last drop of ale she was hot and tired. The still air was heavy with an oppressive heat that seemed to suck the breath from her lungs. She had not gone straight home but had taken a detour intending to pay a call on Betty at the pub and have a chat over a cup of tea. Now that the worst danger was past, she wanted nothing more than to unburden her troubled soul to a friendly ear.

She stopped in the middle of Bow Common bridge hoping to catch a breath of air, but the stench from the factories rose in a suffocating cloud of smoke and dust and the sky was tinged with sulphurous yellow. Below her the canal seemed to boil as it moved slug-gishly, rippling with the bow waves of passing narrowboats. She could hear sounds of merriment emanating from the tavern and she was about to continue on her way when an ominous rumble of thunder made her change her plans. Her first instinct was to get home to comfort Georgie. He was terrified by thunder and lightning and had been left with Dotty who might also be frightened by storms. Effie turned her barrow and set off for Albert Place.

The streets were strangely quiet now that the hordes of workers had gone their separate ways. Although there were several hours before darkness engulfed the city, there was an unnatural twilight and dark clouds of starlings swooped on tall buildings as if homing in to roost for the night. Their head-splitting chorus was both noisy and eerie. A wind had come up from nowhere, buffeting Effie, tugging at her hair and slapping her face with pieces of straw and detritus snatched up from the gutters. She put her head down and threw all her weight into pushing the cart with its heavy oak barrel. The mugs banged together and an even stronger gust almost tipped the barrel off the barrow causing the mugs to clatter in unison like chattering teeth. Then the rain came, falling from the cast-iron sky in steady torrents. It swept through the city turning streets into rivulets and causing blocked drains to overflow. Effie was close to home but she could barely stand and she was forced to take shelter in a chapel doorway.

She was already soaked to the skin but the wind and rain made it impossible to manoeuvre the cart. Any moment it might tip onto the cobblestones and possibly smash into matchwood; she struggled to keep it upright. A flash of lightning was followed almost immediately by a loud crump of thunder. It rolled around the sky, echoing off the buildings and fading into the distance only to be followed by more lightning. Another crack of thunder made the ground shake beneath her feet. Effie huddled against the chapel door covering her ears with her hands. The barrel swayed ominously, caught by the strongest blast of wind yet. It tipped and would have fallen if a dark figure had not appeared and grabbed it with both hands. Lashed by the wind and rain, the man struggled to hold the barrel and Effie left the shelter of the doorway to help him.

His wide-brimmed hat was pulled down over his brow and the howling wind made it impossible to speak as they battled against its mighty force. Effie had no idea who was helping her until a flash of lightning illuminated his scarred features.

'Mr Westlake.' She almost lost her grip on the barrel as the wet wood slipped through her hands.

'It's the day of judgement,' Seymour said, baring his teeth in a grim smile. 'An apocalypse, my dear Effie.'

Dashing the rain from her eyes, she stared

at him dumbfounded. 'I don't understand. What are you doing here, sir?'

'Never mind that now. Let me help you get this contraption home. How far have you to go?'

Effie pointed in the direction of Albert Place. 'Just a hundred yards or so, but I couldn't push the cart against the wind.'

'Don't waste your breath talking,' Seymour said, taking the handles in a firm grasp. 'Lead on.'

Lashed by wind and rain and half blinded by the jagged flashes of lightning, they made their way slowly and with difficulty. Effie steadied the barrel but several of her tin mugs had gone flying off down the road as if flung by angry hands.

'Leave them,' Seymour ordered. 'Keep the keg steady or you'll lose it.'

Eventually, and with much effort, they reached the safety of Effie's back yard. The wind ranted and raged overhead but the high brick walls protected them from the worst of the storm. Across the common Effie could see the wavering lights from the fairground. She could hear the slapping of the guy ropes and the shouts of the men as they dismantled the show tent. She hoped that her friends were safe in their caravans, but there was nothing that she or anyone could do in the face of

488

such wild weather. She entered the kitchen to find Tom and Agnes sitting at the table with Georgie, who was marching his toy animals into the wooden ark. The warmth of the fire and the soft candlelight illuminated a scene of pleasing domesticity in stark contrast to the turbulent force of nature outside.

'Where is Dotty,' Effie asked anxiously.

'She was scared of the storm,' Agnes said with a rueful smile. 'We sent her home.'

Tom leapt to his feet, his eyes wide with astonishment as Seymour followed Effie into the kitchen. 'What's he doing here, Effie?'

'Don't just stand there,' Effie said hastily. 'Mr Westlake is soaked to the skin. There are clean towels in the cupboard, Tom.'

Seymour took off his hat and grimaced as it sent a shower of droplets onto the floor. 'I'm sorry to cause you any bother, Effie. But see to yourself first. You are just as wet as I.'

Agnes rose from her chair, casting a sideways glance at Seymour's scarred face and then looking away. 'I'd best be on my way home.'

'Not in this storm,' Tom said firmly. He took two huckaback towels from the cupboard next to the chimney breast and gave one to Seymour, passing the other to his sister with a questioning look. 'What's going on?'

Agnes laid her hand on his arm. 'Ask questions later, Tom. I'll make a pot of tea.'

'Thank you, Agnes,' Effie said with a grateful smile. 'And thank you both for looking after Georgie. I was really worried about him.'

'No need,' Tom said, grinning at Georgie as he pressed a giraffe into his hands. 'I can remember being scared of thunder when I was a nipper.'

Satisfied that her son was happily oblivious to the storm that raged around outside, Effie turned to Seymour. Now that they were safely indoors she was bursting with curiosity. 'May I ask what are you doing here, sir? I can't believe that it was just a coincidence that you found me sheltering in the chapel doorway.'

'Nellie told me that you knew the landlord of the Prince of Wales tavern. I wanted to find you and I thought it the best place to start.'

'Ben knows when to keep his trap shut,' Tom said, eyeing Seymour suspiciously. 'He's a good man.'

'He is indeed and he took some convincing, but eventually I managed to coax your address out of him. I was on my way here when I saw you standing on the bridge, Effie. I called out to you but those damned birds were making such a din that you didn't hear me, so I followed you.'

'That explains a little,' Effie said slowly. 'But why did you want to see me?'

Seymour looked down at his sodden clothing with a wry grimace. 'I'm soaked to the skin, my dear, as are you, and what I have to say can wait until morning. I think I'd better hurry back to the tavern where I've booked a room for the night.'

'Yes, of course you must change out of your wet things as soon as possible, but you can't leave me in suspense, Mr Westlake. I won't sleep a wink unless you give me some idea why you've sought me out.'

He hesitated and a reluctant smile softened his stern features. 'Let's just say I've had a change of heart. I've returned slowly and painfully to the real world and working the land has made me face certain truths.'

'About Toby?'

'Yes, about my son. Of course I knew that he was my child, but after Mirella died, instead of cherishing him and taking comfort from my own flesh and blood, I turned him out. I think I went a little mad with grief and the suffering caused by my disease. I hated myself and I loathed the world where people could be happy when all the joy had been taken from me.'

Agnes muffled a sob and Tom hooked his arm around her shoulders with a sympathetic murmur.

Effie found herself shivering violently. 'I think I understand, but I could never abandon my child.' She made a move to pick Georgie up but remembered her wet clothes in the nick of time. She ruffled his curls affectionately. 'Georgie is my life,' she said softly. 'And Tom, of course, but I'm afraid I'll never see Toby again.'

'That's why I'm here. I want to visit my son and I need to know where they have him imprisoned.'

'In Millbank, I think. I've only seen him once when he was in the house of detention, and that was weeks ago.'

Seymour rammed his hat on his head. 'We'll discuss this tomorrow. I really must go now.'

Effie nodded reluctantly. She wanted to sit him down and spend the night talking about Toby, but she could see that Seymour was flagging and in desperate need of dry clothes, hot foot and above all a rest. As she saw him out of the house she could only marvel at his sudden change of heart. It seemed like a miracle that he had dragged himself from the brink of insanity and turned his life around. The serious man with a quiet voice and calm demeanour was quite unlike the half-crazed creature she had first come across in Marsh House.

She felt a tug at her skirt and looked down

into Georgie's smiling face. 'Mama,' he said happily. 'Come.' His efforts to draw her back to the kitchen brought a smile to her lips and she knelt down beside him.

'Mama got caught in the rain, darling. Go back to the kitchen and wait for me while I change out of my wet clothes. Then we'll have supper and I'll read you a story.' She watched him toddle off to join Agnes and Tom in the kitchen, and despite her sodden garments she felt a warm glow rushing through her veins. She had her precious family around her and now she had Toby's father on her side. She was no longer fighting the battle alone.

That night Effie slept more soundly than she had for weeks. Next morning she waited anxiously for Seymour's arrival, rushing to the window in the front parlour every few minutes to peer out along the street. The storm had passed over during the night leaving the streets scoured clean of debris. The early morning sunshine glistened on wet pavements and there was a fresh feeling in the air as if the old city had been washed clean by the savagery of the elements. A cursory glance at the common first thing had revealed an empty space where the fair had been, and Effie felt a mixture of relief and sorrow. Frank had gone away and she hoped never to see him again, but she wished that she had had more time with Leah and the others.

When Seymour's tall figure came striding into view Effie could not get to the door fast enough. He was all courtesy and smiles as he followed her into the kitchen and took a seat at the table, but Effie was suddenly nervous. Seymour Westlake was an educated man who had been born into a privileged class. She was a penniless widow and the mores of society were harsh. She was not of the same social standing and it was no use pretending that the barriers did not exist. She eyed him cautiously. 'What is it you wanted to say to me, sir?'

'I think you know me well enough drop the formalities, my dear. I am Seymour to my friends and I owe you much.'

'I don't understand.'

'When we last met I must confess that your words hurt me, but they sank into my thick skull gradually and I realised that what you said was true. I've wasted years by denying my son, and now I'm determined to make amends. I'm going to Millbank prison today and demand to see him.'

'Do you think they will allow it?'

'I don't know, but I'm going to try. I'm also going to visit an old friend who works in the City. He handled my affairs until I was foolish enough to take the bulk of them over, thinking in my arrogance that I knew better than he. I'm hoping he can find some assets left in the ruins of my former fortune. If that succeeds I'll hire the services of the best lawyer in town to put in an appeal on Toby's behalf.'

'That's wonderful, sir – I mean, Seymour. I can't tell you how happy that makes me.'

He reached across the table to lay his hand on hers. 'And you can help by telling me exactly what happened, how the fire started in the narrowboat and, if you can bear to talk about it, how your father-in-law died.'

'I can do better than that,' Effie said eagerly. 'I have two witnesses who overheard Salter admitting that he had lied to the police.'

'Excellent.' Seymour's eyes shone with excitement. 'Tell me more.'

Effie hesitated; it was not going to be easy to tell Toby's father of her previous involvement with Frank, or of the terms he had demanded in order to secure his witness statement. She cleared her throat nervously.

'I don't know where to begin.'

'Why, at the beginning, my dear. I'm a man of the world, Effie. You can tell me anything.'

Seymour left the house intent on his mission and primed with the information that Effie had given him. She watched him striding purposefully down the street and she found it hard to believe how much he had changed since their first encounter. The drug-ridden eccentric who barely knew his own name had been replaced by a man of sharp intelligence and undeniable authority. It was obvious that he was still painfully aware of the scars that marred an otherwise handsome countenance, and she could only imagine how hard it must have been for him to venture out into the wider world after years of hiding away in Marsh House. She wished that she could accompany him on his visit to Toby, but there was only the slimmest of chances that he would gain admission to the prison. He had promised to return later in the day, and until then she would have to be patient and stick to her normal routine.

Having taken Georgie to Phoebe Street where he would spend the morning playing with the younger children under Bella's watchful eye, Effie returned home to start another brew. She was in the washhouse waiting for the water to reach the correct temperature when she heard hammering on the front door. She picked up her skirts and raced through the house, hoping that it would be Seymour bearing good news.

She opened the door and was faced with two official-looking men wearing bowler hats and stern expressions.

'Mrs Grey?'

'Yes.'

'You've been reported for brewing ale without a licence. We're here to issue a summons and to close you down.'

Chapter Twenty-Two

The whole street gathered to watch as the bailiffs loaded Effie's precious barrels onto a dray. Distraught and shocked, Effie could only stand and stare as her living was taken away from her. A flick of a whip and a sharp command from the driver to the shire horse and the dray lurched forward. The sun beat down mercilessly on Effie's bare head but she felt cold and numb inside. She could only guess that it had been the Salters or maybe Frank who had pointed the finger at her, acting out of pure malice and the wish to see her livelihood destroyed. Well, she thought bitterly, they had succeeded. The ale had been confiscated and she had been served with a summons to appear at the magistrates' court on a charge of brewing ale without a licence in contravention of the 1830 Beer Act.

Sniggers from a group of slatternly women who lived across the street in Prospect Place brought Effie back to her senses. 'Stuck up cow,' one of them jeered. 'Thinks she's better than the rest of us, but she ain't.'

'You won't look so neat and tidy after a few days in the Bridewell.'

'Try living twelve to a room and see how you like it.'

Holding her head high, Effie retreated into her house, closing the door behind her. The taunts of her neighbours were upsetting but as nothing compared to the loss of the business she had built up from such small beginnings. The money she had saved was to have paid for Toby's defence, but the younger of the two bailiffs had warned her that the fine would be at least two guineas, and that was almost exactly the amount she had tucked away beneath the floorboards. The rent was due at the end of the week and they would only have Tom's meagre wage to live on. The person who had reported her to the law had done their worst, and yet again she was facing homelessness and ruin.

Once inside the door she felt as though the walls were closing in on her. She had the stark choice of sitting and doing nothing while she awaited Seymour's return, or putting on her bonnet and going to the tavern to seek comfort and advice from Betty. She made herself ready, but a glimpse through the front window confirmed her worst fears. The women were still crowded round their doorways chattering like magpies and casting eager glances across the street as if waiting for another chance to humiliate her. Effie could think of no good reason for their overt animosity; she had kept herself to herself and never exchanged so much as a cross word with any of them. She closed her ears to their cruel jibes as she left the house and made her way down the street. They seemed to think that she was different in some way from them, but they are wrong, she thought sadly; we are all sisters beneath the skin.

Betty was a good listener when she managed to hold her tongue for more than two minutes at a stretch. She was so infuriated by what she heard that she kept interrupting Effie, voicing her opinion as to the characters of the Salters and the punishments they deserved. Ben came into the kitchen demanding to know what was going on, and when he learned what had happened to Effie he was just as outraged as Betty. He offered to accompany Effie to court next day to act as a character witness, and he threatened to bar the Salters from his pub. Betty shook her head and told him it would serve their purpose best to leave them be. Should Toby's case come up for appeal Salter would be a key witness, and they didn't want him to scarper off and disappear.

Effie left her friends discussing what they

would like to do to the Salters and Frank was included in their desire for retribution. Betty had managed to elicit the full details of his appalling behaviour from Effie and she was both horrified and furious. She had lost no time in passing the information on to Ben, and that was when Effie decided that she had had enough. Using the excuse of collecting Georgie from Phoebe Street, she escaped from the fraught atmosphere of the pub kitchen only to bump into Sal Salter on the canal bank outside.

'Well, well. They ain't clapped you in irons yet?' Sal sneered.

Effie held on to her temper with the greatest difficulty. 'So it was you who reported me to the authorities.'

'Well, it was my man, but he done it on my say-so. It's a warning, love. Keep your pretty little nose out of our business. You lost us a fortune and we Salters don't forget a wrong or forgive.'

'If you're talking about the *Margaret* she was not yours to lose. Georgie should have in-herited his grandpa's business, but it's gone now and there's nothing that can be done about it.' Effie made as if to walk away but Sal caught her by the wrist.

'You ain't getting off that easy, missis. I'm going to make you sorry you was ever born.

You won't be so cocksure when you're homeless and living on the streets.'

Effie shook off Sal's restraining hand. 'Leave
me alone, Sal Salter. Go and find some other
innocent family to prey on.'

Sal's jaw dropped and for once she was
speechless. Effie walked off, taking a small
amount of satisfaction from having the last
word.

Georgie was too young to understand, but
Tom was devastated by Effie's news. It was
all that Effie could do to dissuade him from
going out to find Salter with the intention of
beating him to a pulp. Her brother's heart
might be in the right place, but Effie knew
that he stood no chance against a brute like
Salter. Having calmed him down, she assured
him that the fine would be automatic and
minimal.

'But it ain't fair,' Tom protested. 'You've
worked hard and now you're being punished
for it.'

Effie eyed him anxiously. He was seething
with rage and the last thing she wanted was
for him to roam the streets looking for trouble.
'I know it's unfair,' she said softly. 'Life's like
that sometimes but we've just got to make the
best of things.' She could see by his set expression that he was not listening. She tried again.

'Why don't you go round to Phoebe Street and call for Agnes? Go for a stroll along the canal bank and talk things over with her; she's a sensible girl and I'm sure she's a good listener, just like her ma.'

'What if Salter comes round trying to bully you while I'm out?' Tom said, fisting his hands. 'I'd like to see him try anything when I'm here to protect you.'

'He won't,' Effie said confidently. 'He's done his worst for now and he's not entirely stupid. He won't risk getting into trouble with the law. He'd rather creep about behind our backs, telling tales and taking away our living.'

'Just let me get me hands on the bugger.'

Effie glanced at Georgie who was listening intently. She could almost see the swear word forming on his lips. 'Don't worry about me, Tom,' she said, propelling him out of the room. 'Mr Westlake will be back soon, and I pray to God that he'll bring news of Toby. We'll get through this. We always have in the past and we will in the future, but only if we stick together.'

Tom patted her on the shoulder. 'I'll never leave you, Effie. You don't have to worry about a thing when I'm around.'

She kissed him on the cheek, realising with some surprise that she had to reach up in order to do so. Tom had shot up during the last year and he was rapidly growing to manhood. 'You're the best, Tom,' she said, smiling up at him. 'The best brother a girl could have.'

His cheeks flushed scarlet and he stared down at his boots. 'Aw, Effie. Don't talk soft.' He gave her a sideways glance. 'You're not so bad yourself.'

'You'll have me in tears if you keep talking that way.' She gave him a gentle shove towards the door. 'Go and see Agnes. She'll put a smile back on your face, and don't worry about me.'

'I won't stay out late,' he promised as he let himself out of the house, calling over his shoulder, 'Don't open the door to anyone but me or Mr Westlake.'

Effie waited all evening for Seymour's return. She paced around the front parlour where the empty trestles and the smell of beer were the only evidence that remained of her attempts to support her family. The long summer evening slowly darkened into night and Tom returned home but there was still no sign of Seymour. Effie was sick with worry. Anything could have happened to him and not knowing was worse.

Next morning Tom went to work as usual and Effie made herself ready to attend the magistrates' court. She left Georgie with Mary Smith and Dotty, confident that he was in safe hands, and she set off alone for the county court in Bow High Street. The waiting area was crammed with people of all ages. A burly chimney sweep was hanging grimly on to a skinny little boy. The whites of the child's eyes, and the pink of his tongue when he opened his mouth to howl, were the only features visible beneath a thick crust of soot that made him look as though he were made of liquorice.

'What's he done?' demanded a plump, matronly woman.

'Stole tuppence from me,' the sweep said, giving the child's arm a savage tweak. 'Bleeding little animal he is. Ungrateful little beast who don't deserve a good master like meself.'

Effie was about to protest when Ben strode into the room. He came to sit beside her, taking her hand in his. 'I'm sorry I'm late, Effie. Only I was held up by a delivery from the brewery.' He pulled a wry face. 'That wasn't the most tactful thing to say. I'm always putting my foot in it.'

Cheered by having someone she knew to support her, Effie squeezed his fingers. 'You came, that's the main thing.' She winced as the sweep slapped the boy around the head. 'Stop that, mister,' she cried angrily. 'He's little more than a baby.'

'Mind your own business, missis. This limb of Satan might look innocent but he's more trouble than he's worth. If they send him to jail it will be one less of his kind to end up in the gutter.'

'You can't do anything,' Ben whispered. 'You'll only make it worse for the boy if you take the master on.'

Forgetting her own troubles, Effie wanted to snatch the little chap up in her arms and give him a cuddle. He was small and stunted and could have been any age from six to ten. He looked little older than Georgie but his wizened face was that of an old man and her heart went out to him. 'It should be against the law,' she said loudly. 'Sending little boys up chimneys shouldn't be allowed.'

The boy gazed at Effie with eyes magnified by tears. He seemed more like a wild creature than a flesh and blood child.

'Leave little chummy out of this, missis,' the sweep said with a belligerent outthrust of his whiskery chin. 'He gets three square meals a day and a bag of warm soot to sleep on at night. He ain't no worse off than the little varmints living off dust heaps or scavenging down the sewers for silver spoons or similar.'

'You should be ashamed of yourself,' Effie cried passionately.

'You heard the lady.'

The whole room had been listening to this fierce encounter and their heads turned as one to see who had spoken out in such stentorian tones.

Effie half rose from her seat at the sight of Seymour Westlake standing in the doorway. He was an imposing figure but when he removed his wide-brimmed felt hat a muffled gasp rippled round the room as the onlookers observed his scarred face. Seemingly oblivious to their curious stares, he crossed the floor to where Effie and Ben were sitting. One look from Seymour and the plump woman made room for him, moving up a seat and drawing her skirts away from him as if he had something contagious.

'Thank you, ma'am,' Seymour said with a courtly bow from the waist. He turned to the sweep. 'As to you, sir, I imagine you are aware that sending small boys up chimneys has been illegal for many years. I would think very carefully about taking the child before the magistrate if I were you. It might be you who end up in prison for breaking the law, with child cruelty added on for good measure.'

Someone clapped and then everyone, with the exception of the sweep, joined in. The sweep master rose to his feet. 'Damn you to hell, mister.' He dragged the unfortunate boy from the room, slamming the door as he left with such force that the glass panes rattled.

Effie was close to tears. 'That poor child. I can't bear to think what will happen to him now.'

'Nothing changes,' Seymour said, shaking his head. 'I shut myself away from the world for twenty years, but I see little improvement now.'

'It's appalling. It makes my problems seem so small.' Effie took a hanky from her purse and wiped her eyes. She would have followed the sweep master and snatched the child from him but for the fact that she was to be called next into the courtroom.

'Ben told me what happened yesterday,' Seymour said in answer to her unspoken question. 'I arrived back at the tavern too late to call on you, but I am here now and both Ben and I will speak up for you.'

'Aye, that we will.' Ben squeezed her hand. 'Chin up, Effie. We'll have you home in no time at all.'

The two guinea fine was paid and Effie left the court relieved, but angry and with a lighter purse. The magistrate had scolded her for her ignorance of the law, telling her that it was no excuse, and in her heart she knew that he was right. Even so she could not help feeling resentful. Circumstances had forced her into desperate measures and it was easy for a man with a comfortable home and money enough for his everyday needs to look down on the poor who were simply trying to survive. As she walked homewards between Ben and Seymour she could still hear the cries of 'little chummy' in her head. She could visualise his terrified face and the desperation in his eyes. She wished with all her heart that she could make a difference to a world where selfish people, too wrapped up in their own lives to care about others, allowed this sort of cruelty and injustice to continue.

'I wasn't allowed to see Toby.'

Seymour's voice broke into her thoughts and she raised her head to give him a questioning look. 'Is he in Millbank prison?'

'I believe so, but the gatekeeper was not very helpful. He advised me to go through official channels, whatever those might be.'

'It's an excuse for the lawyers to make money out of us respectable citizens,' Ben grumbled. 'Like the beak charging Effie two guineas for an oversight on her part. The really evil characters like Salter get away with it and we're the ones who have to pay.'

'But did you see your friend, sir – I mean,

Seymour?' Effie demanded breathlessly. Her companions were walking so fast that she had to run in order to keep up with them.

'No, my dear. Unfortunately he had changed his place of business several times and I spent hours going from office to office in the City. Eventually I found someone in his club who knew where he'd gone, and I'm sorry to say he's left the country, most probably taking anything that was left of my investments with him.'

'You mean there's no money for Toby's appeal?'

'Unless I can find Forster it seems a hopeless case.'

'Did they say where he'd gone?' Effie clung on to hope, but it was receding fast.

'Argentina.' Seymour drew his mouth down in a wry smile. 'I was told he had gone there to mine for silver, no doubt using my money to fund his expedition.'

They had reached Albert Place and Effie fumbled in her purse for the key. 'If you would both like to come inside I'll make us some tea. I'm afraid I can't offer you anything stronger.' She put the key in the lock but it would not turn. She tried again.

'Here, let me have a go,' Ben said, taking it from her. 'You've been through a lot this morning, my girl. No wonder your hands are shaking.' He put the key in the lock and tried again, to no avail.

'I don't understand it,' Effie said. 'There must be something stuck in the keyhole.'

'No, missis. I changed the locks.'

Effie spun round to see a small man wearing a green-tinged black suit with leather patches at the elbows of his jacket, and a stiff paper collar that threatened to cut his throat each time he moved his head. He took off his battered bowler hat, tucking it beneath his arm. 'I'm sorry, missis. Just doing me job.'

'And what is your occupation, sir?' Seymour demanded in a booming voice that echoed off the dilapidated buildings across the street, causing doors to open and heads to pop out like peas bursting from their pods. A small crowd began to assemble.

'Bailiff, mister. This lady ain't paid no rent this week and the landlord has received information that she's a felon, and been up in court. I've been told to evict her.'

Effie stared at him in disbelief. 'You can't do that. The rent isn't due until Friday.'

'I'm just doing me job.'

The bailiff took a step backwards as Ben uttered a growl of displeasure. 'No need for violence, cully.'

'And taking great pleasure in it, unless I'm very much mistaken.' Ben made a move as if to grab the man by the throat, but Seymour held up his hand.

'Don't touch him, Ben. You'll only get yourself into trouble with the law, which I very much fear is on the side of this villain.'

'Here, mister, I ain't no villain, I'm just . . .'

'Doing your job, I know,' Seymour said severely. 'But you can surely open the door and let this lady pack up her belongings?'

'There must be some mistake,' Effie cried passionately. 'I've got the money indoors. Please let me go inside and get it.'

'Can't do that, missis. I've carried out me duty and everything in the house belongs to the landlord. The contents will be sold off to cover outstanding rent and costs.' He turned and ran, the bundle of keys grasped in his hand jingling with every loping step.

'I'll go after him and make the little bugger open the door,' Ben said, preparing to follow the terrified official.

'No, don't.' Seymour laid a restraining hand on his arm. 'If he's a bailiff he has the law on his side and I think we've seen enough of the magistrates' court.'

'But my things,' Effie protested. 'Everything I own is locked in that house. All our clothes and my pots and pans and Georgie's toys . . .'

'All can be replaced, Effie,' Seymour said gently. 'It's harsh, I know, but how long would you have been able to hold on to the house without the ability to sell ale? It was a brave attempt to support yourself and your family, but it's come to an end and you must accept help from your friends.'

'I'd take you in, but you know how things are with the missis . . .' Ben's voice trailed off miserably and he avoided meeting Effie's troubled gaze.

'There's no question about it,' Seymour said firmly. 'Marsh House will be your home from now on, Effie.'

'I couldn't. I mean, I know how little money you have and . . .'

'I'm a rich man compared to you. I have property and enough income from our efforts at farming to keep the wolf from the door. Can you look me in the eye and tell me that you don't want to be at Marsh House when Toby comes home?'

Effie felt the ready blush flood her cheeks. 'No, sir.'

'No, Seymour,' he said, smiling and placing his hand on her shoulder. 'We're going to be family, Effie. I'll not only have a son, but a daughter and a grandson as well. Where is the little fellow?'

Effie could see Mary and Dotty peering out

of their front room window and the top of Georgie's curly head and his tiny starfish fingers clutching the windowsill.

'Georgie,' she murmured, hurrying to the door and rattling the knocker. 'Mary, it's me.'

'Best bring Effie to the pub, sir,' Ben said gruffly. 'My missis won't have nothing to say if she's with you, but I'd best get back there now. I've work to do.'

'Of course.' Seymour shook his hand. 'We'll follow on when we've got the boy.'

Effie bent down to catch Georgie in her arms as the door opened and he hurtled out to greet her.

Mary eyed Seymour nervously. 'I'd ask you in, but I'm in the middle of a big wash. My house ain't fit to be seen by a gent.'

'I expect you saw what happened just now,' Effie said, glancing over her shoulder at the silent crowd on the far side of the street. 'It will be all round Bow that the bailiff was called in.'

Mary's cheeks, already flushed with heat from slaving over the washtub, deepened in colour. 'Don't take no notice of them over the road. They're sluts and trollops, all of them. They'll gab on about the bailiff throwing you out of the house for a day or two and then it'll be some other poor sod who gets the sharp end of their spiteful tongues. I got no time for them.'

Effie put Georgie down in order to give Mary a hug. 'I'll miss you, Mary. You've been a good friend.'

Dotty tugged at her mother's apron strings. 'C'mon, Ma. We'll never get done at this rate.'

'And we should be going on our way,' Seymour said gently. 'It's a long ride to Marsh House.' He proffered his arm to Effie, ignoring the titters from the women across the street.

'Goodbye, Mary,' Effie said tearfully. 'Take care of your ma, Dotty.' Taking Georgie by the hand, she allowed Seymour to lead them away from the house which she had worked so hard to turn into a home. 'We must find Tom,' she said urgently. 'He doesn't know what's happened.'

Seymour patted her hand as it nestled in the crook of his arm. 'All in good time, Effie. We'll get you and Georgie settled in the parlour at the tavern and I'll send the stable boy to find your brother. I'll need to arrange transport to take you to Marsh House.'

Effie shot him a curious glance. 'Aren't you coming with us?'

'No, my dear, I'll stay a day or two longer. I'm not leaving without seeing Toby and I have the name of a lawyer in Lincoln's Inn Fields who is supposed to be the best in the business.'

'I don't want to be rude,' Effie said tentatively, 'but can you afford his fees?'

Seymour threw back his head and laughed. 'You get straight to the point and that's very refreshing, Effie. The answer to your question is no, but if everything goes to plan that won't be a problem.'

If Maggie Hawkins was dismayed to see Effie walking into her pub, she hid her feelings well. She greeted them with a bright smile painted on her thin features as she ushered them into the best parlour. Seymour thanked her and complimented her on the style and comfort of the room, which to Effie's eyes was over-furnished and fussily decorated. The whitewashed walls were hung with sentimental prints of angelic-looking children playing with fat little puppies, or posing like statues with flower-bedecked hoops held above their heads. Dusty velvet curtains draped the small window and every spare inch of shelf space was occupied by the type of cheap fairings that Leah might have sold from her stall.

'This is our best room, sir,' Maggie said proudly. 'Will you require a meal, Mr Westlake?'

'I'll eat later, Mrs Hawkins, but I'm sure Effie and her child must be famished.' He turned to Effie with an amused twitch of his lips. 'Order whatever you fancy, my dear. I'm going out now but I'll be back soon.'

'You will send someone to find Tom, won't you?' Effie asked anxiously.

'Consider it done.'

There was a moment's silence after Seymour left the room. Maggie stood in the doorway with her hands clasped tightly in front of her. Effie could see the muscles at the corners of her mouth twitching as if she had something to say but was biting back harsh words.

'I don't want to put you out,' Effie said hastily. 'I'm more than happy to eat in the kitchen, and I would like to see Betty if it's all right with you.'

'The kitchen is where you belong,' Maggie hissed. 'But he wants you to be treated like a lady, so that's how it shall be.'

'This has nothing to do with Mr Westlake. I choose the kitchen and I don't think you will be silly enough to make a fuss.'

'Don't you get all hoity-toity with me, you trollop,' Maggie said through clenched teeth. 'You've been after my Ben since the day you first showed up on our doorstep, but now I see you've set your sights higher. Good luck to you, I say.'

Effie sighed, shaking her head. 'I'm really sorry for you, Maggie. You're making your-self miserable with your jealousy, and if anything drives Ben into another woman's arms it will be you.'

'And that woman would have been you if you hadn't wheedled your way in with a toff.'

'I like Ben as a friend and that's all it ever was and ever will be.' Seizing Georgie by the hand, Effie marched past her and made for the kitchen.

'Them Salters was at the back of it,' Betty said when Effie told her what had happened. 'They're out to make your life a misery and that's for certain.'

'I know, Betty, and that's why I have no choice but to accept Mr Westlake's invitation. At least we'll be safe at Marsh House and I can wait there until Toby is released from jail, no matter how long it takes.'

'I wish I could do more for you, ducks. And my poor little Aggie will be heartbroken if Tom goes with you.'

Effie paused with a spoonful of soup halfway to her lips. 'What a selfish creature I've become. Everything has happened so suddenly that I hadn't given a thought to Tom's feelings.'

'He could stay with us. One more mouth to feed wouldn't make no difference, and he could visit you on Sundays.'

Effie put her spoon down as her appetite

deserted her. 'I'd have to talk it over with him. It would be his decision, Betty.' She leaned over to wipe jam off Georgie's chin, receiving a happy smile as he held his hand out for another of Betty's jam tarts.

'I'll miss you both,' Betty said wistfully. 'You're like family.'

Effie broke a jam tart in half and gave one part to Georgie. 'This isn't goodbye, Betty. I'll come and see you as often as I can.' She looked up with a start as the outer door was flung open and Tom rushed into the kitchen, flushed and perspiring, with an anxious look on his face.

'Are you all right, Effie? Seymour came to fetch me and he's told me what happened this morning.'

'Ho, Seymour is it?' Betty said, raising her eyebrows. 'Show a bit of respect to your elders and betters, boy.'

Tom shot her a sideways glance. 'He said I was to call him that.' He pulled out a chair and sat down at the table opposite his sister. 'What are we going to do, Effie?'

'I haven't much choice,' she said slowly, measuring her words. 'But you have, Tom. You can come to Marsh House with Georgie and me, or you could lodge with Betty in Phoebe Street and come to see us on Sundays; that way you could keep your job and still see Agnes every day.'

Tom glanced at Betty and she gave him an encouraging smile. 'You're more than welcome to stay with us. You've done it afore so you know what it's like sharing a room with my boys.'

'But you need me, Effie,' Tom said, frowning. 'I'm the man of the house; you've always said so.'

'Mr Westlake will be your guvner,' Betty put in before Effie had a chance to respond. 'You'll have to do what he says, young man.'

Effie reached across the table to clasp his hand. 'Of course I need you, Tom. But I want what's best for you. If you'd be happier staying in Bow with Betty's family, then that's what you must do.'

Tom shook his head. 'I dunno. I want things to go back as they were. I liked our little house and I was happy being able to walk across the common to work each morning.'

'I know, and it hurt me to leave our home too, but it's gone and we've got to get on with our lives.'

'I don't want to leave you to struggle along on your own,' Tom said slowly. 'And I don't want to leave Agnes either.'

'Mama,' Georgie cried, thumping his sticky hands on the table to attract her attention. 'Mama, more.'

'That's one more word he's learned,' Betty

observed with a fond smile. 'I'll miss seeing him growing up, I really will.'

'He is getting to be a big boy, and a greedy one too,' Effie said, giving him the last of the jam tart. 'He'll miss your cooking, Betty, but I'll bring him to see you as often as I can, that's a promise.'

'I should hope so too.' Betty sniffed, mopping her moist eyes with her apron.

Tom thumped his hand on the tabletop. 'This is a bloody mess. And don't tell me off for swearing because I feel like saying much worse things. I could kill Salter for what he's done to us.'

'We've got to forget about the Salters,' Effie said earnestly. 'It's you I'm most concerned about, Tom.'

He groaned, running his hands through his already tousled hair. 'I just don't know what to do for the best.'

His obvious pain made Effie want to cry but she made an effort to sound positive. 'I can't tell you what to do. You must follow your heart.'

'And what about you, Effie? What will you do?'

'I'll watch Georgie grow into a fine fellow like his Uncle Tom, and I'll wait for Toby to be released from jail.'

'Mr Westlake will find a way to set him free,'

Tom said hopefully. 'And then you'll be together forever.'

'I hope and pray it will be that easy, but Mr Westlake has to find the money for a lawyer and even then an appeal could fail. It might be years before Toby is a free man.'

Betty pursed her lips. 'Let's hope he's ready to settle down then. I'd hate to see you waste your young life waiting for a man who'll break your heart.'

'How can you even think such a thing?' Effie cried passionately. 'Toby loves me and he wants us to be together always; he said so.'

'He's part gypsy, Effie love. He might fly off like a canary let out of its cage.' Betty lifted Georgie from his chair and set him down on the floor. 'Toby Tapper was never in one place long enough to call it home. I'm just being realistic.'

'He loves Effie,' Tom said, frowning. 'I know he does.'

'All I'm saying is, you shouldn't get your hopes up too high, and you should think hard before you throw in your lot with them at Marsh House.' Betty shrugged her shoulders. 'I'm just thinking of what's best for you, Effie.'

This was not a conversation that Effie wanted to have. She knew she would be taking a risk by returning to the house on the marsh, but she realised that her choices were limited.

'I have Georgie to consider,' she said slowly. 'He needs a proper home and a good education. I don't want Owen's son to grow up ignorant and without prospects. I want a better life for my boy.'

Betty nodded her head. 'Every mother wishes the best for their nippers, and you are a good mother, Effie.'

'And a good sister,' Tom said sincerely. 'I don't want to let you down.'

Effie was close to tears but she hid them from Tom by rising hastily to wipe the jam from Georgie's hands and face. She turned with a start as Seymour strode into the kitchen from the stable yard.

'I thought I'd find you all in here. Betty's kitchen is the heart of the pub and her food speaks for itself. I'll be sorry to leave.'

'Are you coming with us after all?' Effie asked in surprise. She was certain he had said he intended to stay on for a day or two.

'No. My plans are still the same, but Champion is harnessed to the dog cart and champing at the bit. It's time for you to go.'

Effie eyed Tom anxiously. 'I'm ready, but it's up to you, Tom. Are you coming with us or are you going to accept Betty's kind offer of lodgings? It's your decision.'

Chapter Twenty-Three

'It's going to be a long winter,' Nellie grumbled. 'If the master don't come back soon we'll be chopping up what's left of the furniture for fuel and living off apples.'

Effie had just come back from the orchard with a basket overflowing with ripe fruit. She took an apple and gave it to Georgie who was tugging at her skirts in an attempt to attract her attention. 'What do you say?' she said as he snatched it from her hand.

'Ta, Mama.' He scuttled off to sit on the tiny wooden stool that Jeffries had made for him.

Effie smiled indulgently. 'Georgie wouldn't mind eating nothing but apples, would you, darling?'

He grinned, his mouth too full of fruit to allow him to speak, and a dribble of juice ran down his chin.

'Well, it's all right for him,' Nellie said darkly. 'He's got all his teeth. Me and Jeffries got nothing but our gums and the odd bit of broken peg. I need soft food and I want meat, even if I have to mince it up small.'

'Tom gets plenty of rabbits and he's a good fisherman.' Effie tried to sound positive but she was well aware that a harsh winter would make life intolerable. They had managed so far by selling their surplus eggs, butter and cheese at market, and she planned to barter apples for flour at the mill, but they would still need coal, candles and paraffin.

'There's precious little left of value in the house,' Nellie went on, ignoring Effie's last remark. 'I daresn't sell the best dinner service without the master's say-so. He'd wring me neck if he came back from foreign parts and found his ma's precious Coalport had gone to the auction rooms. It's the last thing he held on to even when he was desperate for opium or brandy.'

'And it won't be sold,' Effie said firmly. 'We'll manage until he returns from Argentina.'

Nellie pulled a face. 'Gallivanting off to South America like that. What was he thinking of?'

'He hoped to get back some of the money that his friend Forster had invested for him. You know that very well, Nellie.'

'A fool and his money are soon parted. That's what my old ma used to say and she was right.' Nellie moved a little nearer to the fire. 'I could do with a drop of ale, Effie. Is there any left in the keg?'

Effie went into the pantry and filled a tankard. She gave it to Nellie, noting with some concern that the old woman's hands appeared worse today; her knuckles were swollen and hot to the touch and her fingers gnarled like branches on the hawthorn bush outside the front door. 'Here, drink this. Purely medicinal, as you used to tell me.'

'Less of your lip, girl,' Nellie growled, but there was no malice in her hooded eyes. 'Those were the days when I could cure meself with a drop of Hollands. I've almost forgotten what it tastes like, and I'd give anything for a lump of sugar to sweeten me tea. Honey is all very well but it don't taste the same.'

'Honey,' Georgie said, swallowing a mouthful of apple. 'Bread and honey, Mama.'

'Eat up your apple, and you shall have bread and honey for dinner,' Effie said, hoping that there was enough honeycomb left for their midday meal, as Tom was partial to sweet things and she could not begrudge him a treat every now and then. She would not have blamed him had he chosen to stay in Bow, but it would have been difficult to manage without him. He had worked hard all summer, toiling in the walled garden and in the field where Seymour had planted vegetables. They had lived off the crops as they came into season, and Nellie had shown Effie how to preserve food for the long winter months. They had podded peas and left them to dry in the sun. String beans had been sliced and packed in crocks between layers of salt, and root vegetables were stored beneath straw in the cellar. Onions and herbs hung from the beams in the kitchen and anything left over was fed to the animals. Nothing went to waste. The goats ate almost anything and the chickens had roamed freely in summer, but would need grain to keep them going in the winter.

'We need sugar and spices if we're going to make chutney and jam,' Nellie muttered, sipping her ale. 'We can't let the apples and berries go to waste. In the old days this kitchen was busier at this time of year than any other. You could smell the boiling fruit and vinegar all through the house, and we used to make wine from blackberries and elderberries. The master used to complain about the smell, but he was pleased enough to have pickles and chutneys with his game pie and redcurrant jelly with roast lamb or pheasant. And he wasn't too proud to enjoy a glass or two of home-made wine. Those were the days. We'll never see their like again.'

Effie went to the range and took the lid off the saucepan to taste the rabbit stew for seasoning. They were running low on salt as well as sugar and something needed to be done. With September almost over and nights drawing in, autumn was already upon them, and very soon the first frosts would arrive, turning the sedge and reeds into a white wonderland. It might look pretty, but unless she could think of a way to earn money they would be on the verge of starvation before winter gave way to spring.

Nellie supped her ale in silence and Georgie was too busy munching his apple to seek his mother's attention. Effie stirred the stew, taking the brief respite to think. Toby had still not responded to her letters, even though she now wrote to him at least twice a week, and it was three months since Seymour had set sail for South America. They had managed so far, but only because Tom had put the knowledge he had gained in the market garden into providing food for them all. She knew what it had cost him to make the choice, but every Sunday he took Champion and rode to Bow to see Agnes. Once or twice, taking advantage of the long summer days, he had brought her back to Marsh House, and she had been wide-eyed with astonishment to think that one man owned such a large house and grounds. Effie had accompanied Tom to Bow on a couple of occasions and had enjoyed her brief visits. She missed Betty and her large boisterous family,

528

but she did not miss the grime and the filth of the city streets, or the suffocating stench and clouds of flies that made warm weather unbearable.

The East End was expanding at an alarming rate, but Marsh House was protected to some extent by the River Lea to the west and the marsh to the east, although builders were cashing in on the expansion of the railway system. New estates were being constructed so rapidly that the city was encroaching on the countryside day by day; almost minute by minute it seemed to Effie when she took their produce to market. Workers who thronged to the city offices had to live somewhere and as the transport system improved new suburbs were being created.

Thoughts had been whirring around in Effie's head like the bees in the hive, and she paused with the wooden spoon poised above the bubbling pan of stew. 'Nellie, I've got an idea.'

'It had better be a good one, ducks,' Nellie said, draining the last drops from her mug of ale. 'Give us a refill and tell me all about it.'

'I've done it before and it was a great success,' Effie said, placing the lid back on the pan. 'If only I'd known about licences I would probably still be selling beer to the factory workers in Bow.'

'What are you suggesting? If you're thinking of turning Marsh House into a pub, you'd best forget it. The master would have forty fits.'

'I wasn't, but that's a possibility.' Effie pulled up a chair to sit beside Nellie.

Georgie climbed onto her knee, tugging at a loose strand of hair that had escaped from the knot at the nape of her neck. 'I hungry, Mama.'

'I'll get your dinner in a minute, darling. I need to speak to Nellie first.'

'Well go on then,' Nellie said eagerly. 'Don't keep me in suspense.'

'We've got three barrels of ale in the cellar, all ready for drinking. Just a couple of miles away in Homerton and Clapton there are whole streets of houses under construction. Where there's hard work there'll be thirsty men. I'm not saying we could make a fortune, but at least we could earn enough to feed us and keep us warm in the winter.'

Nellie's wrinkled brow knotted into lines of worry. 'But what would the master say?'

'Mr Westlake is thousands of miles away. We haven't heard from him since he sailed for South America and quite honestly, Nellie, I don't care what he thinks. There's no knowing when he'll return and I'm not going to let my child starve.'

'What will you do?' Nellie seemed to shrink

into her clothes like a small tortoise drawing its head in when threatened by danger.

'I'm taking the eggs to market tomorrow. I'll find out how to get a beer licence and we'll go on from there.'

'What's all this?' Tom demanded as he sauntered into the kitchen. 'Did I hear you right, Effie?'

She turned to him with a brave attempt at a smile. 'You did. I'm going to get a proper licence and start selling beer again. We've got plenty made and I can soon brew more.'

Tom selected an apple from the basket on the table and he bit into it. 'Pity you can't make cider as well. We've got tons of fruit that will be fit for nothing but pig food if we leave them lying on the ground.'

'One thing at a time,' Effie said smiling. 'What do you think of my idea, Tom?'

'I think it's a good 'un. Just make sure you get the licence this time.'

Getting a licence to brew ale was easier than Effie had expected. She suspected that living in Marsh House, the ancestral home of the Westlake family, might have swayed the balance in her favour, but whatever the reason she snatched the licence and took it home with a feeling of triumph and high expectations. It was getting dark as she drove homewards and frost sparkled on the rutted track, dancing and gleaming in the light from the lamps hanging on either side of the dog cart. Stars shone down from a clear sky and a large yellow moon hung suspended like a glass bauble on a Christmas tree. Effie breathed the cold air and felt it spike in her lungs. 'Giddy-up, Champion,' she said through chattering teeth. The horse pricked up his ears and obligingly increased his pace.

In the stable yard Effie was met by Tom and Jeffries, both of them grinning up at her as if they could barely wait to give her good news. Her heart gave an erratic bump against her ribs, and for a wild moment she thought that a letter had come from Toby, or that Seymour had returned with a sackful of gold and silver.

'What on earth is it?' she demanded as Tom helped her down from the driver's seat.

'Did you get it?' he asked breathlessly.

'Yes, I did. We're back in the brewing business.'

'That's good, missis,' Jeffries said, grinning and exposing his single tooth. 'That's the ticket.'

'What is all this?' Effie looked from one to the other. 'What's going on?'

Tom grabbed her by the hand. 'Come with me, Effie. You won't believe this. Lead on, gaffer,' he added, nodding his head to Jeffries

532

who loped on ahead carrying a lighted lantern. Following the flickering beam, Tom led Effie out of the stable yard to a set of outbuildings which included the washhouse and the dairy. These were in a reasonable state of repair but the old coach house was almost derelict, with ivy-covered walls and bats zooming in and out of the glassless upper windows.

'Why have you brought me here?' Effie demanded. 'Is this a joke, Tom? Because if it is I shan't be amused. I'm cold and hungry and I don't want to look at rusty old farm implements.'

Jeffries stepped forward to heave the double doors open. He held the lantern up high, flooding the interior with light. 'Go inside, missis. Take a look at the room out back.'

'Yes, come on, Effie.' Tom's voice throbbed with suppressed excitement. 'I'd no notion this was here until Jeffries showed me.'

Her curiosity aroused, Effie followed them into a large back room, partially open to the sky where the tiles had blown off the roof. At first she could not make head or tail of the contents. To her it looked like a jumble of rusty farm implements and a huge, circular stone trough with a mill wheel half protruding from a pile of straw. 'What on earth is it?'

'Don't you see, Effie?' Tom chortled. 'It's a

cider press. There's everything we need to turn the apples into cider.'

'Aye,' Jeffries said, nodding his head. 'That's what the old master planted the trees for. In days gone by we made the finest cider in the whole of Hackney. Folks used to come from miles around at harvest time just for a taste of it.'

'And you've got a brewing licence,' Tom said, giving Effie a hug. 'We're going to make a fortune.'

It was not as easy as Tom had hoped. Effie came up against strong opposition from the foremen on building sites. She had chosen the midday break when the men were allowed a brief respite to eat and drink, but she found all too quickly that strong ale was forbidden. They did not want inebriated construction workers, the gaffers told her when she arrived with a cart laden with barrels of ale, and she was forced to return to Marsh House with not a pint sold. She revised her strategy and next day went out with barrels of small beer, a much weaker ale which was drunk by children as well as adults. This proved acceptable and popular but was cheaper and therefore less profitable. Undaunted, she went out a second time each day with Tom at her side, and this time they had barrels of strong ale loaded on the cart. Waiting a respectable distance from the actual building sites, they peddled their brew to the men who had just knocked off work.

They did not make their fortune as Tom had optimistically predicted, but they made sufficient profit to keep them in essentials, although it was hard work and by the end of November the dark nights had drawn in and the weather was bitterly cold. By the time she arrived home Effie was frozen stiff, with chilblains burning painfully on her lower limbs and hands. Trade began to drop off significantly and hard-working labourers did not want ice-cold beer or cider to drink when there was snow in the air. Ever ingenious, Tom found an old brazier which they took with them on the evening round. He would light it as soon as they reached their pitch, and the heat and warmth always attracted a small crowd of passers-by. If they were expecting to buy roasted chestnuts they were doomed to disappointment, but Effie lit upon the idea of mulling ale and cider with a red-hot poker. She added spices to the warm brew and the fragrant scent of mulled ale drew in many more customers, including office workers on their way home and housewives weary after a day's shopping in the market.

Snow in December halted the building

work, but by now Tom and Effie were a familiar sight in the market squares and with the approach of Christmas people were in a festive yuletide mood and business boomed. Nellie baked great slabs of gingerbread to tempt hungry workers, and it was her idea to add mulled wine to the booming sales of ale and cider. The scent of cinnamon and cloves mingled with the aromatic zest of oranges and lemons and the smell of warm berry wine filled the frosty air, reviving memories of warm autumn days. The mulled wine was a particular hit with women, who might have turned their noses up at the prospect of beer or cider, and Effie soon found she was selling it by the jugful. When they occasionally ventured into more prosperous streets, house-maids would come scurrying from the larger houses, inhabited by bank clerks and junior civil servants, to have pitchers filled with the tempting brew.

They were out in all weathers and Effie was only too well aware that they must earn as much as they could before the snows of winter set in making roads impassable. She spent what profit they made on buying large quantities of staples like flour, rice, sugar and tea, as well as coal, candles and paraffin. She was deter-mined to keep her family warm and fed should the weather close in, isolating Marsh House from the rest of the world. She continued writing letters to Toby, even though she never received a reply. She tried not to think about how he must be suffering in the cold, dank prison cell and she pinned her hopes on the successful outcome of Seymour's long voyage. She put all her faith in him, sensing that now he had acknowledged his son he would move heaven and earth to secure his release from prison.

The longing to see Toby a free man and the desire to keep her small son safe and out of harm's way were the only things that kept Effie going through hard times. She was up before dawn each day, attending to the brewing processes and the more mundane household tasks such as washing and ironing. Nellie did her best to help but her rheumatics were always worse in the cold weather and she spent most of her time in the kitchen. Her devotion to Georgie meant that Effie could leave him safely in Nellie's care while she and Tom went out selling ale, but being constantly exposed to the elements was slowly taking its toll on them both. Tom had developed a hacking cough that reminded Effie of the terrible lung disease that had made her a widow when she had barely become a wife. As for herself, she kept going even when colds and chills racked her slender body. She could not afford to give in, and sometimes it was only the strength of her will that kept her going.

It was Christmas Eve, and Tom was spending the night in Phoebe Street with the Crooke family, having been driven there by Effie. She had spent an hour with Betty, drinking tea in the kitchen and swopping gossip while Georgie was kept amused by Bella and the younger children. Agnes and Tom had gone out to the pub to join Harry and his new girlfriend. He was stepping out with a young lady who worked in the factory office on one of those new-fangled typewriting machines, Betty said, with a hint of pride in her voice. Fred had been promoted to foreman in charge of his particular section of the chemical works, and the rest of the family were doing as well as might be. At the tavern things went on as normal. Ben was his usual self and that went for Maggie too, who never lost an opportunity to nag the poor chap.

It was Effie's turn then to tell Betty everything that had happened to her since they last met. When she glanced at the clock on the mantelshelf she was startled to see that it was five o'clock and high time she was setting off for home. She had not intended to stay so long and now she would have to drive home in the dark. She was about to take her leave of the family when Betty drew her aside.

'I didn't want to say too much in front of the nippers,' she said in a low voice, 'but the fair is back on Bow Common. I daresay Agnes has told Tom, but I thought it best if I was to warn you, just in case you happened to run into Frank.'

The mere mention of his name brought memories of their last meeting flooding back and Effie felt a shiver run down her spine. 'Thank you for warning me. I'll be on the lookout in case I should see him in the street.'

'Just ignore him, ducks. He's not worth bothering about.'

'I'd go down on my knees to him if I thought I could persuade him to give evidence against Salter, but I know it would be a waste of time.' Effie kissed Betty on the cheek and gave her a hug. 'Merry Christmas, Betty dear.'

'I'll see you again soon, I hope.' Betty smiled, but her eyes were moist. 'Take care of yourself and the little 'un, and hurry home. You don't want to be out on the marsh alone in the dark.'

'I'll be fine,' Effie said stoutly. 'Champion knows the way home.'

Betty opened the door and recoiled as fingers of fog curled into the house. 'I knew there was a pea-souper coming. I could smell it in the air an hour ago. Perhaps you ought to stay tonight, ducks?'

Effie peered out into the street. She could just make out the shape of the chemical factory and the hazy glow forming halos around the street lamps. 'I'll be home in an hour,' she said, hoping that she sounded more confident than she was feeling. 'Don't worry about us.'

She began to regret her bold words as she let Champion have his head. They had skirted the common, where muffled sounds and a soft haze of light were the only signs that the fair had arrived in town. The road ran alongside the North London railway line, but as the fog thickened and became so dense that she could barely make out Champion's head, let alone see where they were going, she had to put her trust in his instinct to take them home. She wrapped her cloak around Georgie, tucking him in to her side as she held the reins, and, worn out after his games with the Crooke children, he soon fell asleep. Champion plodded along the road, the fog muffling the sound of his hooves, and an eerie silence descended around them.

The filthy stench of the fog filled Effie's nostrils, making it difficult to breathe, and her eyes ached with the effort of peering into the thick green gloom. Then, suddenly, as if she were in a living nightmare, a figure loomed out of the fog to grab the reins and bring Champion to a standstill. A scream of terror was wrenched from her lips and she reached for the horsewhip, but the man leapt up beside her.

'Don't be frightened, Effie. It's me.'

'Frank!' She made a grab for the reins but he brushed her hand away.

'Don't be a fool, Effie. I've been following you since you passed me by on the road half a mile back. You're heading straight for the river.'

'That's ridiculous,' Effie cried angrily. 'Champion knows his way blindfold.'

Frank flicked the reins, clicking his tongue. 'Walk on, boy.' Expertly he steered the old horse away from the water's edge.

Effie caught her breath as she glimpsed the swirl of dark water just feet away from the wheels.

'You took the wrong turn, girl,' Frank said gruffly. 'You were heading east straight into the Lea.'

'Why were you following me?'

'To save your pretty little neck, you fool.' Frank stared ahead, concentrating on guiding Champion through the narrow streets where abandoned barrows and carts loomed suddenly out of the fog, causing the frightened horse to rear in the shafts. 'Where are you headed, Effie? You shouldn't be out alone in this.'

Effie bit her lip. She didn't want to tell him where she lived, but she knew that she was lost and had little chance of getting home without his help. Frank knew the area quite literally like the back of his hand, and she had little choice other than to trust him.

'The house on the marsh,' she murmured reluctantly. 'Do you know it, Frank?'

'I passed that way once. I think I can find it, even in a London particular.'

Georgie stirred in his sleep and Effie cuddled him to her side. 'Why were you following me, Frank? You didn't really answer my question.'

'I've been looking for you for days. I tried asking at the tavern but I got short shrift from the landlord. I waited until your friend Betty had finished work and I followed her home. Then I saw you and Tom drive up and I hung around, waiting for you to come out. I almost missed you because of the damned fog.'

'Why did you go to such a lot of trouble? What is there left for us to say to each other?'

'Everything, Effie. I still love you.'

'Oh, please don't start all that again.'

'I know I behaved badly. I know I was a brute but I couldn't help myself. I was mad with jealousy and I took it out on you. I'm sorry.'

'At least you admit it.'

'I do, and I'm ashamed of myself.'

She studied his profile, looking for the man she had once loved, but all she saw was an unhappy stranger. 'There's no point in all this,' she said gently. 'I love Toby and you have a wife and child.'

'She left me and went back to her own people, taking the baby with her. It was a mistake for both of us and she knew it.' Frank turned his head to look at her for the first time. 'My God, you are so beautiful, Effie. I can hardly breathe for wanting you.'

'I'm sorry she left you, Frank.'

'I was a fool to let my old man talk me into it, when all I wanted was you.'

Effie said nothing for a moment. She could feel a faint cool breeze on her cheek and the stifling odour of soot and chemicals had been freshened by the scent of damp earth and brackish water. 'We're back on the marsh. I can find my own way from here. You should make your way back to Bow Common now.'

'I'll see you safe home.'

'Don't be stubborn, Frank. It's a long way to walk.'

'And I said I'd see you home. Who knows

543

what villains are lurking ready to steal a horse and trap from an unprotected woman?'

'Villains like Salter, you mean? You could have put him away for years if you'd given evidence in court.'

'I know it, and that's one reason why I wanted to see you. I want to make amends, Effie, love. I'm prepared to testify and so is Jed. All you got to do is find a mouthpiece who can talk the hind leg off a donkey, and then your man will be free.'

Effie stared at him, hardly able to believe her ears. 'You're willing to testify?'

'Salter should have been locked up years ago, and I can't live with you hating me, girl.'

'Why the sudden change of heart, Frank? And what do you expect in return?'

'Maybe I just want to hold my head up again with the fairground folk. I'm sick and tired of dark looks from Leah and Gert and the rest of 'em. One day I'll be the boss and it won't work if the fairground folk don't respect me.'

'You have changed,' Effie said reluctantly. 'I wouldn't have believed it possible.'

His lips curved into a smile that did not quite reach his eyes. 'You loved me once, Effie.'

'Yes, Frank,' she said softly. 'I did love you, but it seems a very long time ago now.'

*　*　*

It was mid-evening by the time they arrived at Marsh House. Nellie was openly hostile when Effie introduced her to Frank, but even she agreed that it was not the weather for a man to roam the marshes on foot. It was the season of peace and goodwill to all men, although she confided darkly to Effie that after the way he had behaved in the past she did not necessarily include Frank Tinsley in that category. However, his promise to testify against Salter went a long way to winning Nellie over and somewhat grudgingly she agreed that he could stay for the night. The only bed available was the one in Seymour's room, although Frank protested that he was quite happy to sleep in the chair by the kitchen range. This seemed to offend Nellie's concept of Marsh House hospitality and she insisted on showing him upstairs to his room. Effie was clearing away the supper things when Nellie returned to the kitchen with a wide grin almost splitting her face in two.

'What have you done?' Effie demanded.

Nellie held up her hand, dangling a key. 'He won't get up to no tricks in the night. I've locked him in just in case he thinks he can get away with anything when there's no man in the house to defend us.'

* * *

545

Effie released Frank from his temporary prison next morning with a murmured apology for Nellie's distrustful nature, but he shrugged it off with a smile. 'I suppose I can't blame the old girl for looking after you. It's obvious she thinks the world of you, Effie, as I do.'

She turned away to hide her blushes and she walked towards the stairs. 'Breakfast is ready and then you'd best be on your way.'

He was close behind her and she could feel his breath warm against the back of her neck. 'Don't I get a kiss, Effie? It is Christmas Day after all.'

'You'll get a bowl of porridge and a cup of tea,' she said lightly. 'And my thanks for your change of heart.' She paused in the middle of the staircase, turning to him with a worried frown. 'You do still intend to testify against Salter?'

'You may not think so, but I am a man of my word.' He caught her by the hand. 'If you ever change your mind about us, or if your man doesn't come up to scratch, I'll be there waiting for you.'

She snatched her hand away and continued down the stairs. 'I trust Toby.'

'I'll kill him if he breaks your heart.' Frank caught up with her in the hallway, taking her by the shoulders and gazing deeply into her eyes. 'You are sure that there's no hope for me?'

'I was never more certain of anything. Please let me go, Frank.'

He hesitated for a brief moment and his eyes burned with desire. 'One last kiss, my love.' He jerked her roughly into his arms, stifling her protest with a kiss. His teeth grazed her lips and his tongue probed her mouth. She struggled but her efforts to free herself only served to excite his passion.

Dimly she heard the sound of a door opening and footsteps reverberating on the floorboards. Suddenly she was free as Frank was dragged away from her and thrown to the floor.

Chapter Twenty-Four

Seymour had Frank by the throat and he dragged him to his feet, but his grip was easily broken by a man used to manual labour. Frank drew back his clenched fist and was about to land a punch on Seymour's jaw when Effie threw herself in between them. 'Don't hit him, Frank.'

'What's going on?' Seymour demanded breathlessly. 'I come home to find this oaf treating you like a common doxy.'

'I dunno who you are, mate,' Frank said belligerently, 'but no one calls Effie names when I'm around.'

'Frank,' Effie said, holding him back with her hands on his chest, 'this is Mr Westlake, the owner of Marsh House.'

'I don't care if he's the Lord Mayor of London. No one calls Frank Tinsley an oaf.'

Seymour picked up his hat, which had been knocked off his head in the struggle. 'I speak as I find, and you were molesting this young woman in my house.'

Frank shrugged his broad shoulders. 'Effie

and me, well, we was more than friends not so long ago.'

Effie could tell by Seymour's ominous expression that this admission had only made matters worse, and she laid her hand on Seymour's arm. 'Frank drove me and Georgie home from Bow last night when we got caught up in the pea-souper.'

'That's as maybe, but it doesn't explain why he is still here in the morning or why he was forcing his attentions on you.'

'I got carried away, guvner,' Frank said gruffly. 'I still got feelings for Effie, but she would have none of it, and I slept in a room that was like the inside of a circus tent.'

'You slept in my room?' Seymour's mouth worked as if he was struggling to keep his temper.

'Nellie locked him in,' Effie said hastily. 'We didn't know you would be coming home today. We'd heard nothing from you for six months, and what Frank hasn't told you is that he's promised to testify against Salter. He's going to help us get Toby out of jail.'

'This is all too much for me, Effie,' Seymour said wearily. 'I've been travelling for weeks and I'm bone weary.' He eyed Frank with a hint of a smile in his dark eyes. 'If I was mistaken, I apologise, but I didn't expect to enter my home and find Effie grappling with a stranger.'

Frank nodded his head, holding out his hand. 'No hard feelings, sir. I'd have done the same in your place.'

'Oh, for heaven's sake,' Effie exclaimed. 'Can't you men settle anything without using your fists first and asking questions later?'

'You're right, of course, and I should know better.' Seymour shook Frank's hand. 'Will you join me for breakfast? I'd like to hear what you have to say.'

'Aye, sir, I'd be honoured.'

'I could light a fire in the morning parlour if you want to talk privately,' Effie suggested, hoping that Seymour would opt for the kitchen where she could hear their conversation without eavesdropping. There were many questions she wanted to ask but they would have to wait until Frank had left the house.

'We'll eat in the kitchen,' Seymour replied, shrugging off his greatcoat and dropping it on the oak settle by the door. 'I'm chilled to the bone and the ride from Bow has given me an appetite.'

Effie stared at him, her curiosity aroused. 'You came from Bow?'

Seymour smiled and his eyes crinkled at the corners. She could almost imagine that it was Toby standing there in the dimly lit hallway and her heart gave an uncomfortable thud against her ribs. But if Seymour noticed her discomfort he gave nothing away by his expression. 'It was too foggy to find my way home so I put up at the Prince of Wales. Your friend the innkeeper was only too pleased to tell me all about your heroic efforts to keep the wolf from the door. I'm proud of you, Effie, but I'm home now and you don't have to bear the burden of my run-down estate any longer.'

His reassuring words came as a relief after months of hard work and worry, and she did not know whether to laugh or cry. 'Let me go into the kitchen first. You might give poor Nellie a heart attack if you walk in unannounced.'

Nellie's reactions were predictable. She scolded Seymour, she cried and then she laughed, throwing her arms around his neck and hugging him as if he were one of her errant sons returning home after years of absence. Frank stood back, twisting his cap awkwardly between his hands, and Effie could see that he was eager to get away from what he obviously considered to be a madhouse. She served them with their breakfast of porridge, and she sat by the fire toasting bread while they ate and talked about the evidence Frank would give at Toby's appeal. Georgie sat quietly on his stool by the fire, eating buttered toast and eyeing the men warily, while Nellie flitted about keeping their mugs filled with tea. Each time she passed Seymour she touched his sleeve or his shoulder as if to make sure that he was real and not a figment of her imagination.

Finally, shaking hands on their arrangement to visit the offices of the solicitor in Lincoln's Inn Fields in two days' time, Seymour insisted that Jeffries should drive Frank back to Bow.

Half an hour later in the lane at the front of the house, Frank took Effie's hand and squeezed it gently. 'We was good together for a time, girl.'

'It would never have worked, Frank, and you still have a wife who might come back to you one day, and a child who needs its father.'

He leaned over to brush her cheek with a kiss. 'I won't forget you, Effie. And if you ever change your mind . . .'

'Take care of yourself, Frank, and give my love to Leah and Zilla and everyone. Tell them I'll come and see them as soon as the weather improves.'

Frank smiled, tipped his cap to Seymour and climbed up on the driver's seat beside Jeffries. Effie shivered, wrapping her shawl more tightly around her shoulders. The fog had lifted but a damp, grey mist hung over the marshes and the only sound apart from the rumble of the cart wheels and the clip-clopping of Champion's hooves was the mournful cry of a curlew.

'That was some homecoming,' Seymour said, relaxing at the kitchen table with a cup of tea. 'It's lucky I walked in when I did, Effie.'

'I don't think Frank would have harmed me,' Effie said stoutly. 'He's not a bad man, but he lets his feelings get the better of him at times.'

'Well, he's doing the right thing by Toby, so I'll have to let him off.' Seymour put his tea down and bent over to ruffle Georgie's curls. 'Have you forgotten me, young man? I'm going to be your grandpa.'

Nellie uttered a screech that might have been of pleasure or pain. 'I never thought I'd live to hear you say that, master.'

'It took me long enough to acknowledge my own flesh and blood, and Effie is going to marry my son, so I hope I may fill that gap in Georgie's life caused by the loss of his grandfather.'

His words made her happy, but even so tiny fingers of doubt clutched at Effie's heart. 'Toby may have changed. He might not want to marry me now.'

'Nonsense, girl. What a lot of balderdash

you talk at times. Why would he not want a woman like you? You're beautiful and clever and you've struggled to keep your family together. Why, if he won't marry you – I damned well will.' Seymour threw back his head and laughed. 'Don't look so alarmed, my dear Effie. I'm teasing you, of course.' He rose to his feet, holding his hand out to Georgie. 'Come and help me find my travelling bag, young man. I've brought you a Christmas present.'

Shyly, Georgie slipped his small hand into Seymour's. 'Grandpa?' he murmured.

'What a bright little fellow you are,' Seymour said with obvious delight. 'Grandpa it is, my boy. Now let's go and get your present. There might be one for your mama and for Nellie too.'

Effie watched them leave the kitchen with a lump in her throat. It was hard to believe that Seymour was the same man who had terrified her by his drunken and drugged attentions when she first arrived at Marsh House. She had fallen in love with Frank, but he had turned out to be quite a different person from the man of her dreams. Then there was Toby, the friend who had always been there for her in time of need; the genie of the lamp who had appeared when matters were desperate. She had taken him for granted then; accepting him at face value as an amusing libertine and a gypsy rover, when she now knew he was none of those things. Or was he? Would his time of incarceration in that dreadful jail have changed him? Would he still want to settle down with a ready-made family when he was released? She could not be sure of anything, but she managed a smile as Georgie raced into the room clutching a wooden horse, beautifully carved with a real horsehair mane and tail. 'Gee-gee,' he chortled. 'Mama, gee-gee.'

Effie bent down to examine it. 'He's beautiful, darling. What are you going to call him?'

'Champion,' Georgie said without a moment's hesitation.

Seymour had followed him more slowly, and he presented Effie with the most exquisite shawl she had ever seen. The black, gossamer-sheer material was embroidered with crimson roses nestling amongst green leaves and edged with a pure silk fringe. 'For you, Effie,' he said simply. 'I believe it's Spanish. I saw ladies wearing similar shawls on my travels. I fell in love with Argentina the moment I set foot on land.' He wrapped another and far more practical shawl around Nellie's thin shoulders. 'This will keep the winter chills from your bones, Nellie, my dear.'

'It's like a cobweb, master,' she whispered, rubbing her cheeks against the deep blue lacy folds. 'It's the best present I ever had.'

Effie fingered the embroidery on her shawl. 'It's lovely. Thank you, sir.'

'Seymour,' he said softly. 'How many times have I got to tell you that, Effie?'

'I'm sorry – Seymour. I'll try to remember.' Effie sat down beside Georgie, who was totally absorbed in his new toy. 'Tell us what happened in Argentina. We'd almost given you up for dead.'

'I'm not much of a hand at letter writing, and I'm afraid Toby takes after me in that respect. You haven't heard from him, I suppose?'

'Not a word.'

'He might not be allowed to write letters, but all that will change soon.'

'You have funds to pay for a lawyer, sir? I mean, Seymour.'

'My friend Forster had invested my money and his in a silver mine. It had taken some time to get the operation going but now the mine is beginning to show a profit. I'm not a wealthy man, but I can afford to hire one of the best lawyers in London to put Toby's case for an appeal.'

'You will stay at home though, master?' Nellie peered over the edge of her shawl with an anxious frown. 'You won't go away again?'

'I shall stay until matters are settled here, but then I intend to return to Argentina. The life out there suits me and I find I am accepted as a human being and not as some freak with a pockmarked face.'

'But what about Marsh House?' Effie could hardly frame the words. 'Will you sell your home?'

Seymour shook his head. 'I'll return every now and then, but I intend to sign over the deeds to my son. I can't make him legitimate, more's the pity, but I can make certain that Toby gets what is rightfully his. You will be mistress of Marsh House, my dear Effie.'

'Maybe, or maybe not,' Effie said slowly. 'None of us knows what Toby feels and you haven't even thought to ask him whether he wants to settle down here. People change, as I've learned to my cost. I'll only believe that Toby still wants to marry me when I hear it from his lips.'

Seymour put the wheels in motion for an appeal and there was little they could do other than wait for the case to be heard. Effie busied herself with brewing and selling ale, and the cider that Toby and Jeffries had made having resurrected the old cider press. Seymour was impressed with their efforts and he was generous with his praise. He applauded Tom for the energy he had put into growing crops and he gave him permission to work the land as he saw fit. The days of pleasure gardens had gone, Seymour said regretfully. Times were hard in the country and every acre of land should be utilised for the production of food. He suggested that they should rebuild the old pigsty and keep a pig or two as well as the goats, and perhaps add a cow to their livestock in order to provide milk, butter and hard cheese. If things went well they might even hire a dairymaid.

To Effie's intense surprise, Seymour seemed keen on returning the land to farming and Tom was delighted with the idea. She said nothing; if Tom was happy then so was she, and more food on the table with surplus to sell could only be a good thing. She went about her daily tasks with renewed vigour, and she was filled with nervous anticipation when, at the end of February, a letter came from Seymour's lawyer to announce the date of the court hearing.

Next morning Seymour left for the city, where he intended to lodge in a hotel near the law courts until the case was heard. He kissed Effie, promising her that he would return bringing his son with him. 'You will be a spring bride, my dear,' he said, taking out his wallet. 'Have a new dress made, and I don't mean a drab everyday gown. You must have something to bring out the colour of your eyes and that glorious sunshine hair.' He pressed a crisp five-pound note into her hand. 'It will be your wedding dress, my dear brave girl. I couldn't wish for anyone better to be my daughter-in-law.' Without giving her a chance to answer, he mounted his horse and rode off towards town.

Effie could not settle. She immersed herself in her work, going out alone on the cart with her barrels of ale and cider while Tom worked hard tilling the fields and sowing seeds. When she was neither brewing nor selling, she threw herself into the spring cleaning. She wanted everything to be perfect when Toby came home and she did her best to make the house into the sort of home he remembered as a boy, and one that he would never want to leave. She ordered a new gown from a dressmaker in Bow that Betty recommended, but being thrifty by nature Effie chose taffeta rather than silk and English lace rather than the more expensive variety imported from Brussels. She spent the rest of the money in the sale-room, purchasing furniture to fill the empty bedrooms and comfortable chairs and a sofa for the drawing room. Everything was second hand, but Effie was not proud and she was happy with her choices.

When the news finally came that Toby's case was to be heard next day Effie's nerves were as taut as the strings on a violin. She had kept herself busy at home until now, but she had suddenly felt the need for company and, using the excuse that she was going for the final fitting for her new gown, she drove the cart to Bow. Ben was in the stable yard when she arrived and he waved to her, giving her all the encouragement she needed to brave Maggie's displeasure by visiting the tavern kitchen. Having confided in Betty and taken comfort from her commonsense approach to all things, Effie was surprised and pleased when Ben joined them, but his expression was serious.

'Take care when you leave, ducks,' he warned. 'Sal Salter's in the bar and she's three sheets to the wind and spoiling for a fight with anyone connected with the court case. Her old man's been arrested for perjury and his ill treatment of Mr Grey, and she blames you for tricking him into admitting his guilt. Frank and Jed's evidence could send Salter to jail for years, so be careful when you go. You don't want to catch her in this mood.'

Effie left the pub soon after Ben's warning

and she thought she had escaped Sal's notice, but as Champion plodded steadfastly along the riverbank a scuffling sound beneath the folded tarpaulin in the back of the cart warned her that she was not alone. She turned her head in time to see Sal lunge up at her with a knife in one hand and a cudgel in the other. Effie opened her mouth to scream but Sal was too quick for her. She brought the heavy wooden club down hard on Effie's skull. Effie felt a dull thud, and tumbled into darkness.

When she came to her senses she was aware only of a splitting headache and terrible cramps in her limbs. She tried to move but she was bound hand and foot. It was dark and she could just make out a chink of moon-light through a gap in the roof. There was an overpowering smell of charred wood, soot and paraffin fumes. As her eyes grew accustomed to the dim light she realised that she was in the burnt-out cabin of a narrowboat. She could feel the rise and fall of the water beneath the hull, and it gradually dawned on her that this was no ordinary barge. Unless she was very much mistaken, it was the hulk of the *Margaret*. She tried to sit up, but her hands were tied behind her back and cramp had set in. She groaned with pain and the sound had barely passed her lips when the swaying glow of an oil lamp preceded Sal Salter's huge bulk as she appeared in the open doorway. She leaned against the charred lintel and her face was ghostly in the lamplight.

'Gotcha, Effie Grey. I got an old score to settle with you and a new one coming up.'

'What do you want, Sal?' Effie did not waste time asking her the reason for her capture. It did not take a genius to work out that in some twisted way Sal thought that by imprisoning her she could free her villainous husband.

'I want to see you suffer for putting the finger on my old man, and I ain't letting you go until they set him free.'

'It's nothing to do with me,' Effie protested. 'I can't do anything to help him.'

'You don't have to, ducks.' Sal set the lamp down on the few planks of decking that had not been burnt away in the fire. 'I sent a messenger to old Westlake telling him to call his lawyer off. If your didicoi lover goes free, my man will end up in clink. I ain't having it, Effie Grey. I'll send you to the bottom of the River Lea first.'

'You won't get away with this,' Effie cried angrily. 'You'll end up in jail with your wretched husband.'

Sal reached for a knife that lay on what was left of one of the bunks. For a moment Effie thought her end had come, but Sal seized a lock of her hair and cut it off with one swipe

562

of the blade. 'There, missis. That should convince them that I mean business and that I have you here where no one will find you.'

Effie was shaken but determined. 'And where are we?'

Sal hesitated and then she smiled. 'It won't do you no good, but Salter had the barge towed to the backwater. Old man Grey willed it to us and Salter says it can be rebuilt. We'll be king and queen of the river yet.' She backed out onto the open deck, her large figure silhouetted against the night sky.

Effie leaned against the bulkhead, staring up through the open roof at the stars twinkling above her head. She had no idea of the time or how long she had lain unconscious on the deck, but her stomach growled reminding her that she was hungry and her mouth was dry. She would have called asking for water but she could hear Sal's footsteps crunching the gravel on the towpath as she strode off into the distance. Effie could only guess that the trap was waiting for her in a lane close to the creek and that Sal would take Champion and drive away. She shifted to a less uncomfortable position and closed her eyes, thinking of Georgie and hoping that Nellie would make up a convincing story to explain his mother's failure to return home. She could only hope that Tom would come looking for her, although he would have no idea where to start and the last place anyone would think of would be the charred shell of the old narrowboat.

She tried to sleep but thirst was worse than hunger and her lips were cracked and dry. In spite of everything she must have drifted into a fitful doze. She awakened suddenly to find her face moist and the sky showing the first greenish light of dawn. She opened her mouth and gulped down the sweet-tasting rain. She closed her eyes and held her face up to catch every last refreshing droplet, but the shower was soon over and her feeling of euphoria ended abruptly as the bitter cold penetrated through her wet garments, chilling her flesh and causing her to shiver uncontrollably. She shifted her position, wincing at the pain in her cramped muscles, but she knew she must keep moving somehow or she would perish from the cold. The ropes that bound her wrists and ankles chafed her skin and every movement hurt, but she dared not give up her attempts to keep warm.

Minutes seemed like hours and the hours felt like days. She had no idea of the time and the only sounds she could hear were birdsong and the musical murmur of the water beneath the hull. They must be in a little used part of the backwater, she thought miserably, and if anyone should happen to be passing they would take little notice of the abandoned hulk left to rot amongst the reeds. A light breeze that began by tugging playfully at her hair had gradually strengthened into a blustery wind. The vessel rocked gently at first, and as the playful March wind grew more blustery in nature it bobbed up and down like cork floating on the water. Then, just as suddenly as it had sprung up, the wind died away and a watery sun forced its way between silver-tipped clouds. Effie raised her face to its welcome warmth and her wet clothes began to steam gently.

Her thirst had been slaked temporarily by the rain but as the morning dragged on her throat became more and more parched. Her stomach cramped with hunger and every bone in her body ached. She began to feel light-headed and as the afternoon faded into dusk she was beginning to hear voices in her head and see phantasmagorical shapes looming over her. She tried to call out but all she could manage was a hoarse croak, and anyway there was no one to hear her cries. She dared not fall asleep for fear of never waking to see the light of day again. She thought of Georgie who would be a poor orphan, and Tom who would have to shoulder the responsibilities of a man when he was still little more than a boy. She thought of Toby and tears trickled down her cheeks. Was he a free man? Or had the appeal failed and he had been sent back to prison to endure the rest of his sentence? She might die here tonight and never know the outcome. She might never see his face or hear him calling her name.

'Effie.' Someone was shaking her. She moaned in her sleep, afraid to open her eyes and discover that she was dreaming yet again.

'Effie, for God's sake speak to me.'

She knew that voice. She must have died and gone to heaven.

The shaking grew more insistent. 'Effie, open your eyes. It's me, Toby.'

The touch of his lips on hers was real. The warmth of his body gave her new life. She opened her eyes and found herself looking into his anxious gaze. 'Toby? Is it really you?'

With a muffled groan, he wrapped her in his arms. 'My love, my only love. I thought you were dead.'

Effie winced with pain as the ropes gouged into her raw flesh. 'Untie me, please.'

He drew away from her, uttering a string of expletives as he examined her bonds. 'She'll pay for this, I swear she will.' He seized the knife that Sal had left out of reach but within Effie's sight as if to torment her even more, and he slashed the ropes that bound her.

'Where is Sal?' Effie murmured.

566

'In custody with that villain Salter.' Toby threw the knife away and bent down to take Effie in his arms. His lips found hers, gently kissing away the pain, all her doubts and fears dispelled in his tender embrace.

'Is she all right?' Tom's voice broke the spell and Toby rose to his feet, lifting Effie in his arms as easily as if she were a small child.

'I'm fine now,' Effie croaked, her voice breaking with emotion. 'But I'm parched and I'm starving and I want to go home.'

Washed, changed into warm dry clothes and with her hair towelled dry and hanging loose in a shining cape around her shoulders, Effie sat by the kitchen range with Georgie on her lap and Toby seated by her side, holding her hand as if he were afraid to let her go.

'So that's how we knew where to find you,' Seymour said, filling his pipe with tobacco. 'Ben overheard Sal boasting about how she'd got you where she wanted you, and that she'd see her old man released without a stain on his character. Ben sent for the police and she spent the night in the cells.'

'But how did you know where to find me?' Effie asked, rubbing her cheek against Georgie's soft curls.

'When she was told that we'd won and that Salter was facing jail, she broke down and confessed everything. She told the police where you were and the rest you know,' Toby said, raising her hand to his cheek and holding it there. 'I've missed you so much, Effie. Every minute of every day you were in my thoughts and in my dreams.'

Nellie had been stirring a pan of stew on the range but at that she turned her head, waving the ladle at Toby. 'Save the soft talk for later, boy. Effie needs sustenance, or d'you want her to fade away like a ghost?'

Tom grabbed a bowl and handed it to Nellie. 'She needs building up.' He cast a reproachful eye in Toby's direction. 'Have you any idea how hard my sister's worked to keep us all fed and warm?'

Toby lifted Georgie from his mother's lap, giving him a hug as he put him down on the floor beside his small pile of toys. 'I'm learning, Tom,' he said sincerely. 'I always thought she was a wonderful mother and a good sister, and I'm well aware that she's too good for me.'

'She is too,' Seymour said, winking at Effie. 'But I'm praying that she will overlook the failings my son has inherited from me, and do me the enormous favour of taking him in hand.'

Toby turned on him in mock anger. 'Just because you're my father doesn't give you the right to beg Effie to marry me. That's my privilege.'

Nellie tossed the ladle into the pan. 'You men!' she exclaimed. 'You can't be trusted to do even the simplest things without a woman's help.' She seized Tom by the scruff of his neck and propelled him, protesting loudly, out of the door into the hallway. She beckoned fiercely to Seymour. 'You too, master. This may be your house but you're coming with me and Tom to give these young people a chance to do things their way.'

'Marsh House no longer belongs to me,' Seymour said, turning to Toby and Effie with a broad grin. 'I instructed my lawyer to draw up the deeds and I've signed the house and estate over to you, my son. I'm going back to Argentina to help Forster manage the mining company.'

'You are?' Effie murmured, rising to her feet. 'But this is your home.'

'And always will be,' Toby said, slipping his arm around her waist and drawing her close to him. 'My future wife and I will keep your room just as it is, Father.'

Seymour threw back his head and laughed. 'You are a chip off the old block after all, but take a tip from your old man and ask the lady first. You may find that Effie has other ideas.'

'Oh, for heaven's sake,' Nellie said crossly. 'Come away, master, and leave the boy to it.'

'Say yes, Effie,' Tom shouted from outside

the door. 'Marry him and I'll stay and work for you both, and one day I'll wed Agnes and we'll be one big happy family.'

'Yes,' Georgie said, tugging at his mother's skirt. 'Yes, Mama.'

Nellie darted into the room and snatched Georgie up in her arms. 'You heard the boy,' she said sternly. 'Don't start acting coy, Effie. You know you've been pining for young Toby all these long months. Don't keep him in suspense.' She hurried from the kitchen, closing the door firmly behind her.

'Well?' Toby said, smiling deeply into Effie's eyes. 'It seems that everyone has proposed marriage except me.'

'Do you really think you could settle down here?' Effie asked tentatively, but she could read the answer in the depths of his eyes and it was like drowning in a happy sea of blue.

'I would live anywhere with you, and Georgie, of course. I love you, Effie. I always have and always will. Does that answer your question?'

'Yes,' Effie said simply.

'And will you marry me, please?'

Effie sealed his lips with a kiss. 'Yes. With all my heart, I will.'